THE CI

A NOVEL

Thomas G. Blacklock

FRANKLIN
SCRIBES™
PUBLISHERS

Blacklock, Thomas G.
The CI/Thomas G. Blacklock
ISBN 978-1-941516-16-4
First Edition
A Novel

Disclaimer:
This book is a work of fiction. Names, characters, places and incidents either are the product of the author's imagination or are used fictitiously, and any resemblance to any actual persons (living or dead), events, or locales is entirely coincidental.

Library of Congress Control Number: 2016946184

ISBN Hardcover: 978-1-941516-19-5
ISBN Paperback: 978-1-941516-16-4
ISBN Ebook: 978-1-941516-18-8

Published by Franklin Scribes Publishers.
Franklin Scribes is a registered trademark of Franklin Scribes Publishers.
franklinscribeswrites@gmail.com
www.franklinscribes.com
Contact the author at www.franklinscribes.com/thomas-blacklock/

Front and back book covers by Thompson Printing Solutions
This book was printed in the United States of America.

Acknowledgments

I would like to acknowledge Judy Watters, my copy editor, writing companion and friend, for her excellent work in editing this book. Her efforts in detecting my errors, as well as giving insight and recommendations made this endeavor more readable and are greatly appreciated.

I would be remiss if I did not acknowledge my loving wife Jeri and her support while I endeavored to write this book and who read this work with a critical eye. Thanks, dear, for helping me bring this book to fruition.

Last, but not least, I would like to offer my humble thanks to all those individuals who have fought and continue to fight the scourge of illegal drugs that continues to invade and degrade our society.

Prologue

The title of this book, The CI, is an acronym utilized by Special Agents of the Drug Enforcement Administration when referring to individuals who are Cooperating Individuals or more commonly known as Confidential Informants. Simply referred to as an Informant or snitch, the CI is both the backbone and bane of a narcotic agent's investigative success. To be successful, the agent needs to understand what motivates the informant and how to control them. The oft-repeated refrain "You can't live with them and you certainly cannot live without them," applies to an agent's dealings with an informant.

An informant's motivation to be an informant usually determines how successful he or she will be and how difficult he or she will be to control. Joe Pesci's role as informant in the movie Lethal Weapon II is an excellent example of the pitfalls of dealing with an informant. His motivation is to eliminate those people from whom he, as an accountant for a large illegal enterprise, has embezzled a large sum of money and who now wants him dead. He is whiny, clingy and a general pain to both Danny Glover and Mel Gibson as they try to work in investigation against those who seek his demise.

Most informants fall into two motivational categories: Cooperating with authorities to preclude going to jail or to reduce their jail sentence for some offense for which they have been or are about to be arrested; and the other, financial remuneration. There are, of course, other motivations such as eliminating the competition by helping to arrest them and revenge for some wrong done or perceived to have been done to the informant. Every once in a while, an informant might be John Q. Citizen who feels it is his or her civic duty to get involved in putting bad guys in jail. In my experience, informants whose motivation is pecuniary were the most reliable and easy to control with the spurned lover or revenge the worst.

In this book, a ruthless drug lord makes Juan, the CI, a job offer characterized by the old Mexican adage "Plata Y Ploma" either you take my silver (money) or you'll take my lead (bullets). The drug lord also threatens the CI's brother and the brother's young family.

Ultimately, the CI has to make the decision whether to continue to work for the drug lord and risk extradition to the United States and prison or to trust the agent who promises to protect him and his brother's young family. This decision carries international life and death implications.

CHAPTER ONE

Hang in there, Marcus, old buddy. I'm coming. Tom Blaine inched his way along a massive stone corridor deep in the bowels of an alien building. Corridor was a misnomer. Tom's surroundings more accurately resembled a tunnel in a mine. The walls, solid rock, glistened with moisture, which overran a green mold blanketing everything. The ceiling, almost ten feet tall at its oval-shaped apex, and the frugal ambient light, barely allowed Tom to see more than a few feet ahead of him.

As he hugged the left side of the wet tunnel soaking him in the process, Tom followed his extended hand, which firmly cradled his black mat-finished Glock .45-caliber pistol, which seemed to be leading him directly into harm's way. *How could I have been so stupid to let those bastards grab Marcus from right under my nose? Well, now it's up to me to save him. I hope I'm not too late.* The thought induced a cold chill that coursed through Tom's body like a wildfire when he considered the consequences of being too late. *Where are you Marcus?*

As if his thoughts were a telepathic cue, a slight and barely audible sound emanated from somewhere ahead of him. The sound ended his forward progress for a moment while he waited for it to repeat itself. Tom listened several minutes for the sound to repeat. When it didn't, he inched his way forward again. When the sound did repeat itself, there was no mistaking it for anything but a scream of someone in intense pain. Paralyzed for a moment again, Tom's ice-cold sense of fear consumed him. "Oh, sweet Jesus!" Tom said aloud. "What are those bastards doing to you, Marcus? Hold on, buddy, help is on the way." He reached for his portable radio. "Can you guys copy? I'm down here in the lower level; I think I can hear Marcus. Do you copy? Tony?" Tom almost yelled into the radio. No response. Tom cursed. *I can't transmit out of this tunnel. The radio isn't powerful enough. I'm on my own here.*

Tom picked up his pace and descended lower into the tunnel. As he did so, he noticed the tunnel appeared to narrow in all dimensions in a funnel-like fashion and tended to meander never-ending first downward to the left and then downward to the right. Tom also noted that as he proceeded, the blackened tunnel began to fade to a dark shade of gray allowing Tom to see further ahead and to move more rapidly without fear of running into something. The light was improving in the tunnel. Tom stumbled and struggled to maintain his balance. Another scream—more intense—reverberated along the walls of the tunnel assaulting Tom's ears.

Panic gripped Tom and his pace became a fast trot and then a full-speed-ahead motion. Faster and faster, he descended into the tunnel.

Suddenly, and when it seemed there would be no end to this tunnel, Tom spotted a light ahead. *The obvious end to the tunnel* he instantly decided. Drawn to the light as a moth drawn dangerously to a flame, Tom proceeded ahead.

The light grew more intense; another scream echoed through the tunnel. Tom accelerated his pace. He ran ahead at full speed—oblivious to the danger that awaited him ahead—focused solely on reaching that light. *That's where Marcus will be.* However, it seemed no matter how quickly he moved he could not reach the end of the tunnel.

In what seemed to Tom an eternity was only a few minutes. Tom burst into the lighted opening at the end of the tunnel and found himself in a cavernous underground room. Partially blinded by the bright light, Tom stumbled and fell to his knees losing his Glock in the process. He fumbled like a blind person. *Shit, where's my gun? My gun.* Frantically, his hands searched the floor around him while at the same time he attempted to take in the room. His eyes became accustomed to the light and his vision cleared. He spotted his Glock just off to his left. Quickly retrieving his pistol, Tom began to rise from his knees. Movement at the far end of the room drew Tom's attention. Several nondescript human forms huddled around what appeared to be a large table. The forms focused on something or someone on the table and ignored his presence.

Slowly and silently, Tom approached the group, again with his Glock pulling him onward. Either the forms did not sense his presence or were disregarding him intentionally. As he approached, Tom watched as one of the forms standing next to the table shoved a long rod-like object at the form lying on the table. Instantly, a shower of sparks overflowed the table and drained to the floor in a crescendo waterfall fashion. Tom saw the form on the table jerk in spasms and immediately he heard a blood-curdling scream.

"Stop that, you bastards," Tom attempted to yell. However, no sound would come from his mouth. *What's wrong? Why can't I speak?* Now in a state of full panic and rage, Tom charged the forms surrounding the table attempting to yell at them to stop. When he was within several yards of the table, one of the forms, the one closest to him, turned to acknowledge his presence. As this form did so, Tom immediately recognized him as one of the comandante's ayudantes. The comandante's assistant acknowledged Tom's presence with a sneer-like smile and then turned back to the form on the table. He jabbed at it with the long prod again. A shower of sparks spewed across the form lying prone on the table. Immediately, the form on the table jerked uncontrollably and screamed. Tom recognized the form and Marcus' anguished scream.

"Stop that, you bastard," Tom screamed finally finding his voice while pointing his Glock directly at the ayudante. Instead of complying with Tom's command, the ayudante sneered at Tom, and again jabbed Marcus with the prod producing the same results.

Consumed with rage, Tom directed his Glock at the mass of the ayudante's chest; with his hand shaking violently, he squeezed the trigger. He heard himself yell, "I'll kill you, you miserable bastard."

Bracing for the familiar recoil and bark from his gun, Tom was stunned when the gun merely went pop and a bullet fell harmlessly from the gun's barrel. *Oh, shit! Something's wrong with my gun. Maybe it's a bad round.* Tom again aimed the Glock at the ayudante who now approached Tom with the same menacing sneer still painted on his ugly face and the electric prod in his outstretched hand. "You're a dead man," Tom heard himself say in an elevated voice as he again aimed his gun at the ayudante's chest. Once again, the Glock responded with a small retort as the bullet dropped from the barrel to the floor. The ayudante closed in on Tom. He jerked the trigger several more times; the gun reacted with the same results.

Tom discarded the Glock and reached for the Spidercoe knife in his boot. Deftly opening the blade with one hand, Tom faced off with the ayudante. The ayudante lunged at Tom landing on his chest. Tom heard himself yell, "Die, you son of a bitch," as he attempted to stab and push at the ayudante. He felt a sharp pain in his right side. He knew he was injured. Tom's screams and thrusting movements had the desired results.

He bolted upright in bed. His actions propelled Manfred, his eighteen-pound orange tabby cat from his favorite early morning sleeping spot, straddling Tom's chest, across the bed to the floor hissing while airborne.

Shit, the dream again. Tom relaxed into a slumped sitting position. With his heart pounding, and a cold chill enveloping him, Tom attempted to take stock of his surroundings.

The rock fireplace in front of his king-sized bed still showed slightly glowing embers, remnants from the night before. Off to the right, French doors led to the large wooden deck that traversed the rear of his house. The antique bureau, to his right against the wall, and the nightstands with matching lamps, bordered the bed. Lying back down, Tom realized he was not in the underground cavern but safe in his own bedroom. He had just endured a recurrent nightmare that seemed to have plagued him since the death of Marcus Rodriguez in Mexico earlier in the year.

As he lay there, Manfred gingerly hopped back up on the bed and only ventured within an arm's distance of Tom. Tom slowly reached for a spot on the cat's head Tom knew was one of his favorites and gently began to tussle with his ears. Manfred responded with a loud purr. "Sorry, little buddy. Didn't mean to give you a scare."

The cat slowly warmed again to the show of Tom's affection.

Tom's heart rate seemed to adjust back to an almost normal pattern as he stroked Manfred's head. He realized his T-shirt and sheets soaked with his sweat caused his chill. Pulling the T-shirt off, he wiped his brow and side of his head and was surprised to see that in addition to removing sweat, he also wiped off blood. Feeling his face and neck, he discovered the root of the blood problem. Evidently, that sharp pain he felt in his dream was one of Manfred's claws nailing him as Tom launched him from his chest. Still too shaky to get up, he considered the dream.

The dream, a variation of a recurrent nightmare, seemed to be increasing frequency. While different in scenario, the result was always the same. No matter what he did, Tom just could not manage to save Marcus from the tortuous death that he had suffered at the hands of those Mexican drug traffickers.

Marcus Rodriguez, a young DEA agent and a member of Tom's DEA Snow Cap Team, had been captured, tortured and murdered while doing covert operations in Mexico. Specifically, ayudantes, working for Comandante Jesus Rubalcaba, had grabbed Marcus off the streets of Guadalajara, Mexico, and had taken him to the Estancia of Miguel Felix-Uriarte, the most powerful drug trafficker in Mexico. There, Uriarte's men brutally tortured and killed

Marcus. The fact that both the comandante and Uriarte had both suffered violent deaths themselves was of little solace to Tom's psyche.

Tom had frantically attempted to save Marcus but had failed. Tom blamed himself even though others who knew the truth regarding Marcus's demise did not. The intense guilt Tom suffered from Marcus's sudden death showed in his recurrent dream. He had heard it so many times in his sessions with Dr. John Malcomb, DEA's contract clinical psychologist. "Tom, you must relinquish the guilt or the dreams will persist." According to Dr. John, the passage of time would eventually heal the wounds of the soul. Dr. John was more concerned about the part of the dream where Tom attempted to shoot the miscreants and his pistol failed miserably. According to Dr. John, this type of dream was consistent with police officers who had endured traumatic events and suffered from post-traumatic stress syndrome. Untreated, according to Dr. John, the stress could become debilitating.

While Marcus's death had a pronounced effect on Tom, he was no stranger to deadly confrontations. As a young Marine sergeant in Vietnam, Tom had seen more than his share of violent deaths. His heroic actions and wounds during his two tours made him a highly decorated Marine. Moreover, as a seasoned DEA agent and supervisor, with twenty-eight years of service, he had endured a number of violent confrontations in both the United States and South America. While Tom appreciated the good doctor's concern, Tom had learned from the violent confrontations that only time would eventually erase the emotional hurt and the dreams would gradually diminish to infrequency.

As his blood pressure and his breathing returned to normal, Tom turned to the large orange tabby, who had inched his way closer to Tom now that he felt it was safe to do so. "Well, old buddy, I suppose you want your breakfast." Manfred gave a short meow, stood up, arched his back, turned and leaped from the bed.

Exiting the bed, Tom passed by a mirror on his dresser and noted the damage Manfred had meted out during the dream. A large double scratch ran from Tom's right cheek down his jaw line, across his neck and ended at the beginning of his shoulder blade. It was extremely red and still oozing blood in several places. "Man, you really nailed me good, you worthless fur ball." Manfred stood in the bedroom doorway staring impatiently at Tom.

In the kitchen, Tom opened a can of cat food, put it in a small saucer and placed it on the floor. While Manfred consumed the fishy-smelling chunks of whatever, Tom leaned against the counter and considered the strange relationship he and his cantankerous feline shared.

Manfred had invaded Tom's life several months earlier along with Libby when Tom had returned from Bolivia and the fateful assignment that had claimed the life of Marcus.

Libby, or Edwina Elizabeth Martin who preferred Libby rather than Ed, was ten years Tom's junior. A pert five foot two, slender but shapely blond Assistant United States Attorney had actually been a part of Tom's life prior to his trip to Bolivia. During their initial meeting, because of philosophical differences on how a case should proceed, they had sparred and the heated exchange ended when Tom called her a "pissy little bitch." The "pissy little bitch" characterization had caused him a whole bunch of grief with his *almost* former Special Agent in Charge, Marsha Grant. Tom used the almost former title because until Grant's promotion and transfer to Washington within the next several weeks, she was still, technically, his SAC. Once she heard the words Tom used with Libby, she became angered—just another nail in Tom's career coffin that Grant was happy to pound home.

Although Tom professed at the time of their argument that he would never work with Libby on a case again, circumstances presented itself on a major investigation that precluded him from carrying out this vow. The case, one involving the drug trafficking by the Bandidos outlaw motorcycle gang, was already underway when he returned to Denver from Bolivia and Libby had been working with his agents on the case for several months.

According to the agents, she seemed to be doing a good job and unlike a number of AUSAs in the Denver office, she was usually available and quickly returned telephone calls. Although strained, they both managed to be at least civil to one another in their first meeting with his case agents.

Libby had taken the first step in attempting to reconcile their differences when over a sandwich at the Chez Fey, the cafeteria in the Federal Building, several hours later. "Congratulations on your well-deserved Attorney General's Award. Those officers who survived have only you to thank for their lives."

This was in reference to a violent shootout in northeast Denver in October of the previous year when black crack dealers shot two Denver police officers. A news crew captured Tom's ensuing heroic actions to save the downed officers. The event made the national evening news.

Not good in accepting praise, especially from a person who had previously engendered his wrath, Tom could merely mutter, "Uh thanks. I just did what had to be done in a bad situation."

Seeing that he was uncomfortable talking about that situation, Libby changed the subject.

Tom was grateful for her concern. Most people he encountered wanted a blow-by-blow description of the shootout and he was weary of retelling the story. Her concern about his discomfort with the situation began to melt the hard cold veneer that he had developed toward her.

As the case progressed, Libby and he found themselves in frequent contact; ultimately, it ended up in almost daily contact. While working late into the evening hours, Tom suggested that Libby and his two agents take a break and join him for dinner. One beer quickly turned into two then three, and before anyone knew it, the work for the night was over and the quartet ultimately poured themselves from the bar when it closed at midnight. Too drunk to drive, Tom offered to give Libby a ride home. She reluctantly agreed to accept a ride from him. However, when they reached her apartment building, she leaned across the center console and gave Tom a peck on the cheek telling him he was *sweet* to be concerned about her getting home and all.

The next day, when Tom saw Libby in her office, she seemed distant and all business. Finally, when they were alone, Tom asked if there was something wrong. Had he said or done something to offend her?

At first, she said no, but after some gentle prodding, she said she was slightly embarrassed about actions the previous evening.

"You did nothing to be embarrassed about," Tom reassured her.

"I was out of line allowing you to take me home and then kissing your cheek. It was an impulsive gesture caused by too much beer and not enough food," Libby explained.

"Hell, I don't see it that way, Libby. In fact, it was nice. The last drunk I gave a ride to snored and farted all the way home and smelled a whole lot worse than you," Tom said trying to make light of her discomfort.

His words caused her to laugh at his attempt at humor, but her neck and face turned a bright pink. "In fact, I was kind of hoping that I could take you to dinner this evening. No drinking, of course. This time we eat real food and not just whatever they serve at happy hour," said Tom.

Tom's casual demeanor about her embarrassment won the day and she readily agreed to dinner.

From that point on, it was only a matter of time before they became an item. Several weeks later, Libby, who was in the final stages of a divorce and needing a place to reside other than her mother's house, agreed to move into Tom's place. Manfred had come with Libby. Manfred immediately developed a strong dislike for Tom, and Tom having always been a dog fan, did nothing to endear himself to the large tabby. However as the weeks passed, their relationship developed into one of tolerance with occasional periods of antagonism thrown in to keep each other off balance.

Unfortunately, Tom's first characterization of Libby being a "pissy little bitch" was prophetic. After just several weeks of cohabitating, Libby began to give subtle hints that she wanted more out of the relationship than the great sex they shared, and fearful of becoming husband number three, Tom resisted the suggestions.

Finally, Libby demanded to know. "Tom, where do you see this relationship going?"

Tom's frustration exploded. "Christ, woman, I don't know. Can't we just take our time and let things take their course."

That's all Libby needed to know. She packed her things, and along with Manfred, moved back to her mother's home in Parker.

Ten days later, Tom had stumbled home late one night, and being just a little too drunk to care, flopped down on the bed without removing his clothes. As he stretched out in the darkness his arm touched something fury which responded with a pitiful slight meow. "Jesus Christ," Tom shouted. Startled to a semi-sober state, Tom sprang instantly from the bed and found the light switch. When the room illuminated, Tom saw the cause of his fright. Lying on the bed was Manfred, but not the overweight, feisty Manfred that Tom remembered. This Manfred was emaciated and his fur was heavily soiled and matted. There were also patches of hair missing from various parts of his now gaunt frame. Tom slowly approached the bed and began to speak softly to the cat, "Hey big fella, what are you doing here? How did you get into the house?" Manfred just meowed softly, barely lifting his head from the bedspread. Gingerly, Tom approached the tabby and with soft words, he began to stroke the cat's head having seen Libby do so in the past. The tabby winced in obvious pain. Tom quickly retrieved his reading glasses from the nightstand and could see several large abscesses on the poor critter's head. Additionally, Tom could also see that Manfred had a large infected wound on his left ear. While checking the ear, he noted that both of his ears were extremely warm. He remembered Libby saying that warm ears were a sign of a temperature in a cat. His emaciated condition and his obvious internal infections were a cause for alarm for Tom. Slowly, so as not to disturb the cat, Tom arose from the bed and made his way into the kitchen where he found a phone book and the number of a local vet who Tom had come to know from some volunteer work he had done with the local Boy Scouts.

A somewhat groggy vet answered her phone on the third ring. After hearing Tom's assessment of Manfred, she agreed to meet him at her office in an hour. Tom hung up the phone. *Thank God for living out here in the country. The vets here are used to late night disturbances.*

Tom found an old beach towel, carefully tucked it around Manfred and carried him to his aging International Scout where he laid the docile critter on the right front passenger seat. In the process, Tom decided Manfred had to be sick; he had never allowed Tom to pick him up before and would never have calmly consented to ride in a car.

While in route to the vet's office, Tom considered what the cat must have endured. He must have run off right after Libby took him to her mother's house in Parker. *He had to travel forty plus miles to my place in rural Elbert County, overcoming both living and non-living obstacles in the process. I wonder why he came back here. We barely tolerated one another.* Several times during the short trip to the vet's, Tom patted the tabby and assured him, "Don't worry, old fella. Everything will be all right."

After an hour and a half of ministering to abscesses, suturing open wounds and administering injections, the vet gave her diagnosis. "He's been through quite an ordeal. The pads on his feet are cracked in several places, and animals he encountered along the way, which I hope were not rabid, most likely caused those abscesses. The fact that his shots were up-to-date and that he had a lot of weight to lose bodes well for him."

"Do you think he'll make it Doc?" Tom asked somewhat sheepishly.

"Yeah, I think so. So long as nothing else develops, he should recover. The key will be to keep him quiet for the next several days and try to get this medicine and these pills down his throat. Let me know if there's any significant change. Call anytime," she said.

"Thanks a lot, Doc," Tom said as he exited the vet's office with Manfred wrapped in the blanket in his arms.

The cat slept through the night at the foot of Tom's bed and shortly after seven the next morning, Tom called Libby and told her of Manfred's arrival.

"Thank God he's alive," Libby responded, "I had given him up. I thought for sure he'd been eaten by the coyotes around my Mom's place."

"Why do you think he came back here, Libby?"

"I don't know, Tom. Maybe he sees something in you that I don't right now," she answered with just a touch of rancor seeping into her tone.

"Well, he should be well in several days; I'll bring him to you then."

"Why don't you just keep him? I mean if he went to such extremes to get to you, he obviously wants to be with you."

"Libby, he's your cat. I don't know why he came here. We hardly ever got along and..."

"No, Tom, you keep him. He obviously has selected you over me, and if you bring him back here, he'll probably just do the same thing again. I'd rather know where he is than worry about what has happened to him."

With that, Tom became the owner of one irascible orange tabby cat who day by day got better and after a few weeks, it was difficult to tell that Manfred had suffered at all.

Since Manfred's return, Tom had actually grown fond of the cat. Healthy, he was stubborn like Tom and appeared to be almost fearless. Tom's effort to make him a house cat was an abject failure. When Manfred decided he wanted out, he merely pushed out a screen of an open window if Tom had forgotten to leave a door cracked open for him. This method of egress was coincidently, the same way he had gotten into Tom's house following his trek from Libby's mom's house. After repairing several screens, Tom conceded his failure and purchased a pet door that allowed Manfred access to the outside world anytime he desired.

Tom's initial fear that Manfred would run afoul with the local wildlife proved groundless. Nothing intimidated Manfred. He took on the local skunks and porcupines and the neighbors' dogs and cats. Tom continually pulled porcupine quills from Manfred, and he had learned to keep a stock of tomato soup on hand to deal with the after effects of the cat's skirmishes with the skunks. Moreover, Tom had paid more than his share of vet bills to mollify some irate neighbor whose dog or cat Manfred had harmed. Tom continually scolded the cat for his bad behavior but his chiding fell on deaf ears. On one occasion after scolding the cat, Tom admonished, "Just you wait, mister tough guy. One of these times you'll meet your match." But Manfred never did.

On one particular Sunday morning, Tom thought his warnings were about to come true. As he sat in the cool morning air on his back deck, he watched across a field as Manfred confronted a larger local resident. The red fox that had lived in a hidden underground den behind Tom's property for several seasons decided he had had enough of the cat's interloping into his domain and decided to take a stand. After a stare down with Manfred, the red fox, twice as big, lunged at the cat. Instead of retreating, as smaller animals would have done under similar circumstances, Manfred deftly leaped aside and then leaped through the air onto the back of the lunging fox. Digging his claws into the back, the surprised fox ran in circles trying to shake the cat from his back. His actions only caused Manfred to dig in deeper. Yelping, the fox shook and ran about trying to dislodge the cat. Manfred soon tired of the bucking ride, let loose of his claw hold and dropped from the fox. As the fox beat a hasty retreat, Manfred chased the fox back to the wood line several acres distant from Tom's property line. At first, when the fox stood his ground, Tom became concerned and was ready to run to assist Manfred, but his concern changed to amusement when he realized that his fears were unfounded.

As Manfred finished eating his fishy-smelling breakfast and began to groom himself, Tom heated up a cup of coffee from a pot left over from the day before. Two minutes in the microwave, and the coffee was steaming hot. "Need to go outside, old buddy?" Tom asked Manfred.

Tom quickly went to his bedroom to don some sweatpants. Following the now swaggering Manfred, Tom grabbed his coffee from the microwave and proceeded to his front door and onto a small covered wood deck. The early morning December air at 7500 feet above sea level felt cold and crisp with a definite bite; Tom shivered as he watched Manfred scamper down the stairs in an apparent hurry to do his duty. Quickly retrieving a fleece lined flannel shirt from the house, Tom returned to the front deck to watch as Manfred disappeared in the tree line adjacent to his property.

Tom leaned on the rail and considered his surroundings. *This is certainly*

God's country up here. He took in the vast panorama that began to unfold before him in the early morning ambient light. With nothing to obstruct his view to his left and south, he could just barely make out the still snow-covered Pike's Peak with its shadows casting a purplish hue on its rugged landscape. On a clear day, he could see north and the distant Long's Peak, not yet visible this morning. *I sure was lucky to happen into this place. If it hadn't been for old Mr. Ellsworth, God rest his soul, I would have never been fortunate enough to be able to afford a place like this. The $35,000 dollars the will specified for me to purchase this twenty-five acre spread in rural Elbert County was possibly one-fourth its actual value. It was certainly worth the court battle with Ellsworth's irate nephews who thought that they should have inherited this place. Like I told them and the court:* "I have been more of a nephew to your uncle in the last two years than you've been in a lifetime. I'm the guy who looked after him and the place when he went into the nursing home, not you," ending his statement with an accusatory finger pointed at the nephews.

December 3, 1996; Elbert County, Colorado

The ringing phone coming from inside the house interrupted Tom's thoughts. "Who the hell is calling at this early hour?" The interruption from his early morning enjoyment of his surroundings annoyed Tom. He proceeded to the kitchen where he picked up the imposing instrument from its place on a counter. "Yeah."

"And a good morning to you too." Tom instantly recognized the voice of his friend and mentor, Roger Grey.

"Well, no crap, Roger. I thought that maybe you broke your dialing finger or something. I haven't heard from you in weeks. And when you do call? It's at six in the damn morning. What's the matter? You afraid my problems with DEA will rub off on you? Not that your career has been stellar."

"I'm good, Tom. Thanks for asking. Before you get any testier than you are, I apologize for not calling for several weeks, but the press of business here in headquarters has been brutal. Getting his nibs, the administrator, ready for his International Drug Summit and all."

"Bullshit, Roger," Tom retorted, "You stayed your distance because you were afraid to call me while I was on this forty-five day suspension. It's as if I had the plague or something. And screw his nibs. That jerk could have intervened and set aside this time off."

"Come on, Tom. You know me better than that. I'd never let my position here in HQ or association with Conway interfere with our friendship," Roger offered as a condolence.

"Well, I suppose I know that, Roger." Tom's tone softened. "But I'm still bitter about this whole suspension thing. Forty-five days off for a misuse of the goddamn government vehicle. Give me a break. That's the only thing that clown Peterson could hang on me. Hell, you could get anybody in DEA for that if you wanted to. Roger, did you know that he had his men pull my bi-weekly time sheets for two years and talked with every informant that worked for my group to see if they could give them some dirt on me. One informant, one that we blackballed because he was untrustworthy, says he saw me using my government vehicle to run a personal errand to pick up my laundry of all things. The OPR clowns take his statement as gospel, and I get forty-five days off without pay."

"Tom, we both know the misuse of the government vehicle was a bogus offense, but it was one easy to prove, I guess. I mean, who hasn't done that sort of thing? And you and I both know that this was payback for crossing Peterson over your refusal to back down from officially blaming Marsha Grant for the deaths of those police officers in that shootout in Denver. You just don't cross senior Executive Service Special Agent James – don't call me Jim – Peterson, the keeper of the Office of Professional Responsibility, and not expect retribution in return."

"You're probably right, but Peterson, and Grant for that matter, has not heard the last from me. I'll have my day in front of the Merit System Protection Board and I'll get those days and the lost money back."

"Give it up, old buddy. You might win minor skirmishes with Peterson, but he'll end up winning the war if you take him on."

"That may be true, but I have no intention of capitulating to the likes of them. When I go back to duty in two weeks, I intend to do everything to make Ms. Grant's last few weeks in Denver a pure hell. She can't hurt me now because before she could officially take any action against me, she'll be gone to Washington. Enough of my problems; how's everything in Special Operations, Roger?"

"We're doing some good things down south but nothing like your team did, Tom. At least I'm getting some decent funding to run my programs. However, that could quickly change with Conway. He blows like the wind at times and you never know when he's going to change and cut your funding to support some other program. Maybe this trip to the Drug Summit will light a fire under his butt and he'll free up some more funds for foreign operations.

"When's he leaving for the Drug Summit?"

"In the next couple of days. Everything about the trip has been hush-hush because of some threats allegedly made by the Colombians. Security surrounding his trip is tighter than a gnat's ass."

"Shit, maybe those cartel bastards will whack him. Whoever we got to replace him, couldn't be any worse."

"Maybe, maybe not, but I wouldn't go around saying that in the wrong places, Tom. If you recall my offhanded comments about sending DEA agents covertly into Mexico last year caused me all sorts of problems with the Attorney General." Roger chuckled.

"Heck, Roger, those were not off-handed comments. You were planning to do exactly that if you recall."

"Yeah, I know, but I'd still be careful on what you say about wishing ill will on the Administrator. Not to change the subject, but how are you doing? Forty-five days without pay is a load, and I know your most recent divorce did not leave you in the best financial position?"

"I'm getting by, Roger."

"You're not saying that you've been violating DEA policy by having unauthorized off-duty employment, are you?"

"Are you taping this conversation, Roger?" Tom asked in jest. "Of course, I'm violating the policy. How else could I survive? Besides, there's no court in the land that would uphold DEA's policy of no off-duty employment for employees suspended without pay. And you can bet the farm that I'd take them to court if they tried to screw with me over making money to survive while I was on suspension."

"So what have you been doing?"

"One of the items that came with this ranch was an aging John Deer tractor with a three point hitch and box blade. Do you know what a three point hitch or box blade is, Roger?"

"I have no idea."

"A three point hitch allows you to attach a brush hog for mowing weeds or attach a posthole digger and implements like that and a box blade is like a plow which is used for moving earth or other materials. I managed to get the tractor running pretty good and hired myself out to some locals digging postholes and plowing, dirt and snow on a strictly cash only basis. Come spring and summer I could mow fields. Actually I did pretty good this past month and just might have found myself a retirement business."

"Speaking of retirement, I think Peterson and the Administrator thought that when they slapped that forty-five day suspension on you that you'd put in your papers and retire. Several others in similar situations have done just that recently."

"Let me tell you something, Roger. Retirement was never a consideration. When I get ready to retire, it will be on my terms and why should I let those clowns force me out under a dark cloud. I don't intend to end my career that way. When I do decide to retire, I want people to remember positive things about me not that I had to retire. Besides, I have a couple more years until I have my thirty years counting my military service; I don't intend to retire before that. It's hard to pass up seventy percent of your highest three years after thirty."

"I agree, Tom. That's what I'm shooting for too. But I'd pull the pin before I thought they could get to me. I don't know if I could have taken the suspension like you did."

"You have other considerations with a wife and two children in college. I don't have those worries. And believe you me, if I thought they could actually fire me I'd retire long before they could put the wheels in motion."

"Well, good buddy, my secretary is signaling that I'm wanted upstairs for the morning staff meeting, so I'll say goodbye."

"Okay, Roger. Thanks for calling and give all those headquarter humps my warmest regards."

"Right, Tom," Roger said chuckling. "I'll be in touch."

It's too bad not all the senior executives in Washington could be like Roger. He's a down to earth guy who really has his shit together. Well, time's a wasting as they say. I need to get a move on and get ready for my day on that tractor.

CHAPTER TWO

December 3, 1996; Dulles International Airport, Washington, D. C.

As Tom Blaine began day thirty-eight of his forty-five day unpaid suspension, several of the players in what Tom referred to as the charade to force him from DEA, were also beginning theirs. The most prominent of the players, John Conway, the current Administrator of the Drug Enforcement Administration sat in a plush Corinthian leather chair in an opulently appointed VIP lounge at Dulles International Airport outside of Washington, D.C. conferring with Raymond Perkins, his number two man. Conway, a short but powerfully built man with a slightly receding hair line, and a lip that curved upwards giving him a permanent sneer was a former FBI agent and U.S. Attorney who had been appointed to his post by a newly-elected president on the recommendation of an old friend, the Director of the FBI. At the time of his appointment, many old timers in DEA felt he had come to DEA with a hidden agenda, which was to orchestrate the demise of DEA and fold its responsibility, and more importantly, its annual one billion dollar budget into the FBI. In the four years that he had been the Administrator, Conway, who had failed in his covert mission to dissolve the agency, had ruled the agency with an iron fist. He had continually demonstrated his open contempt for DEA agents in general, so common in FBI types, and had been the cause of a plummeting morale amongst the rank and file agents. As a result of his antagonism, many of the senior level and more experienced agents had been purged from the ranks of DEA by retirement or involuntary terminations leaving it with only a skeleton of experienced agents and ripe for the pruning by a power-hungry FBI.

"Mr. Administrator," began Perkins, a career DEA agent and former Marine captain and the number two man in DEA, "here are those figures you asked for concerning the funds that we have allocated for the Colombians." He handed Conway a sheet of paper. "As you can see," the graying Perkins said, "We are offering them in the form of money and equipment close to one hundred million dollars over the next two years."

Conway, who was attired in a blue pin-striped suit appeared as if he stepped off the page of an Esquire Magazine. He sipped his coffee from a beige, bone china cup provided by a hostess in the lounge and reviewed the papers. "Ray, does this money come from DEA's operating budget?" Before Perkins could answer, Conway interjected, "This is terrible coffee." He screwed up his face and stared at the coffee cup. Looking around the lavishly appointed lounge, he said, "You think that they could have something better to offer here."

Perkins, accustomed to Conway's numerous petty criticisms, ignored the Administrator's coffee critique. "No, sir. Only about thirty percent comes from our operating budget. The rest comes from the State Department Anti-Narcotics Budget and the remainder from a supplemental appropriations budget offered by Congress through the Department of Agriculture."

"One hundred million dollars," exclaimed Conway looking up from the papers. He met the gray-blue eyes of Perkins and continued with a distinct tone of utter distaste in his voice. "Blood money is what this is, Ray. We're giving this money to a bunch of crooks who couldn't give a shit about our drug problem in hopes that we can solicit their cooperation at targeting the organized crime in their country. Those corrupt bastards have been taking our money for years and what have we received in return?" Conway shook the sheave of papers at Perkins. As his face reddened with anger, Conway continued without waiting for a response from the passive Perkins. "Nothing, I tell you, nothing but a corrupt Administration that takes money from us and the cartels to finance their private interests." In a show of disgust, Conway threw the papers onto a massive oak coffee table in front of him. His frown dissolved into a sneer. "It makes me physically ill to think of the programs we could establish and run here that would be of direct benefit for Americans with the money we have thrown down that shit hole of a country."

Having also grown accustomed to Conway's somewhat volatile temperament and knowing how nothing he could say would shake Conway from his current mood, Perkins replied in an even, placid voice. "Yes, sir. I know how you feel, Mr. Administrator, but if we want to keep a presence in Colombia and recognize some limited success by our continued presence, then I'm afraid the money is necessary."

"Damn it, Ray, I know that for Christ's sake." Conway fumed as his face and visible portions of his neck colored from a slight blush to red. "But I don't like it, and as a taxpayer myself, I resent the extent to which we have to go to solicit the cooperation of a country like Colombia. If the people of this country had any inkling of the extent of the money that we have squandered on our foreign drug enforcement efforts, we'd have a massive taxpayers' revolt. And I for one would not blame them."

Perkins knew Conway had been an outspoken critic of DEA's foreign efforts from day one. He also knew Conway was in one of his foul moods again. Instead of responding to the bait Conway dangled, he merely shrugged his shoulders, neither contradicting nor confirming the Administrator's opinions.

Seeing he could not antagonize Perkins into attempting to defend DEA's foreign drug enforcement role, Conway gave up. "Okay, Ray, I understand our position. Mind you, I don't goddamn like it, but I understand it." He changed the subject. "And where the hell is Peterson?" I told him to be here by seven o'clock this morning to brief me on the OPR matters."

"I don't know, Mr. Administrator. Let me take a look outside and see if he's waiting there." Perkins stood to leave the lounge.

"While you're looking for Peterson, see if you can also find me a decent cup of coffee." Conway held up his distasteful coffee. "There must be a coffee shop somewhere in this terminal that can serve something that does not taste like crap."

Perkins acknowledged Conway's demand with a simple nod of his head. He wondered whose head would roll this time for some perceived minor infraction of the rules and regulations. *I'm sure glad I've decided to take that job offer with Federal Express. At the end of the month, I'm history, and John Conway will have to find someone else to kick around and fetch his own damn coffee.*

Perkins exited the VIP lounge and looked over the small entourage that would accompany the Administrator on his trip to the International Drug Enforcement Conference (IDEC) in Bogota, Colombia. Perkins noted that Peterson, the person for whom the administrator was looking, sat by himself away from the group talking on his cell phone. Perkins made eye contact with him and signaled with his hand for Peterson to come into the lounge.

As Perkins held the door open for Peterson, he quietly cautioned, "Be careful, James, he's in a foul mood today."

Peterson acknowledged the caution with a simple nod of his head and walked directly to where John Conway sat.

Perkins watched Peterson approach the Administrator and then turned to exit the lounge. *Let me see if I can find that clown some coffee.*

James Peterson, the senior Executive Service Agent in charge of DEA's Office of Professional Responsibility, the Internal Affairs entity of DEA, always dressed impeccably. Today his attire consisted of a light gray Armani suit and black Floresheim wingtip shoes. He, like Perkins, was fit, trim, and had been a DEA agent for approximately twenty years. However, unlike Perkins, Peterson's career seemed to be going nowhere until a chance meeting with Conway in Newark where Peterson was the Demand Reduction Coordinator for the Newark Division. Impressed by Peterson's demeanor at a Just Say No Conference and, more importantly, by his Afro American heritage, which made him politically correct with the current administration, Conway had jump started Peterson's rather drab career. With a series of quick promotions, Conway propelled him into his current powerful position. Many in DEA, including most of the other black senior agents, thought Peterson had become a Judas Priest who had served Conway's purpose of ridding DEA of many career agents who differed with Conway's views on drug law enforcement. He approached Conway timidly.

"Sit down, Jim."

Peterson bristled at the name Jim, a familiarization of his given name James that he despised. He took a seat adjacent to the Administrator. Had it been anyone else other than the man sitting adjacent to him, Peterson would have instantly corrected the individual by saying, "Don't call me Jim. My name is James." Peterson had said this so often to unsuspecting individuals that he was known throughout DEA as "James, don't call me Jim" Peterson. What can I do for you, sir?"

"Bring me up-to-date on the current OPR cases, Jim," Conway said as he sat back in the chair and looked directly at Peterson.

Again cringing at the familiarized first name, Peterson began. "We have the New York matter under control."

"And which New York matter are you referring to?"

"The missing $75,000 flash roll from the New York State and Local Task Force, sir."

"The flash roll ripped off by the Jamaicans during that undercover deal two days ago?" asked Conway.

"Yes, sir, that's the one."

"Well, what's the story?" Conway drummed his fingers on the arm of the chair and drilled holes into Peterson's forehead with his penetrating eyes.

"As you know, sir, two New York State cops and a DEA agent posing as would-be buyers attempted to purchase several kilos of cocaine. Heavily armed confederates of the alleged drug trafficker robbed them at gunpoint. One of the state cops was seriously wounded in the fray. He'll survive, but his law enforcement career is over. And one of the Jamaicans was shot and killed by the other state cop and our agent, but not before the other Jamaicans made off with the flash roll."

"So the money has not been recovered yet?"

"No, sir, but according to the ASAC in New York overseeing the task force, they know the identities of several of the perpetrators and are obtaining arrest warrants."

Conway gestured with the hand that had been drumming on the arm of the chair. "Cut to the chase, Jim. The bottom line. Could this have been prevented? Was this poor planning? Was there insufficient supervision?"

"No, sir," Peterson replied quickly sensing the Administrator's impatience with him. "Not that we've been able to determine at this time. It appears the basic game plan was well thought out and there was adequate supervision on the street. The group supervisor is relatively young, but she appeared to do everything according to the book."

"Then explain to me how this happened if everything was so well thought out and by the book," demanded Conway. Before Peterson could reply, Conway asked, "Where the heck is Perkins with that coffee?"

Peterson disregarded the Administrator's question about the whereabouts of his coffee. "The three undercovers had dealt with these crooks on several occasions purchasing up to a pound of cocaine at a time with no hint of any problems. The evening before last, the three UC's did a surprise flash and showed the crooks the money when they were not expecting it. They did this flash in a parking lot of a small strip mall out on Long Island, which was not the home turf of the Jamaicans. It was supposed to be just a meet-and-confer to set up a time and place for the delivery. So the crooks had no idea they would be shown the money or that there was even money present. As the meeting concluded, and after the UC's had shown the crooks the money, which was in a briefcase in the trunk of the UC vehicle, confederates of the main crook came careening into the parking lot and crashed into the rear of the UC car. In a barrage of bullets from automatic weapons, approximately seven Jamaicans exited the van, shot the state cop and stole the briefcase containing the flash roll before surveillance could react. The other state cop and our agent, who were initially dazed from the accident, eventually, returned fire, killing one of the Jamaicans before he could get back into the van. A high speed pursuit of the van then commenced but quickly terminated when the GS decided that the fleeing Jamaicans, who were still shooting from the speeding van, posed great danger to innocent bystanders." At this point, Peterson stopped his explanation and looked at the pensive face of Conway.

"I see, Jim. So what's the follow up so far?"

"We know the identities of several of the Jamaicans in the van, and the New York office is getting warrants for their arrest as we speak. The money is, more than likely, long gone and the state cop survived seven hours of surgery. One round penetrated his spinal column; it's doubtful he'll ever walk again."

Perkins returned bearing a cup of Starbucks coffee for the Administrator and set it on the coffee table in front of him.

With his full attention now directed toward Peterson, Conway commented, "Jim, I'm having a hard time understanding how an incident like this could have occurred if the plan was so well thought out. I want your people to examine the game plan closely and discern how the events unfolded. I would be willing to bet that the GS did not do everything in her power to prevent such an occurrence. Look closely at her and any other DEA types at the scene including our UC. While you're at it, examine if the ASAC was involved in the planning stages. If heads are going to roll, I intend to start at the top and work down and not the opposite."

Peterson looked from the administrator to Perkins for support.

"Sir," interjected Perkins, "from our initial reports, it appears our UC did everything by the book and was quite brave in exchanging fire with seven Jamaicans armed with automatic weapons, while he was only armed with a five-shot Smith and Wesson two inch revolver."

"A five-shot revolver. Where was his service automatic?" Conway demanded with a raised voice and furrows developing on his forehead.

"Sir, in undercover operations, it is necessary to carry a smaller weapon so it can be hidden. And as you know, we have not adopted any of the smaller, more powerful weapons for our agents to use in undercover," offered Perkins.

"That's all well and good, Ray," allowed Conway as he looked first at Perkins and then at Peterson. "But let's not lose sight of the fact that we are missing $75,000 and a cop is paralyzed. Just have your people examine this incident closely. Do I make myself clear?" He carefully tasted his coffee.

"Yes, sir," replied Peterson.

Conway's next question interrupted Peterson's train of thought. "What else have you got for me?" Before Peterson could answer, Conway held his coffee up to Perkins. "Much better, Ray."

"Well, sir, just before I came in here, I received a call from the Chief Counsel's Office. We may have a problem with that federal lawsuit against Marsha Grant and DEA in Denver involving the dead Denver Police Officers and Blaine."

The name of Blaine had an instant effect on the composure of Conway. "What kind of problem?" he demanded looking at Peterson with eyebrows twisted into a frown.

"Well, uh…" Peterson stammered and fidgeted with his hands, a signal to Perkins that Peterson was about to break some bad news to Conway.

As Peterson searched for the right words, a slight sweat broke out at his receding hairline.

Shit, Perkins thought, *I've never seen Peterson this nervous before. I'll bet he's done something to screw up this Blaine matter and now he has to fess up.*

"James, what have you done now?" Perkins asked. Before Peterson could respond, Perkins continued. "I warned you about taking Blaine on. Christ, the guy's a hero in Denver. Several Denver cops are still alive thanks to his heroics at the scene of that search warrant of that crack house that turned deadly. Hell, he recently received the Attorney General's Award for his heroism. Why do you continually try to screw with him?"

"Well, sir," began a now red-faced Peterson. Taking a deep breath, he continued. "It seems the judge in Denver has demanded that the U.S. Attorney in Denver appear in court tomorrow to answer motions raised by the petitioners that DEA is attempting to dissuade a key witness from testifying in their behalf. She's handling the civil wrongful death lawsuit filed by the families of the deceased officers."

"And this witness is Blaine?" Conway asked.

"Uh…yes, sir," replied Peterson meekly. He sat back in his chair attempting to put a little more distance between him and Conway sensing Conway was about the explode.

Peterson's attempt to cower away from him, Conway realized immediately that he had the upper hand and launched into a tirade. "God damn it," he shouted with his voice carrying throughout the relatively quiet lounge. Slamming the coffee down on the table in front of him, some of its contents spilled. "I should have known better than to listen to you about taking care of Blaine." His face reddened, but he got a better grip on his emotions and spoke in a mimicking voice. "Let's find some reason to discipline him. If we can give him thirty to forty days off without pay, he'll retire. He's too proud to serve a suspension. It would also serve to discredit his reputation, if we can find something adverse about his integrity. Do you remember those words Peterson?"

"Uh, yes sir, but…"

"Don't but me. You were wrong again, Jim. I talked with his SAC, Marsha Grant, several days ago and according to her, Blaine has already served thirty-some odd days of his suspension and the only papers Blaine has filed are to the Merit System Protection Board to appeal his discipline formally. If his appeal goes like the majority of the appeals recently filed against DEA disciplinary measures, we'll lose and have to pay his back pay and attorney fees.

"Mr. Administrator…," Peterson attempted in a strong voice.

"No, Peterson. I don't want to hear any more of your excuses. I told you the misuse of the government vehicle was very weak to use against him. I shouldn't have listened to you. I should have relied on my own hunches. You see, I remember a statement Mr. Blaine made during a meeting I attended a year ago in preparation for Operation Snowcap. He indicated an unwillingness to make a permanent transfer from the Denver area. I believe he stated he wanted to retire there. Ray, you were at that meeting, weren't you?" Conway asked as he directed his attention to Perkins.

"Yes, sir, but I don't recall his statement." Perkins lied knowing Tom Blaine had indicated he did not want to leave Denver before his retirement. His lie was an effort to protect Blaine, who he considered to be one of the better supervisors in the agency, and who Conway, was making a career out of chasing off before they were ready to retire.

"Well, I do," pronounced Conway as he turned his attention back to Peterson. "I may not be able to affect his credibility as a witness in his case, but I want him gone from DEA. Do I make myself clear?"

"Not exactly, sir. What would you like me to do?" Peterson asked in a challenging voice but absent his usual authority.

"Transfer his ass," Conway spit.

"Transfer him?" a tentative Peterson asked.

"Yes, God damn it, transfer him. Then I'll bet he'll hurt himself putting in his retirement papers.

"Okay. I could see where a place like Cleveland, Detroit or Newark could force his hand," offered a contrite Peterson.

Conway stared at Peterson for a long moment. "Peterson, are you as dumb as you look? Don't transfer him to some shit-hole assignment. That would play right into his hand." He shook his head in apparent disgust. "Transfer him to some office considered desirable or at least high profile like Los Angeles or San Diego. Jesus, do I have to do all the thinking around here?"

"Mr. Administrator, don't you think that might further antagonize the judge in Denver?" asked Peterson. "I mean, it might look like retaliation against a whistle blower."

Conway hesitated a minute before a slight smirk developed on his face. "Peterson, have you ever read the book the *Peter Principle*?"

"No, sir, but I do believe the Peter Principle is a theory about competence."

"That's correct. Actually, the Peter Principle is a theory about how people ultimately get to a level of incompetence. I'm beginning to think that you could be a poster child for the theory," said Conway, his voice full of sarcasm.

"Mr. Administrator..." began Peterson sheepishly in his own defense.

"Save it, Peterson." He pointed his index finger at Peterson. "I don't want to hear another word from you except 'yes, sir.' I'll just have to make the decisions here, as I don't believe I can trust your judgment any longer on this Blaine matter. As far as retribution against a whistle blower and the judge in Denver goes...well, I know a thing or two about judicial matters and the law." Then turning to Perkins, Conway gave him an order. "Ray, transfer Blaine along with several other supervisors who are eligible for transfer to offices in need of supervisory agents. Make sure Blaine goes to some place like Los Angeles, which I happen to know is short several Group Supervisors. Our response to the Denver judge will be that we simply transferred Blaine, along with several other supervisors, to satisfy some supervisory shortages. We'll also insure the Denver judge that DEA will make Blaine available for any court matter in the pending lawsuit." Conway then turned back to Peterson. "And that's how it's done, Jim."

"Yes, sir," was the simple response from Peterson.

As Conway picked up some papers laying on the oak table in front of him, he signaled the conversation with Peterson was over.

Peterson arose and walked toward the exit of the VIP lounge.

Perkins opened the door for him as they exited together. "I told you he was in a pissy mood, James."

"Yes, you did, Ray, but the Administrator just does not seem to understand there is only so much that can be done in the Blaine matter to accomplish what he wants done and not venture into an area where we could really expose ourselves to legal ramifications."

"I know, James. Now I'll have to upset the lives of several DEA supervisors by transferring them along with Blaine just to satisfy the ego of his majesty. And if I were you, I'd try to keep a low profile for a while as he seems to have you in his sights now."

CHAPTER THREE

December 3, 1996; Hacienda Puesta Del Sol, La Cruz, Sinaloa, Mexico

Juan Cervantes drove his late-model Chevrolet Silverado Pickup through the gates of the lavish estate of Jaime Gutiérrez. He beckoned a familiar "Hola" to the two heavily armed guards and began the gradual meandering ascent to the main house of the Hacienda Puesta Del Sol. As he continued through the almost quarter-kilometer distance from the gate to the main house, Juan considered the similarity of this estate with that of his former jefe (boss), Miguel Felix Uriarte. Miguel's estancia, on the outskirts of Guadalajara, was equally massive and ornate in its own style. Even though Juan had grown accustomed to the obscene amounts of money generated by the drug business that produced these ostentatious displays of wealth, it always created a mild awe within him. This fascination with the monies that the drug business could produce began first with his now deceased former jefe or Don Miguel as Juan used to call him. At one time, Don Miguel controlled the most powerful drug cartel in Mexico. He died violently, along with his immediate family, most likely at the hands of some vicious vindictive Colombians. Now, as an employee of the Gutiérrez brothers, Jaime and Hector, once Don Miguel's fiercest Mexican competitors, this fascination with obscene wealth continued.

Whereas Don Miguel's estancia was set in the lush green tropical rainforest in the verdant hills surrounding Guadalajara, the Hacienda Puesta Del Sol sat on a vast, almost bleak, windswept promontory with an unobstructed panoramic view of the Pacific Ocean from its expansive backside facing the west. Located adjacent to the small town of La Cruz, it was almost equidistant from Culiacan to the north and Mazatlán to the south in the state of Sinaloa on the west coast of Mexico. Comprising just over 4000 Hectares, or 10,000 acres, it was a virtual armed camp with a high wire fence surrounding the entire property with state-of-the-art security cameras and devices. Armed guards, or ayudantes, provided the human security. Many ayudantes had been, or still were, members of other legal law enforcement organizations. Some came from the Mexican Federal Judicial Police (MFJP), Sinaloa State Police and the Direccion General De Investigation y Seguridad the successor organization to the much-feared Federal de Seguridad (DFS),

Mexico's equivalent of the Russian KGB.

The main house of the Hacienda Puesta Del Sol was a more than modest forty-two room, two story beige stucco with red-tiled roof and Spanish edifice. The house, perched a relatively safe distance from a sheer cliff that dropped 100 feet to a rocky coast line below, sat at the end of a long Palm tree lined drive that terminated under a covered portico, which accessed the main house through a closed courtyard.

This was the home of Jaime Gutiérrez and his family. Esteban, Jaime's twenty-five year old mentally challenged younger brother, also resided with him at the Hacienda. Hector, Jaime's Harvard-educated younger brother lived in a suite in a high-rise hotel in Mazatlán, which he and his brothers owned. This seemed to fit his bachelor-playboy lifestyle much better than the estancia so far away from the action of city living.

The overt displays of drug-induced wealth did not cease with their abodes. Whereas Don Miguel had a penchant for racehorses and expensive mistresses, Jaime Gutiérrez collected high-priced sports cars. Several stables and other out buildings that dotted the immense property housed a collection of Maserati's, Ferraris, Lotus, Lamborghinis, Jaguars, Mercedes and Porsches. Jaime also collected Chevrolet Corvettes, and one entire garage housed a collection of fully restored vintage Corvettes. Juan's previous jefe, Don Miguel, preferred to traverse the local streets in an expensive Land Rover. Jaime, the obvious Don of the Gutiérrez family, preferred a Chevrolet Suburban he had a firm in Dallas outfit with armor. This same Dallas Company converted factory-produced Suburbans into bullet resistant vehicles for police SWAT teams throughout the United States. Even the tires were of special quality and could not be easily flatten by sudden punctures.

Security was a big concern for Jaime as it had been for Don Miguel. Both the Estancia de Uriarte and the Hacienda Puesta Del Sol were heavily fortified enclaves with a small army of security personnel. While most of the major traffickers in Mexico operated with impunity and little interference from the government, that is as long as the appropriate mordita—literally translated as the bite, or bribe, was paid, there was a common concern about threats from competitors.

In March 1996, a spectacular event occurred that created a major panic amongst the traffickers causing them to increase their respective security arrangements significantly. An armed highly trained commando unit that kidnapped him and destroyed his estancia attacked Don Miguel's Estancia. Because it was more or less common knowledge that the Attorney General of Mexico, Doctor Jorge Cardenas, shrouded Don Miguel from government interference, a general fear rose up amongst the traficante that anyone could become fair game from this unknown armed group. Even Jaime, who regularly paid large tributes to the Mexican Minister of Defense who controlled the military and the Minister of Justice, retained a genuine fear from this unknown group.

While there had been a lot of speculation following the kidnapping and raid on the Estancia de Uriarte, both the traffickers and the Mexican government came to the same common consensus. They concluded a right wing group much in the fashion of the Minute Men Militia in the United States was responsible for this raid. Some thought the raiders were an adjunct group of the CIA, even though the United States government vehemently denied any involvement in this action.

Juan Cervantes did not share this consensus. Having been present at the time of the raid and the subsequent kidnapping of Don Miguel, Juan knew the armed commando unit was in fact a group of highly-trained DEA agents operating in Mexico without the knowledge of or consent of either DEA or the Mexican government. Their leader, a Señor Thomas Blaine, had allowed Juan to escort Don Miguel's spouse and children from the estancia taking with him a satchel containing in excess of two million dollars. Blaine gave Juan instructions to take the money for himself. He was to share his knowledge of Don Miguel's substantial assets located in the United States with other DEA agents.

Juan, a confirmed forty-two year old bachelor of slight build and prematurely graying hair, had returned to Mexico in August 1996 and, at his insistence, had met with Jaime and his brother Hector at Fonda El Refugio, a moderately priced restaurant in Mexico City.

Understanding Juan's concern for his safety and his fear of Hector and Jaime, the Gutiérrez brothers had agreed to meet him in a public locale. They were quick at the outset of this meeting to attempt to assuage his fears. "Come work for us, Juan, as business manager, the same capacity you worked for Miguel Felix; you have nothing to fear. We will pay double whatever Miguel Felix paid you. However, if you choose not to, we cannot guarantee the safety of your school-teacher brother and his young family in Cuernavaca," advised

Jaime. *The old Plata y Ploma – Silver or lead offer* thought Juan. *I take either your money or the lead from a bullet.* Knowing that Jaime had a well-deserved reputation as a ruthless killer, Juan opted for the Plata, or more precisely, the money the Gutiérrez brothers offered him. He acted quickly to insure his employment would not only benefit the brothers but would also insure the ultimate safety of his own brother and his family.

Since his return in August, Juan had determined that Jaime, and his brother Hector to a lesser extent, aspired to achieve the same dominant position in the cocaine, heroin, marijuana and methamphetamine business that his former deceased boss Don Miguel had maintained. Through a systematic scheme of eliminating the competition and government interference, again using the tried and true Plata y Ploma strategy, the two brothers moved closer to their goal. In the process, they had often littered the streets and countryside of Mexico with bodies of those who opted to resist their persistent efforts. It didn't matter to the Gutiérrez's if you were a drug trafficker, an important politician or even a member of the news media. If you proved to be an obstacle, they arranged for your permanent removal. While they had succeeded in becoming the most feared of the traficantes in Mexico, they had also become the most targeted by those who sought revenge for the killings of loved ones. The news media and certain elements in the federal government branded them as vicious murderers.

As they increased their control and power over the narcotic trafficking, their political influence had also grown. The Assistant director of El Cendro, the National Centre for Drug Control Policy, was now tucked safely in their hip pockets along with several officials in the Attorney General's Office.

The right money to the right person can get you a lot in this country, concluded Juan as he parked his truck under the portico of the main house. He proceeded into the hacienda. *While Jaime and Hector worry me, they also disgust me. Taking a life to them is nothing; it's just business. No matter what they pay me, it will never erase the disdain I have for them and their brutal ways. Given the opportunity, I will get my brother and his family out of Mexico and harm's way. In the interim, I have very little choice but to play the dutiful humble servant and assist them in their drug business.*

"Hola, Juan, Como Le Va?" asked Jaime Gutiérrez. Looking up from his seated position at his desk, Jaime watched Juan enter what served as the office for their drug empire. This room, located on a lower level of the Hacienda, was windowless with dark paneling covering the walls. The dark oak furniture included a massive desk for Jaime and a smaller computer table for Juan. Several computers sat on both the desk and table along with numerous telephones. A large projection-style television occupied one corner of the office always tuned to CNN, which Jaime dutifully watched to keep abreast of world events.

"Everything's good," replied Juan who preferred to speak in English. The Gutiérrez brothers didn't seem to mind accommodating him. Juan crossed the room to his place at the computer table.

Moving back from his computer, Jaime took a sip of coffee from a mug on his desk. "Juan, Hector and I are very pleased that you decided to come to work for us as our business manager. You have done very well in the few months you have been with us. Our accounts are looking good."

Like I really had a choice, thought Juan. He stared at the heavily scarred face of the forty-five year old ruthless traficante. At five feet six inches tall and a muscular build, the dark-haired, rugged-looking Jaime exuded power and certainly had the wherewithal to back up his appearance.

"I am pleased you and Hector are happy with my efforts, Jefe," replied Juan.

Jaime smiled. "I can see why Miguel Felix placed so much trust and confidence in you, Juan. You are very capable."

"Gracias, señor."

"While we still have a way to go to achieve my goal of convincing the Ojeda's we should be their single distribution system in Mexico for their merchandise, we have made great strides, mostly because of your efforts, mi amigo."

"Well, Jefe, it certainly helped that we were able to locate several thousand kilos of their product when Miguel Felix met his demise. The twenty-three million we generated from them went a long way to smooth a working relationship with the Ojeda's."

"Sí, Sí, Juan, I agree. Also your bringing Ramon Acevedo on board really expedited our cash flow from the Norte America."

"As I told you when I recommended him, Jefe, Ramon is an expert in smuggling cash from the United States. During our time when we both worked for Miguel Felix, he never lost money coming south. Also his contacts in the United States always seemed to be able to collect what was due even from those who were reluctant to pay what was owed."

"Yes, yes, I agree he has been a very important addition to our organization and well worth the percentage he gets from what he collects. I have no complaints at all with his work, Juan. He is worth every peso we are paying him."

"Jefe, while we are discussing Ramon, I know that you have relied heavily upon Hector to find outlets to invest your vast incomes from the business. However, in seeing what you have done with your money to date, I would like to make a suggestion. Perhaps you should allow Ramon to find some other investments for you. He has many connections in the United States and many safe and profitable avenues for investment."

A look of concern developed on Jaime's usually stoic face. "I don't know, Juan. Hector's role as this family's investor has proven to be both lucrative and safe. He has a degree in finance from Harvard, you know, and I trust what he has done so far."

"Sí, Jefe, I know how valuable Hector has been in this regard to your organization. I am not finding fault with his efforts. What I am suggesting is that you allow Ramon to search out some other possible investment opportunities. He could then run them by Hector. It seems a shame to have all that money sitting in banks earning just simple interest when it could be working more aggressively for you. Besides that, sometimes two heads are better than one in developing outlets for this money. For example, Ramon aided Miguel-Felix in investing in a small strip mall in San Diego. Within six months, his one million dollars had become two when he sold the property to some Japanese investors. He doubled his money in under six months."

"Let me think about it, Juan." Jaime turned back to his computer suggesting this conversation had run its course. After several minutes of manipulating the keyboard, he turned to Juan again. "Oye, Juan, do you think the time is right to approach the Ojeda's about our plan to increase our percentage of transporting their product?"

Juan thought a moment before he spoke. "We are close, Jefe, but first I think we need to prove to them we are untouchable here in Mexico, just like Don Miguel did when he had that large shipment under your control seized by the federales and the pinche DEA."

"Carajo, Juan, don't remind me of that. That lost shipment cost Hector and me a lot of money to make things right with Carlos and his brother. And then we lost his business to that pendejo Miguel-Felix anyway." By Jaime's change of voice, it was evident it didn't take much to anger him.

"I know, jefe, but maybe we should see if we can do the same with some of our competitors to prove to Carlos and his brother Rafael that he should solely rely on you."

"Okay, Juan, let me develop a plan, and we'll see what we can do."

CHAPTER FOUR

December 3, 1996; Franktown, Colorado

Aiming his vintage 1964 International Scout east toward the town of Elizabeth on State Highway 86, Tom Blaine had just cleared the few stores that comprised the business district of the quaint Franktown, Colorado. As he began the ascent up the hills, he noted there seemed to be very little traffic on this bright sunny day. *It sure has warmed up nicely since that blizzard the other day,* thought Tom. *But then, that's Colorado—snowy and cold one day and sunny and 60 degrees a day later. That old saying if you don't like the Colorado weather, wait a day and it will be different is certainly true,* he concluded.

Tom had just finished delivering his aging John Deere Tractor to the local dealership for an electrical repair job beyond his own capability. After a late breakfast at the B&B Café in Castle Rock, Tom was heading home towing his empty trailer. As he began the ascent on one of the gradual elevation increases, which would ultimately deposit him on a plateau of almost 8,000 feet above sea level, he considered the effect this two-lane road had on him. The well-worn state road caused him irresolute feelings at times. At the end of a particularly trying day, he found the road produced a cathartic effect. As he drove upward and eastward toward his peaceful country home, away from the hustle and bustle of Denver and problems of work, he felt relief from the mental strain. At other times, while he maintained the posted legal speed limit of sixty miles per hour, the road added to his stress. Other drivers, who felt it was their God-given right to drive over the speed limit and unable to pass him on many stretches of the highway, hugged his rear bumper in a subtle effort to urge him to go faster. These tailgaters did little to ease his usually high stress level and on a number of occasions added to it.

On this particular bright, sunny winter day, there was little traffic to aggravate Tom. He motored along, noting the snow-covered pines blanketing the hills. He considered the late breakfast he had just enjoyed. *Hard to beat the eggs and corned beef hash from the B&B,* he decided followed by a slight belch. *Those homemade biscuits are the absolute best,* he concluded.

The B&B Café, where Tom was a frequent customer was located in downtown Castle Rock. It was a historic site having been continually in business since 1899. Upon entering the front door of the café, one could sense its rich heritage. A long marble counter ran parallel to the south wall, and according to the history of the café detailed on the back of the menu, the counter had been imported from Italy right after the turn of the century. Old photographs of Castle Rock and notable patrons of the café adorned the walls. Then there was the bullet hole in the tin ceiling caused by an errant round when a villain shot and killed the town marshal. "Yes, indeed, it was worth the extra fifteen miles out of my way to go by the B&B," he uttered to himself as he pressed eastward.

Several miles east of Franktown, as Tom cleared a slight rise and began his descent to a small valley, he noted the flashing red and blue lights of an emergency vehicle stationary up ahead. "John Law got someone, I guess, or maybe it's an accident. The roads are icy this morning with the melting snow from yesterday and then the freezing temperatures last night," he said to himself.

Slowing down as he approached the emergency vehicle, he noted that it was a Colorado State Patrol vehicle. It had a full-sized commercial van stopped on the narrow shoulder of the road. *I'll bet that's Patrolman Epps. According to his captain that prick would write his mother a ticket if he caught her violating the vehicle code,* thought Tom. He drew closer, and Tom could see the patrolman had two individuals in the leaning search position outside their van. Their hands were on the van and their legs spread out and back at a forty-five degree angle. On closer examination, Tom could see the two individuals were Hispanic, and if he could use his police hunch and not be chastised for profiling he would have deduced that the two individuals were apparent gangbangers.

Just as Tom and his trailer-pulling Scout were abreast of the CSP vehicle, parked some fifteen yards behind the detained van, a tire on the right side of Tom's trailer hit an un-melted chunk of ice. It caused the metal-loading ramps in the bed of the trailer to bounce on the metal frame. The sound of the metal meeting metal distracted the attention of the patrolman.

Turning his head toward the sound of Tom's trailer, the patrolman failed to keep his eyes on the two detained individuals for just an instant. In those few seconds, the two gangbangers, who had in all probability, practiced escape techniques from police custody before, turned on the patrolman. One quickly wrestled him to the ground, while the other, who hadn't been searched, pulled a small semi-automatic pistol from his belt and pumped two rounds into the patrolman's back area exposed while he wrestled with the other gangbanger.

"Holy shit, "Tom exclaimed when he saw the CSP patrol officer slump to the ground. Slamming on the breaks of the Scout, he brought it to a sudden halt. Quickly he reached behind him and retrieved his Ruger Mini-14 Ranch rifle from a rack mounted above the left side rear window where he kept it in case of situations involving four-legged and now two-legged varmints. Tom leaped from the Scout and yelled at the gangbangers in hopes of distracting them from taking further shots at the patrolman. His actions worked, and the gangbanger with the pistol fired two quick rounds at Tom, both of which missed him but struck his Scout.

"Shit," Tom exclaimed again." He ducked for cover behind the front bumper of the scout. As he did so, he observed the second gangbanger reach down and remove the patrolman's handgun, which had remained holstered on his left side.

With both gangbangers now armed, their courage grew, and they decided to leave no witnesses to their shooting of the patrolman. Unaware that Tom had a weapon, the first gangbanger, who had shot the patrolman, charged toward Tom's position using the CSP vehicle as a partial shield. From behind the left rear end of the CSP vehicle, which was within twenty feet of Tom's Scout, he opened fire, sending several rounds in Tom's direction. "You're dead meat, gringo."

"I don't think so, homey," Tom said in a slight voice more of an encouragement for him than as a threat to the gangbanger. Several more shots rang out and as they struck his Scout, Tom decided it was time for him to take action. A relative calm came over Tom. He had experienced this a number of times over the years when thrust into violent confrontations. He first experienced these periods of relative calming, which Tom attributed to a stronger fight than flight mental attitude, as a Marine in Vietnam in combat and then as an Agent for DEA in violent confrontations with armed suspects. This seemingly *never back down from a fight* resolve afforded Tom the ability to think and react to these assaults in a clear and objective manner, which heretofore had insured his safety while at the same time eliminating the risk. With a lull in the firing from the suspect, Tom rose up and saw the suspect visually scanning Tom's position for a clear shot.

"I see you, pendejo," shouted the gangbanger, which he followed with two shots aimed at Tom. However, his aim was poor, and he only managed to strike the Scout. Tom had a fleeting thought. *Jesus, I wonder if they suspended my medical insurance along with my pay and allowances.* He quickly shrugged off his concern, rose up and fired two quick rounds at the suspect. His accuracy with the Mini-14, a smaller version of the M-14, the weapon he carried for a number of years while in the Marine Corps and the weapon that just a year ago he used to complete a weeklong sniper school hosted by a local police department, was marginal but effective. The first .223 caliber round merely produced a flesh wound to the gangbanger's left hip area. However, the second round found a more deadly spot in the gangbanger's chest. Dropping his weapon first, the gangbanger, with a startled look on his face, looked down at the damage done to him by Tom's bullets. As a red spot quickly manifested itself on the chest area of his heavy winter jacket, he looked at Tom and then at his chest. Slowly, he dropped to the ground exhibiting no further life signs.

The second suspect, now realizing Tom had shot his accomplice, decided it would be best to flee to fight another day. He ran to the van and while Tom positioned himself to take the van under fire, the gangbanger started the engine, slapped the transmission into drive and floored the accelerator. With a slight roar, the van first lurched forward and then as it hit a slick area on the shoulder of the road, began to slide sideways. The more gas poured to the engine, the faster the rear wheels spun sliding the van further sideways deeper into the heavy snow that had obscured the shoulder drop off. Realizing his transportation from was now out of commission, the gangbanger exited the van through the front passenger door where he took up a position to shoot at anyone who approached the van.

Tom watched the actions of the gangbanger. *I have to get that asshole away from the van so I can check on the patrolman. He could still be alive and bleeding out while I screw with this idiot.*

A male voice from behind Tom interrupted his thoughts. "Hey, what the hell is going on here?"

Initially startled by the voice, Tom turned and saw a middle-aged man whom he recognized as the chief of the local volunteer firefighters. Having recently given the local volunteers a four-hour class on the hazards they could face with a clandestine meth lab, both Tom and the firefighter recognized each other.

"Get down," Tom ordered.

The firefighter dropped to a crouching position behind Tom's Scout.

"Got a suspect with a gun who shot the CSP patrolman behind that white van. Can you use your CB radio to summon us some help? We need an ambulance also."

"I can try," offered the firefighter. He rose slightly to run back to his truck.

"Hey," Tom called to him, "and back your truck down the road to block the traffic coming east bound. See if you can raise somebody east of here to block the traffic coming westbound."

"Will do," the firefighter said.

As if his final instruction to the firefighter was a cue to add to an already bad situation, a car heading west on the highway appeared at the top of the rise and slowly descended into the valley. As it approached the mired van with the suspect hidden behind it, Tom could see a female driving the Silver Chevrolet Blazer. It slowed to a crawl.

Tom watched the vehicle heading into the danger zone. "Shit! Keep on going, don't stop," Tom said aloud to himself as he watched the Blazer continue to slow down. "Aw crap, she's going to stop." The Blazer came to a full stop. As he continued to watch, he saw the driver's door open and the female driver stepped out of the vehicle.

Not realizing the totality of the situation and the inherent danger to her wellbeing, she hurried toward the downed patrolman, leaving the motor running in her Blazer.

Aw Christ. This is not going to end well. Tom aimed the Ruger Mini-14 toward the front of the white van from a good solid prone position by the left wheel of his Scout.

Realizing he now had readily available transportation to escape the area, the gang banger broke from his concealed position and ran toward the Blazer. He also realized that with the driver of the Blazer in the road between him and the person in the Scout who had shot his partner, her presence would partly shroud his dash to her Blazer.

Tom, unable to get a clear shot at the gangbanger as he charged to the Blazer, maintained his firing position. Willing himself to disregard the ice-cold pavement, Tom aimed the Ruger Mini-14 at the gangbanger as he started across the road, but he couldn't get a shot off for fear of hitting the lady who was now in the middle of the road and approaching the downed patrolman. *I need to get her out of the way so I can get off a shot before he gets in that Blazer. Once he gets in the Blazer, I may not be able to stop him.* "Get down," Tom yelled as loud as he could.

His command did not have the desired effect, and instead of getting down, the Blazer driver merely stopped in the middle of the road, and looked in Tom's direction. Seeing her hesitation and deciding he needed to cover his final distance to the Blazer some forty feet or so, the gangbanger elected to fire several rounds in Tom's direction.

The driver of the Blazer, hearing the gunshots, reacted like a deer frozen in a set of vehicle headlights. She remained stationary in the middle of the roadway continuing to somewhat obscure Tom's aiming ability.

"Get down," Tom repeated his command.

This time the Blazer driver somewhat complied. She crouched and turned as if to run back toward her Blazer. However, now seeing the gangbanger with a gun running for her car, she reversed herself and ran toward the patrolman's car.

Her actions reminded Tom of an arcade game he and his dad played when he was a youth. In this game, a bear ran across the screen until you shot it with a small rifle attached to the machine. It would roar up, and then turn and run the other way until you shot it again and it would reverse its actions. At least her hesitant movements opened a small field of fire for a shot at the gangbanger. Trying to aim at the moving target one hundred feet from his position, Tom adjusted for the gangbanger's movement by slightly leading the target. He knew the success of any shot would be tenuous at best.

Within ten feet of his goal, and just when it looked like he might make it safely to the Blazer, the environment intervened on the side of law and order. The gangbanger, concentrating on Tom's position and not the roadway in front of him, hit a sheet of ice, slipped and fell. Realizing he was now exposed, he fired several more rounds toward Tom from a crouched position.

Tom, who now had a good shot, returned fire, striking the slightly moving gangbanger in the hip or groin area. The impact of the high velocity bullet spun him around, and he ended up in a sitting position on the roadway facing Tom.

In either shock as the result of his wound, a final act of defiance or just plain suicide by cop, he raised his pistol to fire again at Tom. Before he could do so, Tom fired the Ruger a second time. The bullet struck the gangbanger in his chest. He toppled over to the roadway like a dead weight.

Arising from his prone position, Tom first yelled to the Blazer driver, who in mild hysteria attempted to hide behind the CSP vehicle. "It's okay now. It's all over. We're the good guys. You're safe, ma'am." Tom raised his arm and waved for the firefighter to join him. He then sprinted quickly to the patrolman's position. Tom found the patrolman alive, just barely, having suffered considerable blood loss from a wound in the belt area. Tom also discovered the patrolman's vest had saved him from additional wounds to the back, which would have in all likelihood, killed him instantly. As he attempted to tend to the more serious wound, he heard an emotion-filled voice.

"I'm . . . I'm a physician's assistant. Can I help?"

Turning, Tom saw the Blazer driver, still visibly shaken by the ordeal, attempting to gain control of her emotions. "Yes, see what you can do. I'm going to get on his radio and get us some medical help here."

The Physician Assistant quickly examined the downed patrolman. She turned and yelled to Tom as he walked to the CSP vehicle. "See if you can get Life Flight. He's in critical condition; I suspect the internal bleeding is more severe than the external."

Tom picked up his pace to the CSP vehicle where the firefighter joined him. "I've got the road blocked both ways now. There's an ambulance in route, as well as the Douglas County Sheriff's Department. How's the patrolman?"

"He's alive but in critical condition according to the Blazer driver who turns out to be a PA."

"She was almost a dead PA," offered the firefighter.

"Yeah, but thankfully, the good guys prevailed this time," Tom replied.

"Can I do anything further?" asked the firefighter.

"Yes, keep the traffic away and everybody but law enforcement and medical out of the scene."

"In case you're wondering, both dirt bags are dead."

Tom answered with a nod of his head.

Help was not long in arriving. A Douglas County Sheriff's Department Sergeant arrived first. He took charge of the scene, and as more deputies arrived, he assigned them scene and witness security tasks. An EMS unit arrived and concurred with the PA's assessment of the patrolman's condition.

Within twenty minutes, they heard the sound of the Life Flight helicopter in the distance. Shortly thereafter, it landed on the road, received the critically wounded patrolman and lifted off to the hospital.

The PA, extremely concerned about the patrolman's condition, asked to accompany him on the helicopter. "I can attend to him in route and can be available to advise on-call surgeons at the receiving hospital of his condition," she said.

Tom, knowing that his Scout had sustained numerous bullet holes and would be impounded in order to recover evidence, agreed to drive the Blazer to the PA's home, not far from his own residence in Elbert County.

"My husband will drive you home and will pick me up when I get off tonight," she offered.

As more deputies and command-level officers from both the Sheriff's Department and the Colorado State Patrol arrived on the scene, Tom's role, other than offering an initial statement as to his actions in the shootings, was over. Sitting in the front seat of the PA's Blazer, the reality of what had transpired set in. It started with a slight tremor in his hands and developed into an intense chill with more than a mild case of the shakes. This wasn't his first dance with similar life-threatening episodes. Tom knew all the signs of post-traumatic stress. He would have to endure its effects for a number of months. Like the PTSD he suffered from the death of Marcus Rodriguez in Mexico, frequent and graphic sweat-producing dreams and the constant replaying of the situation in his mind would characterize this PTSD. He also knew as time passed, so would the effects of the PTSD. In the interim, however, he had found the remedy to cope with this physio-psychological condition. A good dose of single malt scotch before bedtime would just about eliminate the dreams. *I sure could use a good dose of Dr. Glenlivet right now. As soon as I get home, the good doctor and I will begin our therapy.*

As he sat in the Blazer, the warmth of the heater relaxed him somewhat. He unbuttoned his coat, reclined the seat and began to doze. A slight tapping on the driver's window jolted him from his short nap.

"Hey, Tom, you okay?"

Tom knew Steve Janarous, the Sheriff of Douglas County both officially and socially. Steve, a career cop in his late forties was a tad bit too short for his weight, as he liked to describe his physique. He wasn't too fat; he was just stout. Usually attired in cowboy boots, a western cut sports coat and western shirt, he looked the western dude he attempted to project. However, once he opened his mouth and began to speak, his New England accent gave him away as not a true westerner. Born in a Boston suburb, he had rebuffed the efforts of his Greek father and grandfather to follow them into the fishing business and, instead, enlisted in the U.S. Army upon graduation from high school. After completing Military Police School at Fort Gordon, the army sent him to Vietnam where he spent a relatively uneventful twelve-month assignment to the Military Assistance Command Headquarters in Saigon. Following Vietnam, he was reassigned to Fort Carson in Colorado Springs, Colorado, where he ultimately received his honorable discharge. Steve went directly from the Military Police to the Colorado Springs Police where he served for the next twenty-two years retiring as a lieutenant.

However, retirement at age forty-four was not for him, and after less than a year spent in retirement, Steve joined the Douglas County Sheriff's Department. Two years later, after scandals of corruption rocked the department, Steve opposed the incumbent and ran for sheriff. He won by a wide margin. Now in his second term, he had transformed a mediocre department into an excellent law enforcement agency.

Tom had aided Steve in his efforts to change the department even though Steve, at first, distanced himself from federal law enforcement. "Too many bad experiences with the feds," was a common refrain he used to say when asked why he remained distant to the feds. However, after several encounters with clandestine meth labs in his jurisdiction, he had to turn to DEA and its large hazardous waste checkbook—a checkbook needed to pay for the EPA mandated cleanup. One such site could shatter Steve's annual budget if he had to fund the removal of the toxic wastes.

Tom not only brought the magic checkbook, but he also brought the asset-sharing procedures, which allowed Steve's department to share in monies and other assets seized under federal law. With Tom's help, Steve was able to update his aging dispatch center, purchase new radios and Kevlar vests for his patrol officers and add a number of vehicles to his fleet. With his hesitation to become involved with the feds over, at least with this fed sitting in this Blazer, Steve and Tom had become friends and frequently enjoyed each other's company at both lunches and breakfasts.

Steve signaled to Tom to roll down the window. "You okay, Tom?"

Tom opened the door and stepped out of the Blazer. He held his hand out to shake Steve's hand. "Yeah, I'm okay. A little jittery, but that's common for me following these confrontations."

"Say, you did a good job. If that patrolman survives, he owes his life to you."

Tom merely nodded his head.

"Tom, I want you to meet somebody." He pointed to a group of CSP officers congregated around the downed patrolman's car.

"Sure, Steve," answered Tom.

Steve led Tom to the group of CSP officers. "Gentlemen," began Sheriff Janarous, "This is Tom Blaine of DEA."

One man with the familiar gold railroad track bars on his jacket signifying that he was a captain held his hand out to Tom. "Mr. Blaine, I am Captain Stowell, the district commander. I want to personally thank you for your efforts here today. Speaking on behalf of my men, I cannot begin to express the extent of our gratitude in what you did while trying to save the life of our officer."

Tom shook the Captain's extended hand. "I just did what I thought needed to be done. I sure hope that young patrolman makes it."

"I guess it's in God's hands now," replied Captain Stowell.

"Do we know why he stopped the van, captain?" asked Sheriff Janarous.

"We were just discussing that. He didn't radio in that he was making a stop. Unfortunately, that's one of our older procedures we're trying to change. I had my sergeant here run the plates on the van, and while they reflect that they belong on a white van, they actually belong on a Chevy van, not a Ford van. We suspect the plates, as well as the van, are stolen."

The captain had no sooner explained his theory than there was a slight commotion at the rear of the van. A deputy had opened its rear doors to check its contents. He quickly summoned the detectives handling the shooting.

The lead detective instructed another with a camera to begin photographing the interior of the van. This same detective then approached the sheriff. "Sheriff, you need to see this. You other gentlemen might want to see this also," indicating Tom and the CSP contingent.

A gray canvas tarp, laying on the carpeted floor in the back of the van, had been pulled back to expose two duct-taped, bound and gagged bodies. One was a male, the other a female. Both had gunshot wounds at the base of their skulls.

"Looks like execution style," commented the lead detective.

"I guess that answers the question as to why these dirt bags were willing to kill a police officer," said Sheriff Janarous. The group collectively looked from one blanket-covered gangbanger to the other laying where they fell in the street waiting for the arrival of the coroner.

Sheriff Janarous and Tom walked away from the van. "Tom, do you want me to notify your bosses about this shooting or do you want to?"

"Steve, I'm currently on suspension and not on the twenty-four-hour DEA clock. What I did here today, I did as a private citizen. I used my own weapon. I didn't identify myself as an agent or police officer at any time, and I was driving my own car. Technically, there is no DEA involvement here. As far as I'm concerned, the Special Agent in Charge can go screw herself in regards to my involvement in this shooting. Let her get her information from the Denver Post tonight or the Rocky Mountain News in the morning just like all the other residents of Denver."

Sheriff Janarous chuckled. "It's your call, Tom, but I have to maintain somewhat of a relationship with your office. I'll have to call them and advise them of what happened here today."

Tom shrugged. "I understand."

"Don't you want to reconsider and call them yourself? I mean, you not calling . . . won't it just aggravate your current problems with DEA, Tom?"

"Probably, but I have a good attorney and that's why I'm paying him the big bucks," Tom retorted with just a hint of amusement in his tone.

"You know you could end all this aggravation if you would just retire and come work for me. My offer to place you in my department still stands."

"I appreciate the offer, and I just may eventually take you up on it, but not right now. I have to set the record straight regarding my unwarranted suspension and a number of other things before I retire."

"I understand, Tom. My offer will be there when you're ready. Meanwhile, let me get back to work and see if I can't get them to expedite the processing of your Scout so you can get back to your tractor duties."

Tom divided the remainder of the day at the scene of the shooting and then at the Sheriff's Department giving a detailed written statement. It was dark before he left the station. As he drove the PA's Blazer eastward toward home, he thought *Highway 86 certainly did not work its cathartic magic today.*

CHAPTER FIVE

December 3, 1996; DEA Headquarters, Arlington, Virginia

At precisely the time Tom squeezed off the shot that permanently altered the second gang banger's life functions on Highway 86, twelve hundred miles to the east at DEA Headquarters in Arlington, Virginia, he was the topic of a conversation about to alter his own life.

Ray Perkins, the Assistant Administrator of DEA, followed Roger Grey into his office in the Special Operations Section. "Say, Roger, you got a minute?"

"Yeah, sure Ray, just handling some budgetary matters here." Roger indicated a stack of papers cluttering his desk. "What's up?"

Perkins took a seat in front of Roger's desk. "I wanted to give you an informal heads up on a decision made by his majesty before he departed for IDEC this morning."

"Okay." Roger paused a moment. "Does it affect me personally, Ray?"

"Before I say anything further, I want your assurance that this is between you and me for the time being."

Roger gave a slight nod of his head.

"It affects you only in that you are friends with Tom Blaine."

The mention of Tom's name brought a surprised look to Roger's face, but he decided to remain silent and allow Ray Perkins to continue.

"The administrator has decided to take a more forceful action to force him from DEA."

"What the…? Christ!" Roger's anger to Perkins' statement was instant and vitriolic. "What now?" He tossed the pen he held down on his desk. The pen hit with a force that scattered several documents and paper clips sending some cascading to the floor.

Perkins raised his hands in mock defense to Roger's instant anger. "Whoa there, big fella. Don't kill the messenger."

"Come on, Ray, spill it," said a visibly agitated Roger.

"Conway has decided to transfer Blaine to Los Angeles."

"Los Angeles?" Roger shouted.

"Yes, LA."

Roger lowered his voice. "Why LA?"

"During a conversation with Peterson this morning, Conway remembered a statement Blaine made when he was here at a Snow Cap planning meeting last year. During that meeting he made it clear he wanted to remain in Colorado until he retired."

"Yes, I remember that statement," added Grey.

"Well, based on that statement, and the fact that the forty-five day suspension did not force Blaine to retire, Conway wants to ratchet up the pressure to force him out of DEA."

"Jesus H. Christ, Ray! Why can't he just leave the guy alone? Doesn't he realize Blaine is a bona-fide hero? He saved several lives in the Denver shooting and recently received the Attorney General's Award for Valor for his nothing but heroic actions. The local cops there in Denver also awarded him something for his heroism. Christ, the guy's a war hero, too. He received the Navy Cross for his actions in Vietnam for cramming sakes, Ray. And, yes, I know he has caused Marsha Grant a lot of problems with this lawsuit by the Denver victims' families, but as I understand it, Blaine is just telling the truth. From what I also understand of her role in that shooting, both she and ASAC Sidney Krowell should be held accountable for how that shooting went south."

Perkins held up his hand in the universal stop sign. "Roger, you're preaching to the choir. I know Blaine is a hero." He hesitated a moment. "He won the Navy Cross in Vietnam you say? I didn't know that."

"Well, I didn't either and found out only inadvertently when I met another former Marine who knew of Tom's heroics in Vietnam. Tom is quite closed-mouthed about his Vietnam days."

Perkins scratched his head. "I do know that he is one of the best supervisors we have in DEA. However, the truth of the matter often has very little bearing on how the Administrator makes decisions. In his mind, Tom's actions have caused Marsha Grant and DEA lots of problems regarding the victims' lawsuits. And with the fact that Conway selected her to be the first female SAC in DEA and that she has a close tie to the Attorney General, Conway can't let her fail."

"What about that judge in Denver?" Roger asked. "The one handling the lawsuits and who thinks DEA is trying to dissuade Tom from testifying in the case by constantly screwing with him? How does Conway propose to get around that? From what I hear, that judge is very close to sanctioning DEA and certain people in DEA for their apparent attempts to influence Tom's participation in the case."

"Oh, Conway has a solution to that. He's not only transferring Blaine; he's transferring a number of other supervisors as well. His rebuttal to the judge or for that matter anyone else who challenges him on this issue is that he is not singling out Blaine, but instead, is attempting to fill some supervisory vacancies in offices that desperately need filling. LA, which is probably more appealing than Detroit, Chicago or New York, is one of those offices. After all, as we both know, when we agreed to become supervisors, we also agreed to serve where needed."

"I can't believe this shit, Ray?"

"Oh, believe it, Roger. I've just spent the last three hours down in human resources identifying supervisory personnel who have a similar background as Blaine—close to retirement, have completed their headquarters tour and are more or less in the final office, which in all likelihood, is where they plan to retire."

"And?"

"It's probably going to be less than a Merry Christmas for eight group supervisors and one Assistant Special Agent in Charge who will be on the transfer teletype going out in the morning. Plus, I have a number of backups in case some of those selected for transfer opt to retire."

"So Conway is willing to sacrifice nine other supervisors just to force Blaine out?"

"Absolutely."

Roger stood up from his desk and began to pace. "This is pure bullshit. How can this guy get away with this crap?"

"He has a favored status with the AG and the director of the FBI, who still have desires to assimilate DEA into the Bureau. Correction, assimilate our budget into the FBI. Forcing good people out of DEA plays right into their hands."

Ray shook his head in disgust. "Can I tell Blaine?"

"He is the one exception to my promise I extracted from you not to let loose with this information," said Ray as he stood and turned to leave.

"Remember, Roger, you didn't hear this from me."

"Ten-four, Ray."

CHAPTER SIX

December 4, 1996; DEA Headquarters, Arlington, Virginia

"No, I do not have the details yet, Mr. Administrator, but I'll call Marsha Grant in Denver right away and see what she knows," said Ray Perkins into his phone as Roger Grey entered his office. Perkins indicated with his hand for Roger to take a seat in front of his desk. His usually stoic face showed obvious irritation as he continued talking into the phone. "Yes, I can see how you feel, Mr. Administrator. Nobody likes to be blindsided with something like that. I'll get right on it and get back to you with the details as soon as I have them." Perkins placed the phone back in its cradle. "Jesus, what a mess, Roger."

"What's up?"

"Did you get a chance to talk to Blaine yesterday after we spoke?"

"No, I made several phone calls and left messages on his machine to call me, but he didn't return my calls. Is there a problem?"

"The local news in Denver reported Blaine was involved in a shooting near Denver yesterday."

Roger leaned forward in his chair. "A shooting?"

"Yes, a shooting where he apparently shot and killed two individuals while coming to the aid of a local police officer."

"Holy shit! Is he . . . is he all right? He wasn't shot was he?" The surprise in Roger's tone gave way to concern. "Must be why he didn't return my calls."

"Nothing in the preliminary reports indicates he was injured, but evidently the police officer he was aiding was critically wounded."

"Jesus, Ray," was all that Roger could manage.

"Well, his majesty," as Perkins gestured toward his phone on his desk, "has his skivvies in a knot. He was blind-sided by the AG during a conference call with her this morning from his hotel room in Colombia."

"Didn't the Denver office call the duty officer and report the shooting? I can't imagine them not following the agent involved shooting protocol."

"Yes, they called the Headquarters Duty Agent but claimed the only details they could obtain were from a Douglas County Sheriff's Department press release of the incident. The incident occurred yesterday morning in a rural area southeast of Denver. There's been no further word from Denver, which is very confusing. I know we're two hours ahead of them, and they may not have gotten to the office yet, but the SAC or one of the ASACs should have at least called something in to either me, the director of operations or the HQ's duty agent."

"You would certainly think so," offered Roger. "Ray, let me see if I can get Blaine on the phone. I'll try to find out the details from him, and I'll get right back to you," said Roger as he turned to leave the office.

"Please do, Roger."

Roger was already out the door on his way to call his friend.

December 4, 1996; Hacienda Puesta Del Sol, La Cruz, Sinaloa, Mexico

Since his arrival at the Hacienda in the early morning, Juan Cervantes sensed Jaime was in a foul mood. Instead of his usual upbeat business-as-usual mood, Jaime appeared sullen and upset with something or someone. Sitting in his leather recliner positioned directly in front of the large projection television, Jaime appeared to be engrossed in a special report aired by CNN on drug trafficking in Mexico.

After his return to Mexico and being pressured into working for Jaime and the Sinaloa Cartel, Juan had gone to great lengths to defuse any suspicions Jaime might harbor against Juan regarding his loyalty to his employer. *For my brother and his family's sake, I need Jaime to trust me. At least for the time being until I can decide on how to get my money from the bank deposit box in San Diego and use it to move my brother and his family to a safe location.* Juan decided he needed to lighten Jaime's mood and gain some credibility as nothing but a loyal assistant. "Oye, jefe, I talked with Ramon this morning. He has found an investment that might be of interest to you."

Without looking up from the television, Jaime answered over his shoulder. "Run that by Hector. I want him informed on all investments concerning the business. Like I said yesterday, while I certainly agree Ramon has been a great addition to the business, I still rely on my brother when it comes to investing our money."

"Sí, por supesto, jefe. I just thought you would like to make this decision as it is more of a personal nature for you," answered Juan.

Jaime rose from the recliner and approached Juan. "What do you mean of a personal nature?"

Juan sat back in his chair knowing he had Jaime's full attention. He gave Jaime a big smile. "Jefe, how would you like to be the proud owner of a 1953

Chevrolet Corvette with the VIN #89 which, by the way, originally belonged to John Wayne?"

It was now Jaime's turn to smile. "A 1953 Chevrolet Corvette that belonged to John Wayne? I thought that was in an auto museum in Reno, Nevada. I saw it there myself the last time I was in Vegas."

"Yes, there's a 1953 Corvette there that belonged to John Wayne, but that has VIN #53. This is another one. According to Ramon, John Wayne actually owned two 1953 Corvettes. One is, of course as you say, in the museum. The second one, which he purchased a number of years after selling the first one, is in the hands of a private collector who recently displayed it at the Los Angeles Vintage Car Show in Pomona, California. According to Ramon, the current owner would be willing to part with it for $175,000."

"It's condition? Is it in good condition, Juan?" asked Jaime as he exuded the same excitement in his voice that a young child might on Christmas.

"According to Juan, it is in mint condition and has only a few thousand miles showing on the odometer."

"Yes, yes, tell Ramon to make the arrangements. And Juan . . ."

"Sí, jefe."

"Muchas gracias; many thanks for this, mi amigo."

"Denada. It's nothing, jefe." Juan left the room. *He called me amigo. Maybe I'm making some headway in getting him to trust me after all.*

December 4, 1996; Elbert County, Colorado

Upon arrival at his home just outside of Elizabeth the night before, Tom went directly to his liquor cabinet and removed a half-consumed bottle of Glenlivet, single malt scotch. He poured several ounces of the amber liquid into a tumbler with some ice and took a large swig. The cold scotch initially burned his throat but with a second healthy swig, the burning sensation disappeared and with it, Tom's nerves began to un-knot. *Do your thing Dr. Glenlivet.*

Meanwhile, Manfred, who had been lounging somewhere in the house, made his appearance and demanded to be fed. Rubbing up against Tom's legs, he meowed relentlessly announcing his dinner was long overdue. Even though an ever-present dish of dry cat food sat on the floor, Tom had spoiled the large Orange Tabby with a can of something fishy smelling each morning and evening. He now demanded his evening repast.

"Hey, big guy," Tom asked Manfred, "how was your day? Mine? It was shit, but thanks for asking. I suppose you want something to eat."

He fed Manfred, refilled the tumbler with several more ounces of Dr. Glenlivet, and proceeded to his living room. Hitting the play button on his CD player, Tom dropped into a comfortable armchair. He laid his head back as the sounds of Native American flutist Carlos Nakai filled the semi-darkened room. As the soft, mellow sounds of the Southwest further soothed his nerves, he relaxed for the first time since breakfast. *Breakfast, that was a long time ago,* he thought. *Come to think of it, breakfast was the last time I ate. I guess I should eat something before I get wasted with the scotch. What the hell; screw the food. I don't have anything tomorrow; I'll just take my time facing reality.* And that's precisely what Tom did.

A constant banging sound aroused Tom with a sudden start. Shielding his eyes from the bright sunlight streaming laser-like through his bedroom window, he reclined back on his pillow and attempted to determine the source of the constant repetitive pounding. He finally deduced the pounding he heard was in addition to the dual timpani drums pounding in his temples. He attempted to rise. The clock on the nightstand noted the time was 9:30. The bright sunlight outside convinced him it must be 9:30 in the morning.

He took stock of his situation and realized he still wore the clothes from the day before, minus the woolen shirt. He had no recollection of how he ended up in his bed. The last thing he recalled was sitting in the darkened living room with Dr. Glenlivet and listening to Native American flute music. With his head pounding and his stomach doing flips, he slowly rose from his bed. As he tentatively placed his feet on the floor, he stepped on his woolen shirt, which he must have discarded sometime during the night. The putrid smell of vomit on the shirt gave evidence as to why he had shed it. He then painfully remembered the dry heaves. *Ah, I do recall throwing up, so the night is not quite a total blank. I should have forced myself to eat something. Those dry heaves were worse than the actual act of vomiting,* he decided.

"Bang, bang, bang." The pounding continued. Now mostly awake, but far from what one would consider alert, Tom determined the sound came from the kitchen area. With slow and carefully planned movements and with his head pounding with each step, Tom gingerly made his way from the bedroom to the kitchen.

In the short hall between those two rooms, Tom found the bloody massacre scene where a bird of some type had met its untimely demise.

Feathers, as well as splotches of blood, were everywhere, along with a beak and a leg. Just another method Manfred used to indicate his indignation at being ignored at mealtime.

"Nice, Manfred." Tom instantly regretted using his voice so loudly. He winced at the pain in his head as he continued on to the kitchen using the walls to steady his steps. There, he found the large Tabby sitting facing the cabinet where Tom kept Manfred's canned cat food. The scratches on the woodwork frame around the door, and on the door itself, was all the evidence Tom needed. Continuing his slow and deliberate movements in an attempt to lessen the pounding in his head and the waves of nausea, which were coming with increasing frequency, Tom bent over and removed a can of cat food from the lower cupboard. As Manfred watched patiently, Tom advised, "You worthless fur ball. Why don't you grow some opposable thumbs so you can do this yourself?"

Manfred's simple response was a "Meow."

Opening the can, the smell of the fish parts instantly assaulted Tom's nostrils and with the current state of his stomach, it caused him to gag then wretch. It took all his will power not to throw-up, which Tom knew, due to his lack of food intake, would be nothing but the repeat of last evening's dry heaves. "Oh God!" was Tom's simple response to his present condition. He placed the can of cat food on the floor for a grateful Manfred.

Tom had just made his way back to the bedroom and eased his aching head onto the pillow when the phone rang. Once again, he winced at the pain that racked his aching head. He allowed the answer machine to pick up the call and listened to see if the caller would leave a message. He had previously set the volume loud enough so he could screen calls from other places in the house taking those he wanted and disregarding those he did not.

"Tom. Hey, are you there? Pick up, buddy. It's really important I talk with you."

Tom instantly recognized Roger Grey's voice.

Great, Tom thought as he lay on his bed listening to Roger's message. *I don't hear from you for a month, then all of a sudden, I get calls two days in a row, and now it's really important that we talk. He probably heard about yesterday.* He struggled to sit up and fought another wave of nausea. A return call to Roger would have to wait until he felt better. Lying back down, he instantly felt better and just began to doze when the phone rang again.

"God damn it! That better not be Roger again," Tom said aloud.

"Blaine, this is Dominic Angelini. I really need to talk to you," said a voice full of irritation coming from his answer machine. "Call me as soon as possible."

Dominic Angelini, my illustrious Assistant Special Agent in Charge. I can bet he wants to talk about yesterday. I'm sure it's all over the press by now, and he and her majesty, Ms. Marsha Grant, wants, correction, make that needs, more details. "Hey, Dom, why don't you just send me a memorandum which, since taking over from Sidney Krowell, seems to be your preferred method of communicating with me? Why talk to me directly?" Tom said aloud, disturbing Manfred who had crawled into bed with him. Tom scratched the cat's ears. "Well, ole buddy, I guess they're not going to leave me alone."

With some effort, Tom made it to the kitchen where he first made some coffee. Next, he decided he needed to eat something that might stave-off the persistent attacks of nausea. He made himself some dry toast, drank some coffee and rewound his answer machine to find a number of missed calls. *I don't even remember the phone ringing last night.*

"Tom, this is Roger. I need to talk to you today. Call me when you get this message." Tom noted the first call came in at 9:10 yesterday morning. That would be 11:10 Roger's time in Arlington, Virginia. *Hmm, can't be about the shooting because it hadn't happened yet.*

The next call received at 2:35 p.m. came from the John Deere Tractor dealership. "Mr. Blaine, we will need to keep your tractor for another day or so. The supplier sent us the wrong part. They're overnighting the correct part, and we should have it tomorrow."

They sent you the wrong part. Right, jerk off! You ordered the wrong part, dummy. Why can't you people ever tell me the truth?

"This is John Wiley from over in Franktown," began the next caller at 3:10. "Jim Wilbert gave me your name and number and said you made him a good deal on some snowplowing. I sure would like to get together with you and get an estimate on doing the same for me. Please call me at 303-212-4412."

As the dry toast began to work and his persistent nausea subsided somewhat, he played the next two calls, both potential customers desiring an estimate on some type of tractor work and had been received during the late afternoon.

Another call from Roger Grey recorded at 4:30 p.m. preceded the potential customer calls. "Tom I had hoped to hear from you by now. I guess you're out and about. Please call me this evening at home. You have the number. It's important."

As he massaged his aching temples, Tom played this call a second time. *If he knew about the shooting, he would have said something about it. Not that he had something important to discuss with me. Hell, I wonder what that's all about,*

The next call came in at 5:10 from Sheriff Steve Janarous. "Tom, my guys will be finished processing your Scout and trailer later this evening. I've instructed my detectives to get it back to you tomorrow. You can pick it up any time after 9:00 a. m., along with some forms from the Victims Assistance Law Enforcement fund to reimburse you for the damage done. You might be able to recoup some financial help in repairing your Scout. I also had a rather interesting talk with your boss, Dominic Angelini. Is he always such a big jerk or does he have to practice at it? He pissed me off, so I hung up on him and told him he could get the details of the shooting from you or like everyone else from my news release. Hope all is okay with you. Let's get together for breakfast or lunch in a day or so. I can bring you up to date on the investigation."

The angry tone of the next caller came through loud and clear. "Tom, this is Dominic Angelini. I was advised that you were involved in a shooting this morning. Neither I, nor the SAC, know anything about this. I need to talk to you. Call me at home, page me or contact me through dispatch. I need to talk to you right away." This call, received at 6:25 p.m. the night before, obviously followed the evening news.

The more than agitated Dominic Angelini called twice more that evening, at 8:05 and 10:20, and each time he instructed Tom to call him right away.

"Well, Dom, I'm sorry I didn't get any of these messages until today," Tom said as he talked aloud to the answer machine. "Besides I'm on suspension, dummy, and not in a duty status where I have to be available twenty-four hours a day." He erased the last two calls.

I need some aspirin before I begin to return calls. Tom downed four aspirin with lukewarm coffee, and then decided to make his first call to Roger Grey at Headquarters. *I need to start out with a friendly voice.*

"Mr. Grey's office," a southern belle female voice announced.

"Is he in, Sandy?" Tom asked, knowing full well, that Sandy, Roger's Administrative Assistant, knew his voice and saw no need to identify himself.

"Yes, he is Mr. Blaine, but he's on a call to Bolivia. He instructed me to get a call back number and tell you to stay by that number. He emphasized it was very important he talk with you."

"Okay, tell him I'm at home. Say, do you know what this about, Sandy?"

"You didn't hear this from me, Tom, but I know that the heavies here are concerned about a shooting in Denver maybe involving you. Ray Perkins has been down here as has James Peterson from the Office of Professional Responsibility, and from what I can gather, they're upset that nobody has been able to talk with you about this shooting."

"Okay. Well, tell Roger I'm here awaiting his call."

With the call concluded, Tom realized that the dry toast had worked fairly well alleviating some of the nausea, but his head still pounded. *I almost feel well enough to try eating something else,* he thought. While searching the refrigerator for that something, the phone rang. Tom's initial response was to grab for the phone, but as he did so, he hesitated. *What if it's not Roger? I don't want to speak to anyone else before I talk with him.* He let the answer machine take the call. Tom got a chuckle from Roger's apparent exasperation when he discovered that, once again, he had reached Tom's answer machine.

"Damn it, Blaine, what part of staying by the phone did you not understand? Don't you ever do what you're told?"

Tom picked up the phone. "Only when it's your wife whispering in my ear, Roger."

Roger was not in the mood for humor. "Real nice, Tom. I've been trying to get reach you since yesterday morning. Is everything okay?"

"Yeah, Roger, I was a little busy yesterday and was in no real condition to accept or return phone calls last evening."

"So I understand, Tom. What the hell happened?"

"Roger, are you asking me as a friend or as a senior Executive Service Agent from headquarters?"

"Jesus, Tom, with all our history together and you have to ask me that question. Let's start with being a friend first and should the remote possibility arise that I need to revert to the SES mode, we'll reconsider. Okay?"

"Sounds good."

"Most importantly, are you okay? You sound a little fuzzy around the edges."

"I guess I am a little fuzzy around the edges as you put it, Roger. Physically, I was not injured yesterday, but I did try to destroy as many brain cells as I could last night with some good single malt scotch."

"Well, Jesus, man. Tell me what the hell happened."

"It was just my luck that I happened on a situation where I had to take some action which resulted in two gangbangers being killed."

"You did the killing, Tom?"

"Are we still talking as friends?"

"Shit, Blaine, of course I'm asking as a friend."

"Let me make a very long story short." Tom then explained in abbreviated fashion what had transpired on highway 86 the morning before. During this time, Roger remained silent.

"So you used a Mini-14?" Roger asked when Tom had seemingly finished.

"Yes, I keep it in my Scout for mostly four-legged varmints, but it came in handy on the two-legged variety yesterday."

"Any idea on the identity of the two bodies in the van?"

"No, I don't, but it's probable that the sheriff who is handling the shooting does by now."

"Okay, now for the hard questions, the answers to which I might have to share with the heavies around here. Just so you're forewarned. Okay?"

"Shoot," Tom said with just a hint of amusement in his tone.

"Why did you not report the shooting immediately to DEA? You are after all still a DEA employee and bound by its rules and regulations. And being involved in a shooting, even off duty requires…"

"Roger, let me stop you right there," interrupted Tom. He felt his irritation rising at the course that this conversation was going. "I was not in an off-duty status. I am on suspension, not just merely off-duty. DEA is not paying me, and none of my benefits are in force. Therefore, it is my opinion that I acted as a private citizen yesterday. I did not, at any time, identify myself as a DEA agent. I did not utilize a DEA authorized weapon, and I was not driving a DEA vehicle. Basically, I have no ties at all to DEA; I am just a private citizen."

"Tom, that's not going to wash. You know from suspending agents yourself that you have to advise them that they must still adhere to DEA rules and regulations during the suspension."

"Yes, Roger, I certainly have advised an agent or two of those rules and regulations, but at the time, I felt they were unenforceable. My attorney, who is representing me on my Merit System Protection Board hearing, is of the same opinion. According to him and his research, DEA cannot have it both ways. It cannot enforce its rules and regulations on someone it is not compensating."

"Tom, it's done all the time."

"Yes, but it has never been seriously challenged in a fairly liberal circuit like the Federal District of Colorado Courts. I'm willing to bet if we should get lucky enough to draw the same judge who's hearing the lawsuit from the victims' families against Grant and DEA, I could easily prevail."

"While I can certainly empathize with your position, Tom, I know there are many here who will challenge it."

"Well, let them bring it on, Roger. I did nothing wrong, and as far as I know, there is a young state patrolman still alive because of my actions as a private citizen. I'm sure that will impress the court."

"No argument there, Tom."

Roger's short pause made it obvious to Tom that Roger had something else on his mind. "Roger, your first calls to me came in before the shooting yesterday. You left a message saying it was important I get in touch with you. What's up?"

"Tom." He paused. "It's not good news, I'm afraid. Conway is not happy you didn't elect to retire when you received the forty-five day suspension. He's decided to try another tactic to force you to retire."

"What's he going to do, transfer me to Cleveland?" Tom asked in a tone loaded with sarcasm.

"Close, Tom. Los Angeles, actually."

"Los Angeles!" exclaimed Tom in disbelief. "You've got to be kidding me, Roger."

"No, I'm afraid not. Ray Perkins told me yesterday that Conway knew you wanted to retire in Denver and would more than likely retire if transferred."

"But, Roger, I'm not in the zone to be transferred. I've done my Headquarters time with my Snow Cap tours and have had several transfers during my career."

"I know, Tom, but Conway's position is that as a supervisor you are eligible for transfer at the dictates and needs of the agency. There are several supervisory openings in LA and he intends to use you to fill one of them."

"Doesn't he know the Denver judge is about ready to slap DEA with sanctions for screwing with me, a witness in the Denver shooting lawsuit?"

"Yes, he does, and that's why he has also ordered that a number of other supervisors in your category be transferred. That way he contends he has not singled you out."

Tom's own louder voice aggravated his pounding head. "Roger, this is Bullshit. If that asshole thinks I'm going to take this lying down, he's sadly mistaken. I'll get my attorney to file a restraining order against DEA and demand a hearing in front of the judge who's hearing the lawsuit. I'll bet he'll think this is another one of DEA's underhanded tactics to get me to rethink my position on the September 1995 shooting."

"You might be right, Tom, but Perkins is going ahead as directed and has identified the other supervisors to be transferred. The teletype transferring you guys is going out today."

The bile built up in his mouth and his nausea made a rapid reappearance. His headache was now in full force. "Roger, I'm too pissed to talk any more right now. I'll get back to you later." He slammed the phone back into its cradle and raced for the bathroom. Tom just made it to the commode before he upchucked the dry toast he had consumed. The vomiting denigrated to retching and dry-heaves, a repeat performance from last evening. Tom finally rested his aching head on the toilet seat. *No way am I going to LA. I'll fight you tooth and nail on this, asshole. And if I lose, I'll just retire. Hell, retirement won't be so bad. I can get my tractor work going, and I won't have anyone else to worry about but myself and* "of course you, old buddy," he said aloud to Manfred who had silently moved into the bathroom and was rubbing himself against Tom's leg.

December 4, 1996; DEA Headquarters, Arlington, Virginia

"Were you able to get in touch with Blaine, Roger?" asked Ray Perkins looking up from his desk as Roger entered his office.

"Yes, I did. I just finished talking with him several minutes ago. Of course, when I told him about the transfer, the conversation went downhill rapidly. Actually, he just slammed the phone down on me."

"I figured he would be pissed." Perkins placed his pen beside a document he was reviewing.

"Pissed would be an understatement. I would be willing to bet he is on his phone to his attorney as we speak. He said something about getting a restraining order to prevent the transfer."

"Restraining Order? On what grounds?"

"According to Tom, the judge hearing the Denver lawsuit against DEA and Marsha Grant has threatened to sanction DEA if it continues to harass Tom who is a witness in the lawsuit. Tom, I guess, intends to have his attorney contact this judge."

"I know about the judge's warning. Peterson mentioned that the other day to Conway. Well, Roger, between you, the fence post and me, I hope he is successful and can stop Conway from his harassment. What about the other situation?"

"Tom was involved in a shooting yesterday morning while he was driving to his home in Elbert county. He happened upon a scene where he witnessed two gang members over-power and shoot a state patrol officer. Tom intervened and, in the process, took out the gangbangers with his personal Mini-14. From what details he provided, it sounds like a good shooting to me, Ray, and he probably saved the patrol officer's life."

"Both gangbangers dead?"

"Yep, the .223 caliber that is fired from the Mini-14 is unforgiving. And Tom is a very good shot with both a pistol and a long gun."

"Well, that certainly sounds like a good shooting. I wonder why he didn't advise DEA right away."

"It's his position that because he is on suspension, he is a private citizen and was under no obligation to advise DEA."

"Well, that's not going work," began Perkins. He turned his hands palms up. "He knows the rules and regulations that extend to even those agents on suspension."

"He contends that the rules and regulations cannot apply to someone who is not being compensated. He is ready to challenge that in court also."

"Jesus, Roger. Why does he have to be so obstinate? If it was a good shooting, and it certainly sounds as if it were, what does he have to gain by being so pig-headed about following our rules and regulations?"

Roger answered in a voice dripping with sarcasm. "Oh, I don't know, Ray. I mean, Conway and Peterson have been so above board in dealing with him."

Nodding his head in ascent, Ray agreed with Roger's last statement.

"I guess he wants to cause them as much grief as they have caused him," concluded Roger.

"Yeah, I can see his position. But I'm concerned that if he fails to cooperate with a shooting investigation, Conway could have grounds to place him on indefinite suspension, which we all know is a prelude to termination."

"I thought of that, Ray, but Tom was not in a frame of mind to hear that."

"Look, Roger, I know you and Tom are good friends. Call him back and try to talk some sense into him. What's he got to lose by being cooperative, especially if it's a good shooting?"

"I'm sure his concern will be that he did not advise DEA right away. Could merit some discipline."

"Some discipline, yes, but not termination. If the shooting is as you said it was, DEA would look foolish by disciplining one of its agents for getting involved in a shooting where he saved a local officer's life. Besides, Blaine could always use his excuse that he was confused about his status and did not advise DEA because of his suspension."

"I'll see if I can talk some sense into him. But if this backfires on him, I'll be on his side in any disciplinary proceeding."

December 4, 1996; Bandidos Restaurant Mazatlán, Sinaloa, Mexico

"Juan, try the pescado. It is excellent, fresh from the Pacific and grilled with a lime marinade," suggested Jaime Gutiérrez.

"Yes, Juan, you must try the fish. It is as my brother says," added Hector Gutiérrez who continued to peruse the menu.

Although fish was his least favorite dish, and he preferred something with chicken, beef or pork, Juan knew any other selection would disappoint the jefe. "Yes, I think I'll have the fish. It sounds very good," Juan announced.

With his decision made known, Juan glanced at his surroundings. He had never been to this urban restaurant before but had heard of it from others who raved about its cuisine and atmosphere. Bandidos, located just off the main plaza in central Mazatlán, was an upscale restaurant and featured a diverse menu of Mexican dishes as well as a variety of continental cuisine. Bandidos, a large open and airy-type restaurant, had Saltillo-tiled floors and rough stucco walls with paintings of famous Mexican Bandidos.

I don't see Jaime's picture up there among the collection of Mexico's less than desirable characters, Juan mused to himself as he took in his surroundings. *But then again all of those paintings are of dead hombres; Jaime is still alive. Maybe once he is dead his picture will be on those walls.*

Juan and the brothers sat at a large round hand-hammered copper-top table accompanied by massive oak wooden chairs. The waiters, keeping with a Bandidos theme, sported Fu Manchu moustaches and classical Mexican outlaw clothing with cross bandoliers of bullets across their chests. Soft classical Spanish guitars played in the background adding to the festive mood of the restaurant.

After the waiter took their orders, Jaime took a sip of his water. "The licenciado will be joining us shortly." He snagged a tortilla chip and dragged it thought the salsa verde bowl. He popped it into his mouth and with a mouthful of chip and dip, he continued. "He had a meeting with our friends at El Cendro this morning, and he wants to bring us up to date on what is going on that might be of concern for our business."

"Don't talk with your mouth full, Jaime," admonished Hector in obvious disgust at Jaime's lack of social graces. "You mean the licenciado wants more mordida."

In total disregard of Hector's admonishment, Jaime scooped up more salsa with another tortilla chip and tossed it into his mouth. "That too."

Hector shook his head in obvious displeasure. "Jaime, we pay this guy way too much for what we get in return. Every time he meets with us, he wants more money for some minor information about the pinche, DEA or FBI. And every time we attempt to have him lean on our competitors, he has some reason why it can't be done."

"Hector, you think I am a fool? I know he thinks he can bleed us for money, but we just got our foot in the door of El Cendro; we need to cultivate that source. He is our connection to this source right now; we need to keep him happy. Comprende, mi hermano?" asked Jaime as the smile on his face and the warmth of the tone of his voice disappeared simultaneously. "And one other thing, brother, you are not my mother, so don't ever criticize my eating habits in front of company again." Jaime turned to Juan. "I apologize for our little discord here, Juan, but Hector and I sometimes disagree on certain things. Do not be alarmed. It is just two brothers doing the usual sibling bickering. Besides, he dares to criticize me for my bad habits when I know he has been shacked up with a gringa girl down here on vacation while his fiancé sits at home."

"And how do you know that, brother?" asked Hector.

"Hector, I have my sources who told me you have a blonde beauty from

Wisconsin with gigantic tits stashed in a suite in our hotel."

The waiter arrived at the table bearing platters of fish saving a chagrined Hector a response.

Juan gracefully endured his second bite of the vile-tasting fish when the pager on his belt vibrated signifying he had a call. Viewing the screen, he noted the displayed number was unknown to him but followed by the numbers 999. This number was the code he and Ramon had devised to signify the need for an immediate return call. Excusing himself, Juan stood up. "Jefe, Ramon just paged me. I need to call him back right away."

"But the fish, Juan," exclaimed Jaime indicating Juan's plate with his hand.

"I'll be just a minute, jefe," Juan replied.

"I shall have the waiter remove your plate and keep it warm for you. Hurry back, Juan."

As he departed the table in search of a pay phone, Juan heard Jaime tell Hector, "So tell me about this gringa blond with the big tits, brother."

Dialing the number displayed on his pager, Juan wished there was something readily available to get the fish taste out of his mouth.

"Juan?" asked an anxious Ramon.

"Sí, Amigo," answered Juan.

"We have a problem Juan."

December 4, 1996; Elbert County, Colorado

A combination of the cold-tiled bathroom floor, where Tom had fallen asleep after his last upchucking session, and the constant ringing of his phone, aroused Tom. Just a bit disoriented and shivering like a "dog shitting peach stones" as his old Marine drill instructor would say, Tom decided a hot cup of coffee would warm him up. *Probably make me puke again, but I need the warmth.* As the microwave did its thing to reheat his coffee, Tom reached across the counter and hit play on the answer machine. Tom listened to the first message as he looked out the window at the panoramic view of Pike's Peak. Roger implored him not to do anything rash until they talked and strongly suggested he call him as soon as possible.

The next call was from a highly agitated Dominic Angelini. "Blaine if I do not hear from you in the next couple of hours there will be severe consequences."

Tom turned and yelled at the answer the machine. "What Dom? Like you'll put me on suspension, transfer me to some shithole assignment? You don't have the horse-power to fire me, so save your threats, asshole."

Another call from Roger stated it was very important they talk as soon as possible. Libby, the last call, advised, "Tom I just heard about the shooting. I hope you're okay. Please call me; I'm concerned about you." This last call caused a bit of melancholy to overtake his emotions. He had to sit and drink some coffee before he answered any of the calls.

Manfred's mental telepathy must have signaled Tom needed some consoling. He began rubbing himself along Tom's right lower leg. Then he characteristically jumped into Tom's lap where he settled himself and began to purr.

"Yeah, I miss her too, big guy," Tom whispered to the cat. With his emotions in check and his stomach no longer doing flip-flops, he dialed Roger's number at DEA Headquarters.

After connecting with his office assistant, Roger came on the line. "Tom, I'm sure glad you called me back. Before you go all postal on me, please hear me out, okay?

"Okay," answered a somewhat cautious Tom.

"Tom, you really need to cooperate on this shooting thing."

"But Roger…"

Roger cut Tom off. "Listen, god damn it. Hear me out. I'm talking as your friend here not as some headquarters hump. If the shooting was as you say it was, a good shooting, you have nothing to worry about."

"It was a good shooting, Roger. I have no reason to lie."

"Okay, then if it's a good shooting, why don't you just play along with DEA? You have nothing to lose by being cooperative."

"Roger, it's the principle, I guess. DEA can't disassociate itself from me for things like my salary and benefits and then expect to enforce their rules when it suits their convenience or needs."

"Tom, I completely understand your position. While I don't totally agree with it, I do understand. But if you don't cooperate, you are just giving Conway and Peterson more ammo to come at you."

"They could try, Roger, but I'll bet my attorney will be able to prevent them from doing anything to me."

"Listen, Tom, I was with Perkins earlier after you and I talked. He advised that if you do not cooperate with this shooting investigation, DEA will immediately place you on indefinite suspension which we all know is tantamount to termination."

"They could try, Roger, but…" began Tom before Roger interrupted him again.

"One more time, ole buddy. Listen to me, Tom," began Roger with a hint of exasperation in his voice. "Once again, I'm talking to you as a friend, not as a supervisor. Why put yourself though this crap? Just cooperate and this thing will go away. By being stubborn and digging your heels in, you just make them more determined to screw you."

There was a noticeable pause while Tom continued to stroke Manfred's head.

Tom finally broke the silence. "Roger, you're one of the few individuals I *do* trust and a guy whose opinion I value very much. Let me think about this, okay?"

"Okay, but not too long as I would like to march right up to Perkins and tell him you'll cooperate."

"Like I said," began Tom. "Let me think about it and I'll get back to you. I'll get back to you within the hour, Roger."

"While you're considering your options, Tom, you should also consider your options regarding the rest of your career at DEA."

"My career?" Tom snorted. "My career seems to be over. I don't have too many options, Roger. Either I fight this transfer legally, and if I lose, I retire, or I don't fight it and retire. In either instance, the result is the same. My career is over."

Roger sighed. "Tom, if I were you, I would do whatever DEA was trying to do to me and fight them legally, but I would also do what they directed."

"I don't understand. What do you mean?"

"Simply this, Tom. I would go to LA, the moon, wherever. I'd do whatever those idiots, Conway and Peterson, handed out, and fight them within the system. DEA's record with the Merit System Protection Board is abysmal, thanks to those two, and I know you'll prevail eventually."

"Roger I really don't want to go to LA. When I left there a number of years ago, I swore I'd quit before I was ever assigned there again. Besides, I had hopes of retiring right here."

"I know you hated LA. I remember you telling me that on several occasions, and I know that your intentions were to spend the rest of your time right there in Colorado. I also remember you telling me earlier that you were never going to let those bastards force you from DEA. Your words were that you didn't want to retire under a dark cloud. Remember those words, Tom?"

"Yeah, Roger, I do. But things have changed since I made those comments."

"Bull shit, Tom. Nothing has changed. Conway has just ratcheted up his efforts to drive you from DEA, that's all."

Tom felt more confused. "So you think I should go to LA?"

"Tom, I suggest you do whatever Conway and Peterson direct. I've recently seen too many good agents like you hang up their career on a sour note because Conway and or Peterson had them in their sights for some either actual or contrived disciplinary thing. And when they left, there was always that impression they had to retire before the axe fell. I suspect you're like me and don't want to end your career on a low note because you were forced out. I think that stigma will stay with you a long time and will continually eat at you. You've had a great career, and I know a number of people in DEA consider you one of the best supervisors and a hero. A hero should always be able to pick the time and place he intends to retire and not let bozos like Conway and Peterson alter his course. Enough said."

"Jeez, Roger, I don't know. LA! I really hate LA, and I do think my attorney..."

"Get your attorney working," Roger agreed, "but, for God's sake, Tom, do what DEA tells you to do in the interim. If that means going to LA, by God go to LA. That would certainly bode well for you in any civil proceeding. It will show that you were attempting to play by the rules even if those clowns weren't."

"Roger, I have always considered you a bright guy and a true friend. We've done a lot of questionable things together which could have ended both of our careers if we had been caught. I know you mean well, Roger, but LA. If it were any place but LA. Uh, Cleveland wouldn't be so good either. I need to think about this. I'll get back to you."

"Tom, do so quickly. Time is of the essence."

"I'll call you back within the hour," Tom said as he gently shooed the napping Manfred from his lap.

He refilled his coffee cup and put it in the microwave. While he waited, he considered what Roger had said. "What do I do with you, big guy?" he asked Manfred. He looked at the cat who had found a comfortable spot on the kitchen table that was awash with sunlight. "I don't think you'd do well cooped up in an apartment in LA, and I couldn't afford anything else. I've got just the answer." He dialed a familiar phone number.

"Libby Martin," answered the female voice after just several rings.

"Hey, kiddo, it's me." Tom felt his heart begin to race. A warm feeling enveloped his body as his mind conjured up a mental picture of the alluring woman he had until recently shared his home and life.

"Tom! Are you okay? I heard about the shooting this morning when I came in, but nobody knew if you had been injured."

Her concern tugged at his heartstrings, and he had to compose himself for a few moments before he answered. "No, I wasn't hurt during the shooting. The only injury I sustained was post shooting and self-inflicted."

"What? I don't understand. How did you get injured?"

"Too much scotch last evening."

"Oh," answered Libby. After a noticeable delay, her concern turned to amusement. "Got drunk did we?"

"Yeah, my nerves were jangled, and alcohol, as you know, is my way of coping with the stress, or more precisely the prospect of post-traumatic stress which I know usually accompanies these types of actions."

"Well, you certainly should know about post-traumatic stress-producing incidents, considering your recent history here in Denver, Tom."

Here in Denver? Denver was a piece of cake compared to Mexico. If you only knew the half of it. "You're right about that, kiddo. I'm always in the right place at the wrong time or maybe the wrong place at the right time. I haven't figured that out yet."

"So other than too much alcohol, you're okay?"

"Yep, no physical injuries."

"That's good. I'm so glad you weren't injured. The news around here lacked only the facts that a number of individuals including police officers were shot. Nobody could tell me if you were one of the people who got shot." After a slight pause and hearing no response from Tom, she said, "Well, I'm glad you're okay."

"Yeah, I'm okay and should be better after the scotch wears off."

"That's good, sweet…, uh Tom. Well, I need to get back…"

Tom interrupted her. "How have you been, Kiddo?" Before she could respond, Tom added, "We, that is, Manfred and I miss you."

Libby gave an audible sigh. "I've been okay. I miss you two buttheads too." She waited for a moment to allow herself to regain her composure. "Things are okay, I guess, but I've got to do something about my living arrangements."

"Problems with your parents?"

"Living at my parents' place is driving me crazy. They are constantly into my business and can't understand why a girl my age and with my intelligence has trouble finding a decent husband. Sometimes I think I'd be better off if I could find an apartment near downtown. It would save on the commute and the hassle of my meddling folks. Unfortunately, most of the apartments and condo complexes, in fact none of them, come with a stable. I couldn't leave Miss Nelly, at my parents' place if I'm not living there. And as you know, that rat of an ex left me financially, shall we say, not in the most optimal financial position."

"Yeah, I seem to recall that," Tom said. After a slight hesitation, he continued. "Listen, Kiddo, I have a proposition for you."

"If it's to come back and live with you, I just don't want to get into that again right now. You know how I feel about our relationship. I can't just come and live with you without some, uh, more permanent commitment. At least not right now."

After a heavy sigh, Tom answered. "I know. But my proposition is for you to come live here but not with me."

"What? I don't understand."

"His highness, Conway, has decided to up the pressure to force me from DEA; I'm being transferred to Los Angeles."

"Los Angeles? Why Los Angeles?"

"He thinks he can justify the transfer due to the needs of the agency. I guess he thinks a transfer to someplace like Cleveland or Detroit would be too transparent."

"Jesus, Tom." Her voice octave increased slightly. "Doesn't he realize the judge here is about ready to sanction DEA for its actions which seemed to be designed to dissuade or punish you for cooperating in the lawsuit?"

"Conway doesn't care about the judge. He's convinced that he can justify my transfer because of the needs of the agency. He's transferring a number of other supervisors along with me to kind of shield his real intentions."

"You're not considering going to LA, are you? I mean how many times when we were together did you tell me how much you disliked LA and that you'd resign or retire before returning there?"

"Yeah, I know but while LA is not my favorite place, Roger Grey has almost convinced me that I shouldn't let Conway force me to retire or do something that I'll ultimately regret. He's right about one thing. If I retired now, I'd always feel like I retired under suspicious circumstances and Conway would win. When I retire, I want it to be on my terms and not someone else's."

"Okay, I can certainly understand your position. I wouldn't want somebody dictating my life's decisions. So what is it you are proposing, Tom."

"Careful with that word proposal," Tom said which he followed with a chuckle.

"Very funny, butthead. What are you offering then?"

"You come and live here. Bring your horse like before; pay the utilities and keep the place up. My mortgage is only several hundred a month, so I won't need any help there unless I can't afford to live in LA. I know you're paying your folks to live with them so what I'm proposing would not cost you any more than you're already paying them. In fact, it might be cheaper for you. It certainly would be cheaper than renting an apartment downtown, or anywhere else for that matter, considering the cost of decent rental properties. Moreover, it comes with a stable. Besides, by you staying here, it would resolve my problem of what to do with Manfred. He likes it here and wouldn't like being cooped up in an apartment in LA. So you would be doing him and me a big favor and it would be good economically for you also."

"When would this occur, Tom?"

"Within the month, I'd imagine. I'm going to tell my ASAC to establish a reporting date for next month. I can't see any advantage to delaying this thing. Either my attorney will be successful in negating this transfer or he won't, but I would still probably have to report there until a court or the Merit System Protection Board decides. I guess I'll just go while he's arguing for me. Besides, Roger said something that made good sense to me."

"What was that, Tom?"

"He said that by me complying with these things Conway keeps throwing at me, I'll fair better in any legal proceeding."

"He's probably got a good point there, especially with the Merit System Protection Board. They seem to be very employee oriented, and if the employee is playing by the rules and management isn't, they usually come down hard on management. Plus, you'd also be sending a message to Conway that you keep taking his best shots but haven't thrown in the towel yet."

"Hmm, I didn't think of it that way. If I had, I wouldn't have agonized over the decision of going to LA or retiring. You're right-on about that. My complying with his vindictive demands will really eat at his craw. So how about it, kiddo? Do you want to come live here with at least one of the favorite males in your life – Manfred, that is?"

"Let me think about it, Tom. I'll get back to you in a day or two."

"Okay, but remember one thing. You would be doing Manfred and me a big favor and there are no strings attached."

"I'll call you in a day or two."

"Okay, take care, Kiddo."

CHAPTER SEVEN

December 4, 1996; DEA Headquarters, Arlington, Virginia

"Okay, Roger, I have thought about what you said about the shooting and the transfer to LA," began Tom during a call he made an hour later to Roger. "I'll cooperate in the shooting and will report to LA while my attorney fights for me at the Merit System Protection Board."

"Wise choices, Tom. Let me convey this information upstairs and I'll get back to you."

Hanging up the phone, Roger walked to Ray Perkins' office and upon entering, he said, "Ray, I just got off the phone with Blaine; he's going to cooperate in the shooting investigation. Oh and he'll report to LA when ordered." He took a seat in front of Perkins' desk. "He'll be available to the shooting team any time they direct."

"Okay, Roger, that's good news. I'll let Peterson know he'll cooperate," said Ray Perkins as he reached for the phone.

"I'll bet this will make Peterson's day," Roger joked as a big smile developed on his face.

Perkins rolled his eyes and silently agreed with Roger's sarcasm with a nod of his head.

"James, this is Perkins. Roger Grey has advised me that Blaine will cooperate with the shooting team when it arrives in Denver." Ray paused a moment to listen. "Let's hold off discussing any discipline until after the shooting investigation is completed. Yes, I know he failed to report that he was involved in a shooting, but there might be mitigating circumstances we don't know about yet." After listening to a retort from Peterson, Perkins continued. "James, I don't care what the Administrator has demanded. I'm instructing you not to take any action regarding discipline until your agents conduct the investigation." As Ray listened to Peterson's response to his last directive, he looked at Roger and mouthed the words "indefinite suspension." He then spoke into the phone. "You know, James, it's no wonder we're always getting our asses kicked in the Merit System Protection Board hearings. Don't interrupt me. James, there will be no discussion of discipline until the investigation is completed, understand?" Once again, Ray rolled his eyes as he heard Peterson's response. "Go ahead, James. You go directly over my head to Conway, but remember this conversation, because it could become important in any legal proceeding that might arise because of what you and Conway do to Blaine before the investigation is completed. "Threatening you?" asked a now angered Perkins into the phone. "No, I'm not *threatening* you. I'm *promising* you that if you take a unilateral action against Blaine before the investigation is completed, I'll make sure that Blaine and his attorney know of this conversation which I might add is being witnessed by Roger Grey." Ray paused again.

"You do that, Peterson." Perkins slammed the phone down disconnecting the call.

"Well, that seemed to go well," said Roger with noticeable sarcasm.

"That idiot wants to put Blaine immediately on indefinite suspension, which would be totally inappropriate before an investigation is even conducted."

"Well, Ray, I'm sure he's got Conway on his butt to do something to get rid of Blaine."

"I know, Roger, but what those two are doing affects many other disciplinary proceedings we have on-going. Because of their inappropriate actions in so many of these investigations, we're forced to keep sub-par employees who don't belong in DEA or law enforcement for that matter. We continually lose cases both in the courts and the Merit System Protection Board hearings. Hell, we just lost a case where an agent stole several pounds of white heroin from an evidence locker and gave it to an informant to sell. We nailed him good, but because of inappropriate actions in their haste to rid the agent from DEA, the Merit System Protection Board reversed the firing and ordered him reinstated with all back pay and allowances and attorney fees. This thief is still on the job."

"Jesus, Ray, I sure hope they don't do something like that to Blaine. He's one of the good guys and certainly does not deserve what he's getting from Conway and Peterson."

"I know, Roger. And rest assured, I'll do whatever I can to prevent them from doing an indefinite suspension. But as you know, Conway has a mind of his own and frequently fails to listen to those who offer good advice."

"I know that, Ray, and I appreciate what you said to Peterson. I'm sure Blaine also appreciates it."

"How's he taking the transfer to Los Angeles, Roger?"

"While he's not happy about it, he intends to report to LA next month.

"He's not going to fight us on it?"

"Oh, for sure. But he's going to do it legally, and he'll report to LA while the legal issues are being worked out. He recognizes that by fighting any transfer he'll look like a disgruntled employee. By complying with this transfer, one that is obviously motivated by revenge, he feels he'll look better in the eyes of the Merit System Protection Board."

"Good thinking on his part. I'm sure he'll prevail in his challenge."

"I agree. Well, I need to run." Roger stood to exit the office but turned back to Perkins. "That idiot Peterson. It's no wonder the rank and file, as well as certain management, universally dislike our internal affairs operations. He'll probably end up making Blaine a rich man out of this, if Blaine chooses to sue him and Conway. "

Ray Perkins merely nodded his head in agreement.

December 4, 1996; Bandidos Restaurant Mazatlán, Sinaloa, Mexico

When Juan Cervantes returned to the table to rejoin Jaime and Hector, he noted they had been joined by two other people, one of which he surmised had to be the licenciado.

"Juan, this is Licenciado Jorge Morales." Jaime held his open hand to the gentleman seated directly across from him. "And, Licenciado, this is Juan Cervantes, my business manager."

Initially surprised by Jaime introducing him as his business manager, Juan first looked at Jaime who returned his eye contact. "Juan," continued Jaime, "this is Comandante Miguel Guerra of the Sinaloa State Police."

Standing up slightly and reaching across the table, Juan first shook the licenciado's hand. "Mucho Gusto, Licenciado." He then repeated the same gesture with the comandante. As he took his seat, he considered the situation. *This licenciado is meeting with a known traficante in a public restaurant in plain view. He must be either extremely stupid or arrogant not to be concerned who might see him meeting with Jaime and Hector. It must be arrogance. A stupid individual would not be in such a position as he occupies and has the trust and confidence of Jaime.* "Jefe," began Juan as he turned to Jaime, "I have some important news from Ramon."

"In just a minute, Juan. The licenciado is telling me something important also, something about a problem we had in Los Angeles that has been resolved."

The licenciado looked first at Jaime and then at Juan. With a shrug of his shoulders and then with a wave of his wrist at Juan and in an apparent disregard for Juan's sensitivities, he turned to Jaime. "Can we discuss this business in front of him?"

"Por supesto – of course, Licenciado. Juan has my utmost confidence," said Jaime with more than just a note of annoyance in his tone.

The short pudgy licenciado again stared at Juan.

Juan estimated the licenciado to be in his early forties. He had a ruddy complexion and bushy eyebrows that didn't seem to separate.

"That problem in Los Angeles," the licenciado said, "with that individual who was talking to the Grand Jury has shut his mouth permanently."

The mention of a Grand Jury and taking care of the person who was talking to the jury caused an immediate chill to take over Juan's being.

"This is good, Licenciado. Do we know how much he told the Grand Jury?" asked Hector.

Licenciado seemed nervous to have Juan involved in his conversation with Jaime and Hector. He stared at Juan again. "If he told them his name that is too much, as far as I am concerned."

In an attempt to avoid the unnerving constant and somewhat menacing eye contact by the licenciado, and to mask his own nervousness, Juan's gaze fell to the licenciado's attire. He wore an expensive Armani suit, with a silk shirt finished off with gold and diamond studded cuff links and a diamond tie tack. Juan knew that his first assessment of the licenciado had been right. This was one mean hombre and his stares seemed to be a threat to Juan.

"Yes, of course, Licenciado, I agree," replied Jaime. "But do we know if he gave them information that could hurt us?"

"Jaime," began the licenciado who persisted in his stare at Juan, "We must assume he told them something." He finally turned his focus on Jaime. "But not to worry, Jaime. He cannot repeat anything he said where it counts, in court."

"That is good, Licenciado," said Jaime.

"There was however, one minor problem. A minor problem which acts to our advantage."

"Oh? And what is this problem?" asked Jaime with some degree of concern in his tone.

"The people who took care of the problem are, uh, how shall I say this?

Uh, they are no longer in need of compensation," said the licenciado with just a slight sneer developing on his face.

"Oh!"

"Yes, it seems that some local police in Colorado took care of the need to compensate them," advised the licenciado laughing as he did so.

"In Colorado?" asked Jaime.

"Yes, that is where they found the snitch and dealt with him. According to my information, our problem solvers were interrupted before they could finish their assignment. They were..." he began then stopped to stare at Juan again. "Let's just say they were permanently silenced like the individual they were dispatched to take care of."

"None of this will come back on us, will it, Licenciado?" asked Hector.

The licenciado turned to Hector and adopted an attitude that Hector's question was an insult. "You and your brother bring a stranger to this meeting." He pointed to Juan. "And then you dare question my handling of this matter?"

No sooner had the words escaped his mouth, than Jaime came to his brother's defense.

"Licenciado," he spit with a stern voice, "I realize you are a very important person here; however..." With his face reddening, Jaime leaned across the table and pointed a finger in the licenciado's face. "Never forget, mi amigo, who is paying for those gold and diamond-studded cuff links and that Armani suit. Also, never forget that you retain your important position here because I desire it be that way. If either Hector or I want to question you about something you are doing for us, you will answer it, and do so in a civil and courteous tone. Comprende, Licenciado?"

"Sí, I understand Jaime, but I did not..." began the licenciado.

Jaime interrupted the licenciado and pointed his finger at the comandante. "And you, Comandante, I saw you reach inside your coat when I began to address the licenciado. While your loyalty to the licenciado is commendable, it is misplaced and insulting to me. I am the one whose loyalty you should be coveting. This one time I will give you the benefit of doubt that it was a reflexive action, but if you ever do that again, you are a dead man. Comprende?" asked Jaime. He lifted his napkin several inches above the tabletop to reveal a gold-plated Colt .45 caliber pistol, which had been aimed directly at the comandante during his exchange with the licenciado.

The color drained from the comandante's face making a large horizontal scar that ran the length of the right side of his face more visible. His now meek voice contradicted his facial appearance.

"Sí, Señor. Yo entiendo – I understand. Lo siento, Señor. I am sorry it was…"

"And one final thing, Licenciado," began Jaime interrupting the comandante. "When I vouch for someone like Juan here," as he pointed a finger at Juan, "you do not question my decision to include him in our conversations."

"I understand, Jaime. I do not mean to disrespect either of you. I am only trying to watch out for you and your organization."

"I understand. Just don't let it happen again."

"Sí, Jaime."

Watching this exchange between the licenciado and Jaime, Juan remembered the times his former boss, Miguel Felix-Uriarte, felt the need to remind powerful men as to who was in charge. Juan estimated the comandante to be about thirty-five years of age. *Jaime had better watch this one closely. He is very hostile right now. That perpetual sneer on his face makes me believe the rumors that he is a stone cold killer and one violent bastard. Jaime needs to draw him into his pocket or rid himself of him altogether.*

Jaime took a sip of his wine and calmly turned to Juan as if the preceding confrontation had never occurred. "Tell me, Juan, what is it that Ramon finds it so necessary to interrupt your lunch? By the way, where is that waiter?" Jaime made eye contact with the waiter and with hand signals ordered that Juan's fish that had been removed from the table to keep it warm should be returned.

Carajo! I had hoped he had forgotten about the fish. Juan's stomach churned at the idea that he would have to gag down several more bites of the vile tasting fish. "Ramon said there is a problem with one of the money transporters."

"Problema? Qué problema?" asked Hector.

"One of the load cars was stopped at the border and the money was confiscated."

"Confiscated?" Jaime exclaimed in a voice audible by several tables around them. The diners looked at Jaime. He continued in a softer tone. "Confiscated by whom, Juan?"

"US Customs, jefe."

"Pinche, customs. How much did they get, Juan?"

"Five hundred thousand in U.S. dollars."

"Pendejos," screamed Jaime no longer concerned with the neighboring tables. "How did this happen, Juan?"

Before Juan could reply, Hector interjected. "See, brother, I told you not to trust that Ramon. Now look what has happened?"

Juan looked at Hector but addressed Jaime. "It was not one of Ramon's people, Jefe. It was one of ..."

"Hector's people?" guessed Jaime.

"Sí, Jefe, one of Hector's people." Juan's response sounded sheepish. He definitely did not want to develop antagonism with Hector.

"Tell me, Juan. What happened?" demanded a more contrite Hector.

"Sí, Hector. According to Ramon, who has a contact on the Laredo border. The money was in a car—in a false gas tank. Evidently, Customs had the car on a lookout. The license plate was entered into their computer as a possible load car and when it approached the border, they ran the plate through the computer. The car was diverted to an area where it was searched and the cash was seized."

"How was the license plate in the computer in the first place?" asked Jaime, as he stared contemptuously at Hector.

The licenciado knew he needed to regain the confidence of Jaime. "I can find that out for you, Jaime, through my contacts at El Cendro."

"Jefe," began Juan, as he looked at the licenciado, "Ramon has also determined that the body shop in Chula Vista in California where the money was placed into the gas tank has been under surveillance for several weeks. Following the seizure at the border, Customs did a search on the body shop. Fortunately, no additional money was seized, but they seized documents and several load cars."

The comandante decided to enter the conversation. "Sounds like the work of an informer to me, Licenciado, Jefe."

Both the licenciado and Jaime turned to the comandante. "An informer?" asked the licenciado.

"Why do you think that, Comandante?" Jaime asked.

The comandante answered Jaime first. "Jefe, ask yourself, how is it that they came to be watching the body shop in the first place? Somebody had to tip them off. The surveillance then just copied down all the license numbers and put them in the computer. When the car appeared at Laredo to cross over, it alerted the inspectors. It could also be that the informant is a wiretap."

"Wiretap? On whose phone? Ramon's?" asked Hector.

"Ramon does not use his phone for doing business across the border, Jefe. He uses only pay phones on both sides of the border just as he did when he called me now," interjected Juan.

Jaime turned to the licenciado. "I want to know how this happened. You do whatever you think is necessary to find out. I do not want a repeat."

"I will try Jaime but…" the licenciado began.

"Don't but me," interrupted Jaime. He continued through gritted teeth. "I pay you good money to protect my interests and right now my interests are being threatened by the pinche gringo Customs. I want to know how this happened and assurances that it will not happen again. Random, lucky seizures I can understand, but something like this, I will not tolerate. Am I clear on this, Licenciado?"

Meekly, the licenciado replied. "Sí, Jaime, I will see to it immediately."

Following this promise, the licenciado and the comandante rose, quickly exchanged farewells, and departed the restaurant.

After watching them depart the restaurant, Jaime turned to Hector and with his opened palm slapped Hector on the back of his head. "Idiot. Go back and play with your big titted blonde gringa," Jaime said playfully, "and leave the real business to Juan and me." Then turning to Juan and in a parent-like voice, Jaime said, "Juan, eat your fish before it gets cold again."

December 4, 1996; Elbert County, Colorado

Subsequent to his phone call to Roger Grey, in which he advised Roger he would cooperate with the shooting team and intended to report to Los Angeles while his attorney contested the transfer, Tom placed a call to Dominic Angelini. Angelini, a 49-year-old, New York born and bred Italian descendant, was the Assistant Special Agent in Charge overseeing operations in Colorado. He had replaced Sydney Crowell who had retired shortly after the shooting incident in Northeast Denver amid some speculation that he shared some of the responsibility for the deadly encounter. Angelini, who had spent the preponderance of his career in the New York City office, came with the attitude that anything and anybody outside the city of New York was inferior. Moreover, he seemed to have a large chip on his short pudgy shoulders from not having been selected to fill a vacant ASAC position in New York, but instead, had been sent to what he considered an inferior assignment in the "backwards" Rocky Mountains. This attitude was apparent from the manner in which he dealt with people. He was forever in a bad mood, and he could "piss off the pope," was a common expression heard around the DEA office in Denver. While most of the agents and supervisors tried to avoid Angelini, Tom did not. In fact, he seemed to delight in pissing off Angelini on an almost daily basis.

"Well, no shit! It's about time," Angelini said when Tom announced he was returning his call. "I've called you several fucking times since yesterday and paged you a number of times. Why the hell didn't you return my calls or pages, Blaine?"

Angelini's vituperative response was not unexpected; however, Tom's anger instantly began to boil.

"First off, Mr. Angelini, you can park your New York attitude or I'll just hang up the phone right now. If you cannot be civil and tone down your profane rhetoric, then this call is over. Do I make myself clear?"

"Who the fuck do you think you're talking to, Blaine? I'm not just some…" Angelini spit before a now fully enraged Tom interrupted him.

"Hey, asshole, if you can't treat me with some respect, then don't expect any from me. You know what? I don't need your abuse." With that said, Tom slammed the phone back into its cradle. *Well that certainly went well* he thought as he walked away from the phone. He had not gotten far, when it rang. He let the machine take the call. Tom heard an irate Dominic Angelini threaten him.

"God damn it, Blaine. How dare you hang up on me? You're in deep shit now, buddy boy."

"Think so, asshole? I rather doubt that," replied Tom to his machine, which he followed with a chuckle knowing he had pissed off Angelini.

Ten minutes later, the phone rang again and Tom let the machine answer the call. Tom heard the soft feminine voice of Marsha Grant, the Special Agent In-Charge. "Listen, Blaine, I'm sorry for Mr. Angelini's outburst, but you should not have hung up on him. That was disrespectful…"

Before she could finish her thought, Tom picked up the phone. "I was disrespectful?" he said in a hostile voice. "Listen, Ms. Grant, I will not be treated that way."

"Blaine...uh..."

"I'm not done yet. If he can't be civil, I won't talk to him, and I'll file a formal complaint about his abusive language. If he wants me to be respectful, then he should be respectful to me."

"Uh, yes, I can understand your position. But, uh, uh..." she stammered looking for the right words to express her concerns. "Blaine, you've got to understand. We're under a lot of pressure here about the shooting. We have to answer a number of questions posed by headquarters concerning DEA's involvement and potential liability."

"I understand, Ms. Grant." Tom allowed his temperament to return to some semblance of normalcy. "But let me explain why I hung up. First of all, I will not tolerate Angelini's abusive management style. If he cannot be civil, he should not expect any civility from me. Secondly, I am currently on suspension and not at DEA's beck and call as far as I'm concerned, at least not for another five days anyway. Yes, unfortunately I was involved in a shooting yesterday, but as a private citizen and not a DEA agent. I did not at any time identify myself as a DEA agent nor did I use a DEA approved and authorized weapon. And about paging me—if Mr. Angelini cares to look in his safe behind his desk, he will note that he has my badge, credentials and pager. He would have taken my gun also, but it's mine not DEA's, and I refused to surrender it to him when he placed me on suspension. Ask him if he remembers that?"

"Yes, he remembers now and said he is sorry for his outburst," began Grant. Blaine could hear her apparently talking to Angelini in a somewhat muffled tone. "But Blaine you're wrong about being at DEA's beck and call. Just because you are on suspension does not mean you do not have to adhere to its procedures."

"Well, that's something my attorney and the Merit System Protection Board can decide, Ms. Grant, but in any event, I will cooperate with the shooting team."

There was another slight delay. "Good. I need for you to come in this afternoon and give a preliminary statement?"

"Well, that's going to be a problem."

"Oh, why is that?" with just a bit of annoyance again edging into her tone.

"I have no transportation, ma'am. If you look out your window into the front parking lot, you'll probably see my government vehicle parked in a rear slot, unless it's already been assigned to someone else. And the Sheriff's department has my only personal vehicle which was shot up during yesterday's incident."

"I see. Tell you what, I'll send someone to pick you up. Say around 2:00 p.m."

"That will be fine with me. And while we're at it, you can tell Mr. Angelini to go ahead and establish a reporting date for my transfer to Los Angeles around the first of next month."

Grant seemed more than surprised. "Oh, so you know about that already?"

"Of course, ma'am. I do still have some friends in high places."

"Blaine. You surprise me. I would have thought you were going to fight this thing. At least try to delay the actual transfer date."

"Nope. I intend to report within the month."

You know you're entitled to a ninety day reporting date. Don't you want to take advantage of that?"

"Nope. A reporting date of next month is fine."

"Okay, then, I'll arrange a transfer date and advise headquarters."

"Fine. I'll be in this afternoon." Tom hung up the phone. *I'd like to be a fly on the wall to see her response to my decision not to fight the transfer or elect to retire. Sorry, Marsha, you and your buddies in DC cannot get rid of me that easy.*

CHAPTER EIGHT

December 5, 1996; Denver, Colorado

The headline on page one of the December 5 edition of the Rocky Mountain News read: "Federally Protected Witness Identified as Dead Person Found in Van in Douglas County." The article went on to say:

> The Rocky Mountain News has learned that Ernesto Fonseca along with his spouse Amelia Fuentes-Fonseca, the two bodies found in the van following a shootout in Douglas County on December 3, 1996, was a Federally Protected Witness in a major drug investigation. Fonseca and his wife had been relocated to Colorado subsequent to his testimony before a Federal Grand Jury in Los Angeles. His testimony is not of public record until the results of the Grand Jury are made public. However, an informed source advised that Fonseca was giving testimony regarding the Rodriguez Brothers' drug cartel out of Sinaloa, Mexico. Considered one of the biggest drug trafficking organizations in Mexico, the Rodriguez Brothers have strong ties to the Gutiérrez Cocaine Cartel of Colombia.
>
> Both bodies were found in a van on State Route 86, east of Franktown, following a shootout with Group Supervisor Thomas Blaine of the Drug Enforcement Administration. According to the Douglas County Sheriff's Department, Blaine, who was off duty at the time, happened upon a traffic stop where a Luis Sanchez and Jose Vega, both of Los Angeles, had overpowered and shot Colorado State Patrol Officer William Forsythe. In what witnesses describe as a running gun battle using a high-powered hunting rifle, Blaine shot and killed both Sanchez and Vega. CSP Officer Forsythe, whose condition was upgraded from critical to serious following repeated surgeries yesterday, is expected to survive.
>
> Blaine, credited with saving the lives of several Denver Police Department officers in the Five Points drug shootout on September 28, received the DPD Medal of Valor for his actions in that case. Efforts to contact Blaine and his supervisors at DEA have been unproductive with Denver DEA referring all inquiries to DEA in Washington, D.C.

December 5, 1996; Elbert County, Colorado

Rolling over on his left side, Tom checked the clock radio and saw it was 6:00 a.m. He had endured a night of troubled dreams where his repeated attempts to subdue villains were unsuccessful for a variety of reasons. *I knew I should have used Dr. Glenlivet.* Slipping from his bed, he made his way to the kitchen to brew some coffee. As the coffee maker worked, Tom recalled the events of the previous three days. Which day had been worse – the day he endured the effects of a severe hangover, the shootout on the day before with the two gangbangers, or his meeting yesterday with Angelini and Grant? The bright light to all of it was that he would soon be rid of Angelini and Grant.

As he waited while the coffee dripped into the carafe, he heard a soft meow. Turning, he saw Manfred standing between him and his empty food dish. "Hungry, big guy?" he asked. The big Orange Tabby answered Tom's question with another meow as the cat closed the distance and began to rub against Tom's leg. "I'm going to miss you, fella." He filled the cat's food dish and gently stroked the cat's head as Manfred ate.

Tom poured himself a cup of coffee and walked out onto his back deck. It was a crisp cold morning, and Tom took in the panoramic view of what he had come to conclude was God's Country. He could see ominous clouds in the distance that signaled more snow to come. Parked in his driveway adjacent to the lower level garage, his Scout seemed to have aged. He had retrieved the Scout from the Sheriff's department impound lot following his trip into the DEA office in Southeast Denver. Partially covered with a fresh layer of overnight snow, the Scout still showed some of the damage done by the bullets and the forensic technician's efforts to recover those bullets. "Going to take some extensive body work, I guess," he decided.

Shivering from the cold, Tom reentered his home and contemplated what he should do next. *Make some breakfast or get cleaned up.* The phone rang.

"How you doing today, buddy?" asked the familiar voice of Roger Grey.

"Okay, I guess, but the dreams have started already."

"The gun thing?"

"That's one of them. But then again, I guess you're no stranger to those dreams yourself, Roger."

"Yeah, but unlike the dreams that you've described to me in the past, my consistent dream is that when I attempt to fire my weapon, it falls apart into several pieces, like I failed to reassemble it correctly after cleaning it."

"Same effect though, right, Roger?"

"Yep." Silence filled the line for a long moment. "Say, how did you do yesterday at DEA?"

"It wasn't pleasant, Roger. But, then again, I did nothing to make it pleasant. I sure do get a vicarious pleasure in provoking both Angelini and Grant. However, in all fairness to Marsha Grant, I have to say she was halfway decent to me. Angelini on the other hand was an asshole."

"Tom, unfortunately that's Angelini's managerial technique. He just thinks he has to be that way to get any respect, I guess. You gave them a statement?"

"Sure. They already had a copy of my statement I gave to the Douglas County Homicide Investigators and only had to add a few sentences of why I personally did not contact DEA immediately after the shooting."

"And you stuck by the reasons you had given to me?"

"That, plus the fact that Steve Janarous, the Sheriff, tried to advise Angelini shortly after the shooting, but when Angelini became verbally abusive to Steve, the Sheriff hung up on him and refused to take any further calls from DEA."

"And how did that go?"

"Well, Angelini first got red in the face, and then he tried to dismiss his actions saying it was my responsibility and not the Sheriff's. When he became verbally abusive to me, Grant intervened."

"Oh?"

"Yeah, evidently Dom had failed to tell Grant he had talked with the sheriff right after the shooting and when he had pissed off the sheriff, he couldn't get any further details for DEA. It then became clear to her why her own calls to Sheriff Janarous had gone unanswered. Man, she was pissed, and when Angelini tried to defend his actions and shift the blame to me, she instructed him to leave her office. She then went on to apologize for Angelini's actions. I really think my not contacting DEA will be a dead issue when it comes to holding me accountable. My attorney thinks the same, by the way."

"I think you might have just skated on that, Tom. You could argue that you were trying to advise DEA through the Sheriff."

"Those are my attorney's precise thoughts, Roger."

"I think I'll mosey over to Peterson's office and see how his attitude is doing. I'll bet he'll shit a brick when he finds out that Angelini is mostly at fault at DEA not being informed about this shooting."

"I sure would like to have a bug on his phone when he calls Conway to tell him the news."

"Me too, buddy. Well, got to run. Take care and I'll be in touch."

December 5, 1996; Hacienda Puesta Del Sol, La Cruz, Sinaloa, Mexico

Juan's pulse raced at a rampant pace as he read the faxed copy of the newspaper account of the killing of an old associate, Ernesto Fonseca, in the Denver area on December 3, 1996. The licenciado Gorge Morales sent it to Jaime as proof of his statements at lunch that "the problem in Los Angeles had been taken care of in Colorado." Juan knew Ernesto and his wife Amelia for several years when both he and Ernesto worked for Miguel Felix-Uriarte. At the time, it was thought Ernesto had used a small fortune he had accrued during his employ with Uriarte, to leave the drug business to open a restaurant with a cousin in Los Angeles. However, subsequent information received by Uriarte, which he shared with Juan, determined that in reality, Ernesto had joined with his major competitor, Jaime Gutiérrez, and the restaurant that he opened in Los Angeles was nothing more than a front for Jaime's drug trafficking and money laundering operations in the United States.

Juan broke into a cold sweat and his hands trembled as he continued to read the article. Suddenly, an uncontrollable ice-cold dread replaced his racing heartbeat when he saw Ernesto had possibly testified before a grand jury. *That could have easily been me if I had continued down the path I was heading. Had it not been for my forced return to Mexico by Jaime, I would have probably suffered the same fate* thought Juan. He continued to read the fax without Jaime noticing his trembling hands and nervousness. Jaime seemed intent only on the CNN News. Juan's heart missed a beat when he read in the news clipping the name of the person who had allegedly shot the Fonseca's assassins in a gun battle south of Denver on December 3, 1996, Agent Thomas Blaine of the DEA. Recognizing Tom's name caused a surprised Juan to utter spontaneously "Carajo."

"What's that?" asked Jaime who now focused on Juan.

"Nothing, Don Jaime. I was reading a fax the licenciado just sent." Juan attempted to regain his composure.

Jaime approached Juan. "Juan, your hands are trembling. What has upset you so?" Before Juan could answer, Jaime reached out for the paper Juan held. "Here, let me see the fax."

Handing it to Jaime, Juan tried quickly to develop a plausible reason as to why the information in the fax had disturbed him.

After reading the fax, Jaime merely passed it back to Juan. "Of course, Juan, I should have known. You knew Fonseca right?"

"Sí, Jefe, we worked together with Miguel Felix."

"Does it upset you that he had to be dealt with in this way, Juan?" Jaime extended his hands toward Juan, palms up. "What would you have me do with a traitor who wants to destroy me and my business?"

The initial shock passed, Juan gained control of his emotions. "Don Jaime, it is not that Ernesto had to be dealt with so much, but that he would consider cooperating with the pinche DEA. I just never thought he would become a snitch. He had considerable knowledge about my activities with Miguel Felix and now with you. Enough to get me indicted and possibly extradited to the United States. I do not possess the money or power to prevent this. Not like you."

Jaime laughed slightly in amusement at Juan's concern about his indictment and possible extradition. "Juan, you have nothing to worry about as long as you work for me. Nobody who is loyal to me has to ever fear being extradited to the United States."

"Well, it does worry me, Jefe."

Jaime put an arm around Juan's shoulder in an open gesture of friendship. "Juan, mi amigo, trust me. You and anybody else who remains loyal to me have nothing to fear from the pinche Norte Americano cops." With a slap on Juan's back, Jaime returned to his leather chair to watch CNN.

As long as I am loyal to you, I am safe, huh? Juan thought. *Where have I heard that before? Oh, yes, Miguel Felix Uriarte, my former jefe said the same thing on a number of occasions. Well, those DEA agents who raided his estancia in Guadalajara must have forgotten what an important man he was. And Jaime, what would be your position if you knew how close I was to appearing before a grand jury myself?* A cold shiver worked its way down his spine. *I'd probably be joining poor Ernesto and his wife.*

December 6, 1996; DEA Headquarters, Alexandria, Virginia

James Peterson waited through the long silence at the other end of the line. He anticipated Conway's explosive response to the news that Peterson had just told him about Thomas Blaine. As the silence continued, Peterson felt the perspiration develop under his arms. *I wonder what his response will be that Blaine has agreed to the transfer to LA and has not elected to retire like he thought he would. Will he blow up? That's his normal response to bad news, especially when it involves those employees that Conway deems are problem employees. And Tom Blaine sure qualifies in Conway's mind as a problem employee. On the other hand, will he accept the information and try to develop an alternate plan to force Blaine from the roles of DEA or just forget about Blaine. I sure wish I was not the one to have to give him this news. Why is he taking so long to respond? Maybe I've lost the connection. These international connections are lost all the time. Finally, with the perspiration under his arms beginning to soak through his white shirt, the angst of waiting for a response got the better of him.* "Are you still there, Mr. Administrator?"

"Of course, I'm still here," was the terse reply from John Conway. "Don't interrupt me again when I'm thinking."

"Yes, sir."

"Peterson?"

"Yes, sir," said Peterson. *It's never good when he uses my last name.* This thought provoked the re-start of his sweat glands.

"What's the story on the investigation of his recent shooting in Denver? Can we begin proceedings to place him on an indefinite suspension?"

"Sir, the investigation is not complete, but unfortunately for our purposes, it looks like a good shooting; I don't know about his failure to expeditiously notify DEA."

"What do you mean you don't know?" asked Conway.

"Well, uh, sir, it's kind of a convoluted issue?"

"Jesus Christ, Peterson, don't make me drag this out of you. Tell me what's going on. Can't anyone in this agency speak in direct terms?"

"Yes, sir," said Peterson meekly. "Blaine is claiming he was under no obligation to report this shooting to anybody other than the local authorities based on his being on suspension at the time, he did not use a DEA weapon, and he was not in a DEA vehicle."

"That's bullshit. He is still on the roles of DEA and as such is bound by its policy and procedures."

"Yes, sir, I agree, but the courts may not. We recently lost a case before the Merit System Protection Board involving an agent who, while on suspension, obtained outside employment. When we tried to discipline him for violating policy and procedures prohibiting outside employment, the Merit System

Protection Board ruled that our policy was unreasonable and we could not prohibit him from such employment as long as he was not being paid by DEA or receiving benefits."

Conway's irritation showed in his voice. "Am I missing something here, Peterson? We're not talking about an agent working some off-duty job; we're talking about an agent who was involved in a shooting where two suspects were shot and killed by the agent. An agent who failed to advise DEA of said shooting."

"Sir, that is not quite correct," said Peterson.

"Now what the hell does that mean? Did he call DEA right after the shooting or not?"

"No, but the Sheriff of Douglas County called Dominic Angelini, the Denver ASAC, right after the shooting to inform him that Blaine had been involved in a shooting."

"And?"

"According to Marsha Grant, the SAC in Denver, evidently Angelini was not too cordial to the sheriff, and the sheriff terminated the call before giving Angelini any details of the shooting. This sheriff, who, according to Grant has always been a good friend to DEA and has two investigators on our task force in Denver, then refused to accept any further calls from Angelini. Angelini failed to tell Grant about his terminated call with the sheriff; it only became known when she interviewed Blaine herself.

"Son of a bitch. Who is this ASAC?" asked Conway.

"Dominic Angelini," said Peterson.

"Angelini? I don't recall hearing that name before."

"He's a New York guy who spent most of his time in New York and a very short time in headquarters before getting the ASAC position in Denver."

"So in essence, what you're telling me is that technically Blaine's covered on the notice to DEA, and it's basically this Angelini's fault that there was not a timely notification to DEA Headquarters."

"Yes, sir. Policy and Procedures do allow for a third party notification if the agent is incapacitated or for some reason unable to conform to the rule to immediately notify DEA of any shooting in which he was involved."

"Well, this is all bullshit. I don't feel that he was incapacitated or unable to conform. I think that he was duty bound to do the notification himself."

"Sir..." began Peterson."

"Shut up and listen, Peterson."

"Yes, sir."

"I want you to find some way to begin proceedings to place Blaine on an indefinite suspension. If you can't do it for this shooting, then find something else. Any infraction of the rules and regulations will do."

"But, Sir I…"

"Don't but me, Peterson," said Conway. "I want that man gone from DEA by the time I leave for the Mexican Cendro Conference next month, and trust me, he will be gone even if it's the last thing I do as the administrator of this organization. Now if you can't do it, Peterson, I'll find someone who will and you'll find yourself spending what's left of your career in some place like Detroit or Cleveland. Do I make myself clear?"

Conway's voice came across so loud that Peterson had to hold the telephone at arm's length. "Uh, yes, sir."

"Okay, now connect me to Perkins. I'm going to fix it so ASAC Angelini learns how to deal with other police agencies on a more cordial basis. I think a transfer to the El Paso Intelligence Center where he will be required to deal with local police agencies on a daily basis will be just what the doctor ordered. Let's see how that New Yorker clown enjoys that South Texas shit hole."

Hanging up the phone Peterson thought *Maybe Cleveland or Detroit might not be so bad.* Then sitting back in his high-backed leather chair his submissive attitude changed to anger. He allowed himself an uncharacteristic profanity. "Damn that Blaine. No way he's going to ruin my career." *Conway is absolutely right. Blaine will be a constant thorn in our sides until he is gone from DEA. Well, I'm the one who is going to pluck that irritating thorn from this agency.* Sitting back in his chair, Peterson contemplated what course of action he would take in an attempt to satisfy the demands of the administrator and his own personal agenda. "Only one thing I can do," he said aloud as he reached for the phone and dialed a number. "Get in here," he ordered into the phone.

Several minutes later, Senior Inspector Riley Wilson presented himself to Peterson. "What's up, boss?'" asked the six-foot-two-inch black former basketball player from Georgetown University.

"Riley, I want you and McReynolds to go to Denver."

"Denver? What's up in Denver?"

"If you listen a minute, I'll tell you," answered a mildly irritated Peterson.

"Sorry, boss," offered a contrite Wilson.

"I want you and McReynolds to take a very close look at Thomas Blaine."

Wilson was not surprised it was Blaine again. *Why can't they leave the poor guy alone?* "And what are we looking for this time, boss?"

"Anything that will allow us to place him on indefinite suspension. Check his paperwork again, his time and attendance reports, his vehicle reports, his travel vouchers. You know the drill, Wilson. That man needs to be gone from DEA before he embarrasses this agency any further."

I see a classic Peterson witch-hunt. It's not as if we don't have enough legitimate work to keep us busy, thought Wilson. "Uh, boss, we still have that thing in New York to finish. McReynolds and I are scheduled to go up there for several days next week."

"No, Wilson, this is more important. I'll reassign the New York case. I want you and McReynolds in Denver this week, and I want something on my desk by the first of the year. Understand?"

I can't believe this crap. This guy is possessed with getting rid of Blaine. Wait til McReynolds hears about this. He was planning to take some time off for the holidays starting the week after next. Man, will he be pissed when I tell him we might be in Denver then, thought Wilson. "Okay, boss, I'll make the travel arrangements. Will you call the SAC and let her know we'll be coming her way?"

"I'll deal with the SAC," answered Peterson. With a dismissive gesture of his hand, he indicated toward the door signaling the conversation was over.

Wilson walked back to the office to explain their assignment with his partner. *Thank God the career board meets the second week in January. With any luck, I'll get selected for one of those open ASAC positions, and I'll be out of here and free of this idiot.*

December 6, 1996; Franktown, Colorado

"Mr. Wiley, this is Tom Blaine," Tom said into a pay phone at the John Deere Tractor Dealership in Castlerock. "We talked the other day about me doing some snowplowing for you. I just got my tractor back from being repaired, and I can drop by and do the job this afternoon if you want me to."

"Gees, that would be great, Mr. Blaine. I really need to have the road to my barns cleared what with all this drifting snow we've been having, and I don't have a plow of my own. Do you know how to get here?"

"I think so. You have the property adjacent to Jim Wilbert, don't you?"

"Yes, that's right. It's the next ranch gate just south of his property. You'll see the mailbox with my name and the name on my gate is the Double Lazy J Ranch. Two J's—one for me and the other for Jan my wife."

"I know right where you are, Mr. Wiley. I'll be over in about an hour."

"I'll be waiting," said Mr. Wiley.

December 6, 1996; DEA Headquarters, Alexandria, Virginia

"You're shitting me, Riley!" exclaimed the pudgy William McReynolds. With his fiery Irish temper turning the color of his face and neck to match the color of his hair, he bolted up from his desk sending his chair against the wall behind him. "Doesn't that jerk know that I have annual leave scheduled for the week after next?" Before Wilson could respond, McReynolds flayed his arms about. "I haven't taken leave all year so I could take the holidays off and take the family up to my dad's place in Boston. I'm in a use or lose category. I'll lose almost fourteen days of leave if I don't use it by the end of the year. And, Jesus, I've got airline tickets that are non-refundable."

"Mac, I don't think Peterson cares about you or your leave. He has a single focus right now and that is to get Blaine fired."

He pulled his chair back to his desk and sat back down slumping his head into his folded arms on his desk. After several minutes of silence, he raised his head to look at Riley. "You know what, Riley? I'm sick and tired of Peterson and his vendetta shit. You'll leave Headquarters as an ASAC so you won't have to worry about having to deal with many of the people we investigated on a daily basis, but I probably will go back in the field as just a Group Supervisor somewhere. How am I supposed to win their trust and support as their supervisor if I go out of my way to screw them while here in OPR? And, sweet Jesus, how am I going to explain to my wife about our trip? She's been planning on this for months."

Wilson stared pensively at the sullen McReynolds for several minutes. He wanted to say something to ease his partner's sullen mood. "Look, Mac, maybe if we put out heads together, we can figure something out that we can give Peterson and will limit our time in Denver. Spend a few days there, and then return in time for you to take your bride to Boston."

"Jesus, Riley, we've already examined Blaine's time and attendance sheets and his travel vouchers. We already got him on the vehicle abuse thing. And we also talked with his group's informants, so there's not much left that we can do."

"Well, maybe there's something else we can look at, Mac. What's one of the basic unwritten tenants we usually follow in drug investigations?"

"Uh, I don't know, Riley? Putting powder on the table?"

"Besides that, think financial investigations."

"Geez, Riley. I don't know. I'm too upset right now to think."

"Look, man, don't they always tell us to follow the money in a drug investigation."

"Well, yeah. I don't see how that would apply to Blaine. We have no reason to suspect that he's been stealing money or taking payoffs."

"Mac, could you take a forty-five day suspension right now? That's forty-five days without any income."

"I could probably squeeze by if I tapped into the kids' college fund, but it would really be a drain financially. My mortgage here is a lot higher than it was in New Hampshire, and Alice's income wouldn't even equal what she spends at the mall during the month."

"Most people could not lose their income for forty-five days without having a significant savings or another source of income," added Riley.

"You think Blaine just might have another source of income? One that DEA does not know about and one that just might violate the no outside employment without approval of DEA?"

"Mac, it wouldn't be the first time somebody on suspension found non-approved outside employment. But it's something we should check."

"I don't know, Riley, the last agent we investigated for doing that had his case reversed by the Merit System Protection Board."

"So what, Mac? It's still a DEA rule and if Blaine is earning an income from unapproved outside employment he is in violation of the rule."

McReynolds answered Wilson's last statement with a slight nod of his head indicating that he agreed with Wilson.

"Besides, who cares if the Merit System Board reverses what DEA does? His majesty in there," as Wilson used his hand to point in the direction of Peterson's office, "wants something on Blaine, and maybe we can just give him that without a lot of time and effort."

"Okay, but how do we get the info? It's a cinch he won't admit to working a non-approved job."

"Follow the money, Mac. Follow the money. We look at his bank account.

I'd be willing to bet that if he were receiving money from non-approved outside employment that he would deposit it in his bank account. I don't see him trying to hide his money."

"I guess we could subpoena his bank account records; first we'd need to know which bank he uses. How do you propose we find that out without asking him?"

"When you settled your last travel voucher, did you reimburse the government for the unused portion that you drew in advance in cash?"

"I wrote a check," said McReynolds. His face lit up indicating he just realized the answer to where they would get the necessary banking information on Blaine. "We just need to go downstairs and check his travel vouchers again and see if we can find his banking information." McReynolds jumped up quickly. "I'm on it. Why don't you make the travel arrangements for Denver?"

December 6, 1996; Hacienda Puesta Del Sol, La Cruz, Sinaloa, Mexico

Jaime's snake-skinned cowboy boots clicked on the Saltillo tiles as he entered the office. "Juan, get the licenciado on the phone, por favor. He's been calling Hector about some matter; I sure hope he's not trying to get money out of Hector by going around me."

The licenciado always wants money. He's greedier than Jaime. The ring of the phone interrupted Juan's thoughts.

"Policia."

"Licenciado Morales, por favor," said Juan.

"Who is calling?" demanded a curt male voice.

"Jaime Gutiérrez."

"Momentito, por favor, Señor," offered the voice whose tone had instantly dropped the arrogance.

"Hola, Jaime, que tal?" asked Licenciado Morales as he answered his phone.

"One moment, Licenciado," said Juan. He then turned to Jaime. "Jefe, I have the licenciado on the line."

"Licenciado, how goes it today?" asked Jaime taking the cordless from Juan.

"All is well, Jaime, and you?"

"I'm good, unless you have been calling me to give me a problem."

"Not really a problem, just a slight annoyance," replied Morales.

"Oh. What is this annoyance, Licenciado, and more importantly, how much is it going to cost me and my brother?"

"Jaime, I'd rather discuss this with you in person. Shall I come by the hacienda or would you like to meet elsewhere?"

"Let's do lunch around two today. I have to meet with Hector at the hotel, and we could eat there."

"Certainly, Jaime. I'll see you at two then."

After hanging up the phone, Jaime turned to Juan. "The licenciado wants to meet in person, so I know this is going to cost me money. Please call Hector and make sure he is available for lunch. You will come with me, Juan, so I can confer with you and Hector about money if necessary."

"Sí, Don Jaime."

December 6, 1996; DEA Headquarters, Alexandria, Virginia

"Back so soon?" asked Wilson as McReynolds walked into their office and took a seat at his desk.

Laying a single sheet of paper down on his desk, McReynolds raised his head and looked at Wilson. "Piece of cake, my man. Several of Blaine's last travel vouchers were liquidated with a check drawn on the United Bank of Parker, Colorado. I have the address and account number. I also went by personnel and had one of the assistants call the finance center. She was able to determine that Blaine's payroll checks were automatically deposited in the same account."

"Hey, that's good work, Mac. I didn't even think about payroll."

"I keep trying to tell you, Riley, I'm not just a pretty face, no matter what Peterson says."

Wilson smiled at McReynolds' comment. "For a dumb Mic, you're not too bad. I'll get with Chief Council's Office and have them get a Federal Court Subpoena today. And look, Mac, I know you want to get this thing done so it won't screw up your leave. I've already made travel arrangements for us to fly to Denver on Sunday. That way we can be at the bank when it opens on Monday morning.

A spark of light appeared in McReynolds' eyes. "Man, that's great, Riley. I've already been banished to the couch with just the mere mention of a disruption of our leave plans. I hate to see what would be in store for me if we can't go to Boston for the holidays."

December 6, 1996; Hotel Los Mares Azul, Mazatlán, Mexico

Patrons entered the hotel's up-scale restaurant through a darkened tunnel-like aquarium surrounding the customers on both sides and overhead by all varieties of fish swimming lazily in the backlit waters. The interior décor of the restaurant was in keeping with its name: the Blue Seas. The floor-to-ceiling windows offered a panoramic full-length view of the Pacific Ocean on the west side. Nautical artifacts such as large fowled ropes and wooden pylons, anchors of several sizes and a variety of large mounted fish adorned the remaining light blue stucco walls.

Preceding Jaime, Juan noted Licenciado Morales sat with Hector at a corner booth in the rear of the restaurant. From the collection of empty dishes on the table, it was evident that the portly licenciado had already availed himself to a healthy portion of the hotel's excellent cuisine.

The licenciado wiped his mouth with a white cloth napkin as he rose slightly to greet Jaime. "Jaime, good to see you. Hector insisted that I try some of the new items being added to the menu." He gestured toward the empty dishes on the table.

"I'm glad to see we did not hold you up," said Jaime as he shot a menacing glance at his younger brother. "Please sit down and continue your food, Licenciado." Jaime turned to the waiter who had appeared as Jaime seated himself. "I'll have today's fish special. What do you want, Juan?"

"I think I'll have the chicken, Jefe."

"Nonsense, Juan, you weren't able to enjoy it the last time. You must try it again."

Fish again. I hate fish thought Juan as he accepted his plight with a "Sí, Don Jaime."

"Did you get the news article I sent you about that problem up north, Jaime?" asked the licenciado.

"Sí, I did. It seems you took care of the problem, but then again, that is what I pay you and Comandante Guerra to do, Licenciado. Speaking of the comandante, I am surprised he is not here enjoying yet another free meal at my expense."

"He had planned to come and sends his regards, Jaime," began the licenciado.

Jaime interrupted him. "I'll bet!"

"Well, yes, anyway he's trying to resolve a slight problem that developed as a result of that money thing up north the other day."

"What kind of a problem?" asked Jaime.

"It seems that the comandante was correct, Jaime."

"And how is that, Licenciado?"

"He has learned there was a snitch involved in identifying the load cars from that auto body shop that were carrying the items back here to Mexico."

"Do we know the identity of this pinche snitch?" asked Hector interjecting himself into the conversation. He sat up in his chair and made eye contact with Jaime who indicated his displeasure with a frown.

"No, unfortunately, not yet. That is why the comandante has remained in his office; to try to, uh, pressure his highly placed sources to determine the identity of this person."

"I see, Licenciado," said Jaime in a contrite voice. "And how much money is this going to cost me, uh to uh, determine this identity?" His mocking voice was still calm, but in reality, did not divulge his growing agitation with the licenciado."

The waiter appeared with a tray bearing salads and bread causing the licenciado to refrain from speaking. With the departure of the waiter, Jaime forked some salad into his mouth. "Go on, Licenciado. Please continue."

Jaime's statement, through a mouthful of salad, drew a disgusting look from his brother Hector that caused Jaime to shrug his shoulders.

"That's the slight problem, Jaime," began the licenciado. "The best source with the information is inside Customs and will require a significant amount of mordida to determine the identity of the snitch for us."

"How much, Licenciado?" demanded Jaime almost shouting the words at him.

Realizing Jaime's anger, the licenciado sank back in his chair. "US $250,000, Jaime," he offered meekly.

"Carajo! $250,000!" shouted Jaime who, in a fit of apparent rage, threw his fork down on the table striking the salad dish sending salad across the table. Jaime pointed a finger at the cowering licenciado. "I don't believe you."

Unfamiliar at an accusation of lying and without his comandante to back him up, the licenciado was speechless. His face reddened in embarrassment and a hint of anger showed as he stared first at Jaime and then at Hector. He fidgeted with his water glass as he quickly contemplated his response.

Juan sat back watching the scene unfold. *Wow! Jaime has some huevos calling an important person such as the licenciado a liar.*

While the licenciado tried to formulate an appropriate response to Jaime's accusation, Hector decided to play peacemaker and assert some of his authority. He placed his hand on Jaime's arm in an effort to calm him. "Licenciado, I don't understand. Why is it so much money? It seems a simple task for someone in your position. A few questions to the right person should be sufficient to get what is needed to determine this person's identity."

"Hector, Jaime, it's a little more involved than that." the licenciado wiped the perspiration from his brow with his napkin. "I cannot simply go to the pinche Customs and ask for the snitch's name. I must rely on a well-placed source in the Customs Office in San Ysidro to get the information, and it will cost money to bribe the right people. The comandante has talked with this source and they are confident they can get the name of the snitch for the right amount of money."

"And the right amount is $250,000?" asked Jaime in a voice with slightly less anger than before.

"Sí, Sí Jaime, I swear this is the figure quoted to the comandante this morning," said the licenciado extending his palms toward Jaime in a gesture of openness.

As Jaime considered what the licenciado was asking, the licenciado attempted to bolster his position. "Then there is also the problem that without his identity this snitch might be in a position to continue to hurt your business further, Jaime."

Jaime's anger instantly flared again. "Don't you think I know that, Licenciado?"

"Sí, sí, por supesto—of course, Jaime, I was just trying to assure you of the need to act quickly. I did not mean to insult you." A strained period of silence followed the licenciado's apology during which time he made a conscious effort not to look at either Jaime or Hector.

Jaime, on the other hand, sat staring a hole in the licenciado's forehead. The silence was broken when Juan's pager sounded.

"Lo siento, señores," apologized Juan as he quickly muted the pager and noted the number. "Don Jaime, it's Ramon. I should call him back."

Nodding his head in assent, Jaime excused Juan with a dismissive wave of his hand and Juan went in search of a payphone.

Returning to the table five minutes later, Juan noted that things seemed to be a bit more cordial. "Okay, Licenciado. For $250,000, I want this problem completely taken care of. Not just a name. If you and the comandante can't manage this, then I'll find someone else who can. Entiendo? Understand?"

"Sí, Jaime. Yo entiendo."

"Jefe," began Juan, "may I offer something?"

Still showing the visible signs of anger with the licenciado, Jaime snapped. "What is it, Juan?"

"Lo siento—I'm sorry, Don Jaime, I don't want to interfere, but I've just spoken with Ramon, and he has determined that the person responsible for the problem you and the licenciado were discussing is possibly one of these persons." Juan passed Jaime a slip of paper.

Jaime looked at the piece of paper and then at Juan. "Juan, how does Ramon know it's one of these three people?"

"Uh, yes, Juan, how is it this Ramon person can determine this when the comandante has been unable to?" interjected the licenciado with an air of disbelief. Jaime instantly rewarded the licenciado's question with a disgusted look.

"Don Jaime, Ramon met with the attorney appointed to represent the auto body shop owner who was arrested following the seizure of the money and the search of the body shop. Ramon paid the attorney a $25,000 retainer to represent the auto body shop owner and promised him another $25,000 if his client could give up the name of who he suspected was the informant against him. This morning, Ramon met with the attorney again and got these names. The body shop owner feels confident it's one of these three people. All three have much knowledge regarding the activities at the body shop."

The licenciado was the first to speak. "Jaime, this is unbelievable that this Ramon person would contact the body shop owner's attorney. He could jeopardize your whole operation by doing something so cavalier and without your consent."

When Jaime was slow to respond, Juan elected to defend Ramon's actions. "Jefe, Ramon would never do anything to jeopardize our operations. During all the time he acted for Don Miguel, not one seizure was made, and he quickly collected and funneled his end back to us so we could disperse it properly. He also told me to tell you he will personally pay the $50,000 for the attorney, because he felt it necessary to act right away in order that no more seizures or arrests can be made using this informant's information."

Jaime shook his head in agreement. "Ramon was right to do what he did and tell him I will make sure he is reimbursed for the attorney fees." Jaime turned to the licenciado. "I see no need for you to contact your source in Customs..."

"But, Jaime," interrupted an anxious licenciado who realized the $250,000 Jaime just agreed to pay, a significant portion of which was going into his own pocket, was not going to happen now.

"Don't but me, Licenciado. Oye!—listen!" demanded Jaime. "You have the comandante call me immediately, and I will give him the names of these possible snitches. He can then contact them and use his clever interrogation methods to determine if Ramon's information is good. If the information is not good, then we can discuss the other option of paying the source in Customs."

"Jaime, I don't think that is a good plan. I think my source in U.S. Customs can be more productive," countered the licenciado as he cast menacing looks at Juan.

"I disagree, Licenciado, and right now I don't care what you think," said Jaime. "Just do as you are told, and if I am wrong, you can be the first to tell me so." Turning to Juan, Jaime winked signifying he was very appreciative of Juan's efforts in this matter.

December 6, 1996; Franktown, Colorado

What had started out as a cold, dreary day turned into one of those Colorado winter days where it could go from single digit early morning temperatures to a balmy forty degrees in only a few hours. With the sun high in the sky and reflecting off the glistening snow making it difficult to see without sunglasses, Tom deftly maneuvered his tractor into the many snowdrifts that obscured the road from the entrance to Mr. Wiley's ranch to his several barns. The ease at which the aging tractor managed the weight of the snow now made heavy by melting always impressed Tom. As he moved the snow from the roads, he considered the days of his youth when he made money for scout camp by shoveling sidewalks. *Back breaking work that was and I did it for peanuts,* he remembered. *Now days, with gas and electric powered snow blowers, nobody shovels snow. I sure could have used one of them when I was a lad and shoveled the seemingly never-ending Masonic Temple sidewalks for my grandfather.*

He took a break to determine where he would next stack the snow removed from the roadways. Stripped down to a woolen shirt, he sat with his arms folded over the steering wheel and admired the picturesque scenery. Pine-covered and snow-blanketed hills surrounded the ranch set in a small valley that had several cleared pastures currently occupied by a remuda of quarter horses. Watching the horses frolic, Tom drifted into a state of melancholy and realized, *I sure won't see scenes like this in Los Angeles. Man, I'm really going to miss this country. Maybe I should just rethink my decision, retire and stay here. I can do well enough with my retirement and this tractor gig. Then of course, there's the ranch. If Libby won't agree to move into the ranch while I'm gone, I don't know what I'll do. Poor Manfred will go stir crazy in an apartment in LA.* Shifting the idling old beast back into gear, Tom inched forward to resume his snowplowing task. *I sure do hate to give up this business now that I seem to have a steady stream of customers,* he thought as he attacked the next snowdrift. It consumed the better part of two hours to clear the roads of Mr. Wiley's ranch. Tom was tightening the come-along chains to secure the John Deere tractor to his trailer when he heard Mr. Wiley's voice.

"You sure made quick work of that snow Mr. Blaine."

Looking up from his crouching position, Tom acknowledged Mr. Wiley. "Hey there, Mr. Wiley.

How are you today?"

"My dang gum gout is acting up again," said the seventy-four-year-old rancher attired in a faded salmon-colored snowmobile suit. "Must be this cold." He looked from Tom toward his Scout. "Say, it looks like somebody used that Scout of yours for target practice."

"Yes, they did, Mr. Wiley. Fortunately, their aim was bad because they were shooting at me," Tom said with a slight chuckle as he went back to tightening the chains.

"Yes, sir, Ethel and I heard all about that shooting. You're quite a hero around here, Mr. Blaine, saving that poor state trooper's life and all. Heck, none of us even knew a DEA man lived out here until the television news said you were. After you bought ole Hank Ellsworth's spread over yonder and when Jim Wilbert and I first saw you driving that old Scout around town with your tractor, we thought you were one of those dang gum city guys who are moving out here to do weekend ranching. Lots of them are doing that now. But after you did that work for Jim, we weren't sure about you."

"Well, Mr. Wiley, it's just something most of us in law enforcement like to keep to ourselves. Never know who's listening."

"Well, I'm pleased to know you, Mr. Blaine."

"Thanks, Mr. Wiley, and please call me Tom. Mr. Blaine was my dad, and it's too formal."

"Okay, Tom." He turned and looked at the roadway that Tom had cleared. "You sure did a fine job with the snow, Tom, and I'll be sure to call you again. In fact, this spring I need to replace some fence lines and Jim Wilbert says that you do post holes."

"I did, Mr. Wiley…"

"Please call me, John," interrupted Wiley.

"Sure enough," said Tom as he nodded his head in agreement. "I'm kind of getting out of the business for a while."

"Well shucks, Tom. Why you giving up on the tractor work, if you don't mind me asking?"

"It's a long story, John, but the bottom line is that around the first of the month, I'm moving to Los Angeles."

"Los Angeles? Why in tarnation would you want to go there, Tom?"

Tom chuckled and scratched his chin. "It's not that I want to go there, it's because DEA is transferring me there."

"Oh," was Wiley's simple reply.

"Yes, I kind of wanted to finish out my career in the Denver area and then retire to my ranch here," volunteered Tom.

"Don't you have a say in this, Tom?"

"John, it's a long story and…"

"Say, Tom," interrupted Wiley, "this cold is aching my bones," he volunteered while pulling his one-piece suit tighter around his chest area. "How about a cup of coffee? Ethel just made a fresh pot, and she just took some cinnamon rolls out of the oven."

Glancing at his watch first to check the time, Tom then looked to Wiley. "That sounds great. I could use a cup of coffee."

"Nothing fancy like them coffee shops, just plain old coffee, you understand," warned Wiley.

"Even better, John. I don't care for the fancy coffee places. The coffee is usually too strong and the pastry tastes just like what it is. Something made months ago and frozen until being used."

They walked the short distance to the single-story ranch house. "How long have you lived here, John?"

"Most of my adult life. I purchased it right after I came back from Korea."

"You fought in Korea, John?"

"Yep."

"It was Vietnam for me," volunteered Tom.

"What branch of the service were you in?"

"Marines," was Tom's simple reply.

Stopping short just before reaching the front wooden steps, Wiley looked at Tom. "Semper Fi Marine. Me too. I was in the First Division in Korea."

"I was in the Third Division, the 4th Marines," offered Tom.

"I was Fifth Marines myself. So you must have seen your fair share of combat?"

"Yeah, I sure did. How about you?"

"I made that trek out of the Frozen Chosen Reservoir. In fact, I think it was that danged cold there that's causing my problems now," said Wiley as he began a gingerly assent up the stairs to the front porch.

Tom followed right behind him. "Geez, John, my hat is off to you. I don't know how you guys could have functioned in the subzero cold fighting all the way back to Hungnam. At least in Vietnam we didn't have to contend with the cold."

"On frost-bitten feet, placing one foot in front of the other, basically," said Wiley. Wiley opened the front door to the ranch house. "Ethel, we got company. Come on in, Tom."

Kicking the snow from his work boots, Tom removed his hat and entered the ranch house. A quick glance and Tom could see immediately that the interior of the ranch house in contrast to the exterior had been remodeled and was very modern. The living area they had entered had an open beam natural wood ceiling and there was a large stone fireplace on the wall to the right of the front door. The fire not only warmed the room but also gave off that burning wood aroma. Mixed with the smell of cinnamon, it made the house seem cozier. Western artifacts and pictures decorated the walls.

Wiley excused himself to go find his wife. "She's a little hard of hearing," he offered. "Make yourself at home."

Tom unbuttoned his heavy woolen shirt and looked at the pictures on the walls. One picture was not really a picture at all but was a framed Silver

Star Certificate, accompanied by a Purple Heart Certificate. *The Silver Star, John is a combat hero himself and like me has the Purple Heart,* thought Tom. The remaining pictures were obviously of children and grandchildren.

"Ethel will be right with us, Tom," said Wiley as he reentered the family room. "That's our family. A boy and a girl and six grandchildren."

"Do they live around here?"

"Son and two grandchildren live in Fort Collins. He teaches at Colorado State. Our daughter and husband and four grandchildren live in Colorado Springs. He's an Air Force officer and teaches at the Air Force Academy."

"Wow, you must be really proud of them."

"Yeah, we are. They both turned out okay. Couldn't wait to get away from the ranch though."

"Say, John, I see you were awarded the Silver Star in Korea."

"Yes, I was. I didn't see how I earned it though. Just doing what needed to be done to stay alive," said Wiley with his modesty becoming evident.

"I know that feeling all too well, John," admitted Tom as a slight blush developed on his cheeks.

"So you were decorated also, huh, Tom?"

"Yes, I was, and like you, I got recognized for doing what needed to be done to survive."

"What award did you receive, Tom?" asked Wiley.

With the slight blush deepening to an almost crimson color, Tom's shyness showed. "Well, I was awarded the Navy Cross, and of course, I have some of these two." He tapped the glass frame that contained the Purple Heart.

"The Navy Cross! I'm honored to know you, Tom," said Wiley extending his hand to Tom.

"Same here, John."

"I see he's bragging about our family," said a small white-haired lady who entered the living room from the direction of what Tom surmised was the kitchen. Attired in jeans, a woolen shirt and boots and with her hair pulled back into a ponytail, she crossed the room to greet their visitor. Tom guessed she was in her early seventies, but she retained much of the beauty that she obviously enjoyed as a younger lady.

"No, Ethel, we were talking about our Marine Corps time," said a mildly defensive Wiley. "Tom here got the Navy Cross in Vietnam," he added.

"Really? That's commendable. Now I can see where you got your bravery to take on those Mexicans who were trying to kill that poor state trooper."

"Tom, this is my better half, Ethel," said Wiley.

Tom extended his hand. "Glad to meet you, ma'am. I was admiring your family."

"Why don't we move to the kitchen?" Ethel said. "I have some hot coffee and fresh cinnamon rolls."

"Ethel, Tom here tells me that we won't be able to use his services any longer?"

Ethel set a plate of warm cinnamon rolls on a large wooden table in the kitchen. "You're getting out of the business, Tom?"

"No, Ethel, the dang gum government is transferring him," said Wiley answer for Tom. "Just my luck too. I find somebody who does good tractor work and is reliable, and he gets transferred."

"Is this a promotion or something like that, Tom?" asked Ethel.

"No, ma'am, not a promotion. It's a long story but the simple version is that I have angered the powers to be in Washington, D.C. This transfer is either payback for taking a position contrary to theirs or meant to force me to retire. But like your husband here and his walk out of the frozen Chosin in Korea, I refuse to quit or surrender."

"Does your transfer have anything to do with the shooting of those two Mexicans that were trying to kill that state trooper?" asked Ethel.

"Not directly, ma'am. But it does have to do with another shooting in which I had an active part.

"Do say!" exclaimed Wiley.

"Wow!" exclaimed a distracted Tom. "These cinnamon rolls are great!" He finished one and started on a second one. "Do you recall the shooting that occurred in the Five Points area in Denver in September two years ago that involved the Denver Swat Team? Several Denver officers were killed and wounded?"

"Vaguely," replied Wiley.

"Yes, somewhat," offered Ethel. "Oh!" she exclaimed, as her face brightened. "You were involved in that shooting also weren't you. In fact, now that I recall, I think you were the hero there also and saved the day."

Again, with his face flushed red in embarrassment. "Like your husband says about his heroics in Korea, Ethel. I just did what needed to be done to prevent more killing."

"Well, I don't understand why what you did there would get you into Dutch with Washington?" said Wiley.

Tom let out a big sigh. "John, the whole incident could have been avoided had my bosses here in the Denver office allowed me to take the actions I wanted to take. I wanted to do a search warrant early in the morning when all of the crooks would have been asleep. I had a plan I believe would have put us into the house before the bad guys could have reacted. But my bosses refused to listen to my plan and dictated that I opt for using the Denver Swat Team. I guess I was quite vocal about my feelings after the shooting. Now I find myself as a witness against the government in civil proceedings in Federal Court here in Denver. And, of course, that didn't play well with the hierarchy in D.C."

"So this transfer is a way of getting back at you then?" asked Ethel.

"Well, yes. In fact, there has been a concerted effort by Washington to drive me from DEA because of this. As we speak, I'm finishing up a forty-five day suspension without pay and benefits which I believe is directly related to their efforts to drive me from DEA and basically muzzle me. They listened to a less than forthright person who said I abused my take-home car privilege and that's the actual reason for my suspension. While I am guilty of stopping by a store on the way home one evening while driving the government car, I didn't do anything that all agents have done in their career. It certainly did not merit forty-five days off without pay."

"So that's why you've been doing the tractor work?" asked Wiley.

"Got to eat and pay the mortgage, John," Tom said shrugging his shoulders.

"So the other day when you got involved in that shooting, you weren't on duty then?" asked Wiley.

"No, I acted as a good citizen. Well, maybe as a good citizen who is a little more equipped to handle those kinds of situations."

"Tom, that makes your actions even more commendable in my eyes," offered Ethel.

"If you served your forty-five days as punishment, then I don't understand why they are trying to transfer you," said Wiley.

"I think the brass in Washington felt that once they imposed the forty-five day suspension, which by the way is so far out of line with the alleged offense which usually results in a five-day suspension, and I did not retire, then they decided to do something more drastic to force me to retire."

"Can they get away with this?" asked Ethel with more than a bit of surprise in her tone.

"I guess they'll try, but I intend to fight it before the Merit System Protection Board and courts, if necessary." He shrugged his shoulders. "But in the interim, I'll have to go to Los Angeles."

"Say, Tom, have you thought about contacting your congressman about this?" asked Ethel.

"No, Ethel, not really my style, I guess. Most Congressional complaints I've seen in DEA are by problem employees who should never have been hired in the first place. I don't want to be considered as one of those."

"Nonsense, Tom! Congressmen are there to help people in situations such as yourself, and I think you should consider contacting your senator," said an adamant Ethel.

"I think I'll just let my lawyer sort this out for me, Ethel," said Tom with a smile.

"Tom, I think you should listen to Ethel. She knows what she's talking about here," said Wiley.

"Oh! You guys had a problem that was solved by your Congressman?"

"Yep. When I had problems with the Veterans Administration, she contacted our Senator and he got right on the case and resolved my problem in less than a week," said a defiant Wiley.

"A week. Now that was fast," a surprised Tom offered.

"Yes it was, and if he had not acted fast enough for us, Jessup would not have been welcomed here on Thanksgiving."

"What? Senator Collins was here for Thanksgiving?" asked Tom as his face developed into a look of confusion.

"Dern tooting. Brother-in-law or no brother-in-law, he would not have been welcomed here if he had not got me my VA benefits."

"Wait. Senator Jessup Collins is your brother-in-law?" Tom asked Wiley.

"Yes, Jess is my younger brother, and I know he would be willing to help you out on your case. He does have a lot of power in Washington, you know," answered Ethel.

"Yes, I know," said Tom. "I do believe he's on the Judiciary Committee which oversees federal law enforcement budgets," he continued.

"Tom, just say the word, and I'll call him today," said Ethel. "He's still here on the holiday recess."

"Ethel, I really do appreciate your efforts to help me," said Tom. "Let me try to work this out with my attorney first."

"Okay, Tom. It's your call," said Ethel. "But just say the word, and I'll get him on the case."

Tom rose from the table. "Well, thanks again folks for the offer and the excellent cinnamon rolls and coffee. They really hit the spot, Ethel."

"Wait one minute," said Ethel as she grabbed the plate of cinnamon rolls. "Let me wrap up a couple of these for later."

Wiley objected as she began to place several rolls into a plastic baggie. "Ethel, make sure there are a couple left for me for later too."

Ethel waved her hand in a dismissal manner. "Oh quiet, you old fool. There's another plate full for later."

Tom smiled at the two bantering. "Well, I need to be running along. John. When you get ready for the postholes, give me a call. I just might be back here by then."

Wiley handed Tom a check that he had already written for the snowplowing. "Here's for today, Tom, and I will sure call when I need some tractor work done. In addition, listen, young fella, let us know if we can get her brother involved. I'm sure he could remedy your problem."

"Thanks again Ethel, John," said Tom.

In the cold confines of his Scout during the trip back to his home, Tom thought about this lovely couple. *I sure envy them and their lives here. Maybe I will just have to take them up on their offer to contact the senator if my legal actions fail.*

As John Wiley watched the departing Scout pulling the tractor-laden trailer, he turned to Ethel. "That's a fine young man, Ethel. A brave and decent human being who is being screwed by dern Washington bureaucrats."

"John, maybe I should just call my brother and drop a hint about Tom and his problems."

Screwing up his face, John considered her last statement. "Might not be a bad idea, Ethel. But let me speak to him, okay?"

December 9, 1996; Hacienda Puesta Del Sol, La Cruz, Sinaloa, Mexico

The mild on-shore breeze made it seem colder than the actual 64-degree temperature on the back veranda. With no trees or shrubs to block the panoramic view of the Pacific Ocean, Juan felt the chill and sting of the breeze as he escorted Comandante Guerra from the front entrance of the hacienda to the veranda where Jaime sat. *I don't know if it's the weather or the icy personality of this man that's causing me to shiver,* thought Juan.

"Welcome to my humble home, Comandante," said Jaime as the comandante appeared on the veranda with Juan. They shook hands. "Please have a seat." He waved his hand toward a dark leather chair to his right. He turned to Juan. "Coffee for our guest, Juan." He looked back to the comandante. "Or would you like something stronger to ward off this chill?"

"Uh, no, Don Jaime, the coffee would be fine," said the comandante using the polite title of Don for Jaime.

"The breeze is a little stiff today," Jaime said as they waited for the coffee, "but then again, it is January, and one would expect the weather to be cool."

"Yes, it is cool today, but it's not as bad as some days," answered the comandante.

Jaime sat forward in his chair. "We could move inside, Comandante, if it is too uncomfortable out here."

"It is fine, Don Jaime."

Accompanied by a servant, Juan returned with the coffee. After it was poured and distributed to Jaime and the comandante, Jaime took a sip and began. "Comandante, I think perhaps you and I got off on the wrong foot the other day at the restaurant and I wanted to meet with you to clear the air between us without the licenciado."

Acknowledging Jaime's statement, the comandante merely nodded his head in ascent.

"I realize that the licenciado is a very important man in your eyes, Comandante, but I think you are somewhat confused as to who has the real power here," said Jaime with a very casual demeanor in his tone.

"Uh, Don Jaime…," began the comandante tenuously before he was interrupted by Jaime.

"Please, Comandante, listen to what I have to say before you respond."

"Sí, por supesto—certainly," acknowledged the comandante.

Jaime's casual tone gave way to a more serious one. "The licenciado only is the licenciado because I allow it. With a simple phone call from me, he would no longer hold that position. But I allow it because it suits my purpose right now, and he is occasionally of value to me and my operations. However, recently he has become extremely greedy, and it is beginning to anger me.

For example, when I asked him to resolve that problem we had at the border the other day, he advised me it would cost $250,000 to get the necessary information, information that I got from another source basically for free. I suspect that a good portion of the $250,000 would have gone directly to one of his offshore accounts. If he or anyone else thinks they can extort that kind of money out of me, they are sadly mistaken, Señor."

The comandante set down his coffee cup so the slight tremor in his hands could not be detected. "Don Jaime, I had no knowledge of this $250,000 demand. I merely instructed the licenciado that I might need some money to get information from a source inside the pinche U.S. Customs. No sum was ever discussed as I had not made contact with the source."

"It's as I suspected, Comandante." Jaime sat back in his chair and allowed a long silence between the two. The only sound was the waves breaking against the coastline to their front. Jaime ended the silence with a voice that, once again, had become more casual. "Comandante, I want to make you a proposition."

"Sí, Don Jaime, and what is that?" asked the comandante with the tenuousness still evident in his tone.

"I no longer wish to deal with you through the licenciado. I wish to deal with you directly."

"Sí, Don Jaime, but the licenciado has the power to discharge me if he wishes and if he thought I was dealing directly with you, he would get rid of me."

"Trust me, Comandante. That will not happen. I will deal with the licenciado, and I can assure you that your efforts in my regard will be of great benefit to you."

"Don Jaime, I am somewhat concerned with the licenciado and his contacts. He is a powerful man," pleaded the comandante.

With a look of agitation developing on his face, Jaime looked directly at the comandante. "I am somewhat disturbed that you question my abilities, Comandante. The licenciado's power is nothing without me. However, I guess I need to make myself clear on this subject. This is not a negotiation. This is how it is going to be. You either take your directions from me or I will find someone who will."

Instantly, he realized he had no alternative to Jaime's offer. "Don Jaime, por favor, I meant no disrespect. I will do as you say."

"Bueno." The causal tone once again appeared in Jaime's voice. "I'm glad that we could come to an agreement." Jaime turned to Juan. "Give the comandante the names Ramon provided us." Juan passed the paper to the comandante. "I want you to deal with this yourself, Comandante, and determine which one is responsible. Take care of the problem how you see fit." Once again, Jaime turned back to Juan. "The envelope." Juan handed the envelope to Jaime who held it out for the comandante. "This is for you for taking care of the problem. When you tell me the problem no longer exists, there will be another envelope. And for your services, there shall be a monthly envelope containing a like amount."

The comandante took the envelope and with the meeting over, Juan escorted him back to the front of the hacienda and his waiting car. He paused by the open door. "Juan, I guess I was just handed the Plato y Ploma. With the choice of silver or lead what else could I do?"

"You chose correctly, Comandante," said Juan.

December 9, 1996; DEA Denver, Colorado

With equal amounts of anticipation and trepidation, Tom approached the Denver DEA building. He guided his aging Scout into his usual spot at the rear of the parking lot. He figured it would be almost vacant at 7:30 a.m., and it was. Tom felt a chill that was not due to the frosty air on this December morning. He sat with his hands on the steering wheel and stared at the squat stone three-story building. A sudden shiver caused him to contemplate *I wonder if it will be as frosty inside as it is outside.*

Tom looked forward to catching up on what had occurred in his enforcement group during his forty-five day absence. However, beginning the process of turning over the group to someone else before his departure for Los Angeles was another matter. It was not due to any problems that might be facing him with his group or his impending transfer, but instead, the initial encounter with Dominic Angelini that he would have to endure. As Tom's immediate supervisor, he was required to report to Angelini on his first day back to duty. Additionally, Angelini held Tom's badge and credentials that he had taken from Tom when placing him on suspension.

Oh well, only one way to do this, he thought as he exited his Scout. "Might as well go face the music right off," Tom said to himself after noting the lights on in the ASAC's office. Another chill caused him to pull his heavy sheepskin jacket closed.

As he made his way to the third floor office of Dominic Angelini, Tom noted there had been little change to the building since his last day here, except maybe for the Christmas decorations in the various offices.

It was still too early for Angelini's administrative assistant to be in the office, so Tom presented himself at the opened door and knocked lightly on the frame. Angelini sat at his desk writing on a pad and looked up when Tom knocked. "Come on in, Blaine," advised Angelini as he raised the left shirtsleeve and glanced at his watch. "A bit early, aren't we?" he asked.

"Just wanted to get in before the phones began to ring and take care of the paperwork I know is awaiting my return," said Tom.

Angelini acknowledged Tom's last statement with a nod of his head, moved toward the door and shut it behind Tom. "I don't want us to be disturbed."

The chill that Tom had experienced in his Scout returned.

Reaching behind his desk, Angelini retrieved a large envelope and handed it to Tom. "Here's your badge and credentials, Tom. I've also instructed your group assistant to have one of the junior agents to service your vehicle. It should be gassed and good to go."

Everything after "Tom" was completely missed by Tom whose entire focus was *He called me by my first name. He's never done that before. How bad can this be?* Angelini seemed ill at ease with what he was about to say, so Tom decided to make the first move. "Boss, I'm sorry you got screwed in this deal."

Angelini cleared his throat. "Some shit, huh?" He seemed to relax somewhat with Tom's apology.

"Yeah, I guess so, but knowing Conway and Peterson as I do, I can't say I'm not surprised."

"Look, Tom, I'll admit I was pissed at you over this shooting incident and then the transfer to El Paso. That is, until I talked with Roger Grey at Headquarters."

"Oh?" Tom exclaimed.

"Yeah, Tom, Roger convinced me it was Conway and that asshole Peterson's fault and not yours. I guess I should have been a bit more low key with Sheriff Janarous. So some of this is my fault." Angelini hesitated and looked at Tom for several seconds. "You're not married, are you, Tom?"

"No sir, not at the present."

"I know I come on kind of strong at times, and this is really no excuse, but

I'm married to a full-blooded Sicilian woman who thinks her whole world revolves around New York. All her family and friends are there. When I did my tour in HQ, she stayed in New York. I commuted when I could. She came to DC for visits, but hated it and would never consider moving there. When I got a good score for promotion, I just knew I'd be getting a slot in New York or Jersey. Well, of course, I didn't. Oh, she came out here for a househunting trip with me, but decided she just couldn't make the move. So I'm here on my own, and she bitches at me daily. I haven't even told her about my transfer to El Paso.

Tom nodded his head signifying he understood Angelini's predicament.

"I know that's not really a good excuse for my bad behavior," said Angelini.

"Well, it sure does make your life miserable when the wife is not happy. So believe me, boss, I do understand," Tom offered.

"So look, I'm trying to say, I'm sorry for what has developed on this thing."

"There's no reason for you to apologize. Roger is right on, boss. Conway went to a lot of trouble to transfer me to Los Angeles. He's willing to disrupt the lives of nine other supervisors who have done absolutely nothing wrong just so he can get to me," said Tom.

"Roger pointed that out to me, Tom, and candidly, I had not considered it until he pointed that out. Conway is destroying this agency by driving out all the good people who have the audacity to question him. Roger also told me of several other instances where he has done the same thing to guys like us."

"You're absolutely correct in your assessment of Conway and his motives. That is exactly why I won't cave in and allow him to force me from DEA. I intend to fight him every time he screws me. I'll choose the time and place that I decide to retire and will do so with my head held up high. I, for one, do not want to be known as a guy who left DEA under a black cloud of controversy."

"So you're going to fight this transfer then. We all thought you had already agreed to report to LA."

"Oh, I'll report to LA, but I'm going to fight this thing. In fact, even as we speak, as they say, my attorney is exploring what avenue is most likely to be successful. I'll be filing a formal grievance, which in all likelihood will end up before the Merit System Protection Board. My attorney is also exploring the fact that Conway may be trying to influence a witness in a federal lawsuit filed against DEA by the families of some DPD officers who were killed because of alleged DEA incompetence. Lastly, there is the possibility of a lawsuit that Conway is using his position to seek retribution against a whistle blower. What about you, boss? Are you going to fight this transfer?" asked Tom.

"I don't know that I have an argument. I just may have to gut it out for the next eighteen months when I'll be eligible to retire and then pull the pin.

Tom reached forward and took one of Angelini's business cards from a holder. He wrote the name and number of his attorney on the back of the card. "This is my attorney. He's very adept at beating the government in front of the Merit System Protection Board. Give him a call and explain your circumstances." Tom handed the card to Angelini. "I'll bet he'll link your problem to mine."

"What about the cost? I've got a son in college and a daughter who will begin in two years."

"This guy will want a retainer, but you'll get it all back plus his fees when he wins at the Merit System Protection Board."

"Thanks, Tom. I'll think about it."

"Tell you what, boss, I'll call him later this morning and let him know you might file a grievance. You can call him and discuss your problem. He'll tell you straight away if he can help you. It won't cost you anything to talk to him."

"I'll do it, and thanks again, Tom."

"Don't mention it, boss."

Tom excused himself and made his way to his enforcement group on the first floor. *Thank you, Roger. Once again, you bailed me out of a tough situation. I owe you one, my friend.*

Tom would spend the better part of the week wading through the mountain of paperwork that needed to be completed and catching up on the ongoing investigations of the group. He also had to respond repeatedly to the curiosity among his fellow co-workers and associates, who had not sought him out right after the shooting, and more importantly, how did he feel about his transfer to LA. Then there were those who were curious but kept their distance. Tom felt their invasive inquiries with their stares.

CHAPTER NINE

December 9, 1996; Elizabeth, Colorado

"Well, that certainly was a great waste of time," commented Senior Inspector Riley Wilson as he carefully guided the rental car down a snow-covered two-lane country road.

McReynolds looked out the window at the pine tree and snow-blanketed hills. "Actually, I didn't think we'd find out much by checking with Blaine's neighbors. Hell, his closest neighbors were a quarter of a mile away and only knew him to wave at him."

"Well, let's hope the bank records we get this afternoon will be more helpful. The sooner we get something to make Peterson happy, the sooner we can be on a jet out of here," said Wilson.

"Amen to that." McReynolds rubbed his stomach. "It's past lunch time. I'm starved; what you say we find some place to grab a bite?"

"Mac, you're always hungry," Wilson said with a smirk on his face. "But I could use something to drink."

"I didn't see anything that resembles a restaurant when we passed through this berg while in route to Blaine's neighborhood. But I recall seeing a market there. Maybe we can grab something to drink and munch on until we can find a restaurant," suggested McReynolds.

Entering the town of Elizabeth, Wilson almost drove past the market. He wheeled the rental car sharply to the left and aimed it into the parking lot. With just a slight fishtail from a pack of ice, Wilson corrected for the skid and angled the sliding car into a parking slot. "The eagle has landed," said McReynolds providing a commentary on Wilson's driving.

"Hey! You can drive, if you think you can do better on this crap, Mac," answered a slightly annoyed Wilson.

"Naw, you're doing good, Riley. We haven't gotten stuck yet considering all the snow out here."

The market in Elizabeth was more than just a market. It was a combination food and meat market with a laundromat and video store all compacted into a single story low-slung rustic building. Entering the market, Wilson and McReynolds were pleased to see that fresh-made deli style sandwiches could be purchased in the butcher shop area and several tables sat adjacent to the laundromat and video shops. While he waited for his sandwich, McReynolds, partly out of a combination of curiosity and boredom, perused a bulletin board located on a back wall. The bulletin board held a large variety of notices of locals offering items for sale, as well as a myriad of services people were willing to perform for compensation. "Hello, what's this?" he exclaimed.

"What you got, Mac, somebody who's willing to deliver you a cord of wood or stuff your elk?" kidded Wilson.

McReynolds pulled a small three-by-five card from the bulletin board. "Better than that."

"Light Tractor Work in Elbert, Arapahoe and Douglas Counties— culverts, post holes and light grading my specialty. Call Tom at (303) 458-5675," read Wilson from the card handed to him by McReynolds.

"Yeah, so what, Mac?"

"The number on the card, don't you recognize it, Riley?"

"Don't tell me it's Blaine's?" asked a mildly surprised Wilson.

"Bingo. I remember it from looking at his toll calls we subpoenaed," said McReynolds.

Wilson stared at the card for several seconds. A large smile developed on his face. "Mac, you just might have found the smoking gun we need to get Peterson off our backs and us out of Colorado in time for you and your bride to spend your Christmas holidays in New England. Talk about fortuitous luck."

"Riley, I know the outcome of many good cases were the result of fortuitous luck," said McReynolds."

"Quite true, my man, but first we have to ascertain if he really performed any tractor work for compensation while on suspension to prove he violated the policy about non-approved outside employment," said Wilson.

"He had to do something with the money people paid him for the work, Riley, and I'm willing to bet he deposited it in his checking account. So when we check the records later on this afternoon, I'll bet there's a number of either cash or check deposits over the period he was on suspension."

McReynolds scratched his head while considering Wilson's last statement. "That may be true, but just because he deposited money in his account while on suspension, doesn't mean he got it from doing unauthorized off-duty employment. I would be willing to bet that Blaine is a little smarter than that and will have a plausible excuse for the monies appearing in his account. No, we need someone to tell us they paid him for his tractor services."

"Sandwiches up," shouted the butcher from behind the meat counter.

The men gathered their sandwiches and returned to the table.

"Man, look at the size of this sandwich," McReynolds said. "There's got to be half a side of beef in this thing." McReynolds quickly changed the subject. "Look, Riley, I think I should go undercover and ask around here about someone reliable to do some tractor work for me."

"Good idea, we could ask around…" began Wilson before McReynolds interrupted him.

"Let's face it, Riley, you're not going to fit in here. I mean how many blacks have we seen since we left Denver."

"Yeah, I guess this is definitely a white bread area," said Wilson.

McReynolds didn't waste time. After consuming his sandwich, he asked some of the market patrons about local contractors who did tractor work. Once again, fortuitous actions intervened on his behalf when he questioned an older rancher, who identified himself as Hank Ellsworth. Ellsworth voiced his opinion of Tom Blaine's tractor work. "I had him drill a bunch of post holes on my spread right before all this dang gum snow. He did a good job, and he was reasonable. What do you need him for?"

"I got a culvert I need to put in," said McReynolds dropping into an undercover role. "I'm building a house east of town."

"Kind of bad time to do it right now with the ground frozen and all, ain't it?" asked Ellsworth.

"Yeah, but I'm up against a construction loan deadline and need to do it so the construction guys can get into the property," said McReynolds.

"I see. Well, Tom did a fine job for me, and I know he also did some plowing for John Wiley over near Franktown last week. Besides, he's a local hero around here, you know?"

"You don't say?" asked McReynolds.

"He's that DEA man who killed those two Mexicans that were trying to kill the state trooper over near Franktown last month."

"Oh yeah, I heard about that. He's that guy huh?"

"Yup, so I think he's real reliable, but you best act quickly, cause John Wiley told me yesterday at church that Tom's getting out of the business soon. He's been transferred to Los Angeles."

"Really, well I hope he can still get me in, cause I need the work done right away."

"I'd call him right away. If he ain't at home, leave a message on his phone, and he'll call you right back as soon as he can," said Ellsworth as he turned to walk away.

"Well, thanks for the info Mr. Ellsworth, but let me ask you one more question if you don't mind," said McReynolds. "Will he take a check or does he prefer to deal in cash?"

"Don't seem to matter none to him," said Ellsworth with just a slight shrug of his shoulders. "I wrote him a check and he seemed happy with that."

"Okay, then. Thanks for your information," said McReynolds.

"Glad to help you, young feller," said Ellsworth.

While in route back to Denver, Wilson and McReynolds listened to the conversation with Hank Wiley that McReynolds had taped using a hidden Niagra tape recorder. "Mac, I think you just assured yourself that you'll be going home for the holidays. Say, how did you come up with that thing about a short time frame and construction loan? I certainly would not have been able to come up with anything as spontaneous as that."

"Simple, Riley. When I had my home built in New Hampshire, I had a similar problem and just figured it would work here also."

"Well, good job, my man. Now if the bank records show deposits, we should have a good enough case for Peterson to go forward against Blaine for unauthorized off-duty employment."

"Yeah, but I sure hope that unauthorized off-duty employment is enough to satisfy Peterson," said McReynolds. "Remember, the Merit System Protection Board has ruled against DEA on this same issue."

"I know but it's all we've got, and I think I can convince Peterson we have left no stone unturned. Besides, I think Peterson can pitch a case to Conway that Blaine has a repeated history of violating DEA rules and regulations and should be terminated for cause. I mean, the guy was on suspension for another infraction while he was violating the authorized off-duty employment rule."

McReynolds nodded his head in agreement. "I sure hope so, Riley."

December 10, 1996 Hacienda Puesta Del Sol, La Cruz, Sinaloa, Mexico

"Hola, Juan." Juan Cervantes recognized the voice on the phone as that of the comandante.

"Buenos dios, Comandante. How are you today?"

"Juan, I have a slight problem and need to speak with Jaime as soon as possible."

"A problem?" repeated Juan. His concerned tone caused Jaime, who was sitting in his leather chair, to sit straight up and reach for the remote to mute the CNN broadcaster. He quickly approached Juan and signaled for the phone.

"Comandante, this is Jaime. What's the problem?"

"Oh, Don Jaime, I have a slight problem, a problem that maybe I should not talk about on the phone. Could I come by and talk with you directly?"

"Sí, of course, Comandante. You are always welcomed in my humble home. What time can I expect you?"

"I can be there within the hour, Don Jaime.

"Bueno, Comandante, I will see you then."

Forty minutes later, the comandante was escorted from the front foyer area of the estancia to Jaime's office where Jaime was once again seated in the leather chair watching CNN. The comandante's long face, slightly shaking hands and clipped speech announced his nervousness, which was uncharacteristic of one who had such a violent reputation.

Jaime did not rise to greet him but merely indicated with his hand toward the leather chair opposite him. "Have a seat, Comandante."

"I have a problem with the licenciado, Don Jaime."

"And what is this problem, Comandante?"

"He learned through one of my ayundantes, that I was dealing with that potential snitch on the money seizure thing without first going through him. He came screaming into my office a little while ago and said I was done working for him, and he was making the phone call to have me replaced."

"I see. Who was the ayundante who told him, Comandante?" asked Jaime with a calm voice that belied his true angry feelings.

"A newer ayundante, a relative of the licenciado who was hired by him. I suspect he was hired to spy on me."

"I see," said Jaime again. He looked straight ahead for several minutes, which seemed like an eternity to the nervous comandante. Jaime then turned his attention back to Comandante and smiled. "Not to worry, Comandante. Go back to attending to that thing I asked you do up north, and I will take care of the licenciado. I think after I talk with him, he will agree that he was a little premature in trying to fire you."

"Sí, Don Jaime." The comandante rose to leave.

"Oye, Comandante, una momento por favor." Jaime grabbed a slip of paper from Juan's desk.

"Write the name of this ayundante on this slip of paper."

The comandante did as Jaime requested, turned and left.

Jaime returned to watching CNN. After a few minutes, Jaime, once again, muted the television. "Juan, call my brother and have him set up a late luncheon meeting with the licenciado."

"Sí, jefe, for this afternoon?"

"Yes, Juan."

December 10, 1996; DEA Denver, Colorado

While those who would conspire to violate the federal drug laws of the United States arranged for a late luncheon, several thousand miles to the northeast, those who would enforce the drug laws were planning likewise. "Tom, I decided to take you up on your offer to move into your house while you're in LA," came the soft voice of Libby Martin over his phone on his desk."

"Libby, that's great," said Tom with obvious relief at hearing this bit of news. "Now I can stop worrying about Manfred and my ranch while I'm gone."

"I think we should get together and discuss how this is going to work and some ground rules," said Libby.

"Ground rules? Okay, I guess. Can you do lunch today?"

"I'm in trial right now, Tom, but I could get away for a quick lunch. Could you come by the court and then when King March breaks for lunch we could go someplace close by."

"Judge March, huh? Lucky you. Is he ruling over his fiefdom like he normally does?" asked Tom.

"Worse, I'm afraid, and right now, it seems to be open season on assistant United States attorneys."

"Geez, I'm sorry, I know what a jerk he can be. But then what can you expect from someone who was a criminal defense attorney and got appointed to the bench because of hefty campaign contributions to a presidential candidate."

"Listen, I've got to get back into the courtroom. Come by around noon. Okay, Tom?"

"Sure, I'll be there, Libby."

After hanging up the phone, Tom sat at his desk and assessed his instant reactions to hearing Libby's voice. His mood had instantly switched from morose to happy, and he felt an excitement deep within that had been missing since they had parted ways. Just the conjuring up of a mental image of her in his mind as she sat in her office on the phone caused a stirring within that Tom had only experienced when he was with her. He sighed audibly. *Libby, Libby, why does this have to be so damn difficult. But right now, I'll take difficult to nothing at all.*

"Got a minute, boss?" asked one of Tom's young agents sticking his head in the door.

"Sure, what's up?" he asked.

The agent walked into Tom's office and handed him a manifold form. "I need a signature on this 103 to get some PE/PI funds for that deal later this evening."

"Have a seat," Tom said. He quickly reviewed the form. "This is only for the purchase of the evidence. What about payment to the informant?"

"He doesn't get anything unless the deal goes. That's our agreement. He gets the one ounce of meth, or he gets nothing."

"And we suspect the source of meth is connected to Sons of Silence?" Tom asked.

"Yes, boss, and with any luck, surveillance might be able to tie it to the Sons' clubhouse in Greeley."

"That should be great for paper on the place."

"Yes, but we'd like to do some more deals first before we consider a search warrant. I want to tie up some more players," said the agent with just a hint of a plea in his tone.

"Okay. Sounds good to me, keep me advised about the deal and I should be available to help tonight."

With obvious relief, the young agent stood and turned toward the door. He stopped abruptly and turned back to Tom. "Thanks, boss. It sure is good to have you back. It's been miserable around here without a real supervisor while you were gone."

"It's good to be back," said Tom.

December 10, 1996; Federal Courthouse, Denver, Colorado

Forty minutes following his phone call with Libby, Tom walked into Judge March's courtroom and slid into an aisle seat in the sparsely populated gallery. Tom noted he was among the regular court watchers, a group of elder citizens who routinely attended courts for daytime entertainment, and a number of obvious homeless people who had traded the cold outside for the warmth of the courtroom and who would remain until court security removed them. Just the sight of Libby even in her muted navy blue business suit caused his heart to race. She stood at the prosecution's table at a lofty five-four in her stiletto heels. Her normally luscious brown-flowing hair, now pulled back into a bun, didn't help. He felt himself getting warm with anticipation about being with her even for a short lunch. He then noticed the man in a business suit to her right seated at the prosecution's table.

"You're in contempt, Ms. Martin. That will be one hundred dollars," announced an angered Judge March."

"Fine, at least somebody will be held accountable for a crime in this courtroom today," retorted a defiant Libby."

"That will be two hundred dollars, and if I hear one more word out of you, counselor, it will be jail," responded the judge whose face had turned a beet red.

Wisely heeding the judge's threat of jail, Libby remained silent.

"We're in recess until 1:00." The judge rose and stormed from the courtroom.

Libby continued to stand at her table as her male companion stood, patted her on the shoulder and walked toward the rear of the courtroom. Tom recognized the companion as a Secret Service Agent from the local office. They exchanged nods as they passed in the limited-spaced aisle.

"What was that all about?" Tom asked realizing something must have occurred prior to his entering the courtroom.

"He's being his usual self. Always siding with the defense on their objections and motions. I called him on it, and he got pissed and held me in contempt. He's probably on the phone right now to the U.S. Attorney. I'll be lucky if I don't get fired over this."

"Libby, they're not going to fire you for sticking up for the government. That's what they pay you to do, for Christ's sake."

Libby turned to Tom for the first time and faltered for words for a moment. She quickly gathered her thoughts again. "Tom, I know that, but I just get so frustrated in March's courtroom because it's so blatant."

"But there's not much you can do except take him up on appeal every time you feel you have been unfairly treated. Maybe if enough of you assistants would do that, he'd get the message when he suffered enough reversals or when the Judicial Review Board got involved."

"I guess you're right. It won't help me here on this case, but maybe in the future, if I have a future." Libby pushed papers into her briefcase. "Come on, let's get out of here." She grabbed her briefcase and purse.

The two headed toward the rear of the courtroom. "Besides, if the U.S. Attorney fires you, you could always hang out your shingle and go into criminal defense work and become rich."

Libby gained her resolve and smiled. "I'd rather quit the law before I did that buster." She punched Tom slightly on the arm. "Let's go eat, big guy. I might as well get fired on a full stomach."

"Where to, kiddo?" he asked.

"Let's go to Chez Fe. It's close and fast," she suggested.

"And don't forget my favorite adjective—cheap?" A large smile emerged on Tom's face.

The employees had labeled the Federal Cafeteria on the third floor of the federal building as Chez Fe. It sat adjacent to the federal courthouse. The large open dining area allowed for several food stations along two walls offering sandwiches, hot meals, prepared salads and a large variety of desserts. Tuesday was meatloaf day at the hot food entrée station, and Tom settled for that with mashed potatoes, gravy and green beans. Libby opted for a prepared chicken salad. Carrying their meals to a table toward the rear of the cafeteria, Tom nodded to several acquaintances.

Libby caught the looks of several patrons who offered muted comments to their lunch partners. "You seem to be a hit here at Chez Fe."

"Yeah, I've found there's nothing like a good shooting to get you a few minutes of fame. Then, of course, they could be looking at you saying isn't that the former U.S. Attorney who called King March on his impartiality."

"Shut up, butthead," replied Libby. With a short swift kick, she attempted to make contact with his leg."

"Hey, watch it, those pointed shoes are lethal weapons," yelped Tom who deftly avoided a second kick attempt. Their antics got them both laughing and seemed to turn the previous somber mood a little more lighthearted.

They found a small table at the back. One bite of the meatloaf caused Tom to contort his face in a grimace. "This tastes like something I would feed to Manfred. On second thought, he'd turn his nose up on this too. He spun his plate around and commenced to work on the mashed potatoes, slightly more palatable than the meat loaf.

Libby picked at her salad.

"Okay, kiddo, I know you're still upset about this morning, but do you think we can discuss your concerns about our arrangement."

"Oh sure, Tom. Sorry, I was still thinking about the courtroom." She smiled. It was only the second time she had done so this morning.

It caused an immediate reaction in Tom and sent his heart racing. "What's up, Libby?" asked Tom.

"When are you leaving for Los Angeles, Tom?"

"I'm leaving on the second of January in the early morning. That gives me several days to get organized before I have to report to work." He began working on the green beans.

"Wow, that soon, huh?" asked Libby.

He nodded his head.

She shoved her salad she had hardly touched to the side. "I'd like to move my stuff to your place at the end of the month. I have plans for New Year's Eve. So could I do it on the twenty-eighth instead of the thirty-first?"

"Sure, that's fine with me. Plans for New Year's Eve, huh? Some stud, I'll bet," Tom suggested with just a bit of jealousness in his tone.

"No," Libby said dragging out the o in no. A group of us from the office has rented a condo at Beavercreek for the night. We'll ski during the day and ring in the New Years in the condo. Anyway, as I was saying, I'll move my things then if I can find someone to help me."

"Well, it just so happens that I'm available, and as a lad, I worked for Bekins Moving and Storage. Are you going to rent a truck?"

"No, I think I can get everything I need into my horse trailer and truck," she answered.

"I also have a trailer we can use. I can pull it with my Scout," said Tom.

"What about the financial arrangement, Tom?"

"I thought I would continue to pay the mortgage and taxes and any maintenance that might be necessary. Maybe you could pay the utilities like the electricity, propane, phone and trash."

"You don't want me to pay something in rent?"

"No, Libby, I don't. I really appreciate you moving in to take care of

Manfred and my place while I'm gone. If my transfer gets rescinded, or I decide to retire, we can work something else out."

"Okay, then," said Libby, "that sounds good. I certainly could not find a place where I can keep my horse for something like this." Then as an afterthought she added, "My Mom won't like it though."

"Your Mom, why not?"

"Because she won't be able to meddle in my life, that's why not."

"A little problem there, kiddo?"

"Oh yeah, since I moved back in with her and dad, she's been constantly into my business and cannot understand why her forty-three-year-old daughter is not married and giving her grand babies."

"Just a normal parental concern, I guess," Tom offered.

"Yeah, I know, but she is smothering me. I feel sorry for my poor brother."

"Oh, I thought your brother was away in the Army."

"He was, but he got home last month. The war in Iraq convinced him that a career in the military was not a good option right now, so he's trying to find work to tie him over while he pursues a career in professional rodeo. Of course, my mom is driving him crazy too."

"Say, Libby, if I recall, he was in the engineers in the Army, wasn't he?"

"Yes. He worked on heavy equipment when he wasn't out searching for explosive devices. That's what caused him to reconsider his career choice. He lost several friends to those devices and came close to ending his own life a couple of times."

"Hey, you know what? During my suspension from DEA, I started doing some tractor work with my old John Deere. Nothing major, things like postholes, snow plowing, driveways and putting in culverts. I found that there is a real need out there for somebody local who's dependable. I've been doing pretty good money-wise and was seriously considering retiring and doing it full time. Do you think he'd like to take over my work? He can use my tractor and trailer."

"I don't know; I can ask him, Tom? It would get him away from my Mom during the days, and it would put some money in his pocket while he pursues the rodeo thing."

"If he wants to do it, let me know so I can notify some of my customers who I've already told I'm getting out of the business because of my transfer. Plus, I have some other people who want work done."

"Let me check with him tonight, and I'll get back to you." She turned her head toward the beeper alerting her to a message. "Shit! She exclaimed; it's the First Assistant looking for me. I bet I know what this is about. I'd better go."

"Okay, kiddo. Hope everything works out," Tom offered.

As they stood to leave the cafeteria, Libby turned to Tom and moved closer to him so that those sitting at nearby tables could not overhear. "Listen, big guy, my moving in while you are still there does not come with fringe benefits, comprende?"

"Why, whatever do you mean, Ms. Martin," Tom said feigning ignorance.

With a slight grin on her face she whispered, "I mean it will be a strictly plutonic relationship, Blaine. There will be no hanky panky." She punctuated the last part with a finger jabbed into his mid-section.

"Ouch, watch that thing. It's got a nail in it." Tom drew back away from her with a smile on his face.

"I'll be in touch," she said over her shoulder as she walked away.

Damn, this is going to be a lot harder than I thought, Tom silently decided.

December 10, 1996; Hotel Los Mares Azul, Mazatlán, Mexico

As Libby and Tom finished their lunch in Denver, several thousand miles to the southwest, Jaime Gutiérrez was about to have his. Entering the hotel restaurant with Juan trailing slightly behind him, Jaime walked like a man with a purpose. He hesitated slightly and cursed "carajo" when he spotted Licenciado Morales seated at his booth with Hector. The cause of his expletive was two-fold. First, there were several dirty dishes containing partially consumed food in front of the portly licenciado. This angered Jaime because the licenciado did not seem to have the good graces or respect to wait for his host to arrive before he availed himself of free food. The second cause of his inappropriate language was the large breasted blonde sitting next to Hector. This Norte Americano female appeared to be maybe twenty-four years of age, and there was more protruding from her skimpy bright yellow polka-dotted halter-top than there was contained within it. While she was not a real beauty, her physical attributes more than compensated for her comely looks.

He stopped in front of the booth, and Jaime's scowl, along with a slight shake of his head, gave enough of a non-verbal cue to his brother that he was not happy with this arrangement.

Hector sought to assuage Jaime's feelings. "Hola, mi Hermano, este es Emma – this is Emma. She's from Iowa."

Jaime simply replied with a nod of his head in her direction. He then turned toward the licenciado and, with more than mild irritation in his tone, asked: "Get enough to eat, Licenciado?" Jaime did not wait for a response from the licenciado whose mouth was full of food. "I'm glad to see you did not stand on ceremony and wait for the host to arrive."

The licenciado's face reddened slightly. He swallowed the contents of his mouth and answered while pointing an accusatory finger at Hector. "Jaime, perdone, but it was Hector's idea that we sample some new dishes while we were waiting for you."

Jaime glared at Hector until he felt uncomfortable and got the message that Jaime was angry.

Hector withdrew a hundred dollar bill from his wallet and gave it to Emma. "Why don't you go check out the hotel boutiques while I visit with my brother? I'll meet you out by the pool in an hour or so."

"Okay, bye Hector; bye Mr. Morales," said Emma to Hector and the licenciado as she slid from the booth. She merely nodded to Jaime and Juan, both of whom had remained standing beside the booth.

"Sorry about that, bro," said a more contrite Hector.

Jaime took a seat, and before he could respond to Hector, the waiter had appeared. "Buenos tardes, señores." He handed both Jaime and Juan oversized menus. "Tomar, por ustedes?" "Something to drink for you?"

"Ramon," said Jaime addressing the waiter by his name, "I'll have a Mezcal and the el pescado del dia—the fish of the day, por favor." Jaime looked over the top of the propped up menu in front of him. "Juan, what do you want today?"

"Don Jefe, just some chicken soup, por favor. I'm not real hungry right now."

"Juan, if I didn't know better, I'd think you did not like the food here in my restaurant," said Jaime with a mixture of both humor and irritation in his voice.

"Oh no, Don Jefe. I like the food here; it is very good, it's just that I am not feeling real well today."

"Do you need to lie down, Juan? I can arrange for a room for you." interjected Hector before Juan interrupted him.

"No gracias, Hector. I'll be fine in a while."

Jaime gazed around the restaurant and nodded his head in recognition to several acquaintances. He then focused his attention to the licenciado. "Licenciado, how is the comandante coming on that thing up at the border? Has he made any progress with those names we gave him?" Knowing the licenciado had fired the comandante, Jaime wanted to see how he would attempt to squirm out of this predicament.

The licenciado took a drink of water as he felt the perspiration develop on his forehead. "About that, Jaime. I'm afraid I had to replace the comandante."

"You had to replace him? Why is this, Licenciado?" Jaime asked faking an element of surprise in his tone.

"I discovered he was doing things behind our backs, and I cannot have that in my comandantes, Jaime. I am sure you would agree with me on that."

"Oh, most certainly, I would agree with that, Licenciado," said Jaime in a tone dripping with sarcasm. "We cannot have people doing things behind our backs. But what about the names we gave the comandante? One of those people has already done harm to me and cost me much. He could do further harm if he is not stopped quickly," Jaime suggested.

"Jaime, I am dealing with that matter personally. Do not concern yourself with that," said the licenciado with a dismissive wave of his hand and a little more assurance in his voice. His protruding stomach gave an audible rumbling; he rubbed his stomach. "Excuse me, señores."

"So the problem is no longer a problem then, Licenciado?" asked Jaime.

Instead of responding to the question, the licenciado looked furtively around the room. His stomach rumbled again and beads of sweat broke out on his forehead. "Excuse me, señores, a sudden and urgent call of nature beckons me."

Jaime waited until the licenciado had disappeared in the direction of the restrooms before turning to Hector. "Hector, I think the licenciado has forgotten who is in charge here. And you do absolutely no good allowing him to gorge himself at our expense." He playfully slapped the back of Hector's head with his palm.

"But, Jaime, it was your idea to meet here," said Hector in his own defense.

"It was not my idea to feed him a mega kilogram of food before I arrived," said Jaime as he gestured toward the many partially consumed meals on the table in front of him. "I think we should go check on the licenciado. Juan, you stay here and drink some coke to settle your stomach."

Jaime and Hector entered the large marble-tiled men's room. The brightly lit restroom contrasted to the subdued lighting in the restaurant. Fancy cream-colored ceramic urinals, separated by carpeted partitions, occupied one wall. A bank of similar colored sinks with gold faucets lined another wall, and stalls for commodes lined yet another wall. A distinct fragrance of flowers, provided by an automatic air freshener along with the soft music of flamingo guitars, completed the ambience of the upscale facility. Quickly searching the restroom, Jaime and Hector noted that the only occupant was connected to a pair of legs that showed beneath a metal stall door. Signaling to Hector to lock the restroom door, Jaime approached the occupied stall and tapped lightly on the door.

"Ocupado!" announced the licenciado from within the stall.

Waving off the foul smell wafting from the stall occupied by the licenciado, Jaime took in a large breath, which he held. Rearing back with his right leg, Jaime executed a short compact and forceful kick to the stall door, causing the door to spring open as the simple slide lock gave way. The stall door swung inward and slammed into the sidewall causing it to bounce back at Jaime with a loud bang. In a fast and fluid motion, Jaime parried the closing stall door with a forearm keeping it from closing and revealing the licenciado sitting on the commode with his pants down.

"Jaime! Que Pasa? What's happening?" screamed a startled licenciado at the intruding Jaime.

Without uttering a word, Jaime reached into the stall and grabbed the licenciado by the necktie. Jerking the licenciado forward like one would drag a dog on a choker chain, the licenciado came forward off the commode, and fell to his knees choking and gagging as he did so. Dragging the wide-eyed licenciado from the stall and across the polished marble floor, Jaime kept a strong grip on his tie while the licenciado, with his arms flaying about trying to keep his balance and to prevent Jaime from choking him further emitted gagging noises. When they reached the approximate center of the restroom, Jaime reached behind his back and pulled his gold plated .45 caliber pistol from his belt. Pressing the pistol against the temple of the licenciado, whose choking sounds were reduced to a gurgle, Jaime released his grip on the tie slightly so that the licenciado was able to gasp for air and did so as he slumped to the floor.

Jaime bent down close to the licenciado. "Now, we talk, Licenciado. I hope I have your full attention."

The licenciado made gulping sounds as he took in air.

"I'll take that as a yes. You seem to have forgotten, Licenciado, that I am the boss here. When I tell somebody like the comandante to do something for me, I expect it to be done, and not countermanded by someone like you, Licenciado. Comprende?"

The licenciado quickly responded with a furious nod of his head.

"Also, I do not like somebody doing anything behind my back, and if you ever cross me again in this manner, I will not act so kindly to you. Comprende?"

Again, the licenciado's response was a quick nodding of his head.

"Furthermore, if I do not have your complete cooperation from this point forward, I shall have to take steps to have you removed. Rest assured that my steps are much less forgiving than your attempt at firing the comandante. And, mi amigo, I would also hate to see something happen to those two lovely twin girls you have in that private academy up in San Diego for which I am sure I am paying." After a short pause, Jaime patted the licenciado on the cheek. "I'm glad we had this little talk, Licenciado. I feel much better about our relationship. Now get yourself cleaned up and get back to your office where you will rescind the firing of the comandante. I want an answer about those names, pronto." Without waiting on the licenciado, Jaime and Hector exited the restroom. "Hector, have maintenance see to that restroom. You might also go to the parking lot and alert the licenciado's ayudantes that he is having some stomach distress. Then, why don't you go see to your big titted blonde gringa. I'm going to enjoy my lunch."

December 10, 1996; DEA Headquarters, Alexandria, Virginia

The constant hum on the phone line annoyed Senior Inspector Riley Wilson. "Mr. Peterson, are you still there?"

"Yes, Riley. I was contemplating what you just told me," replied Peterson.

"Well, sir, what do you think?"

"I don't know, Riley. While it is something, I just don't know that it is enough for our purposes here."

"Sir," Wilson said in a mildly defensive tone, "I think we have a good case against Blaine for unauthorized off-duty employment. We have the original bulletin board card advertising his tractor services from the market in Elizabeth, Colorado, which is near where Blaine resides. Then we have the recorded undercover conversation made by McReynolds with the citizen who claimed Blaine had recently done tractor work for him for pay. Lastly, we have Blaine's bank account statements that reflect weekly and bi-weekly deposits of several hundred dollars each—deposits made during the time he was on suspension. And, I have checked with personnel; there is no record of him being approved for off-duty employment.

"Yes, I understand what you and McReynolds developed, Riley, but I just don't know that it's enough for placing him on indefinite suspension pending termination actions," challenged a less then convinced Peterson.

"I don't know about that, sir," countered Wilson. "The fact that he was already on suspension for another infraction seems to me to aggravate this most recent infraction. I think a case could be made that his actions are wanton enough to require his termination. It surely demonstrates his open defiance of the rules and regulations of this agency. Besides, sir, I'll bet Blaine will elect to retire if he thinks termination is a possibility. I know if I were eligible, I'd certainly pull the pin and retire before they could even begin termination proceedings."

"You could be right, Riley, but we all thought he would retire before he accepted a transfer to Los Angeles, and he doesn't appear to be fighting that," said Peterson.

"Yes, sir, you might be right, but he also has not reported to Los Angeles yet, has he? He could just be baiting us and retire at the last minute."

"Yes, there is that possibility."

"Mr. Peterson, I cannot think of anything else we can do on this end right now. We have covered all bases on this matter, and there just isn't anything else to hold him accountable for."

After a hesitation, Peterson said, "Yes, I agree, Riley. I don't think there is anything else that can be done with the Blaine matter. Go by and brief his SAC; then you guys come on back here."

"Will do, sir," said Wilson.

After his conversation with Wilson, Peterson walked the short distance down the hall to the administrator's office. *I sure hope he's in a good mood today. I know he'll be less than convinced that we could not find anything else on Blaine.* At the door, he hesitated slightly and then took a deep breath.

With a sigh, he muscled up his resolve and entered. He approached the administrator's assistant, a middle-aged woman who could best be described as matronly. "Is he available?"

"He's on the phone to the AG right now, Mr. Peterson," replied the assistant in a short clipped tone, her common demeanor for anyone of an inferior rank beneath the administrator or the assistant administrator. Like most assistants in government in a similar position, she seemed to take on the power of her boss with those she considered inferior. "He should be done in a few minutes. Would you care to wait?"

"Yes."

A few minutes actually became ten nervous minutes of sitting there where he and the assistant remained mute. Just as Peterson was about to excuse himself to return to his office, the assistant said, "He's off the phone now. Let me see if he'll see you." She picked up her phone. "Mr. Peterson to see you." She listened for the reply, and then hung up the phone. "The administrator will see you now."

Conway sat coatless behind his massive wooden desk devoid of anything but his prominent marble nameplate and a sheaf of papers. A quick glance at the administrator's face caused Peterson to flinch slightly. He had become adept at reading his boss's face to gauge his mood. Peterson was disheartened to see that he wore a determined frown that almost appeared to be a snarl. *Not a good sign.*

"Sorry to bother you, sir," Peterson said tentatively.

Without so much as a greeting of even a casual comment, Conway spat, "Get on with it, Peterson."

"Yes, sir." Peterson was now more than nervous. "Mr. Administrator, I've just heard from Riley Wilson who is with Bob McReynolds in Denver looking into the Blaine matter."

"Yes, Peterson?" interrupted Conway with a certain rudeness in his manner. "What have they found?" he demanded.

Peterson detailed what Wilson had related to him about Blaine's apparent unauthorized off-duty employment. He punctuated his details with "I think that Wilson and McReynolds did a really thorough job and have left nothing undone in this matter."

Contemplating what Peterson had just conveyed to him, the administrator sat for several minutes with a menacing glare directed toward Peterson. As the seconds elapsed, Conway's piercing eyes caused Peterson's nervousness to increase. He could feel the perspiration developing under his arms. He was instantly glad he always wore his suit coat, which in this instance concealed his noticeable discomfort.

"That's it? That's all you could come up with?" demanded Conway.

"Yes, sir, I'm sorry," replied Peterson meekly.

Throwing a pen down on his desk in apparent disgust, Conway rose from his desk and walked over to a bank of windows, which offered Conway a panoramic view of the nation's capitol across the Potomac. Even in the dead of winter without the greenery, the scene was majestic and inspiring to those in power or who sought power. As Conway stared at the vista in front of him, Peterson offered, "Mr. Administrator, while I recognize that unauthorized off-duty employment is a minor offense, when it's coupled with the fact that Blaine brazenly defied DEA rules and regulations while serving a suspension for another infraction, we could make the case for termination."

Conway turned back from his view of the seat of government. A frown replaced his previous sneer.

However, Peterson's hope that Conway would be more congenial was soon dashed.

"Well, you are right about two things Peterson—you are sorry, and I now regret pulling you out of that no-nothing job in Newark, and second, what you have offered here is a minor offense. However, I suppose what you have said about coupling this offense with the fact that it was committed while Blaine was on suspension for another trivial matter does tend to show his disregard for our rules and regulations. And, if and when we confront him on the issue and he elects to lie about it, we could add questionable integrity. It will just have to do, I guess."

Sensing a weakening in Conway's resolve to be disdainful of his abilities, Peterson decided to offer something that might diffuse the administrator's antagonism toward him. "Mr. Administrator, might I suggest we wait on pursuing this matter to see if Blaine actually reports to LA."

"What?" asked a distracted Conway.

Borrowing the words used by Riley Wilson previously, Peterson offered, "Blaine may be baiting us, Mr. Administrator."

"How so, Peterson?"

"Telling us that he will report to LA and then at the last minute decide to fight us on it or just retire. Even if he does report to LA, we could always impose an indefinite on him at that time."

Contemplating Peterson's last statement for several seconds, Conway broke into a slight smile. "You know, you might be right. He could be baiting us. Even if he's not, we could impose the indefinite on him in LA, which would conceivably cause him more of a financial hardship than if he were back in his familiar home grounds of Colorado. It could probably push him over the edge and force him to retire."

"Yes, sir, those were my thoughts," said Peterson.

"I like it. Let's make this our strategy toward Blaine, Jim."

Conway's use of the nickname Jim for his given name of James that he demanded others to use caused Peterson to cringe, but the fact that he had offered something that pleased Conway tempered his irritation of the misuse of his given name. Excusing himself, Peterson departed the administrator's office and a headed to his own office. *He is one malicious individual; must be the attorney in him. I need to keep a low profile around him for a while.*

December 18, 1996; Hacienda Puesta Del Sol, La Cruz, Sinaloa, Mexico

"Buenos Dias, Don Jaime," greeted Comandante Miguel Guerra as Juan Cervantes escorted him into the large office of the Hacienda. Attired in his usual black leather jacket, sports shirt, jeans and cowboy boots, the comandante moved quickly across the office where he extended his hand to Jaime.

Shaking the comandante's hand, Jaime said, "Good morning to you, Comandante. I trust all is well with you and you have good news for me. Please, Comandante, have a seat." Jaime gestured toward a large leather chair adjacent to his massive wooden desk. Before the comandante could respond, Jaime asked, "Coffee, Comandante?"

"Sí, Jefe. Coffee would be fine.

"Juan, have them bring us coffee, please. And see that the comandante's ayudantes are comfortable."

"Sí, Jefe," replied Juan.

The comandante waited until Juan had departed the office. "Don Jaime, like I told Juan on the phone two days ago, that problem up north has been permanently taken care of and will not cause us any further problems. Unfortunately, to get truthful answers to our most pressing questions, it took a little more persuasion than I would have liked, but such things happen when individuals become stubborn and elect to place themselves above other family members."

"Oh?" questioned Jaime.

"Sí, Don Jefe," said the comandante as he accepted a cup of coffee from Juan. The comandante placed several packages of sugar into the coffee. "The person with the big mouth attempted to hide behind his espousa." The comandante stirred his coffee. "We had to send him a strong message that she did not have the ability to cover for him."

"I see. There shall not be any consequences for us regarding this will there, Comandante?" asked a mildly concerned Jaime.

"No, Jaime, both the pinche snitch and his puta wife have disappeared permanently and shall be of no further problems to us," said the comandante. "And the two young children, I'm told, did not witness anything that could identify my associates."

The mention of two young children caused an instant icy feeling of dread to consume Juan's total being. Ceasing his computer work for a moment, he positioned himself to face both the backs of Jaime and the comandante. *These ruthless bastards! They casually sit here and discuss murdering two people leaving their children orphans as if it were an everyday necessary business occurrence. What am I doing here? Don Miguel never did this type of business in front of me. Oh, I know he did similar things; he just shielded me from it I guess. I can't be a party to this much longer. I have to plan a way to get my brother Roberto and his family out of Cuernavaca and somewhere safe. Then I can disappear to some place like Costa Rica where with the money I took from Mexico after Don Miguel's demise, I can live comfortably for the rest of my life.*

The comandante's answer to Jaime's question interrupted Juan's thoughts. "Comandante, the licenciado is not causing you any problems is he?"

"Oh, no, Don Jaime! The licenciado has not been a further problem for me. In fact, since rescinding my termination, he has been very gracias. He was very apologetic and said it was just a major misunderstanding. He had acted on some faulty information and has assured me he is behind my efforts to aid you in every way."

"Bueno, Comandante. But should he become a problem, I insist that you contact me directly and I shall have another, uh, talk with him about our arrangement."

"Sí, Jefe. While the licenciado is not a problem right now, I did hear something about that other problem we had to take care of up north, however, the one in Colorado involving that pendejo who talked to the grand jury."

"Oh?" exclaimed Jaime who sat up in his chair and faced the comandante. "And what is the problem."

The mention of the problem in Colorado got Juan's full attention too and caused another icy chill to traverse his spine.

"I have learned from a very good source that the brother of one of the people we sent to Colorado to take care of that problem and who was shot by that DEA puta is very upset and has vowed to seek revenge on this DEA agent. At the time, I can't remember his name, Don Jaime."

"It's Blaine, Thomas Blaine," blurted Juan spontaneously and then instantly regretted his action.

Both Jaime and the comandante simultaneously turned their heads toward Juan, whose face quickly registered surprise. Juan waved the newspaper article faxed by the licenciado to Jaime in the air. "I recently reread the article about the shooting in Colorado, Don Jaime, and I remembered the agent's name."

"You must have a photographic memory, Juan," advised a slightly skeptic comandante.

"Juan knew the problem that was taken care of in Colorado, Comandante. They both worked for Miguel Felix before Miguel Felix's problems. Isn't that right, Juan?"

"Sí, Jefe."

Jaime turned to the comandante. "Why should this concern us, Comandante?"

"I do not think Ernesto Fonseca, Juan's friend, was acting alone." The comandante's face developed into a sneer-like smile. "I think there were others giving information about your business to the grand jury."

Jaime first looked at Juan, who was using every ounce of willpower to maintain an outward, relaxed appearance while his insides were in upheaval. "Why do you think that, Comandante?"

"According to our information, the licenciado's and mine, Fonseca told the people we sent to deal with him that there were others talking to the Grand Jury. While he didn't know who they were, he said that because of the questions asked of him at the Grand Jury, these others had good information about your business Don Jaime."

"And we are sure he didn't know who these others were, Comandante?"

"Sí, Don Jaime. Rest assured he would have given up his mother if she had been involved by the time we were finished talking to him. Our interrogation techniques can be very persuasive." The comandante accompanied his remarks with a slight chuckle.

Using all his resolve, Juan continued to maintain an outward relaxed bearing. He felt he had to defray any suspicion directed at him. Jaime looked at the comandante but spoke to Jaime. "Don Jaime, Ernesto Fonseca was not my friend. We both worked for Don Miguel but in different capacities. I did not know him that well. I do know that when he left here to go to California, Don Miguel was not unhappy he was leaving. Had I known he was working for you when I came here, I would have cautioned you not to trust him. I had no knowledge that he was working for you."

"I see, Juan." Jaime continued to stare at Juan.

Juan turned his head back to the computer to hide the sweat on his forehead.

"I don't know why this brother should be a problem for us, Comandante," continued Jaime. "Let him do what he wants to do. Maybe there will be one less DEA puta that we have to deal with."

"Don Jaime, there is no way they can tie the Fonseca thing to us, but I am afraid that if the brother kills this agent, there might be some heat on some of our associates in the United States.

"I still don't see how what this brother does can affect us, Comandante. We've had no contact with him, and there is no way the Norte Americano cops can connect us to whatever he does. In reality, I really don't care if they connect us to him or not, and I don't really care if he does cap this DEA agent, uh, what's his name, Juan?"

"Blaine, Thomas Blaine," answered Juan.

"Yes, Blaine. I don't care what he does to this agent Blaine, Comandante."

The comandante turned to Juan in an effort to draw him into the conversation. "Don Jaime, don't you remember the problems created when that DEA agent was grabbed and killed several years ago in Guadalajara. It affected all of us here in Mexico, business wise."

"Sí, Sí, it did, Comandante, I know that only too well. But that was because that foolish act was done here in Mexico. Why would someone shooting a DEA agent in Colorado have any effect on us here in Mexico? I think you are over-reacting and we should not concern ourselves with what this brother wants to do."

"But Jaime..." began the comandante.

"I don't want to hear another word about this, Comandante," said Jaime. His voice rose slightly indicating his developing irritation with this subject. "I'm not spending a dime, and I know that's where this conversation is heading. Do I make myself clear on this?"

"Uh, Sí, Sí Jaime. Entiendo—I understand."

"Good. Anything else, Comandante?"

"No, Don Jaime. Everything is fine. We are preparing for another shipment by the end of the week and have plans in place to protect it before you have it moved north."

"Bueno. That is good, Comandante. Juan will show you out. Call me if there is a problem."

"Sí, Don Jaime." The comandante rose and exited the office following Juan. "Juan, you are close to the jefe. What does he think of me?" asked the comandante.

"I think, Comandante, that he trusts you as far as he trusts anyone in this business. Just don't ever give him a reason not to trust you. He is not a forgiving man."

The comandante responded with a nod of his head.

Juan and the comandante shook hands at the front door. Juan headed back to the office. *What should I do about this information? Something tells me I should try to get word to Blaine about this so-called brother's intentions so he could at least be prepared. But why should I care? Then again, I do owe him for allowing me to leave Miguel Felix's estancia with that bag of money and my life. I need to consider this carefully. If Jaime found out I was talking to Blaine or anybody in DEA for that matter, I'd be joining poor Ernesto and his wife. And my brother and his family also. Jaime has already demonstrated that they would be expendable as far as I am concerned.*

The more Juan contemplated this dilemma, the more he became convinced that he should at least try to warn Blaine to be careful. He had a feeling that at some time in the near future he might need the help of Blaine to extricate him and his brother's family from Mexico should he no longer enjoy the protection of Jaime.

Later that afternoon, Jaime offered Juan an excuse to leave the hacienda and an opportunity to contact Blaine. "Jaime, I need for you to go to the hotel and see Hector. He has something Ramon needs to see up north. Some new idea he has discovered about moving money. He wants to implement it, but I told him that I wanted Ramon to look at it first."

Jaime's statement told Juan two things. First, Jaime was now trusting Ramon's financial arrangements more so than Hector's and that Juan had brought Ramon into Jaime's business. And second, a trip to the hotel would allow him an opportunity to use the pay phones off the lobby to make calls without being noticed.

An hour later, Juan placed the first call. He dialed the phone number from memory. He had met with this agent in LA before he was forced to return to Mexico. Juan waited for the connection to be made.

"Group Three answered a female voice."

"Agent Henderson, por favor," said Juan.

"Lo siento, señor, No está aquí," replied the bilingual female.

Juan switched to English. "When will he return?"

"Not until after Christmas, señor, Can somebody else help you?"

"Uh, no, I guess not."

"Do you want to leave a message sir?"

"Sí, por favor. Tell him Juan called."

"Can I tell him what this is about?"

"No, I just need to talk with him."

"Okay, well then…"

Juan glanced furtively around the lobby. "Excuse me, señora. Do you have the number for the DEA office in Denver?"

After receiving the number, Juan dialed it and waited nervously as the connection was made.

Another female voice answered. "Drug Enforcement."

"Thomas Blaine, please," said Juan.

A short pause followed, and a male voice answered. "Group One."

"Thomas Blaine, please," repeated Juan.

"He's out of the office right now," replied the male voice. "Would you care to leave a message?"

"No, I guess not," began Juan tentatively. He nervously looked around the lobby again. "Wait, tell him Juan called, and I have something important to tell him. I will try to call later."

"I'll make sure he gets the message."

After a short meeting with Hector, a despondent Juan departed the hotel for the hacienda.

December 18, 1996; DEA Denver, Colorado

Tom Blaine stared at the phone message. "Hey, Junior, did you take this call from somebody named Juan?" he shouted from his office.

The agent got up from his desk outside Tom's office and stuck his head in the doorway. "Yeah, boss. I did."

"He didn't say anything else?"

"Nope, just that it was important, and he would try to call later just like it says there on the slip."

"Was there anything else about the call you can remember? I know how difficult it is for you to focus on things now that you're in love," replied Tom with a hint of amusement in his voice.

Tom's comments got the attention of several other agents in the group, and they felt it was necessary to add their two cents to the conversation.

"Yeah, boss, you'd think he'd be more responsible now that he's getting it regularly," quipped one.

"That's what happens when the little head does the thinking for the big head."

"Leave the poor guy alone," added the middle-aged group secretary who often showed her motherly care for the agents.

"The only other thing about the call, boss, was that it sounded like it was long distance," offered junior.

"Okay," said Tom.

CHAPTER TEN

December 28, 1996; Hacienda Puesta Del Sol, La Cruz, Sinaloa, Mexico

Morose would be the word that best described the atmosphere that pervaded the hacienda. While this time of the year should have been festive, such was not the case. In spite of the Christmas decorations that filled every void in the large home, a very dark mood had descended on the hacienda brought on by an event that occurred just outside of Disneyland in Anaheim, California, the day before. Against Jaime's better judgment, Hector had decided to take their younger brother Esteban to the popular theme park as a late Christmas present. Esteban, who was twenty-five in chronological years, had the mental capacity of an eight-year-old. A good-looking young man, who favored his dark handsome brother's features more so then he resembled Jaime, would catch a lady's eye until he opened his mouth or did something strange. He had been pleading with both Jaime and Hector for several years for a trip to the Magic Kingdom much as any eight-year-old might pester his parents.

When Hector broached the subject with Jaime about his quick "in and out" trip to LA and Disneyland, Jaime was against it. "Hector, it's too dangerous for us to travel north. I think we should wait and see if that Grand Jury our former associates apparently talked to has plans for us."

"Jaime," sighed an exasperated Hector, "I had the licenciado check. There is nothing for us to fear at the present according to his inside sources at El Cendro. Besides, I will take the Lear Jet, and we'll fly out over the coast and drop in from the west of LA to the airport in Orange County as if we are coming from Hawaii. I have a passport in another name to use if stopped by the pinche Customs. It will be a quick in and out trip—airport to Disneyland and back to the airport. Nothing more, I promise. Besides, poor Esteban has had his heart set on going there for a couple of years."

While it was true that Esteban had been pleading with both Jaime and Hector to take him to Disneyland for several years, Hector had failed to mention he had his heart set on meeting with Emma, his lady friend who now resided in the Los Angeles area.

"I don't like it at all," were Jaime's final words on the subject.

Hector and Esteban flew in the Lear Jet to the Orange County airport successfully avoiding U.S. Customs. Upon checking into the Disneyland Hotel on the twenty-sixth, they were joined by the lady friend, the vivacious and well-endowed, blonde-haired aspiring actress, Emma Watson. The trio enjoyed a wonderful fun-filled day at Disneyland.

Later that night, Hector and Emma enjoyed a late dinner at an upscale restaurant. On their return to their hotel, Hector, while driving Emma's Toyota and being playful with Emma's upper thigh, cruised through a red light. Unfortunately for Hector, the traffic violation caught the eye of an officer of the Anaheim Police Department. Yielding immediately to the red lights of the police vehicle, Hector was very cordial and cooperative with the officer, surrendering his Mexican driver's license and passport when requested. In his haste and possibly suffering from the effects of one-too-many martinis at dinner, Hector surrendered a driver's license, which bore his true identity and a passport, which had a pseudonym. The confusion as to his identity caused by two official documents in different names set the stage for major problems for Hector. His failure of a field sobriety test did nothing to ameliorate this mounting problem. The police officer arrested Hector for being under the influence and transported him to the Orange County Jail pending arraignment for the DIU offense and a determination as to his true identity.

Unknown to the Gutiérrez brothers, nor to the licenciado and his sources at El Cendro for that matter, a sealed federal indictment of both Jaime and Hector in the U.S. Central District of California Federal Courts awaited their arrest. They were jointly charged with violations of the Racketeering Corrupt Influenced Organization or the RICO statute. United States officials also knew the two brothers as heads of a Continuing Criminal Enterprise (CCE), responsible for the distribution of large quantities of controlled substance and the conspiracy to distribute controlled substances. Based on these indictments, U.S. officials had issued arrest warrants for both brothers and a number of their associates. When a fingerprint check by the FBI's National Crime Information Center (NCIC), determined Hector's true name, the computer also responded with an active warrant. While Hector would be eligible for bail on the DUI offense in the morning, bail for the federal offenses would not be established until he appeared before a federal magistrate. Because of the holiday season, it could be several days before the U.S. Marshals would move him to federal custody and before an appearance could be arranged.

When the Anaheim Police detained Hector, Emma, who had no knowledge of Hector's drug business, had agreed to return to the hotel to stay with Esteban until Hector could be released. After being booked into jail and learned he would not make bail, Hector used his one phone call to contact Emma.

"Emma, I need you to call my brother Jaime in Mexico and tell him I'm in jail. These charges against me are a big mistake. I'm just a successful businessman who has been wrongfully charged." He gave Emma Jaime's personal phone number. "This is all a big mistake."

Fearful of what and with whom she had become involved, Emma, instead of calling Jamie, as Hector had directed her, called her dad in Iowa. "Dad what am I going to do? I don't want to be associated with major drug traffickers. It could be dangerous and seriously affect my chances of landing a role in a movie.

"Dear, if you don't do as they ask you never know what people like this might do. Just call the brother and then disassociate yourself from any further contact with of the Gutierrez's," he suggested.

She waited until the next morning to call Jaime's personal number. "Hello, is this Jaime Gutiérrez?" asked a pensive Emma.

A gruff voice answered the phone. Instead of answering her question, an irritated Jaime responded with his own question. "Who is this?"

"I'm, I'm," began a now very nervous Emma. "I'm Emma, a friend of your brother, Hector," she replied hesitantly. "We met in the restaurant in your hotel earlier this month."

"Yes, I remember you, Emma," he said with a little more cordiality in his tone. "And why is it you are calling me?"

"Jaime, I'm afraid I have some bad news."

"Oh?" exclaimed Jaime, rising slowly from his seat at his massive oak desk.

"Yes, Hector's been arrested here in Anaheim, and he asked me to call you right away."

"Arrested?" shouted Jaime not masking his surprise. His shout immediately got the attention of Juan who rose from his computer and approached Jaime's desk.

In an effort to downplay her involvement in Hector's predicament, she elected to give Jaime the shortened version of Hector's arrest. "Yes, we were returning from dinner, and he ran a red light. When he gave the police officer a driver's license with one name and a passport with another name, they took him to jail to identify him. When they identified him as Hector, they said there was a federal warrant for his arrest, and they would not release him on bail."

Jaime's first reaction was mild shock, which quickly gave way to intense anger. "Stupido!" he screamed into the phone.

"Uh, excuse me. Are you talking to me?' asked Emma timidly.

Jaime quickly regained his composure. "No, excuse me, señorita, I did not mean to scream at you. When did this happen?"

"He was arrested last evening when we were returning from dinner and..." began Emma.

Jaime interrupted her. "Where is Hector now?"

"He called me from the Orange County Jail, so I guess he's still there. He asked me to come back to the hotel and take care of Esteban and call you."

"So you have Esteban with you?" asked Jaime.

"Yes, he's sitting here eating cereal and watching cartoons. But look, Jaime, I need to go for an audition in a couple of hours. And we need to be out of the hotel by noon."

"Give me your phone number and a gentleman named Juan will call you in a few minutes to make arrangements concerning Esteban, entiendo?"

"Okay, I'll wait for the call, but please remember I have that audition in a couple of hours and need to get going soon."

"I understand," replied Jaime as he hung up the phone.

"Stupido! Pinche pendejo!" ranted Jaime as he began to pace back and forth in the office. His face reddened with anger. "I told him not to go there. Now look what's happened?"

"Don Jaime, what's wrong?" Juan asked.

Now in a full rage and his face growing redder by the minute, Jaime, instead of responding to Juan, exclaimed, "Pendejo! I told him not to go to Los Angeles. I had a bad feeling about going up there. But he chooses not to listen to me and now look where he is."

"Don Jaime, what's wrong?" asked Juan.

Jaime turned to Juan. "That stupid brother of mine has been arrested in California and is now in jail."

"Arrested? What for Don Jaime?"

"I don't know what for." He pointed to the phone on his desk "That blonde gringa he brought to lunch two weeks ago. Somehow, she and my idiot brother were driving back to the hotel when the police stopped and arrested him. She said he's in the Orange County jail, and he instructed her to call me. She has Esteban with her at the hotel. I want you to call her and arrange for someone to take care of Esteban and get him back here as soon as possible. Do whatever is necessary, Juan. Here's her phone number." Jaime passed her number to Juan. "But before you do that, get me the licenciado on the phone. I want to know what's going on."

"Sí, Don Jaime," said Juan as he dialed the phone.

December 29, 1996; Elbert County, Colorado

Swatting at the persistent and irritating pawing at his cheek, Tom knew Manfred's way of communicating it was way past his breakfast time. Tom's hand, instead of connecting with the elusive feline, came in direct contact with the soft bosom of his female bedmate. The slight grunt from the bedmate, as well as the surprised contact with her female anatomy was enough to wake Tom from a wine-induced sleep. While this unexpected contact with the private parts of a female was a surprise, the fact that there was a female in his bed was even more of a surprise. A pleasant one, but nonetheless, a surprise for Tom, who had recently been living a monastic life. As his eyes began to clear and become accustomed to the semi-darkness of the bedroom, Tom was able to make out the diminutive but shapely form of Manfred's former owner. Libby made his Denver Broncos T-shirt look better than he ever did.

"Aw crap," Tom softly uttered as he looked at the sleeping Libby. But as he watched her sleep, his irritation with himself began to melt, and a smile developed on his face. He considered her pronouncement when she had agreed to move into his house to play caretaker while he went on to his new assignment in Los Angeles.

This plutonic arrangement and her resolve to avoid hank-panky did not survive the consumption of a bottle of her favorite wine and very little to eat yesterday after Tom helped her move into his house.

Moving day had been a long one. Tom made several trips in his aging Scout, which still bore the bullet scars from the shoot-out. He pulled a horse trailer with her two horses while Libby packed her pickup truck. The mere thirty-mile move from Parker to Tom's ranch should have taken just several hours. Tom took the series of flat tires on Libby's aging horse trailer in stride sensing his criticisms would only further anger an already agitated and tearful Libby. Tom decided to remain mute that she should have replaced the tires on the trailer years ago, before the dry rot caused them to disintegrate when subjected to significant weight. Finally, they had the horses boarded and settled into stalls in his barn, and Tom and Libby had sat down in front of the fireplace in Tom's cozy family room.

Several glasses of wine with just a snack of cheese and crackers quickly affected Libby. Her resolve to avoid hanky-panky soon melted and further wilted during their trip down memory lane during which each shared mostly fond memories of their short but highly electric relationship. The effects of the alcohol, the warm feelings she still harbored for Tom and a slight chill of the room coaxed Libby closer to Tom, and soon they were snuggled close together. And the rest, as they say, was history.

A persistent banging, coming from the kitchen, interrupted Tom's reminiscence of last evening. After covering the sleeping Libby with a blanket and donning a pair of sweat pants and a shirt, Tom walked to the kitchen where he found Manfred sitting in front of the kitchen cabinet that housed his canned cat food.

"Hungry, big guy?" Tom immediately realized the absurdity of his question. "Of course, you're hungry. You're always hungry, you worthless fur ball."

Tom's less than charitable characterization of the large Orange Tabby was met with a simple "Meow."

Tom filled a plate of fishy-smelling cat food and set it down for the anxious Manfred. He then turned his attention to making a pot of coffee. *Funny, I don't have a headache this morning. And I did drink more than my share of wine last night. And I didn't have any of those dreams. Maybe good sex is the answer to PTSD and not wine or single malt scotch for that matter, as I previously thought.*

As the coffee pot began to fill, Tom slipped his cup under the brew basket. He then walked out on the front deck of his home. Stepping out in the crisp December morning, Tom took in the panoramic view beginning to emerge as the dawn awakened. As Pike's Peak to the south became visible and bathed in the early morning sunlight, Tom pondered aloud. "Man, I'm going to miss this place." He watched as the darkened mountains of the front-range began to appear. "Maybe I should just retire and stay here. Naw, I can't let Conway and his flunky, Peterson, win. That's what they want, and I couldn't live with myself knowing I retired under a dark cloud. I'll retire on my timeline, not on theirs."

"Having a nice conversation with yourself?" Libby interrupted Tom's thoughts. With a slight start, he turned and saw her standing in the open doorway. Tom's favorite Pendleton wool shirt covered her body to just above her knees, and again, looked better on her than on him. "It's too cold out there; come on inside and talk to me."

"Is there a *please* in that statement that I missed?"

"Get in here, jerk-off," Libby said in a playful tone.

As Tom stepped by Libby who remained partially blocking the doorway, he reached around and patted her bare butt in the process causing her to jump back. "Damn you, Blaine."

"And a good morning to you, sunshine." Tom gave her a quick kiss on the cheek.

"Don't *good morning* me, you jerk. You got me drunk last night and took advantage of me," Libby kidded jabbing him in the chest with her forefinger.

Tom fended off her playful attack. "Well, as usual, in that warped attorney sense of what's right and wrong, you've got it all wrong. I was the model of platonicy, if there is such a word, and it was you, after several glasses of wine, who took us right to the, in your words, hanky panky."

"I see. So you have absolved yourself from the responsibility of what happened last night?"

"Heck, no. I think I performed my responsibility quite well in fact," Tom said with a large smile.

"That you did, big guy." Libby as moved closer to allow Tom to take her in his arms. She nestled her head against his chest. "I thought I would get over you, Tom. But I can't, and I've decided that if I can't get more of a commitment out of you, then I'll just settle for what I can get. My feelings for you have not changed since we've been apart. In fact, I was hoping there would be some way we could get back together." She sighed.

Tom moved his head back to look Libby in her eyes. "Libby, I've missed you, too, and I can't count the number of times I started to dial your number just to hear your voice. This place has been very lonely without you. Oh, I have a part of you with Manfred, but to be honest, every time I see him, it reminds me of you. And while I at least had a little of you here with him, I missed you even more."

His words caused Libby to tear up. "So where does that leave us, Tom?"

"Well, I for one would like to forget the plutonic relations bit and the *no hanky panky* rules you imposed and go back to being the couple we once were. If memory serves me right, we had quite a good relationship. It only became strained when you wanted more of a commitment that I wasn't willing to give at that time. It wasn't my idea or desire to end our relationship."

"I know. But I would still like to think that somewhere down the line we could get married. I think that's what most women would expect out of a similar relationship."

"I know, Libby," Tom said. "It's not an unreasonable expectation, and marriage for us is a very distinct possibility. It's just not something I can commit to right now. My life is too unsettled."

"I understand. Do you still love me Tom?"

"Very much, sweetie, and I want us to be together, even if we are apart while I'm in LA."

"I guess I'll just have to settle for that for now. I've tried the other alternative and living without you in my life sucks."

Realizing they both probably suffered from morning breath, they settled for a strong hug. Tom augmented the hug with a kiss on her cheek.

Libby shivered from the chill in the house. "You haven't seen my panties, have you? I can't find them anywhere."

"Manfred," said Tom. Don't you remember how he used to steal parts of your clothing and hide them from you? I'll bet you'll find them somewhere near his bed. But if you want something warmer, I've got some other sweats you can slip into."

Libby followed Tom to the bedroom and slipped on the sweat pants he offered. "So how is this going to work?"

"What work?" asked Tom.

"Our arrangement."

"Well, like I proposed. I'll pay the mortgage and any expenses relative to the upkeep of the house. You handle the utilities, phone and the satellite TV expenses."

"But what about us, Tom? Are we exclusive or what?"

"Libby, even with you gone, I've been exclusive. I see no need or desire to change that."

His last statement earned him another hug. "Careful there, kiddo. I just might have to let you take advantage of me again."

"Breakfast first, big guy. I haven't eaten anything since breakfast yesterday. Oh, other than the cheese and crackers last night."

"Breakfast coming right up," Tom replied.

December 29th, 1996; Hacienda Puesta Del Sol, La Cruz, Sinaloa, Mexico

"Don Jaime, I have the licenciado on the line," said Juan as he rose from his desk bringing a cordless phone to Jaime. Jaime muted CNN and grabbed the phone from Juan. Juan had given Jaime some space since the phone call this morning informing him of Hector's arrest in Los Angeles. Since joining Jaime's organization, Juan had learned when it was best to leave Jaime to himself. To attempt to engage him in conversation when he was in a foul mood would only engender his wrath more, which at times could erupt into physical violence.

Juan could see from the frown on his forehead and the pain in his eyes that Jaime's disposition had not changed much since the phone call this morning. The curt tone in his voice verified Juan's belief that Jaime's attitude had not changed at all. "What have you found, Licenciado?" demanded Jaime without so much as the usual polite social greeting.

"Uh, Jaime," began the licenciado tentatively. "I'm afraid not much."

"What do you mean, not much?" shouted Jaime, his face and neck reddening in anger.

"Jaime, it's the weekend, and the courts in the United States are closed, so my sources cannot get access to the necessary files," said the licenciado in an effort to defend his negative efforts.

"What about El Cendro, Licenciado? Surely they know something by now."

"Jaime, my sources in El Cendro can only advise that Hector's arrest was obviously based upon a sealed federal indictment out of Los Angeles."

"What does that mean? I don't understand. I thought in the United States they could not keep someone in jail without telling him why."

"Yes, that is true in the United States; unfortunately, they can hold Hector until the courts resume business on Monday. That's when the indictment will be unsealed, and we shall get the details then."

"So why can't Hector get bail?"

"Unfortunately, also, according to my sources, bail cannot be set until Hector appears in front of a federal magistrate. That will not occur until Monday afternoon." After a long pause, a nervous licenciado continued. "I don't think there is much we can do until Monday, Jaime."

"I can't believe that neither you nor your sources at El Cendro have any information on why this happened. It was no secret that certain people were talking to a grand jury. Am I right about that, Licenciado?"

"Sí, Jaime."

"Then why don't you, the guy I'm paying a lot of money to protect my interests, know more than you do right now?"

"Uh, Jaime…" began the licenciado before Jaime interrupted him.

"Save your breath, Licenciado. Right now you're useless to me." Jaime disconnected the call and threw the cordless phone across the room where it struck a wall and dropped to the floor in pieces.

Juan retrieved the cordless phone, reassembled it and placed it back in its cradle. He then went back to work at his desk.

After several minutes, Jaime turned to Juan. "Juan, what's happening with Esteban?"

Juan welcomed the opportunity to give Jaime some good news. "Don Jaime, I have made the arrangements and the pilot of the Lear jet should be at the hotel right now getting Esteban. He will take him to the jet and fly him right back here later this morning."

"That is good, Juan. Gracias. I am sorry if I have been short with you."

"Don Jaime, it is understandable."

"Thank you, Juan," said a more contrite Jaime.

"Jefe, may I offer a suggestion?"

"Sí, por supesto, Juan."

"Ramon has many contacts in the United States. Let me call him and see what he can find out."

"Yes, please do that, Juan. I'd be very appreciative of his efforts."

Juan dialed Ramon's number. *I'm sure glad I am not in the licenciado shoes right now. I need Ramon to find something out for Jaime or I'm afraid heads will roll.*

December 30, 1996; DEA Headquarters, Alexandria, Virginia

"I wish I could say his arrest was due to the diligent efforts of my agents, Mr. Administrator, but it actually was a fortuitous traffic stop by an Anaheim police officer. When Hector Gutiérrez surrendered a driver's license and a Mexican passport in different names, the officer became suspicious. And then, of course, Gutiérrez failed a sobriety test," said Hugh Gilbert the Special Agent in Charge of the Los Angeles Division of DEA.

"Is Hector the main player in the Gutiérrez Cartel, Hugh?" asked Conway.

"No, sir. He has a significant role, but according to our sources, he's more involved in moving money around. Jaime Gutiérrez, his older brother, is the main man of this cartel," replied Gilbert.

"So you think he was in California on a money thing then?"

"No, sir, as far as we can determine, he was here on a pleasure trip. Our sources have told us that he is kind of a playboy and when my agents interviewed the arresting officers, they said he was accompanied by a very pretty young lady who we are trying to locate and interview right now. Hector was actually driving a car registered to her."

"I see. So are you planning a press conference for today then?" asked Conway with noticeable impatience edging into his tone.

"No, sir, not until we have all the details and have interviewed the girl. If he was up to something and she knows what he was doing, I don't want to jeopardize further possible arrests or seizures."

"Listen, Hugh, do you think this is a significant enough event that I should do a press release from here? The Attorney General has indicated we need to demonstrate to the public that we are having success in this war on drugs. An arrest of this magnitude demonstrates our success."

"Yes, sir, we can do that. However, we might do a short release indicating his arrest. The press will be all over his arrest, which is of public record at the Orange County jail. We just won't give any details, and we can stall a few days with the indictment, especially with the New Year's holidays and all."

"That's good, Hugh. On another note have you heard anything about Thomas Blaine and if he is going to report out there this week?" asked Conway.

"As far as I know, he's scheduled to be here next week, Mr. Administrator. I sure hope so because three of the five other supervisors that were on the transfer list have elected to retire. One has contacted his Senator claiming it was an unfair transfer. That leaves me just Blaine; I need supervisors badly."

Don't count on having him too long thought Conway. "I see. Well, call me immediately if Blaine's status changes," instructed Conway.

"Yes, sir, will do," replied Gilbert.

Conway disconnected the call and punched the button for his intercom. "Grace, get hold of Perkins; I need to see him ASAP," he instructed his administrative assistant.

Several minutes later, Grace buzzed Conway's intercom. "Mr. Administrator, Mr. Perkins for you, sir."

"Send him in, Grace."

"Good Morning, Mr. Administrator. How are you today?" asked Ray Perkins.

Conway ignored Perkins' social graces. "I'll be doing a press release on the arrest of this Gutiérrez fella."

"Oh?" exclaimed Perkins as a look of surprise developed on his face.

"Yes, Ray, I think it's a good idea for us to show the citizens of this country that we are doing something positive in the war on drugs," Conway said showing a bit of irritation in his voice. "Do you have a problem with that?"

"No, it's just that we've always left that up to the local SACs and ASACs."

"Well, not this time, Ray. I want to demonstrate to the public this administration's dedication to eradicating illegal drugs from our society."

"I see," said Perkins. *You're just trying to kiss the AG's ass.*

"I'll need a briefing on the Gutiérrez Cartel or whatever it is we call his organization."

"It's the Sinaloa Cartel, Mr. Administrator."

"Whatever," replied Conway. He gave a dismissive hand gesture to Perkins. "That's all." Perkins rose to exit. "Wait, Ray," Conway said. "I just talked with Gilbert in LA. He said three of the five supervisors we transferred there decided to retire. I guess one has contacted his Senator. What do you know about this?"

Perkins sat down again and took a minute to compose his thoughts. "He's correct, Mr. Administrator. Three of the five supervisors on the transfer list with Blaine have opted to retire instead of going to LA. We already have a Congressional Inquiry on another. That leaves only Blaine on the original transfer list who is going to report."

"Well, Jesus Christ, Ray, when were you going to tell me this?" Conway threw his pen down on the desk.

"I was going to bring it up at the staff meeting on the second, Mr. Administrator. But as long as we are discussing it now, I might as well tell you. Of the ten supervisors we transferred, only three, including Blaine are reporting. The rest have opted to retire or are contesting their transfers."

"What's wrong with the people in this organization? Where's their loyalty?" demanded Conway His face and neck reddened. Haven't they ever heard of doing what's good for the agency?"

"Mr. Administrator, I'm sure these supervisors, many of whom are close to their thirty years, feel they have done what's good for the agency for all their careers. Now they are at a position where they want to do what is good for themselves. I can't say I blame them, sir."

Conway screwed up his face in disbelief. "Ray, I can't believe I'm hearing this from you? You, of all people, should know we are bound to do what is good for the agency." He shook his head. "If you find you can't support this position, maybe it's time for you to consider moving on."

Perkins stared at Conway in disbelief. He wondered if he should speak his mind or keep his job. In the end, he decided it was about time for him to call a spade a spade. He calmed his voice as best he could. "You know what, Mr. Administrator? I think that is a very good idea. I will do just that. I'll move on. Don't go spouting loyalty. You have no loyalty to anyone but the AG and yourself. I refuse to continue to be a part of your ass-kissing efforts to drive good people like Tom Blaine, a true hero in every sense of the word, from this agency. You only care about looking good to the AG and this liberal administration. So save that loyalty crap for someone else."

Instant anger registered on Conway's face. He stood up and pointed his finger at Perkins. "Who do you think you're talking to, Perkins?"

A slight grin developed on Perkins' face. "I'm talking to you, Mr. Conway. And you know what else? I should have done this a long time ago."

"I'll have your job for this, Perkins," Conway screamed.

Perkins laughed. "I'll save you the trouble. I'm leaving here, walking right down to personnel and putting in my retirement papers. And you, sir, can kiss my ass." Turning, he started toward the door, but stopped short and turned around again. Conway's face was bright red with rage. "Furthermore, if you attempt to interfere with my retirement, my first phone call will be to the press. I'll make sure that Blaine and the senator who is questioning the transfer of that other supervisor know the truth behind these transfers. Let's see how that plays out with the senator and the Merit System Protection Board." He walked out and left a seething DEA Administrator. As he walked to his office, he considered, *I should have done that a long time ago.*

December 30, 1996; Elbert County, Colorado

"Guess what, ole buddy?" asked Roger Gray when Tom answered his home phone.

"Let's see, Roger, I don't know. Your wife has decided to divorce you so she can be with her midget lesbian girlfriend," replied Tom sarcastically.

"Real nice, butthead. No. Ray Perkins just left my office and is headed down to personnel to put in his retirement papers."

"Hmm, kind of unexpected, wasn't it?" asked Tom.

"Actually, he's been waiting to hear about a corporate security job with Federal Express, but he just had a blow out with that idiot Conway and told him he was fed up with how he was treating the agents. Perkins told me Conway was ranting and raving about the lack of loyalty of senior personnel in this agency, and Perkins decided he couldn't take any more of his crap and told him so."

"I wonder what brought that on, Roger?" asked Tom as he reached for his coffee.

"I'll tell you exactly what brought it on. Your transfer to Los Angeles, for one thing."

"My transfer?" exclaimed Tom. "Why would that cause Perkins any grief?"

"Well, you see, of the ten people on your transfer list, six have elected to retire early and one has sought congressional intervention. Only you and two other supervisors are accepting the transfer. I guess when Conway started ranting and raving about the lack of loyalty in the agency, Perkins had just about enough of his bullshit and fired back. One thing led to another, and Perkins basically told him to do something with himself that is anatomically impossible."

"Damn, Roger, isn't Perkins afraid that Conway might try to screw with his retirement? After all, Conway does have friends in high places."

"Perkins figured Conway might try something, so he put Conway on notice that if he screwed with him, he'd make sure the Merit System Protection board and the good Senator, who's acting in behalf of another transferred supervisor, knew the truth about your transfer.

"Holy crap, Roger. Do you think Perkins will come to my aid at the Merit System Protection board?"

"For sure, Tom. In fact, he told me to tell you that you can count on his support if it becomes necessary."

"Well, this just might be a Happy New Year's after all, Roger."

"Yes, I think it will be, Tom. I just wanted to give you the news, old buddy."

"Who will they get to replace Perkins?"

"I don't know right off hand, but I sure hope it's somebody from our ranks and not an outsider which Conway certainly could do."

"I sure hope it's not Peterson," said Tom.

"You and me both, buddy." Roger gave a slight nervous laugh.

After a short pause during which neither Tom nor Roger said anything, Roger said, "Oh, and by the way, did you hear they grabbed Hector Gutiérrez of the Sinaloa Cartel in Los Angeles? Actually, it was Anaheim, I guess."

"Oh!" exclaimed Tom, with less enthusiasm in his voice than what Roger expected.

"Yeah he was with some starlet and got stopped by a local for drunken driving. He gave the officer phony ID."

"I hadn't heard that. But I've not been in the office since Friday."

Roger chuckled at Tom's apparent lack of concern. "Tom, you have no idea who Hector Gutiérrez is, do you?"

"No, not really. I've been too busy working on biker groups since I returned from down south. I haven't kept up with the Mexican Cartels, or even the Colombian Cartels, for that matter."

"Tom, the dead guy found in the van after you shot those two Mexicans was a Los Angeles CI who had testified at a grand jury against the Sinaloa Cartel. Hector Gutiérrez is the number two man in the cartel. So, you see, you do have a connection to the case."

"That's all very interesting, Roger, but my connection certainly wasn't as a result of my keen investigative ability. Instead, I just happened to be in the wrong place at the wrong time. Like so many good investigations. Major breaks often are the result of some fortuitous actions."

"Ain't that the truth," answered Roger. "Are you and the next Mrs. Blaine planning a big New Year's bash?"

"Nope, she has a prior commitment which doesn't include me. And cut that crap about the next Mrs. Blaine," said an irritated Tom.

Roger laughed at his own joke. "This prior commitment. Is it with another guy?"

"Naw, she and some friends from the U.S. Attorney's office have rented a condo at Beaver Creek in the mountains and are going to ski and celebrate there."

"And she didn't invite you?"

"Nope. Besides, skiing is not my thing, Roger, so I'd probably decline if she asked anyway. What are you and your significant other doing?"

"Not much, just a quiet night at home, I guess. I really don't like to go out on New Year's Eve any more. Too many crazies on the roads."

"That's exactly how I feel, Roger. Well, have a happy one."

"Right back at you, Tom."

December 30th, 1996; Hacienda Puesta Del Sol, La Cruz, Sinaloa, Mexico

When Juan arrived at the Hacienda at 7:00 a.m., he noticed the somber mood of the day before had not changed. Jaime was already watching CNN on the big screen in the office. Unshaven and in a maroon silk dressing robe, his blood-shot eyes demonstrated he had not slept much. Instead of coffee, he appeared to be drinking straight Mezcal, a bad omen in Juan's estimation.

Jaime slurred his speech slightly as he waved his hand to Juan. "Que tal, Juan—What's happening?"

"Buenos Dios, Jefe." Juan walked over to Jaime sitting in his leather chair and reached for the half-consumed glass of Mezcal from the table. "Why don't I get you some coffee, Jefe, and then maybe some breakfast?"

Jaime grabbed the glass from Juan, and in one gulp, drank the remainder of the Mezcal. He handed the glass back to Juan. "Sí, breakfast would be good. Mi amigo, what have we heard about my poor hermano, Hector?"

Mi amigo, huh? He's a lot drunker than I thought, was Juan's instant assessment of the situation. Juan picked up the phone. "Bring some coffee and breakfast for Don Jaime," said Juan into the phone. He turned to Jaime. "Jefe, I plan to call Ramon first thing this morning. He flew over to Los Angeles last night to confer this morning with the lawyer we've retained for Hector. He told me last evening that he had talked with the attorney on the phone, and Hector should be arraigned in court this afternoon. That's when the judge will decide on bail."

"Decide on bail?" asked Jaime.

"Yes, Don Jaime, but Ramon advised that according to the attorney, the warrant specified no bail, so he will have to contest it at the arraignment. It might be in a special hearing in front of a different judge, the judge who will handle Hector's case."

"No bail?" shouted a drunken Jaime. "Can the pinche American courts do that?" he demanded as he attempted to stand.

Juan moved quickly to assist Jaime back into his chair. "Careful there, Jefe." Just then, a servant wheeled in a food trolley with a pot of coffee. Juan poured a cup of hot black coffee for Jaime. With a wave of his hand, Juan dismissed the servant and handed the coffee to Jaime. "According to Ramon, the no bail stipulation is common and can be overcome in court."

"I see," said Jaime as he sipped the hot coffee screwing his face up at its bitter taste.

"But, Don Jaime, Ramon also said that according to the lawyer, the judge might deny bail because of who Hector is and because he is not a citizen of the United States," advised Juan as he set a plate of Huevos ala Mexicana, bacon and corn tortillas on the table for Jaime.

"Deny bail? Because of who he is?" repeated Jaime. "I don't understand, Juan," said Jaime.

"Jefe, and again this is according to the attorney, the Norte Americanos consider Hector a major trafficker and a flight risk and as such might deny him bail."

"They can't do that, Juan. They cannot just hold him hostage like that."

"Lo siento—I'm sorry, Don Jaime, but according to the attorney, they can, and have done it in the past."

"Carajo!" shouted Jaime as he slammed the coffee cup down on the table spilling the coffee that remained in the cup. Struggling to his feet, he swayed slightly and finally got his balance. He pointed a finger at Juan. "I will not allow that. If this pinche attorney cannot get mi hermano out of jail, I will take matters into my own hands and get him out myself."

Juan decided he needed to calm his boss realizing Jaime was slipping from a friendly drunk to one of his mean moods. He held up the palms of his hands toward Jaime. "Don Jaime, please, let's not get upset until we know what the judge does today. We need to think rationally about this. Have some breakfast, and I'll call Ramon." This had the effect Juan desired.

Jaime wavered back and forth. " , Juan, as usual you are right, mi amigo. Let us wait and see what the pinche judge does this afternoon, and then I can do what needs to be done." Slumping into a chair at the table, Jaime began to eat his breakfast.

Juan sensed he had calmed the situation for now. *Wait until he finds out that according to Ramon, the attorney had already said there is no chance they will release Hector on bail. One crisis at a time, I guess. I wonder what the jefe meant that he will do what needs to be done. Surely, he does not think he can buy Hector's freedom with mordida like he can here. And certainly he does not think he can forcibly free Hector. Then again, judging from his past, maybe he thinks he can.*

Juan's subsequent call to Ramon did nothing to assuage Jaime's poor state of mind. According to Hector's attorney, he would not get bail at the afternoon hearing and it was highly doubtful that a Federal District Court Judge would negate the Magistrate's ruling on no-bail. Ramon concluded, "We shall just have to wait and see."

When Juan conveyed this information to Jaime, he went into an instant fit of anger. Slamming his fist on the desktop, he cursed, "Carajo! Pinche Norte Americanos! Pinche judge, that Pendejo! Who do they think they are treating mi poor hermano like this?"

"Don Jaime, calm yourself," pleaded Juan.

"No, Juan," Jaime said in an elevated voice. "I'll not calm myself. I will show them who they are dealing with. Get me the licenciado and the comandante. I want to talk with them right now."

Juan knew that trying to reason with Jaime would be useless. "Sí, Jefe," Juan said as he reached for the phone.

December 30, 1996; DEA Headquarters, Alexandria, Virginia

"Uh, Madam Attorney General," began a very nervous John Conway, "I just wanted to give you a heads up on something I don't think will cause a problem, but I did not want you to be blindsided if the press got wind of this."

"Okay, and what is this potential problem, John?" asked Marilyn Thomas the Attorney General of the United States.

"Ray Perkins, my assistant, and I had a disagreement regarding some loyalty issues with some senior DEA employees; he unexpectedly decided to retire."

"I see. And why would you think it might affect me or this administration?"

"Uh, well, like I said, Madam Attorney General, I don't think it will cause any problems…"

"John, you wouldn't be calling me if you didn't think there might be some fall out, so why don't you just tell me what's going on," interrupted Thomas.

"Perkins quit because I transferred several supervisors, including Thomas Blaine, the supervisor in Denver who has caused Marsha Grant so many problems."

"John, I don't understand why he would quit over some transfers of several supervisors unless there is something going on that you're not telling me."

"Well, uh, ma'am, the truth of the matter is that I was hoping by transferring Blaine he would just elect to retire and that might end our continuing problems with him. However, he hasn't done so, but several other supervisors I transferred along with him, so that it would not look like I wasn't singling him out, have put in their papers, and one has contacted a member of Congress."

"Sweet Jesus, John. So there will be a congressional inquiry on this?"

"There could be, Madam Attorney General, but fortunately the one supervisor who has contacted his senator was in the zone for transfer anyway, so we will be able to answer any inquiry with clean hands, so to speak."

"Well, maybe we dodged a bullet on him, but what about Blaine? He could make a case that this is retaliation for whistle blowing."

"I think we would have heard that by now, Madam Attorney General, but Blaine has been real quiet, and I just talked with the SAC in LA. Blaine is scheduled to report there around the first of the year."

After a short pause, Thomas asked, "I'm confused. Why would Perkins be upset over these transfers, John?"

"I think he has a case of misplaced loyalty to Blaine and these other supervisors who elected to retire instead of accepting a transfer," said Conway. The conviction returned to his voice after realizing he would be able to lay the blame of any backlash on Perkins. "These supervisors accepted their positions knowing full well they could be transferred according to the needs of this agency. They really have no valid complaint. Perkins evidently did not see it that way."

"I see. Do you think Perkins will cause us any problems, John?"

"No, ma'am, I don't think so as long as we don't interfere with his retirement. He has just as much to lose as we do by going public with his allegations. I'm told he is being considered for a corporate security management position with Federal Express, and I know the Director of Security there. He's a retired FBI agent, an old friend. I could have a word with him about Perkins if he decides to play rough with us."

"All right, John. Please keep me advised on this and if anything develops that could give us a black eye."

"Yes, ma'am, I will certainly keep you advised."

"I know it might be a bit premature, but have you given any consideration on Perkins' replacement," asked Thomas.

"Yes, Madam Attorney General, I have decided that James Peterson will temporarily assume Perkins' position as the assistant administrator. I'll keep him in that role for several months until Marsha Grant gets settled in here at Headquarters and then I'll move Peterson out to a SAC's position and make her my number two if that's okay with you and the administration."

"Peterson? What's his status right now?"

"He's my Chief of the Office of Professional Responsibility and has been for some time now. He's a career DEA Agent who is very capable. I have all the confidence in him, and being black, he would look really good in our efforts at diversification."

"Yes, I quite agree. That will be fine with me, and again, I know the President will be happy with these selections, John. Thanks for the heads up on the Perkins matter and keep me posted."

"Yes, ma'am," said an eager Conway. He disconnected the call and felt a sudden rush of relief. He was once again in good graces with the AG and the Administration.

December 30, 1996; Elbert County, Colorado

With a cordless phone in his hand, Tom stepped out onto the front deck of his home immediately feeling the chill of the mid-morning air. Shivering, he pulled his open Pendleton wool shirt closed against the mid-twenties temperature. He dialed a number. While he waited for the connection, he admired the view of the Front Range to the west. He noted that Long's Peak to the north was bathed in sunlight. *There's not too many winter days when I can get such a clear view of Long's Peak. Lots of snow up there right now which means a good run off and good fishing later this summer. Sure hope I'm back here to enjoy it.* The snow-capped mountains were spectacular. Swinging his view to the south, he saw that a low cloud cover, west of Denver and south to Pike's Peak, hid Mount Evans. In all likelihood, it was probably snowing on the summits. Looked like he might be getting snow later on.

"Libby Martin's office," answered a female voice.

"Hi, is she in?" asked Tom.

"Is this Tom?" the female voice inquired.

"Yes, ma'am, it is," he answered.

"Wait one minute, please," came the reply.

As he waited for Libby to take his call, he noted his heart beat just a little faster, and he could sense the excitement building with just the thought of talking with her. *Calm yourself boy*, he told himself.

"Hey there, big guy, what are you doing?" asked Libby in a jovial voice.

"Just standing out here on the front deck admiring God's country, kiddo. I'm sure going to miss this place."

"Just the place?" asked Libby feigning hurt feelings.

"Well, no, not just the place. I'll also miss Manfred," said Tom jokingly.

"You butthead. So what's up?"

"I was wondering how your day was going and if there's a chance you can get out early. I thought we might drive over to that steak place in Parker for dinner."

"Sorry, Tom, I've got several defense motions I need to answer, and I'm off tomorrow, so I don't think I can get off too early. Maybe we could meet at the steakhouse; I could stop there on my way home."

"Sure, that sounds good. Call me when you get ready to leave, and I'll leave here then. It should put us both in Parker at about the same time."

"Okay, sounds good. So what are you going to do with the rest of your day?"

"Just some things around here I've been putting off. Need to get ready for my trip to LA. Oh, by the way, Roger called me and told me that Ray Perkins, the number two man in DEA, had a major falling out with Conway and decided to retire. He told Roger he'd gladly offer his support to my case against Conway. He can share with them the real reason behind this transfer."

"Wow, Tom, that's really great. If he'll say that Conway is retaliating against you, then you'll definitely win your case at the Merit System Protection Board."

"Yes, I thought so too, and I'm going to call my attorney this morning and get him working on it. Maybe my stay in Los Angeles won't be so long after all."

"I'm counting on it, cause if it is, I just may have to transfer to the U.S. Attorney's Office out there."

"Geez, kiddo, I don't think that will be necessary."

"Tom," she began with her voice cracking, "I don't want to be separated too long. Just the thought of you leaving in a few days is more than I can bear."

Tom felt the onset of melancholy. "Yes, I know, Libby, I feel the same way, but I promise you, it won't be for a long time. If I don't win, I'll just retire and move back anyway. So we're just talking a few months at the most."

"Promise?" asked Libby who Tom sensed was close to tears.

"Yes, sweetie, I promise."

Libby stifled a sob. "Tom, why don't you go with me to the mountains tomorrow? I checked with the others, and they don't mind one more. We'd have to share a bed in a loft area, but I don't see that as a problem. Do you?"

"It depends on who we'd be sharing the bed with," Tom kidded.

"You know what I mean, you jerk," Libby retorted.

"I don't know, Libby, I don't ski, and I'd probably be a wet blanket on your attempts to have fun."

"No, you won't," Libby pleaded. "You could just relax in the lodge. There are other things to do besides skiing. I've just about decided that if you won't go, I won't either."

"Geez, girl, don't make me feel guilty."

"Well, then, come with me. It would be fun, and we'd get to spend more of our last few days together. We could at least ring in the New Year together. I mean unless you have other plans you haven't shared with me."

"Nope, no other plans. I was just going to sit here with Dr. Glen Livet and Manfred and wish I wasn't going to LA."

"Then come with me. I'll make it worth your while, big guy. I can give you some things that Manfred can't."

"Right down to the hanky panky, huh, Ms. Martin?"

"Damn straight, if that's what it's going to take you to go with me."

"Naw, while the hanky panky promise is great, I'd go just to be with you."

"Then you'll go?" squealed Libby.

"Yes, I'll go," Tom answered in a mocking fashion.

And Tom would have gone had it not been for Mother Nature's interference. His earlier speculation that he might get some snow proved to be accurate. By early afternoon, the low clouds that obstructed Mount Evans and Pikes Peak had moved northward and blocked the complete Front

Range from view. At 3:00 p.m., the snow began. While it started with just a few scattered flurries as Tom exited the local hardware store in Elizabeth, it became almost a white out blizzard by the time he drove the several miles to the ranch. When he turned on the television, he learned a massive storm had settled in over the Front Range extending from Cheyenne to the North, to Pueblo in the south. Weather reports predicted snow accumulation for the Denver area to be a foot or more. A quick glimpse out his front French doors revealed the snow was beginning to accumulate.

Tom picked up the phone and called Libby. "Hey, it's really snowing here, maybe you should leave early. If the conditions there are as bad as they are here right now, I wouldn't try coming this far. Maybe you should head toward you parents' place."

"Wow! I just now looked out the window; it's really coming down. I'll wrap up what I was doing and head toward Parker. But if the roads aren't bad, I'm coming to your place."

"Our place," Tom corrected. "But don't take any chances; the visibility is zilch here, kiddo."

"Damnit, I wanted to have dinner and a nice evening with you, Tom. We have so few days left before you go to LA," said an almost tearful Libby.

"Yeah, me too, kiddo, but please don't take any chances. The roads might really be impassible here in Elbert County."

"Okay, Tom, I'll let you know once I get to Parker."

Libby made it to her parents' place in Parker and was forced to stay there while the snow continued through the night and most of the next day. When it finally stopped, fourteen inches of snow had fallen in most of the Denver area with more in the outlying suburbs. The roads were all but impassible, and the highway department had closed all the mountain roads. Both Tom and Libby had to settle for a quiet New Year's Eve at home—he at his home in Elbert County and she at her parents' home in Parker.

January 1, 1997; Hacienda Puesta Del Sol, La Cruz, Sinaloa, Mexico

It had not been a festive New Year's at the hacienda. While Jaime had consumed more than his share of Mezcal, it was not in celebration but more to assuage his mood, which vacillated between despondency to anger. He remained intoxicated following the news on Monday that Hector would not be released on bail and was to be held at the Federal Correctional Facility on Terminal Island pending trial. Additionally, the federal judge, who had drawn the case, in an emergency motions hearing on December 31 requested by Hector's attorney, denied his attorney's motions to set bail citing the gravity of the charges against Hector. Another factor against Hector was that he had no ties to the United States making him a severe flight risk.

The bad news did not stop there. The sealed indictment, when provided to the defense in court, was more comprehensive than anticipated. In addition to Hector, and of course Jaime, being named as co-conspirators, numerous others in Jaime's organization, including Juan, were also listed. It also ordered the seizure of a number of properties allegedly purchased with drug proceeds. The alleged overt acts were all encompassing. Just by reading the indictment, it was obvious to all that the witnesses against the cartel were more extensive than originally thought.

Arriving at the hacienda late in the morning on New Year's Day, Juan found Jaime in a dark mood, the result of too much bad news and too much Mezcal.

"Hola, Juan," uttered Jaime. He struggled to speak and slurred his words. "Has the comandante located the licenciado?"

The office smelled of alcohol. Juan began picking up empty Mezcal bottles and other trash Jaime had discarded. "No, Jefe. Not as of an hour ago when I talked with the comandante. But he is still trying to locate him."

"Nobody knows where he is?" asked Jaime sweeping his arms around and with doubt evident in his tone.

"Don Jaime, I think that the licenciado is afraid of you right now and does not want to be found," said Juan.

"Afraid of me?" questioned Jaime. He turned his head toward Juan and gave a puzzled look. "Why would he be afraid of me?"

"Don Jaime, I think the licenciado feels you will hold him responsible for Hector's arrest. He probably also feels he let you down and should have known there was an indictment."

"Hector was stupid; he was thinking with his dick again. I don't blame the licenciado for that. I do think the licenciado should have known about the indictment though. His position at El Cendro should have given him insight to what the pinche gringos were up to."

"Don Jaime, please don't take this as I am defending the licenciado. Like you, I think he became very greedy and that interfered with his role to protect us, but according to Ramon and Hector's attorney, the sealed indictment was a well-kept secret. Yes, we suspected certain people were talking to the grand jury, but no one knew the extent of what was being said to them. Had we been able to contact any of these witnesses and convince them to tell us about their testimony, we would have been better prepared. For example, the witness hiding in Colorado. The people sent to deal with that witness got careless or stupid and were eliminated themselves before they could tell us what the witness had told the grand jury."

"Sí, Juan, you are right, amigo."

"We still need the licenciado as a source in El Cendro and his direct access to the Attorney General, Don Jaime, until we can develop someone else."

"Sí, Sí, I agree," said Jaime shaking his head in agreement. Then placing his forefinger to his lips Jaime hesitated, obviously in thought. "Have the comandante put out the word that I do not hold the licenciado responsible for Hector's arrest or the indictment. I do need his support in dealing with the Norte Americanos and how I respond to what has happened to mi hermano and those of us in the indictment which includes you, Juan."

"Sí, Sí, Jefe." Jaime's comment on how he would deal with the indictment distracted Juan for a moment. The distraction caused a burst of fear to spread quickly through his body, and he realized Jaime was planning to use his old brutal methods in dealing with those who had caused him problems. Just being named in the indictment was overwhelming to Juan. If Jaime began using violence against those who had given testimony, or God forbid against the American police officers and judges involved, it would only aggravate the charges already existing against him. And when things turned bad in Mexico, like they were sure to do just as they did when he was working for Miguel Uriarte, he would not have his avenue of escape. And that avenue of escape, San Diego, California, was where he hid the money from Uriarte's estancia. *Maybe I should talk to that pinche DEA agent in Los Angeles. Maybe he could get the charges against me dropped if I cooperate with them against Jaime's organization. First, I'd have to get my brother and his family out of Mexico and somewhere safe or maybe I should keep my mouth shut and see what happens.*

"Juan, Juan, are you listening to me?" asked Jaime.

Juan broke out of his distracted thoughts. "Lo, Siento – I'm sorry, Don Jaime, I was just trying to think of what we could say to convince Licenciado to come out of hiding."

"Yes, Juan, I was just saying while you were day dreaming, I want you to instruct the comandante to locate the licenciado and tell him no harm will come to him or his family so long as he continues to help me in this matter."

"Sí, Jefe, I'll call the comandante right away. He should be here in a couple of hours anyway so maybe you should get cleaned up a little."

Jaime laughed at Juan's comments. "Juan, mi amigo, do I look and smell that bad?"

"Uh, I just thought with the comandante coming, you should look like the Don Jaime that everyone respects."

"As usual, Juan, you are correct." Jaime headed toward the office door but stopped and turned back to Juan. "I know you are concerned, but this is only a minor setback. You are right, of course, that I need to be clear headed to plan what my strategy will be for dealing with the pinche Norte Americanos who think they can hold my brother hostage."

"Sí, Jefe, and I'll have the cook make some fresh coffee."

"Coffee would be good and some pan sucre – sweet bread would also be nice.

"I'll see to it, Don Jefe," said Juan as he reached for the phone.

Two hours later, Juan escorted Comandante Jesus Guerra into the office of the hacienda. Dressed in jeans, western shirt and snake-skinned boots, the comandante wore his ever-present menacing sneer on his pockmarked face. "Juan, how is Don Jaime today? I'm sure he has taken this arrest of his brother and the indictment very poorly."

"He was in a very foul mood when I got here this morning. But with coffee, food and no more Mezcal, he is better now. Have you heard from the licenciado?"

"Sí, Juan, I suspected all along that he was across the border in Bonita, California, at some relative's house. I had him contacted there; he will be returning tonight. He is very fearful of Jaime; afraid that Jaime will kill him."

"I don't think that will happen if the licenciado can do some things to help Jaime. He is in a good position at El Cendro to find out who the witnesses are against us…"

"Oh, that's right, Juan," interrupted the comandante. "You were also indicted."

Sí, Comandante," replied Juan as a shiver of fear ran through his body. *I just cannot get used to the fact that I'm included in a group like Jaime and*

Hector or that I'm a wanted man, thought Juan.

"Good, you're here," said Jaime as he entered the office. Showered and shaved, he had shed his silk robe for a bright red guyabera shirt with black slacks and ostrich skin boots. While his eyes were still red, he appeared now to be completely sober.

"Buenos tardes, Don Jaime. I would wish you a Happy New Year's but somehow I feel that it is inappropriate with what has transpired over the past several days. I am very sorry about your hermano, Don Jaime."

"Thank you, Comandante. Please have a seat." Jaime indicated a large brown leather chair that faced the massive rock fireplace. "Have you heard from the licenciado?"

The comandante sat in the chair Jaime indicated. "Sí, Don Jaime. He was in California visiting some relatives and promised he would be back this evening." The comandante revealed a noticeable lack of conviction and some nervousness in his tone.

"Visiting relatives, huh?" mocked a disbelieving Jaime. "Well, bueno. I want him to identify the witnesses who have spread these lies about us to the grand jury. Once he does so, I want them to be convinced they were incorrect. If they won't, I want them convinced not to offer their testimony at trial."

"Sí, Don Jaime, entiendo – I understand. But the witness identities will be protected by the pinche gringos, and it may take some time and some..."

"Money!" exclaimed Jaime.

"Uh, Sí, Don Jaime," said a subdued comandante.

"You just find the witnesses, Comandante, and then tell Juan what you need."

"Sí, Don Jaime, I will get on it right away." He stood to leave.

"Momentito - a moment, Comandante," said Jaime. "I have more. I have decided that if the pinche gringos can hold mi hermano Hector as a hostage, I can do likewise."

"You want to take a hostage?" a skeptical comandante asked.

"Sí, if we take somebody very important to them, we can make a trade. Hector, for my hostage. And if they refuse, they'll never see the hostage again."

Juan answered this time while the comandante looked on with a surprised look on his face. "Don Jaime, I don't know if this is a good idea," he began very tentatively. "Remember the response from the Norte Americanos when those fools kidnapped that pinche DEA agent in Guadalajara."

"Of course, Juan. It had a serious impact on my business, but that was different. Those fools who grabbed that pinche DEA agent were seeking revenge for what he had done to their business here in Mexico. Nobody came forward to take responsibility and make demands that the pinche gringos would have to honor for his release. I feel they allowed it to drag on too long. I shall do neither. I will state my demands right up front, the outright release and return to Mexico of my brother along with a specified time limit to meet my demand."

"Who do you propose to take as a hostage?" said a nervous comandante. "The pinche judge in the case?"

"Even better, Comandante." With a smile on his face, Jaime rose to his feet. "Come over here; I'll show you."

Juan and the comandante followed Jaime to the big screen television.

Sliding a cassette into the VCR, Jaime fiddled with the buttons on his remote until the picture of John Conway filled the screen. The video, made by Jaime from CNN, was of a speech that Conway had given several months previously to Congress about what DEA was doing about the Mexican Drug Cartels and the violence that seemed to stem from the competition amongst them. Neither Juan nor the comandante recognized the person in the picture and indicated this by looking at first one another then at Jaime. They shrugged their shoulders to indicate they didn't know who this person was who filled the large screen.

"Pendejos," chided Jaime shaking his head in mild disgust. "This is Juan Conway, the head of the pinche DEA."

Both Juan and the comandante were shocked by what Jaime proposed.

The comandante responded first. "Don Jaime, I do not mean any disrespect, but are you sure about this? Do you realize the ramifications this will have if we do this?"

"Don Jaime, can we rely on your contacts in our government to protect us?" asked Juan.

"I have thoroughly thought this through. First, Comandante, I realize the ramifications, and it's not if we can accomplish this, it's when we accomplish this. I am willing to deal with the ramifications, and, Juan, I have no fear from our government. Too many people in high positions in our government count on my mordida to cross me. And if they do, I'll deal with them on a more personal basis." Jaime looked from Juan to Comandante then softened. "Listen, amigos, I know what I am doing. I have a plan, and when it is executed, it will be quick and if the pinche Norte Americanos know what's good for them, they'll return Hector home in order to save their John Conway."

"Again, not meaning any disrespect, Don Jaime, but what if the Norte Americanos will not deal? They've never bowed to pressures like this in the past."

"Oh, I think they'll deal on this. They've never had someone like pinche John Conway taken hostage before. It's always someone who lacks the status of a guy like Conway. And just think what this will say to the world. It will show them that we Mexican businessmen are a force to be reckoned with. And I'm sure that I'll get the support of our allies in Colombia."

"Yes, I can see where we would get the world's attention, Don Jaime, but I'm not so sure that this is a good thing," said a somber Juan.

Jaime moved closer and put an arm around Juan's shoulder. "Juan, trust me, I know what I am doing. I have thought this thing through. In fact, I have been planning something like this for months now, so it is not a knee jerk reaction to Hector's arrest. Besides, this will make your indictment go away also."

"Don Jaime, how do you propose to take the hostage?" asked the comandante.

"He makes many trips. When he's on one of these trips, we'll grab him from his hotel. It would be impossible to do this in Washington," replied Jaime.

"I see, but how will we know in advance of these trips and where he will be staying?" asked Juan.

Jaime turned to Juan and smiled. "Like all things we do, we shall pay for the information. I am sure there are sources willing to give us such information if the price is right." Jaime focused on the comandante. "I want the licenciado and you, too, Comandante, to cultivate such a source. Further, I want you to make this your priority. Entiendo usted?"

"Sí, Jefe, I understand," replied the comandante. Then as an afterthought he offered, "I'm sure he will be accompanied by body guards, Don Jaime. What will we do about them?" asked the comandante.

Jaime looked at the comandante in apparent disbelief. "Comandante, I am positive that a man of your talents can figure out a plan to neutralize any resistance. And rest assured, I will give you all the financial backing you need on this." A slight smirk developed on Jaime's face. "I might also add, Comandante, that upon successful completion of this mission, you will be a very rich man. Oye, amigos, I love my brother. As stupid as he is sometimes, he is my blood. I will do anything to get him back here to Mexico."

Juan and the comandante remained silent as Juan escorted the comandante to his car. Upon reaching the front door, the comandante turned to Juan. "What do you think, Juan? What are the chances we can carry this off?"

Juan considered the question for several minutes. "I think Jaime believes he can do this with or without our help. And as for the consequences, well, they could be successful in getting Hector returned to Mexico or cataclysmic for all of us involved."

The comandante nodded his head in agreement before he entered his dark Suburban. Juan watched him depart the hacienda. *What Jaime is proposing is pure lunacy but something he is certainly capable of doing. I need to reach that DEA agent in LA and warn them of Jaime's plan. If he is successful, this could turn out very bad for all concerned. I'd rather take my chances with the pinche DEA than with Jaime. But before I can do anything, I need to have more than just talk about the planned abduction. They might not believe me and think that this is something I contrived to get out of the charges against me. No, I must wait to call them after I have more specific details about the abduction. More importantly, I need to get my brother and his family to a safe place. Somewhere out of Mexico. I need to visit him and convince him to leave. But I must be very careful. If Jaime even suspected what I was planning, he would kill my family and me without hesitation.*

When Juan returned, Jaime was waiting for him at the office door. "Juan, please call Carlos and Ramon in Colombia."

CHAPTER ELEVEN

January 22, 1997; Los Angeles, California

The traffic congestion on the multi-laned freeway to his left caused Tom to chuckle. *Johnny Carson sure hit the nail on the head,* he thought. *The California freeway system is without a doubt the best bargain in the world. Where else in a large city can you park for free?* Watching the gridlocked traffic inch along the freeway, Tom waited for the surface street stop light to change.

With just a few days shy of a month under his belt of living in an East Los Angeles motel off Interstate 10, Tom took no solace in the fact that the miserable image he harbored in his mind of returning to LA had been vilified. Just as it was in 1978, when he left the city with the vow he would retire or resign before returning, the conditions had not improved, and instead, seemed to have become more aggravated. A heavy blanket of smog still hung over the LA basin like a dirty brown cloud. And the traffic, well it appeared that gridlock on the freeways had worsened if that was possible. Tom had learned his lesson when he was stationed here in the late seventies—avoid the freeways during the morning and evening rush hours. After some trial and error, he had developed a route to the DEA offices on South Figueroa in downtown LA using surface streets and completely avoiding the freeways.

Navigating his self-designed route to the office, he was amused at the contrasts that the city presented. Along with the stately palms that lined the streets and boulevards, the multi-colored succulent plants flourished everywhere and created a certain appeal. That was, until you looked closer and saw the overwhelming number of ill-kept houses, festooned with burglar bars complemented by junker cars abandoned on the lawns and vacant lots. And, of course, the ever-present graffiti seemed to occupy every available inch of both buildings and other stationary structures.

Tom gave an audible heavy sigh. *This place is a far cry from my ranch in Elbert County. Oh, to be home again, away from this traffic nightmare and the squalor.*

Tom had arrived in the City of the Angels on January 3 flying into Los Angeles International Airport. By prior arrangements with his new ASAC, Clifton Wallace, a decent guy who was cruising until retirement later in the year, a member of the Enforcement Group of which he would assume control met Tom at the airport. The group member, a relatively young agent who sported a beard and long hair, had driven Tom first to the suite-style motel east of LA where Tom had made prior arrangements. Renting rooms by the day, week and month, the motel offered accommodations that included a small kitchenette. Not having taken the usual government-funded house-hunting trip, Tom could draw up to ninety days of temporary living allowance, TLA, which he planned to use to pay for this lodging. Hopefully, his tenure in LA would not extend beyond this time frame, but if it did, he would have to make other living arrangements. He couldn't afford the monthly rent on the motel without the TLA. After checking into the motel, the young agent drove Tom to the DEA office where he reported to ASAC Wallace and received his assignment and a government vehicle. Like his living accommodations, Tom figured he could get along without a personal vehicle during his stay in Los Angeles. He would have to make other arrangements if his stay went beyond a couple of months. He didn't want to make a case for James Peterson and his headhunters from OPR for misuse of a government vehicle.

During his initial meeting with his new boss, Tom developed an immediate affinity for his ASAC. Wallace, a fifty-seven-year-old black, had short graying hair and steel gray, deep-set eyes. His sturdy build complemented his tailored blue pinstriped suit telling Tom his ASAC pumped iron. While plaques and certificates adorned the walls of Wallace's office attesting to his significant achievements, Tom knew from talking with Roger Gray that Cliff Wallace had been an outstanding agent in his time, making many significant heroin cases. In fact, he had been shot during an undercover operation in San Francisco. According to Roger, Cliff could have been a SAC, but like Tom, he was prone to tell people how he felt without regard to political correctness. Because of that, his promotion beyond GS-15 would not happen in the current DEA.

"Tom, your group, Group III, is a mixture of both highly energetic young agents and some older agents who think that DEA owes them a living and have basically assumed the position I like to call 'being retired on active duty.' They will be a challenge for you," said Wallace during their initial meeting.

Tom looked at the graying Wallace as he sat behind a large oak desk. "I like a challenge, Cliff, and it's been my experience that it takes just the right motivation to encourage those types who seem to have forgotten how to make a case. Hurt them in the pocket book, and they usually come around or move on. Nothing like denying them an in-step pay raise to get their attention."

"They'll fight you on that, Tom. In the past, nobody has ever challenged them like that," warned Wallace as he looked at Tom above a set of short squat reading glasses.

"Good, Cliff, cause you know my history in DEA. I don't usually shy away from a fight."

Cliff chuckled first, and then paused for several seconds. "And that's why I chose you to take over that particular group. While you will certainly have my support as long as I am here, don't expect much out of his nibs next door." Wallace pointed his finger to a wall to the left, the other side of which was the office of the Special Agent in Charge. "He'll only support you so far. He caves in especially if an issue becomes or even threatens to become litigious. I think he has a direct line to Chief Counsel's Office and will not take a stand unless he has their full backing."

"Like I said, I like a challenge," replied Tom.

To familiarize himself with the group and its activities, Tom spent the better part of a week at his desk reviewing active, inactive and the recently closed investigative files of the group. When he finished with that task, he pulled and reviewed the groups' Confidential Informant files. He had almost finished reading these files when one inactive informant file startled him.

"Holy shit," he exclaimed aloud. Sitting upright in his chair, he nervously began reading several debriefing reports of this informant made by one of the younger agents in his group. As he read, his nervousness increased and he noted his underarms had soaked his dress shirt. The informant's name had initially startled him. The nervousness was caused by how the informant came to the attention of DEA with information about Mexican drug traffickers. In the initial debriefing report, this informant, Juan Cervantes, claimed to have been closely associated with the Miguel Felix-Uriarte drug cartel and could provide detailed information regarding the deceased Felix-Uriarte's financial holdings in the United States as well as information regarding other members of his organization. Tom breathed a sigh of relief when he read that Cervantes had come to DEA to offer his assistance because he feared indictment in his role with Uriarte and he wished to remain in the United States. There was no mention of his conversation a year ago with Tom at Uriarte's estancia in Guadalajara when Tom and his team of agents secretly raided it seeking to find their kidnapped fellow agent. Nor was there any mention of the fact that

Tom had allowed Cervantes to depart the estancia with a large canvas bag containing over a million dollars in U.S. currency.

According to the status reports in his file, shortly after coming to DEA, Cervantes disappeared without a trace and did not come to the attention of DEA until several informants identified him as a major member of the Gutiérrez run Sinaloa cartel. He recently had been indicted for his role in that organization. Agent Henderson, who had been handling Cervantes, enumerated his unsuccessful attempts to locate or contact Cervantes. Tom noted the last update was last November.

"Henderson, get in here," Tom yelled from his office taking the chance that Henderson was in the group work area.

"He's in the field, boss," replied a male voice.

January 22, 1997; Hacienda Puesta Del Sol, La Cruz, Sinaloa, Mexico

To Juan, it appeared that Jaime had snapped from his sullen mood once he made his declaration of his intent to kidnap John Conway, the "pinche jefe" of the DEA. For the next week, he arose early each morning, shaved and showered, and was neatly attired in one of his trademark tailored bright guayabera shirts, dark colored slacks and lizard-skin cowboy boots when Juan arrived at the hacienda. Gone too was the Mezcal having been replaced with Mexican coffee. Jaime preferred the strong bitter Mexican coffee grown on one of his plantations to the south.

Juan had to admit that the aroma of the freshly-brewed coffee, which hung in the office air, was tantalizing. He glanced at Jaime who was watching CNN. *Since his crazy decision to do this thing, he has become like the old Jaime. He is more focused and alert. I guess it's because he now feels like he is back in control of this situation and not at anyone's mercy. I pity the poor fool who attempts to stand in his way or block his efforts to get Hector freed and returned to Mexico. I need an excuse to give Jaime so that I can travel to Cuernavaca and prepare my brother to move his family.* Remembering a conversation he had at Christmas with Isabella his sister-in-law, he knew that he could not accomplish this with a simple phone call. "I hold you personally responsible for putting us in danger Juan. Roberto and I have tried to live a comfortable decent life on a modest teacher's salary and you are ruining that. What are we to do? It's not possible on our meager means to move somewhere safe and it would mean uprooting the children. And is there really any place safe from the people you work for?"

Juan sat down at his computer and waited for his computer to boot up. *I need to find a way to get access to that money that I have stashed in the bank box in San Diego. Roberto could use it to move his family out of Mexico.* Juan also thought about what had transpired in the almost three weeks since Jaime's decision. During this timeframe, he had agonized over calling the DEA agent in Los Angles. On several occasions, when he was out running errands and away from the hacienda and Jaime, he had serious thoughts of using a pay phone and making the call. However, on each of these occasions, he had decided to wait. He still lacked any specific information about the proposed abduction of John Conway and, more importantly, because of his concern for his own safety and that of his brother and family, he had elected not to make the call.

Jaime's first order of business since declaring his intent was to determine where and when he could accomplish the abduction. By contacting various governmental officials under his influence, members of his organization and even the Ojeda's in Colombia, he made it known that he would pay handsomely for any information concerning the travels and routine of John Conway. In a conversation with the Ojedas in Colombia, Carlos Ojeda offered their qualified support but questioned what would happen to the hostage once Jaime successfully obtained the release of Hector.

"Oye, mi Amigo," began Carlos Ojeda, "Rafa and I will support you in these efforts to do this thing, but we do not agree with your plan to release the hostage once you have succeeded in the release of Hector."

"Oh!" exclaimed Jaime. "What is it you two think should be done with the hostage?" he asked.

"Jaime, it has always been our intention to kill that pendejo if and when we got the opportunity."

"Sí, I understand, Carlos, but your intentions are somewhat different than mine. You want to send the strong message that even the Jefe de Jefe's cannot escape the consequences of interfering with your business. And this message will be sent anonymously. Por supesto – for sure, they would suspect you but could not prove it was you who orchestrated his death. In my situation, I will have to be up front in demanding the release of mi hermano so there will be no doubt who is behind the kidnapping. While I am confident I have enough empathetic friends in high places here in Mexico who will support me in my efforts to seek the release of my brother, I am not as confident that I could weather the storm that would arise if we killed him on Mexican soil."

"Entiendo, Jaime," replied Carlos. "It just seems like too good of an opportunity to waste."

The promise of money for information regarding the movement and suspected movements of John Conway resulted in a plethora of reports. However, it was the licenciado who, fortuitously, came up with the information regarding the movements of John Conway that would most likely allow Jaime to be successful. During a meeting at El Cendro, the licenciado learned during a casual conversation with an associate, who held a high-ranking position in the Minister of Justice Office, that he, the associate, would be attending a conference regarding better cooperation concerning drug trafficking across the border. This conference was to be held at the El Paso Intelligence Center in El Paso, Texas, during the week of February 3. John Conway, the DEA Administrator, so advised the associate, would be hosting the conference.

This piece of information not only provided Jaime with what he needed to put his plan into action, but it also put the licenciado back in the good graces with Jaime. With his confidence somewhat restored, the licenciado also took it upon himself to insure that the right people in the government were sympathetic to Jaime's cause and would support Jaime in the event that the fallout from the abduction turned ugly like it had when the DEA agent in Guadalajara was kidnapped and murdered. With the promise of money, coupled with veiled threats, the licenciado felt confident that Jaime, and those who aided him in using whatever means he felt necessary, would weather any international pressure brought on by the abduction.

"I have been in touch with my sources at the Minister of Justice's Office in Mexico City," the licenciado advised Jaime in a meeting at the hacienda office. "I have been assured that the Minister himself, while not actually sympathetic to our cause, understands your position. He has suggested in a confidential meeting with my source that while outwardly demonstrating an outrage that such a thing occurred, he would also insure that the investigative efforts of his office would fail to demonstrate that his office lacked sufficient evidence to cause your arrest. It will be important for us to keep the hostage's locale a secret if we bring him to Mexico. This would allow the Minister to claim that, while the kidnapping violated the laws of the United States, no Mexican law was violated. Therefore, it would prevent him from arresting you or holding you for extradition to the United States." Allowing a few seconds for Jaime to digest this information, the licenciado, who started out with a conciliatory tone and furtive eye movements, now looked directly at Jaime and addressed him with more authority. "Jaime, I believe the Minister was sending us the message that we should not hold the hostage here in Mexico. If it was proven that we did so, then he might be forced to act."

Jaime paused several minutes to consider what the licenciado said. He looked out of the large windows at the panoramic view of the Pacific Ocean. Jaime then turned his eyes back to the licenciado. "Bueno – You have done well, Licenciado. Turning to Juan, Jaime asked, "Juan what are our financial arrangements with the Minister's Office."

"Every several months, I wire between five hundred thousand and one million dollars to an account in the Grand Cayman Islands," said Juan. "It depends on our level of operations for those months."

"Licenciado, please convey to your source in the Minister's office that for his cooperation in this matter, we shall double our usual payments to his account when this thing happens and five million once Hector is safely back here in Mexico."

"Sí, Jaime…" began the licenciado.

Jaime raised his index finger as a signal he was not finished. He looked at the licenciado for a moment while he collected his thoughts. "I want you also to convey that I consider this offer generous, and it is not negotiable. Any failure to cooperate or interfere on anyone's part in the government will be dealt with, uh, how shall I say this?" He paused and placed his fist to his chin; he appeared to be in deep thought. "They and their families will be dealt with in a most unpleasant and permanent manner, entiende?"

"Sí, Jaime, I will see to it immediately. And I will continue to get as much information as I can about the jefe de DEA's trip to El Paso.

When the licenciado had departed the hacienda, Jaime approached Juan who was at his desk. He waited for Juan to look up from his work. "Juan, mi amigo, what do you think?"

"I think the licenciado did good, Don Jaime. So long as we do not violate any Mexican laws regarding this abduction, I think you will not have anything to fear from the Mexican Government."

"Yes, I agree, but I do not trust taking the hostage someplace where I do not exercise control. We shall bring that puta here to Mexico, and when they release Hector, we shall release the hostage in Costa Rica. They do not honor extradition treaties."

"I understand, Jefe," said Juan.

With his government safety net, so to speak, in place, Jaime enlisted the aid of the comandante to develop the abduction plan. By the end of January, a plan had been fully developed. Jaime felt good about it. "Esta Bien – that's good. Now all we need to know is where that pendejo will be staying in El Paso."

"Not to worry, Don Jaime," responded the comandante. "I feel confident my men, who shall be staged and ready in El Paso on February 3, shall be able to determine this once he arrives through some local well-placed sources. The only problem will be if he decides to stay on the army base at El Paso."

"Is that a possibility, Comandante?" asked a concerned Jaime.

"Sí, Don Jaime, it is possible, but my sources advise that it is more probable he will stay at a hotel in town where accommodations are more suitable to his taste. Evidently, the accommodations on base, even for high ranking military and government officials, are somewhat lacking and most choose to stay in an upscale hotel in town."

"When will we know, Comandante?"

"We will know the day before he arrives because of the security arrangements that are afforded him. Our sources are in a position to tell us about the pre-arrival security arrangements."

"Esta bien – that's good, Comandante," said Jamie nodding his head in approval.

Following this meeting, Juan approached Jaime. "Don Jaime, uh, would it be possible for me to take a few days and go south to see my brother and his family. I have not seen them since my return to Mexico. We have been so busy here. It would only be for a couple of days."

"Juan, this is not a good time right now. I know how important family is, but I need you here until this thing with Hector is resolved," replied Jaime. A look of suspicion developed on his face. "I am surprised you would ask at a time like this, knowing how much I am dependent upon you. Are you not concerned for mi hermano?"

Jaime's suspicious questioning caused an instant shot of fear to overtake Juan. Juan forced an inner calm, while at the same time, he attempted to project a feeling of indignation. "Don Jaime, of course I am concerned. I am as concerned about Hector as you are. I just thought that it has been such a long time since I have seen my own brother and his family that I could get away a few days before this thing happens. That is all."

"Juan, mi amigo, once Hector is back here, you can take all the time you need. But right now, I need your total concentration here and not in Cuernavaca. Entiendo usted – Do you understand?"

"Sí, Don Jaime," Juan knew that the mention of Cuernavaca, the town where his brother and family resided, was yet another one of Jaime's veiled threats. This implied threat disabused him of any thoughts of his calling the DEA agent in Los Angeles. *While I can take care of myself, I need to get my brother and his family to safety before I can make that call.*

January 22, 1997; DEA Headquarters, Alexandria, Virginia

An uncomfortable silence descended upon the large conference room only interrupted by a slight cough or throat clearing and the shifting of attendees in their large oak and crush red velvet cushioned chairs. During this painful silence, John Conway stared at one person, Senior Executive Service Special Agent Enrique Salazar, the current Country Attaché, DEA's top agent in Mexico. The un-nerving silence, enhanced by the windowless rooms and sound-suppressing acoustic-tiled ceiling, made those in attendance realize that John Conway's temper was about to manifest itself. SES Salazar was going to get his butt blistered in the upcoming outburst.

"So, my friend," began a patronizing John Conway, "you think I am wrong with my decision to inform the Mexican Attorney General that unless we get better cooperation targeting the major cartels thriving in his country, that DEA will withhold the additional thirty-four million dollars we were given by the CIA for use in Mexico?"

Salazar, a thirty-two-year veteran of the drug wars with DEA and its predecessors, had spent a large percentage of his illustrious career either in Mexico or along the U.S. Mexican Border. He looked up from staring at the highly buffed conference table. "Yes, sir, I think you are wrong, and your challenge will only exacerbate a tentative alliance we have with the government of Mexico."

"So instead, Salazar, you expect me to go to the meeting next week and play nice with the representatives from the Mexican Attorney General's Office, pat them on the back and congratulate them for the wonderful job they are doing," said a sarcastic Conway.

"Mr. Administrator, with all due respect," began Salazar, "this is not the way we get things done in Mexico, sir."

"Get things done in Mexico?" spat Conway. "The way I see it, the only thing getting done in Mexico right now is the coddling of the Mexican government by you and others in this agency. Meanwhile, the Mexican cartels flood our streets with drugs, corrupt local law enforcement, poison our youth and foment violence. So spare me the diatribe about getting things done in Mexico."

"Mr. Administrator…" began Salazar whose dark Hispanic features began to deepen in either embarrassment or anger.

"Shut up," interrupted Conway. His brow furrowed and his neck turned crimson in a full rage. He pointed his finger at Salazar. "I've heard all I want to hear about how to deal with the Mexicans. For several years, I listened to the likes of you about how to handle the Mexican government, and all I have to show for it is an increasing drug epidemic in this country, brought in great measure by our friendly country to the south."

"But Mr. Administrator…" pleaded Salazar.

Conway jumped to his feet and waived his hand dismissively. "Out, out of this conference room right now, Salazar. I don't want to hear any more of your bullshit on how to deal with the Mexicans."

Rising to his feet, the five-foot-seven and slightly pudgy Salazar slowly collected his papers and binder and started toward the conference room door. Halfway to the door he turned and addressed Conway. "You are making a big mistake, Mr. Administrator. And if you don't want to heed my recommendations on how to deal with the Mexicans, then I guess it's time you replaced me."

Sitting back down, Conway looked back to his papers on the conference room table, refusing to make eye contact with Salazar. "Consider it done."

As SES Salazar opened the door to leave, Conway turned to Peterson, his acting Assistant Administrator. "Peterson, find a replacement for Salazar."

"Yes, sir," offered Peterson meekly.

Following the meeting, Roger Grey, who was also in attendance, went in search of his old friend Enrique Salazar and found him in the first floor cafeteria nursing a cup of black coffee.

Enrique looked up from his coffee. "Some shit, huh, Roger?

"Jesus, Henry, I can't believe what happened up there."

"Well, I can't say I'm surprised. For a while, I've had the feeling that Conway was not pleased with how I handle the Mexicans."

"Conway's an idiot and can't seem to fathom the concept that we have and need guys like you in positions like in Mexico to advise him on how to deal with the particular problems of that country. I have a feeling he's also heading for a disastrous end with Javier Clemente in Colombia. He thinks he can bully cooperation from those governments by controlling the purse strings," said Roger.

"Yes, I know. I've had to deal with him on almost a daily basis, and it always ends with his way or the highway. What he doesn't seem to understand is that the Mexicans allow us as guests in their country only because of the money we give them; money, which I know does not always go toward our goals. But if you remove or attach conditions to the money, they'll just tell us to leave their country. And that would be a grave mistake. We derive a lot of intelligence about the drug traffickers in Mexico from local sources we're able to recruit because we are there. Remove us, and that timely intelligence will dry up, and if he thinks the drug situation in this country is bad now, wait and see how bad it gets without that timely information."

"Henry, I know what a great job you were doing in Mexico. I, for one, in Special Ops am appreciative for all the timely intelligence we get from our agents in places like Mexico and Colombia. But I'm afraid, like you, that with the idiot Conway and his stupidity and blind arrogance, we'll lose this source of timely intelligence.

Salazar shrugged his shoulders as he raised his cup of coffee to his mouth. "Not my problem anymore, Roger."

"Now what, Henry? What do you intend to do?"

"Actually, my health has begun to deteriorate lately. I was thinking about requesting a reassignment here in the states where I could get better health care. Conway just made that decision for me. I'm going up to personnel and put my papers in. I'll retire and go back and raise a few long horns on my forty-acre ranchita in South Texas."

"Henry, I'm sorry for you and the way your career is ending; I'm sorry for this agency, which will suffer a great loss with your decision," offered Roger.

Salazar responded with a simple appreciative nod of his head.

January 22, 1997; DEA Los Angeles, California

"Jesus, Roger, how long are we going to have to put up with Conway's bullshit? Doesn't this Administration realize what a detriment he is to our international drug enforcement efforts? And never mind what he's doing to the morale of this agency." Roger Grey's summation of his morning staff meeting and the resignation of Enrique Salazar only served to frustrate Tom Blaine further.

"Tom, I think he's got the AG convinced that our problems with Mexico are because they have not been dealt with properly, and it is he, who has the answer. I also firmly believe, as many others here in HQ feel, that by ridding this agency of the competent and knowledgeable leadership, he is following the game plan established by the AG, the Director of the FBI, and him to meld DEA, and more importantly, its annual budget into the bureau. In his short tenure, he has driven a good number of DEA leaders from our ranks, leaders he knows who have the experience and knowledge to effectively counter any serious suggestion to disband DEA in favor of the FBI."

"Yeah, I know, Roger. It's causing a serious morale problem among the DEA troops here in the field. I can't tell you how many times a young agent has asked me what was going to happen to him if DEA ceased to exist. As a leader whose job it is to keep up the morale, what am I supposed to tell these young agents when they ask me that? Am I supposed to lie to them and tell them not to worry, that everything will be fine, and if there is a merger, they'd still have a job?"

"I guess you just have to tell them the truth, Tom, that the outcome of these merger rumors is unknown. If the merger does occur, they might keep their jobs if they gave up concessions like their changing from a career civil servant to a schedule B employee, which in effect will relinquish their legal rights of tenure."

"I've tried to maintain a positive approach with the agents, Roger, telling them that many of us have been through this before, but it's getting more difficult each day with what Conway is actually doing and what the rumor mill is generating. I've also tried to use the positive approach by telling them to stay focused on their job and forget about the rumors. As I've pointed out, the one thing that has always boded well in our favor is that we in DEA do a better job at narcotic enforcement than does the FBI, and we do it cheaper. And we can prove this with our record."

"I guess that's the right approach, Tom. I hope that this Administration will realize that nobody can do the international thing like DEA does. Besides, their espionage missions have caused many foreign government officials not to trust the bureau; they really don't want a bunch of them running around their country.

"Personally Roger, I'll be damned if I would become an FBI agent if DEA were disbanded. But then again I doubt that they would want the likes of me and my track record toward higher management types. Well, at least unlike those young people out there in the group area, I have the option of retiring at any time."

Tom, my assistant is signaling me; I have to run. Talk to you later."

With the call ended, Tom sat stoically at his desk for several minutes. Rising from his chair, Tom went to his opened office door and stared out into the working bay. "Henderson, got a minute?"

"Be right there boss," replied the young agent.

The young man's demeanor impressed Tom. From Henderson's file, Tom knew he was thirty-one and had spent six years in the Marine Corps rising to the rank of First Lieutenant before leaving to join DEA. A muscular young man, his five-foot-eleven frame easily carried his 180 pounds of body weight. Like many other young agents, Henderson spent numerous hours in the gym, and it showed. Nicknamed Hawk, Henderson was divorced, and it was common knowledge that he was quite the ladies' man. Judging from his rugged good looks, Tom could see why he was a hit with the Los Angeles ladies.

"What's up boss?" asked Henderson as he entered Tom's office.

"Have a seat. Forgive me, Henderson, I've forgotten your first name," said Tom somewhat sheepishly.

"It's Harold, boss, but everyone around here calls me Hawk."

"Hawk? Oh yeah, Hawk. Why Hawk?" asked Tom.

"It's a long story, boss, but it involves an invitational golf tournament for the California Narcotics Officer Association where my less-than-adequate golf skills caused a red tail Hawk to tumble from the sky. I felt so bad about hitting the poor critter with my golf ball that I managed to corral it with my windbreaker and get it to a Birds of Prey Sanctuary up the coast. Of course, those bozos out there," as he pointed to the agents' work area, "gave me all kinds of flack over the incident and from that point on, I became known as Hawk."

"Damn, and I thought maybe it was because of your rugged good looks, or better yet, a reflection of the ferocity on how you attack drug traffickers," Tom said as he chuckled.

"Don't I wish," began Hawk. "It's gotten even worse now. With every case we handle that has an animal, I get the assignment," replied Hawk with just of hint of regret in his tone.

Tom smiled and changed the subject. "Look, I called you in here to talk about one of your old CI's."

"I know I'm delinquent on some of my CI status reports," interjected Hawk.

"Yeah, that too, but I'm interested in this one." Tom shoved the folder containing the dossier of Juan Cervantes across his desk to Hawk.

Hawk looked at the CI number labeled on the file. "Him. He was a strange one, boss. He called out of the blue one day and wanted to give up a lot of details about the financial holdings of Miguel Felix Uriarte, a former major Mexican trafficker."

"I know who Uriarte was," offered Tom.

"We met several times, and he seemed to have really good information about properties we could seize here in the US. According to him, Uriarte purchased these properties with drug proceeds. But before we got too far, Cervantes just disappeared."

"Disappeared?" asked Tom.

"Yep, just vanished, boss. I detailed it in one of my last status reports. I checked the address he gave when I registered him. The apartment building management claimed they never heard of a Juan Cervantes. Then, all of a sudden, Wiley, over in group five who's working a major conspiracy case on the Gutiérrez organization, contacts me. According to Wiley, several informants identified Cervantes as a major player working for Gutiérrez. I guess their information was good. They indicted him along with about twenty members of the organization, including the top leaders. There's a warrant for his arrest based upon the indictment."

"I see," said Tom. He pondered this last piece of information.

"What's your interest in Cervantes, boss?"

"I was wondering why he just seemed to vanish. But you've answered that with his being indicted. I guess he decided to work for the Gutiérrez's instead of us."

"I guess so, boss," said Hawk. "You know, just before Christmas, while

I was on leave, I think he tried to contact me. At least somebody named Juan called here looking for me. I think I still have the message on my desk." Hawk quickly left Tom's office and retrieved the yellow telephone message from his desk. He held it up to Tom as he walked back into the office. "Yep, a Juan called on December 18 while I was on leave. He didn't leave a call back number. At least Alicia didn't write one on this slip."

"Alicia, come in here a minute, please," Tom yelled.

Alicia, a short rotund female of Mexican descent appeared at the door. Attired in a large dress to hide her obvious girth, she smiled at Tom. "Yes, what can I do for you?"

Tom took the telephone message from Hawk and extended it to Alicia. "Do you remember taking this message for Hawk?"

She looked at the message. "Yes, I think it was from one of his CI's. I remembered his voice; he had called here on several occasions." She placed the message form on the corner of the desk. "I spoke with him in Spanish."

"Did he give any indication as to why he was calling?" asked Tom.

"No, he didn't. If he had said something, I would have put it on the message," Alicia answered with a bit of defensiveness in her voice."

"Okay," said Tom. "Thanks."

She turned to leave then stopped and turned back to Tom and Hawk. "Wait, I remember he also asked me for a telephone number."

"A telephone number?" asked Tom.

"Yes, I thought it was strange, but he asked me for the telephone number for the DEA office in uh …" She hesitated a moment to think. "I believe it was Detroit, Des Moines or Denver, one of the D city words."

Tom instantly remembered the phone message he had received when he returned to work in the Denver office following his suspension in December. It was from somebody named Juan. While it didn't make sense at the time, it was clear now that Juan Cervantes had attempted to call him.

"Are you sure?" asked Hawk. "I don't recall him saying anything about having contacts in Detroit or Denver."

"Yes, I'm sure because I thought it strange, also," said Alicia.

Tom didn't want to tip his hand about knowing Juan. "Thanks, Alicia. That's all for now."

"He never mentioned anything about those cities to me," Hawk said. "I wonder what or who he wanted?"

"Never mind, Hawk. If he calls back, let's see if we can arrange for him to surrender and get him to cooperate for consideration on his indictment."

"Ten-four, boss," replied Hawk as he exited the office.

CHAPTER TWELVE

February 4, 1997; Los Angeles, California

While every major news source in the country led off with the story, the Los Angeles Times seemed to capture the major news event succinctly beginning with the front-page bold headline: "DEA Administrator Kidnapped." The storyline followed.

> In a brazen act, several heavily armed and disguised men kidnapped John Conway, the Administrator of the Drug Enforcement Administration, from a downtown El Paso hotel. According to informed sources, the armed suspects aroused the hotel residents at around 2:00 a.m. CST by setting a fire on the fourth floor where Conway was staying. When the residents, including Conway and his two Special Agent bodyguards, began to evacuate the hotel, the suspects met them. A gun battle ensued with one bodyguard killed and the other critically wounded. He clings to life in an El Paso hospital. One suspect was shot and killed and left at the scene when his cohorts departed with Conway. A police source said the dead suspect is believed to be a Mexican National but had no identification on his body.
>
> While it is unknown at this time, who masterminded this kidnapping, speculation is that the Mexican cartels have elected to expand their influence of violence from Mexico to the United States. No ransom demands have been received nor has anyone come forward claiming responsibility.
>
> In an early morning press conference, Attorney General Marilyn Thomas decried this heinous act, praised the courage of the two DEA body guards and vowed she would invoke the full power of the Federal Law Enforcement community to seek the safe return of John Conway and to bring to justice those individuals involved in this act.
>
> Mr. Conway was in El Paso hosting a joint conference with representatives from the Mexican Attorney General's Office about better cooperation between the two countries regarding drug trafficking. This reporter learned that the planned two-day conference had ended abruptly when the Mexican Attorney General's party stormed angrily from the conference room. The cause of their sudden departure from the conference is unknown at this time, which might have played a role in this kidnapping.

February 4, 1997; Main Justice Building, Washington, DC

The mood in the Attorney General's conference room was somber as Roger Grey accompanied James Peterson, who, because of the kidnapping of John Conway, was now the acting DEA Administrator. Several other DEA executives were also in attendance. Taking a seat at the large oak conference table, Roger noticed this conference room was much like the Administrator's conference room at DEA, large heavy oak furniture, acoustic tiled ceilings and plush carpeting on the floor. Unlike the DEA conference room, which had no windows, heavy floor to ceiling drapes blanketed the windows in this room. Roger found it amusing that he would be sitting here at the acting Administrator's request. He figured after he had given this AG a piece of his mind on how the drug war should be fought that he would never see this room again.

The entrance of the Attorney General Marilyn Thomas broke Roger's train of thought. Roger was taken aback at how bad she looked compared to the last time he had personal contact with her. With her face, drawn and haggard, it was obvious that she had given up trying to improve her comely looks by wearing absolutely no makeup and devoting very little attention to her hair. Moreover, she appeared to have lost a significant amount of weight with her plum-colored pants suit hanging on her large framed body. He had heard rumors of the AG being in the first stage of dementia. Maybe the rumors were more fact than gossip.

"I want to thank you all for coming here on such short notice," began Thomas. Several Associate Attorney Generals assembled with a collection of senior or executives of the FBI, DEA, and U.S. Customs. She followed her greeting with a forced a smile. The smile evaporated into a slight frown when she spotted Roger. "I know it's early, but I wanted to gather as much information on this horrendous situation so I can get the right people coordinated and moving in a uniform direction. And let me make myself clear on this; our efforts to locate and free John Conway from his abductors shall be done jointly without petty agency politics or bickering," she continued. "Do I make my clear on this matter?" she asked.

The assembled senior executives nodded their heads. Only one head failed to nod in agreement.

Randall Walsh, recently elevated from the Head of the FBI Counter Terrorism Branch to Assistant Director of the FBI, voiced his concern.

"Madam Attorney General, while I quite agree we need to work jointly, I must point out that kidnapping is the venue of the FBI. Therefore, we should be the lead on this investigation. All efforts should be coordinated through my office."

Thomas stared at Walsh and took a moment to control her irritation before she spoke. "Mr. Walsh, I am sure all of us here are well versed in the federal law and know that the FBI has the responsibility for kidnappings, but this is not a normal kidnapping. It involves an executive of this administration, and therefore, I have promised the President, in an early morning phone conversation, that we," as she lifted both hands to indicate the collected attendees, "would not only work together to bring John Conway back safe and sound, but we will also apprehend those individuals who played a role in this treacherous act. If it is your intention to not accommodate my wishes, then I shall seek from Director Williamson, uh, who by the way is where?"

"Madam Attorney General, Director Williamson is with Mrs. Conway. They are old friends; Director Williamson recommended Administrator Conway for his position. He thought it best that he be with her this morning," said Walsh a bit tentatively. He sensed that the Attorney General was not happy with the Director's absence.

"Okay. As I was saying, if it is your intention not to accommodate my wishes that this be a joint effort, I shall seek from Director Williamson someone who will."

"Please, Madam Attorney General, don't mistake my statements that we do not plan to cooperate," said a slightly chagrined Walsh. "I just want to establish that the FBI should have the lead in this investigation." Walsh turned to James Peterson, the acting DEA Administrator. "Just as I am sure that DEA would insist on being the lead if this were a drug investigation."

James Peterson nodded his head in agreement. Roger Grey had other thoughts: *When has the FBI ever acknowledged that we were the lead agency on drug matters. He is so full of shit. And he's the one that's going to lead this investigation into the abduction of Conway? Yeah, he'll be the lead until something bad occurs. Then he'll distance the bureau from the investigation and blame a lack of cooperation on participating agencies for the failure. And look at that bozo Peterson agreeing with him. He should be at least interjecting that Conway is one of us and we should be equal partners in this investigation. We have a memo of understanding about internal affairs matters with the bureau where we investigate crimes committed by DEA agents. Why doesn't this apply to crimes committed against DEA agents as well? And let's not forget the fact that DEA, not the FBI has a major presence in the countries from which these kidnappers might have originated. We are in a much better position to collect intelligence than is the bureau.*

The Attorney General turned to Randall Walsh. "Okay, Mr. Walsh, the ball is in your court. What do we know so far?"

"Madam Attorney General, ladies and gentlemen," began Walsh as he acknowledged the other attendees, "As you all know, approximately 2:10 this morning, Administrator John Conway was kidnapped by several heavily armed masked men from the Wyndham Hotel in El Paso. One of his bodyguards was shot and killed during this kidnapping and the other was seriously wounded. This wounded agent was able to provide some information to local police before passing out."

"The agent's name is Jason Boyd," interjected an irritated Roger Grey.

"Uh, yes. Agent Boyd and the deceased agent were able to return fire killing one of the suspects. The other suspects who fled the scene dragging Conway with them left this suspect. The dead suspect had no identification on him, whatsoever, and is described as of possible Mexican descent and attired in military commando-style combat gear. A balaclava covered his face. Several witnesses outside the hotel described a white-panel van exiting the parking lot at a high rate of speed just after the shooting. There have been no demands from the abductors and nothing to indicate their intentions at this point in time."

"So right now we have no idea who is behind this abduction or their motives?" asked the AG.

"Not at this time, Madam Attorney General, but we are awaiting a fax of the fingerprints of the deceased suspect to run through our data base. If it yields an identity, we might be able to establish who is behind this kidnapping."

"Madam Attorney General, if I may," began James Peterson. "Before coming over here I had my Office of Professional Responsibility check to see if there had been any recent threats directed against the Administrator."

"And?" questioned the Attorney General.

"Other than what we have determined to be nuisance type threats, there is nothing that would lead us toward any one or group who might be responsible for this kidnapping."

"Madam Attorney General," said Roger Grey, "let me offer something we might consider."

The Attorney General had dealt with Roger Grey on several occasions dating back to when she was the District Attorney for Cook County, Illinois, and then as AG of the United States. She frowned at Roger. "What is it, Mr. Grey?"

"I don't think we should rule out groups like FARC or Los Zetas."

"FARC? Los Zetas?" repeated the Attorney General.

"Yes, Madam Attorney General, the FARC or Fuerzas Armada Revolucionaries de Colombia is the Revolutionary Armed Force of Colombia and is a para-military guerrilla organization that has aligned itself with the Colombian Drug Cartels for financial support. They're in a battle with the government of Colombia and actually control certain areas of Colombia. They could gain a lot of leverage by demonstrating they have the power to kidnap the head of DEA. If you remember, they were behind the bombing of that Avianca flight several years ago. And as for the Los Zetas, they are developing into the para-military wing of the Gulf Drug Cartel. They are comprised of a number of ex-Mexican Army Special Forces types. We at DEA have received intelligence that they have been expanding their area of violence north from the Gulf coast. What a perfect way to establish themselves as a force to be reckoned with in Mexico than to grab the Administrator of DEA in a military style commando raid. It would surely send shock waves through those in the Mexican government who stood in their way."

"But we have nothing more definitive that would point toward them other than speculation at this time," commented Randall Walsh.

"No nothing other than the military-style commando raid, and the fact that one of the suspects appears to be of Mexican or Latin descent."

A slight smile developed on the Attorney General's face. "Thank you, Mr. Grey. While I was somewhat leery when you interjected your thoughts, based upon our past history and all, I find that your suggestion about the FARC or Los Zetas being involved, a good suggestion and one that we must seriously consider."

The Attorney General's comments affected three members at the meeting. Roger, himself, was buoyed by the AG's comments in light of their tumultuous past association; James Peterson was delighted that someone from DEA had offered a possible suggestion for who might be responsible for John Conway's kidnapping; Randall Walsh was more than mildly irritated that he had not had similar information to render to this group.

"Anything else? Anybody?" asked the Attorney General.

"Yes," began Walsh. "There are reports that the conference had ended when the representatives from the Mexican Attorney General's Office abruptly left the conference room obviously in disagreement with something being proposed by DEA."

"I can address that issue, Madam Attorney General," offered James Peterson.

"Please do so, Mr. Peterson," said Thomas.

"The Administrator wanted to seek more cooperation in our efforts to target the Mexican cartels and had planned to use a $34 million dollars of foreign aid grant as leverage for this cooperation. Evidently, the Mexican government representatives balked at his proposal and were irritated that DEA would suggest that the Mexican government was not doing everything in their power to target the Mexican traffickers. DEA hopes to assuage their feelings and will seek another meeting with these representatives."

"Could this have something to do with his kidnapping?" asked Walsh.

"Certainly you are not implying that the Mexican government is behind the kidnapping?" asked Thomas with noticeable shock on her face and in her tone.

Walsh's answer was a simple shrug of his shoulders.

"I don't want any more talk of complicity by the Mexican government unless we have definite proof to substantiate the claim. Do I make myself clear?" said Thomas. She looked at all in attendance.

"All right then, I want to establish a command center here at main justice that is to be manned twenty-four hours a day until we return John Conway. Secondly, I want a briefing at 9:00 a.m. every day until this thing is resolved. And, of course, I want to hear right away, no matter what time of the day or night of any major developments."

With that said, the Attorney General concluded the meeting.

February 4, 1997; Hacienda Puesta Del Sol, La Cruz, Sinaloa, Mexico

The slight smile on Jaime's face could only be described as smug. Juan watched this slight smile spread on Jaime's face as he intently watched the CNN report of the kidnapping of the DEA's Administrator. In Juan's estimation, only a treacherous individual would have no feelings regarding the death of his own men. He sat in the large leather chair positioned in front of the projection TV.

"The question has yet to be answered. Who is responsible for the kidnapping of the DEA Administrator?" the anchorman asked.

Sitting upright in the large leather chair positioned in front of the TV, Jaime clapped his hands together once. "I kidnapped that pinche pendejo, you maricón." He jumped to his feet and turned to see Juan at his desk. "Juan, mi amigo, have we heard from the comandante yet?"

"No, Don Jefe. I would imagine he has been real busy this morning and will call when he gets a chance."

"Yes, you are right, of course. Be sure to put him straight through to me when he calls, Juan."

"Sí, Jefe, por supuesto," Juan had already heard that at least five times. He wished the comandante would call just to shut up Jaime.

At that moment, the phone on his desk began to ring. Jaime approached his desk as Juan answered.

"Hola." He held up his hand to ward off Jaime, and he mouthed the words "The licenciado, not the comandante."

Jaime grabbed the phone. "Licenciado, have you been watching the news?" He paused a moment to listen to the licenciado's reply. "I understand. I don't want to discuss this type of business on the phone. When can you be here?" After another short pause, he said, "Okay, within the hour." Jaime hung up the phone, and turned to Juan. "The licenciado wants to come by and discuss some concerns he has about our success. He probably smells more money."

Within the hour, the licenciado arrived at the hacienda and was escorted from the front portico to the office where Jaime was, once again, riveted to CNN reports of the kidnapping of John Conway. Rising from his chair, Jaime jubilantly greeted the licenciado. "Buenos Dias, Licenciado, Como le va?"

"I am good, Jaime, and you are obvious in a good mood because of the apparent success of the comandante. I am, however, a little concerned about the two deaths that occurred during the kidnapping. It could muddy the waters a bit with our friends in high places," said the licenciado. Today, the usual Armani suit had been replaced with a black silk shirt, black trousers and Gucci loafers. He also had a small fortune in gold hanging around his neck.

"Collateral damage," said Jaime. "But I will not know until I talk with the comandante. Speaking of the comandante, you have not heard from him have you?"

"No, Jaime, not since he went north to El Paso two days ago," answered the licenciado.

"Okay, tell me what is on your mind, and why you think this collateral damage might affect me." Jaime indicated for the licenciado to take a seat in front of his large oak desk.

The licenciado seated himself and developed a concerned look. "I've talked with my contacts at both the Ministers of Defense and Justice Offices and they have expressed their concern about the ramifications these deaths might cause if the Norte Americanos can make a case that John Conway was brought to Mexico. Right now, the crimes occurred in the United States and no Mexican law has been violated, but they are concerned. If Conway ends up here in Mexico, they will be forced to take some action."

The licenciado's words instantly irritated Jaime. "Are they concerned enough that they don't want to take my money?" Before the licenciado could answer, Jaime continued. "I think not. But in any event, please advise our contacts that the pinche DEA Jefe will not be brought to Mexico as I promised."

Instant relief registered on the licenciado's face. "This is good, Jaime. I'm positive our contacts will be delighted to hear this. If you don't mind me asking, where is the comandante taking the DEA Jefe?"

"Licenciado, I think it best to keep that information limited to only those who need to know. At least until we hear of the release and return of mi hermano to Mexico. The fewer people who know, the less chance that something will go wrong. If you are confronted by someone investigating this matter, you could truthfully say you do not know but were told he was not to be brought to Mexico."

"Jaime, I would never tell anyone about our business," offered the licenciado.

"Well, in any event, if you do not know, you do not know. Entiende usted?"

"Sí, Jaime," was the licenciado's simple response. He realized he should not pursue this subject any further.

"Please contact me if you need for me to intervene in any way."

"I will do that, Licenciado. In the meantime, I want you to stay in close contact with your people in the Minister's Office and let me know the minute you see a problem developing."

"It will be done, Jaime." The licenciado stood to leave. "I shall be in touch."

Juan accompanied the licenciado to his car.

"Juan, is Jaime telling me the truth about this kidnapping? Is he planning to bring that DEA Jefe to Mexico?"

"Licenciado, it is like Don Jaime has said. Only those who really need to know have been told this location. I am not one of those who need to know," said Juan. While this was true, he wished he did know. That could be his bargain chip with the DEA.

When Juan returned to the office, Jaime was sitting at Juan's desk talking on the phone.

"Esta Bien," Jaime said. "Don't say anything more until you get here. And don't talk about the location on the phone to anyone. See you in a couple of hours." Jaime hung up the phone, after tossing a wadded scrap of paper into the wastebasket. He looked up at Juan. "That was the comandante. All is well; he will be here later today so we can plan our next step." Jaime hummed to himself, a practice Juan had never before witnessed. He returned to his leather chair and turned up the volume on CNN.

Look at him, thought Juan. *He is extremely happy with what he has done. Right now, he thinks that he is invincible but I do not. Look what happened to Miguel Felix Uriarte. He thought he was invincible and yet the DEA got to him. No, I need to protect my family and myself. I must find out where they are holding the DEA Jefe and contact that agent in Los Angeles. That is the only way that my family and I will survive this thing.*

The next commercial break on CNN gave Juan his opportunity.

"Juan, I need to go piss," Jaime announced. "Call me if CNN comes back on with anything about my abduction."

"Sí, Jefe." *My abduction. The arrogance of this man.* Juan noted the pad of paper on his desk had an obvious indentation. He could make out a single letter—J. He took a quick look toward the door, reached down into the trash and retrieved the crumpled sheet of paper. A single letter J in black ink. J— Juan wadded up the paper again and returned it to the trash. He sat straight and rigid at his desk. The significance of the letter J gnawed at him. *What is the significance of J. Suddenly it came to him. Janos—the ranchita near Juarez. Suddenly it came to him. It's a perfect place to hold the hostage. It's close to the border yet remote enough to conduct our drug business. Has its own airstrip not too far from the ranchita. Do I wait for the comandante to arrive here and see if I can determine if my assumption is correct? Or, do I try to call that agent in Los Angeles. If I am correct, this location is the perfect bartering tool for me with DEA. I'll trade the location of their Jefe for my safety and the safety of Roberto and his family. No, I cannot wait. I need to get away from here to make the call and see if that agent is willing to help me. Some place I can talk freely and not get caught by Jaime. I need to come up with an excuse to get away from the hacienda.*

February 4, 1997; Janos, Chihuahua, Mexico

John Conway had never experienced anything like this in his forty-eight years of life. His emotions ranged from a paralyzing terror to abject despair with mind-numbing shock, anger, self-pity and a deep sense of hopelessness. *I wish they had killed me along with those two agents.* The thought of death caused him sob again. He tried to gain control of his emotions but the thought of being tortured made him shiver all over.

Conway tried to retrace the last ten hours. He could still hear the claxon horn blaring and the emergency lighting in the corridor. At first, he hadn't thought much of it – just a fire somewhere in the hotel. But as he reached the first floor, flanked by his two bodyguards, all hell broke loose. Several armed men, attired in commando style combat gear and armed with automatic weapons, opened fire, striking the agent to the front of him. The agent to his rear reacted quickly forcing Conway to the concrete floor. He covered Conway with his body and returned fire at the commandos. The volume of rounds increased and the agent on top of Conway recoiled as he was shot numerous times. Conway soon felt the agent's body go limp.

Terrified and numb from the shock but feeling no obvious pain, Conway's first thought was to remove the dead agent from him and flee. As he pushed against the weight of the agent's body, it was suddenly pulled from him and several pairs of hands grabbed his arms. With the multiple hands trying to restrain him, Conway's survival instinct switched from flight to fight. He tried to escape the grip of the commandos who he could now see in the limited light wore balaclavas to cover their faces. His efforts were answered with numerous painful punches to his midsection and head and a rapid series of shouts in Spanish.

Realizing his resistance was futile, he succumbed to the directions of one of the commando abductors. "Alto, alto, pendejo." The abductors then affixed plastic cuff restraints to his hands wrenched behind his back. They slapped a piece of duct tape across his mouth just before a black cloth bag was stretched over his head.

A van-like vehicle waited for their get-away. They drove for the better part of an hour on what Conway figured was a highway, based on the smoothness of the road and their speed. The driver soon lessened the speed and drove in a slower manner for almost another hour before the van stopped for several minutes with the engine idling. Conway heard a large sliding door open. The van drove forward and stopped again. The van's engine cut off, and Conway heard the sound of the large sliding door being closed.

Then the van door opened, and men dragged Conway out and dropped him to the cement floor. He estimated it was thirty minutes before he was pulled to his feet.

"Move."

When Conway hesitated a moment to get his bearings, hands shoved him forward.

"Rapido, pendejo."

He walked a short distance before numerous hands grabbed him and shoved him down what appeared to be a shaft descending to what he estimated was the bottom of a ten-foot hole. He remembered his thoughts. *This is it; this is where they're going to leave me to die.* This was the first time he audibly cried.

His sobs earned him a head slap from one of the abductors. "Silencio, maricón."

Shoved slightly forward, several pairs of hands forced Conway into a prone position on what appeared to be a small rolling platform. Conway realized he was on some type of cart on tracks. *I must be in one of those tunnels that the traffickers use to move drugs under the border. If they're going to this much trouble, I guess they're not going to kill me yet.* He weighed the thought of death with the possibility of torture like what they did to that poor agent several years before. The tears began to pour from his eyes. *Poor Emily; she'll be devastated. And the grandkids.* He realized crying wouldn't remedy his situation; he needed to get a grip on himself. Finally, it came to him. *I'm still alive; there's a reason they need me. That's it! They need me alive for something.*

Twenty minutes later, the process through the tunnel was reversed. Once again, strong hands pushed him into a van. Conway estimated this trip to be in excess of an hour with the last twenty minutes spent traversing a rough road. When he felt that his already aching kidneys could take no more pounding from the rough road, the van stopped, and once again, hands jerked him from the vehicle. Shoved forward, he walked just a short distance and then was pushed up several steps and into a building, tripping and falling to one knee in the process. Hands guided Conway to a room where he was forced to the floor. His captors then exited the room closing and locking the door behind them.

Conway righted himself to a sitting position. With his back to a wall, he took stock of his situation. *I must be in Mexico. It's obviously a rural area because of the rough road, and I heard no sounds of traffic. Their attire and actions indicate a well-planned abduction.* Conway had heard only two names mentioned – Comandante and Teniente. *But why me? What can they expect to extract out of the government by grabbing me?*

The abductors allowed Conway to remain alone for the next several hours, a technique used to create doubt and confusion as to their intentions. Conway's thoughts ran wild with all sorts of images of what they might do to him. Finally, he heard the sound of the door opening and somebody approached him and stood by his feet.

"Oye, mi amigo," said a heavily-accented voice, "I am going to remove the bag from your head. If you try anything stupid, it will go right back on. Comprende?"

Conway shook his head vigorously signaling he understood. The limited light in the room assaulted Conway's eyes causing a temporary instant blindness. Closing and opening his eyes along with some squinting, he slowly acclimated to the light, and he could see his abductor.

A middle-aged man, wearing dark sunglasses, squatted in front of him. The abductor had changed his clothes from the combat gear at the hotel to jeans, a western shirt and snakeskin cowboy boots.

Conway took in his surroundings. The small room had a single window covered with a sheet of plywood. A dim overhead light bulb gave the walls a dingy shade of yellow. The room contained only a small bare mattress with a single gray dirty blanket, a plastic patio chair and a large bucket in the far corner.

"If you will behave, I will remove the tape from your mouth," advised the abductor.

Conway nodded his head in agreement, as he braced himself for the pain he knew would accompany the ripping of the tape from his face. He was not disappointed. The sharp pain caused by the ripping tape made Conway's eyes tear and he gave an involuntary yelp.

"Lo siento, amigo – I'm sorry, my friend, there is no other way," said the male who then took a seat in the plastic chair.

"Could I have some water, please?" Hearing his own hoarse voice surprised Conway.

His abductor yelled toward the door. "Emilio, agua, por favor, por mi amigo."

A man, still wearing his commando-style clothing and the balaclava, soon entered the room and handed a bottle of water to the abductor. "Aqui esta, Comandante," he said.

Comandante, thought Conway. *He must be the leader.*

Placing the water bottle on the floor the comandante removed a large knife from a pouch on his belt and leaned toward Conway. Seeing the instant fear in Conway's eyes as he drew back, the comandante grinned. "Relax. I am going to cut off the plastic restraints, but if you get any funny ideas of escape, Emilio here," as he indicated with his free hand to the commando behind him, "will shoot you, entiende?"

"Yes, I understand," managed Conway through his parched throat.

Reaching around Conway's back, the comandante cut the plastic restraints from Conway's wrists.

Conway rubbed his wrists to reestablish circulation. He watched as the comandante returned the knife to its scabbard on his belt. He then retrieved the water bottle from the floor, removed the cap from the bottled water and handed it to Conway. Conway consumed over half of the bottle in one drink. "Thank you."

"De Nada – you're welcome," answered the comandante.

After taking another long swig, Conway set the bottle on the floor and looked at the comandante. "Am I permitted to ask a question, Comandante?"

"Sí, por supesto – yes of course," answered the comandante.

"Why me? What do I have to offer you?" Conway sounded more like a whiney child than an adult.

"Your government, Conway, has something my jefe wants returned to Mexico. And if this something is returned, you will probably be returned to your country," said the comandante in a voice devoid of passion.

"So I am a hostage until your jefe gets what he wants?"

"Sí, es correcto."

"Am I permitted to ask what it is that your jefe wants from my government?"

"Unfortunately, I am not at liberty to tell you that."

"And what happens if my country refuses to deal with your jefe? I guess I am a dead man, huh?"

"Otra vez es correcto. Lo siento…I'm sorry you do not understand Spanish. Once again, you are correct, Señor Conway," replied the comandante.

"Well, I guess I'm fucked then. My government doesn't usually bargain with kidnappers," said Conway.

"I think this time they will," said the comandante. A slight smirk developed on his heavily-scarred face.

"Why do you say that, Comandante?"

"In the past, your government has never had to deal with a problem of this magnitude. In those other cases you refer to, the person held captive was not somebody of your esteemed position. Do not worry, Conway, your government can't afford *not* to concede to the dictates of my jefe."

"May I ask where I am?"

"No more questions now, Conway. I shall have my men bring you some food shortly. If you need to relieve yourself, until we can trust you not to do something foolish, you can use that bucket over there. I shall leave your hands free and the mask off, but if you become trouble, they will be put back on."

"But…"

The comandante abruptly interrupted Conway. "No more questions, Señor." The comandante stood and walked to the door. Knocking slightly on the door, the comandante said something in Spanish and the door opened. He exited the room, and Conway was alone, once again, to consider his fate.

February 4, 1997; DEA Los Angeles, California

"Some shit, huh Roger?" Tom Blaine sat perched on the edge of his office desk.

"Can you believe it, Tom? I mean, it's unreal, something like out of the movies. I could better understand it if it were done in some foreign place like Colombia or Mexico, but Christ, not the United States."

Tom felt a cold chill at the thought of what Roger just said. "I know, Roger. It's hard for me to imagine something like this happening here. I know it's sent shock waves through the troops here in LA. The kidnapping was bad enough, but the killing of an agent and wounding of another agent on American soil is just unbelievable.

"Jason Boyd died around noon today. He never regained consciousness. Just shot too many times; it's remarkable he survived as long as he did."

The phone line was silent between the two men for a moment. Tom sighed. "Aw, man, I'm sorry to hear that, Roger. Sorry, and at the same time, angered. How dare these assholes come to this country, kidnap the Administrator and kill two agents. What's headquarters doing about this? We've not heard much of a response from Peterson who I assume is now the acting Administrator. Shit, I've gotten more information from the local all-news radio station here in LA than I have from DEA."

"Yeah, Peterson's the acting, unfortunately. The AG has convened a task force consisting of FBI, DEA, Customs and any other agency that wants to participate. Of course, the FBI has demanded the lead because of the kidnapping."

"Who's taking the lead for DEA, Roger?"

"Guess, Tom? An old friend of yours."

"You've got to be shitting me! Not Marsha Grant!" exclaimed Tom. "Please tell me it's not Marsha Grant, Roger."

"I'd be lying if I told you any different, old buddy."

"Jesus, Roger, why not you? It would make more sense for someone who knows the international scene like you do to put you in charge."

"The key word in your last sentence Tom was *sense*. Peterson has none, and he's totally in over his head as the Administrator. He didn't even have the balls to stand up to the FBI Assistant Director when he demanded that the FBI be the lead. We have a memo of understanding regarding matters like this, and we should have at the least shared the lead."

"Roger, if we wait on the bureau to solve this case, Conway will be dead, and we'll be no closer to bringing those assholes who killed the two agents to justice."

"I know, Tom, but putting Peterson in charge is not much better. In fact, as soon as I hang up, I'm going to see the Chief of Operations, Doug Cameron, and propose that we create a Mobile Task Force, much like we did when they grabbed Kiki in Mexico."

"Well, at least somebody back there is thinking, Roger. God help us if we leave this thing up to Peterson and Grant. "So, tell me, Roger, are there any leads? Has anyone come forward and claimed responsibility?"

"No, Tom, but because of how well planned and coordinated this attack was, I would wager it's a well-armed and trained para-military type group like FARC from Colombia or Los Zetos from Mexico."

"I'd put my money on Los Zetos. Say, wasn't one of the attackers killed and left at the scene?"

"Yeah, but unfortunately, he had no ID on him. The bureau's waiting on prints to see if they can identify him."

"If he's either FARC or Los Zetos, his prints are probably not going to be on file here."

"I'll bet you're right, Tom."

"Just a minute," Tom yelled to an agent in the background. "Roger, I've got to run. We got a deal down in Orange County and need to leave now to beat the traffic."

"Okay, Tom. Talk to you later."

"Roger, it goes without saying, if there is anything I can do on the Conway matter, let me know."

"Tom, I'm surprised. I thought you and lots of others in DEA would be celebrating that Conway can't harass them right now."

"Yeah, Roger, I know. Conway and I don't exactly exchange Christmas cards, but while I really don't give a shit about Conway, I'll be damned if I'll just sit by and let these assholes get away with killing two agents and taking Conway captive right here in my country. It's like they are thumbing their noses at us. You know how I am when somebody disrespects me."

"Oh yeah, Tom, I know how you can get."

February 4, 1997; Bandidos Restaurant Mazatlán, Sinaloa, Mexico

The perfect excuse, which would allow Juan to get away from the Hacienda to make the call to the DEA, actually came when Jaime decided to celebrate his successful kidnapping of the Jefe de Jefe's of DEA.

In the early afternoon, an upbeat Jaime approached Juan. "Juan, the comandante will be here in a couple of hours. Call the licenciado and have him meet us for dinner at Bandidos. I want to drink to our success and plan our next step in getting mi hermano back to Mexico. And call the restaurant and have them reserve my favorite table."

"Sí, Don Jaime, I shall make the calls," replied Juan.

Within the hour, a report by a CNN anchor caused Jaime's jubilant mood to turn angry and then sullen.

> This just in from Washington. According to a spokesperson in the Attorney General's Office, three groups have come forward and have claimed responsibility for the kidnapping of the DEA Administrator. The first group, thought to be headed by the Burmese War Lord Khun Sa, has demanded one hundred million dollars in exchange for the DEA Administrator. According to the Attorney General's spokesperson, Khun Sa had long been targeted by DEA as a major heroin violator. A second group, thought to be Colombian, demanded the release of several Medellin Cartel members incarcerated in the United States and twenty-five million for Conway's release. And yet a third group calling itself the Green Earth Movement had, in a hand-delivered note to the New York Times, laid claim to the kidnapping of John Conway and demanded that when the possession of Marijuana was totally decriminalized, John Conway would be released.

Jaime instantly sprang to his feet and screamed at the television. "Carajo! Who are those pendejos?" Red faced and with the blood-coursing veins in his neck threatening to rupture, Jaime picked up a heavy ceramic ashtray and flung it at the television. It struck the wood framed cabinet and ricocheted harmlessly to the floor. "They cannot do this to me."

Juan jumped to his feet and walked to the bar area where he poured some Mezcal into a shot glass. Retracing his steps, he approached Jaime and extended the shot glass to Jaime. "Don Jaime, drink this. It might calm you."

Jaime reminded Juan of a raging bull ready for a fight as the CNN news anchor continued.

> While each of these demands is taken seriously, the Attorney General's office is in the process of determining if any of these demands are legitimate and if they are from the actual kidnappers of John Conway.

"How about I cut off his pinche fingers, or even better, his dick, and send it to you as proof that I have the pinche pendejo," shouted Jaime still in a full rage.

"Jaime's anger and his statement about cutting off the Jefe de Jefe of DEA's body parts sent a cold shiver down Juan's spine. He silently prayed *I hope Jaime doesn't do something stupid before I can contact that DEA Agent.*

By the time he and Juan entered the Bandidos restaurant, Jaime's anger had subsided somewhat. As they walked through the packed dining room, Jaime acknowledged several patrons. One, a high ranking elected official, stood and greeted Jaime with an embrace. "Jaime, mi amigo. I am sorry about Hector. What have you heard?"

"Not to worry, amigo. I have it on good authority that he shall be home soon," replied Jaime.

Both the licenciado and the comandante, seated at Jaime's favorite table, had drinks in their hands.

Attired in one of his trademark Armani suits with white shirt and dark blue tie, the licenciado quickly stood. In a hushed tone, he said, "Jaime, congratulations. You succeeded in doing what I think many thought couldn't be done. It will be just a matter of time before the Norte Americanos will be forced to return Hector to Mexico."

Jaime acknowledged the licenciado's words with a simple nod of his head and turned to the comandante who had risen slowly from his seat. "The real congratulations should go to the comandante here.

The comandante's face looked drawn and concerned when Juan and Jaime approached the table. He smiled slightly with his menacing smirk. "Yes, Don Jaime, we were successful, but it cost me one of my trusted ayudantes to do so."

"I am sorry about your ayudante, Comandante. Did he have a family?"

"Sí, Don Jaime, an espousa and three niños."

"Carajo!" exclaimed Jaime. "Comandante, see that they are taken care of." Jaime turned to Juan. "Give the comandante whatever he thinks would be appropriate for his ayudante's family."

"Gracias, Don Jaime," said the comandante.

"Other than that unfortunate event, everything went smoothly, Comandante?" asked Jaime.

"Sí, Don Jaime." The comandante gave a heavy sigh. "There would not have been any shooting at all if those DEA putas had not started shooting first. I cautioned my men before we entered the hotel not to shoot unless necessary. I was fearful we'd hit Señor Conway and that would have been then end of our effort."

"I see, Comandante."

"But other than that, it went smoothly, and we were able to use the tunnel."

Jaime put an index finger to his lips to silence the comandante. "Let us not discuss those operations here in public, Comandante."

The comandante looked around the restaurant. "Lo siento, Don Jaime."

"No problema, Comandante," Jaime smiled at the comandante then turned to the licenciado. "So what have you heard, Licenciado?"

The licenciado felt the cold glare of Jaime's eyes and paused for a moment. "Uh, not much, Jaime. It is too early yet, and there has been nothing to indicate the kidnapping to be connected to Mexico. Uh, but I am concerned about something the comandante just said about using the tunnel."

Once again, Jaime put his forefinger to his lips. "Silencio! We shall not discuss those operations here, Licenciado."

"Sí, Sí, I understand Jaime." The licenciado searched for words that would not irritate Jaime. "As I said prior to this, uh…event, the person would not be brought to Mexico. As I explained, my high-level contacts want a plausible deniability, that no crime has been committed in Mexico, Jaime. Don't you remember me telling you this?"

"Sí, Licenciado, and as far as your position to your contacts on this matter, you will be adamant that you have it from good sources that he was *not* brought here to Mexico, but instead, was taken to a Central American country. If that is not enough, I can send them a strong signal not to concern themselves with this matter. Entiende usted?"

"Sí, Jaime. I just need to be able to advise my contacts that there is no reason to believe the man is here in Mexico. My contacts will feel pressure from the Norte Americanos once you make the demands known."

"Yes, I am sure. But it is your job to remind them of my generosity they have willingly accepted over the years and the pressure I can bring on them and their families here in Mexico. You will need to remind them that *my* pressure, well let's just say, it will not just be threats or token actions." Jaime stared at the licenciado for several long seconds before his face broke into a smile. "We are here to celebrate. Let us celebrate." Jaime signaled a waiter, who closely resembled Pancho Villa himself. He approached the table.

"A bottle of your best Mezcal for my compadres," announced Jaime.

Watching this exchange between the licenciado and Jaime, Juan knew two things to be definite. The licenciado *best be careful. Don Jaime also meant him when he suggested he would bring pressure on those who interfered with his effort to bring Hector home. Second, mention of a tunnel proved his guess that the DEA Jefe was taken to the ranch at Janos. They would have used the tunnel near Agua Prieta that goes under the border to Douglas. Very clever of the comandante. I need to call that DEA agent in Los Angeles right now.*

Juan glanced at his pager as if he had received a page. "Ramon," he said to Jaime. "He was expecting something large for us. I better go call him."

"Sí, of course. Don't be gone long. I am hungry," answered Jaime after he drained his first glass of Mezcal.

CHAPTER THIRTEEN

February 4, 1997; DEA Los Angeles, California

Like many drug deals, the one in Orange County had not gone as planned. Instead of the agreed upon simple exchange of cash for the three kilograms of cocaine at a restaurant parking lot, the two suspects had arrived at the arranged location and first demanded to see the money. They wanted the money fronted to them so they could get the kilograms of cocaine to do the deal. Lacking the authority to authorize the fronting of over one hundred thousand dollars, and more importantly the suspicion that these traffickers didn't have the dope, Tom instructed his undercover agent to demand a sample first and authorized the purchase of an ounce of cocaine for twenty-two hundred dollars. By doing this, Tom hoped the dope dealers would go to their source followed by surveillance. Once they delivered the cocaine, a search warrant could be obtained to search the location for the ounce of cocaine. But it was not to be. Instead of going to one location, the crooks had gone to several locations, and it became obvious to the surveillance that they were, as one of the agents said over the radio, "shopping for dope."

Tom made the decision that when they returned with the cocaine, they would be arrested and the cocaine and money seized.

After an hour and a half, and when it became apparent that the dope dealers had not yet "scored the coke," Tom made the decision to stop the crooks and recover their cash. This was done and surprisingly, the crooks did have a half an ounce of cocaine on them. When offered the opportunity to lead DEA agents to the source of the cocaine, the suspects declined and opted to go to the Orange County jail to await prosecution on the state charges of possession of cocaine.

Because it was getting late, Tom offered to take the large flash roll of cash back to the office and lock it in his safe for the evening, while the agents working the case booked the suspects or went home. He arrived back at his office in downtown LA just after 7:00 p.m. With the money secured in his safe, he decided to call Libby.

"Hi, big guy," Libby said. "I wondered when you would call."

"Hi, kiddo…wait…one of the group phones just started ringing. It might be one of the agents calling about a problem with our recent arrest. "I'll be right back." Before Libby could say anything else, Tom punched the hold button and answered the other line. "Group Three."

"Agent Henderson, por favor," said a male voice.

"No está aqui," Tom said in his less than perfect Spanish.

The caller switched to heavily accented English. "Señor, it is very important I talk with him."

"I can page him and have him call you. Do you have a number where he can reach you?" asked Tom.

"No, Señor, I cannot receive a call. It is very important for me to talk to him."

"Well, look, I'm his boss, maybe I can help you." After a long day and his desire to talk with Libby, Tom's patience had worn thin.

After several seconds, the caller then said, "I can wait by this phone for several minutes. Can you have Agent Henderson page me at this number, and I will call him right back." Juan then gave the number to Tom.

Tom recognized the number as an international number. "Can I tell him who's calling him?"

"Sí, señor, tell him, Juan called."

Instantly, Tom recognized the voice on the other end of the line. *An international phone number, possibly Mexico. Could it be this is the informant, Juan Cervantes, who had vanished?* Taking a chance, Tom asked, "Juan, your last name is not Cervantes, is it?"

There was a long pause at the other end of the line. "Do I know you, Señor?"

"I think you do, Juan. If this is Juan Cervantes, we've met once before."

Again, after a significant pause, Juan asked, "Who am I speaking with, please?"

"Juan, this is Tom Blaine. We might have met last year ago in Guadalajara, at Miguel Uriarte's estanica."

"Señor Blaine, Sí, sí, I remember," said an anxious Juan quickly. "I have tried to call you in Denver before. You are now in Los Angeles?"

"Yes, Juan. I have been here for a month."

"Senor Blaine, I read about the killings of the Fonseca's in Colorado. That could have easily been me if I had continued to provide agent Henderson there in Los Angeles with information about the Mexican drug business. Had it not been for my forced return to Mexico, I would have probably suffered the same fate. With Miguel Felix dead, the only other people of significance I could give up were Carlos and Rafael Ojeda in Colombia. While I didn't have significant information about Jaime and Hector Gutierrez, I guess I had the ability and contacts to develop more information. I could have developed enough information at least to make Agent Henderson happy. When I met with him, he didn't seem pleased with just the historical background information about Miguel Uriarte's hidden assets in the United States and wanted to expand his investigation to include Miguel's association with the Colombians and any information I had or could develop about Mexican traffickers including Jaime and Hector Gutierrez."

"Okay, I understand," began Tom. "Well, Juan, Agent Henderson works for me. So what's so important tonight that you need to talk with him immediately? After all, you start to cooperate with us then just up and disappear. Agent Henderson has not heard from you in months?"

"Señor Blaine, I had no choice. I was forced to return to Mexico."

"Forced to return to Mexico? Seems to me, Juan, you returned to Mexico, and according to your recent indictment, you began to work in the same capacity for the Sinaloa Cartel that you did for Uriarte."

"Sí, that is correct. But had I not returned to Mexico, my brother, his wife and children would have been killed. I had to make the choice to either return to Mexico to work for Jaime and Hector Gutiérrez, or they would kill my brother and his family."

"I see," said Tom. "Why did they want you so badly, Juan?"

"Señor, Tom, I do not have the time to go into great detail right now. Let me just say Jaime and Hector needed the Colombian contacts I had from working with Don Miguel.

"I see," said Tom. "So tell me, Juan, why didn't you just take some of that money I left you and leave Uriarte's Estancia and move you brother and family somewhere safe. There certainly was enough money in that bag to allow them to live comfortably for years."

"Sí, Sí, Señor Blaine, that is correct, more than enough money. But I put it in a safety box at a bank in San Diego. My return to Mexico was so sudden I did not have time to get it or arrange for it to be forwarded some place where I could access it. And now with that indictment, I cannot return to get it."

"Okay, I think I understand. What's the emergency right now?"

"Before I say any more, I need your promise to help me and my brother and his family."

"Help you how, Juan?"

"Help me with the charges against me in the United States, so I can get to my money in San Diego. I can then move my brother and family some place safe."

"The indictment is pretty serious, Juan. You would have to do something very significant before the U.S. Attorney would consider dropping or reducing the charges."

"What if I could tell you where your jefe is being held?" asked Juan.

"My jefe?" Tom asked not understanding at first.

"Sí, Señor Blaine, the Jefe de Jefe of DEA."

Tom sat upright in his chair. "What! Jesus Christ! You know where our Administrator is being held?"

"Sí, Señor Blaine," said Juan.

"Juan, stop this Señor Blaine crap and call me Tom. Jesus, Juan, you know where they're holding John Conway?"

"Sí, Tom, I know where he is."

Tom tried to hide the excitement in his voice. "Juan, I can just about assure you that if your information is correct that indictment against you will go away and you'll be able to get your money and move your brother and his family wherever you choose." After several seconds, when Juan did not respond, Tom said, "Juan, you'll have to trust my word on this that I can get the indictment against you dropped. I think you know from our encounter in Guadalajara last year that I am a man of my word."

"Sí, Tom. I believe you when you say you'll do what you can."

"Okay, so where is Conway being held Juan?"

"I am pretty sure he is being held at a ranch in Janos. Janos is about 80 kilometers south of Agua Prieta, which is right on the border. Jaime's organization uses this ranch to store drugs from Colombia. He then hides drugs in trucks carrying farm produce like melons to the United States."

"Juan, do you have a better address for the ranch. There are probably a number of them in the area. How would I know which is the right one?"

"I have never been there, Tom, but I have learned through conversations between Jaime and the comandante that it is called Tierra Del Sol and has a large stone front gate guarded at all times by ayudantes hired by the comandante."

"Okay? Why is he being held there?"

"It is close to the border; I heard the comandante mention to Jaime something about the tunnel. They use the tunnel to bring drugs under the border at Agua Prieta into Douglas, Arizona. I think they took the DEA Jefe through the tunnel to Janos."

"Why did they kidnap Conway, Juan?"

"It was Jaime's plan to take your jefe hostage to exchange for his brother Hector. The comandante and his men are the ones who took him from the hotel in El Paso and brought him to Mexico."

"The comandante? Who is this comandante you keep talking about, Juan?"

"His name is Jesus Guerra; he is very vicious. Look, Tom, I cannot talk much longer. I am using a pay phone at a restaurant. Jaime, the comandante and the licenciado are with me having dinner."

"Juan, how can I get in touch with you?"

"You can page me, but I cannot call from Jaime's hacienda and will have to wait until I can get to a phone away from Jaime and the hacienda."

"I understand, Juan. Take this number down. It is the number of our twenty-four hour communications center. When you call, they will patch you through to me at almost any phone." Tom then gave him the number.

"Tom, you must act quickly on this information; I am afraid Jaime will do something bad to your jefe. He has threatened to cut off his fingers and send them to the DEA as proof he has him."

"Okay, Juan. I've got to make some calls to get things going."

"What about my brother and his family?"

"Juan, go about your regular routine as if nothing has happened. I'll let you know when it's time for you to make your move. Okay?"

"Okay, Tom."

"Uh, one more thing, Juan. How much influence do you have with Jaime about matters like the kidnapping of Conway?"

"He trusts me pretty good on business things. I have helped him with his Colombian contacts and with moving money like I did with Don Miguel, but I have not been a part of any type of things like this kidnapping."

"I need for you to try your best to discourage him from harming Conway. That would be very bad for all."

"I will try, Tom. In fact, this dinner with the comandante and the licenciado is to decide the next step. They need to decide how to make their demands known so they are believed."

With Tom's quick thinking, he hit upon an idea. "Juan, suggest that they have Conway tell the U.S. Attorney General the conditions of his release."

"I don't understand, Tom."

"Suggest they have Conway make a videotape of why he was kidnapped and the terms of his release. The people in Washington who make the decisions couldn't argue with such a demonstration."

"Sí, Tom. I think that could work. I will suggest it. I must go back to dinner."

"Okay, but call when you can if you have any more news. And, Juan, trust me. I will do everything in my power to protect you and family."

"Gracias, Tom."

As Tom hung up the phone, he realized Libby was still holding. "Shit, I forgot about Libby," Tom said aloud. He punched the blinking line. "Libby, I'm sorry," but his reply was met with a dial tone. *Crap she must have gotten pissed and hung up. But I really need to talk to Roger about what the CI said and what we should do with this information.* He decided that whatever he would face with Libby, he had to call Grey immediately.

February 4, 1997, Bandidos Restaurant Mazatlán, Sinaloa, Mexico

"There you are, Juan. What took you so long? I was about to send the comandante's men in search of you."

"Lo siento, Don Jaime, but I had to page Ramon and wait for him to return my call," replied a nervous Juan.

"Is everything okay with Ramon?" asked Jaime.

"Sí, he just wanted to tell me that because of the kidnapping of the DEA Jefe the Norte Americano customs and police are searching all cars departing the United States for Mexico. He was not going to have that large shipment sent until he was sure it would be safe to do so."

"Esta Bien, Juan. It should be safer in a few days, if not, we can use another route." Jaime poured Juan a glass of Mezcal and one for himself. "I took the liberty of ordering the fish for you, Juan."

Juan felt his stomach churn.

Jaime quickly downed the glass of Mezcal. "Okay, where are we now?"

"We were discussing how to make our demands known to the right people in Washington," said the licenciado.

"Yes, and because of these other maricóns who have attempted to claim they have the DEA Jefe, we shall have to make our demand so that they know we are ones who really have him."

"How about we send a letter to an important newspaper in Washington, New York or Los Angeles? We could take his inked fingerprints and put them on the letter so they could verify we have him," offered the licenciado.

"That's good, Licenciado, but it might take too much time to do that and I want to do something quick," replied Jaime.

"How about I slice off his right index finger and deliver that along with a letter stating our demands to a TV channel in El Paso or Los Angeles. That might get their attention quicker," suggested the comandante.

The comandante's suggestion got a slight laugh from Jaime. "Yes, I thought of that also while all those other pendejos were claiming they have the pinche DEA jefe. But let's save that for later if we need to up the pressure."

The icy cold shiver that ran through Juan when the comandante made his suggestion quickly melted when Jaime deferred on this course of action.

"Sí, I agree with Jaime on this, Comandante. We should wait to see what the gringos' response is to our demands before we up the ante, so to speak," offered the licenciado.

"Don Jaime, perdone, if I may speak," began Juan."

"Sí, of course, Juan,"

All eyes focused on Juan. "Why not have the DEA jefe himself make the demand for the release of Hector," Juan said. "They could not say that the demand was not legitimate if it came from his own mouth," he continued.

"And just how do you propose to do this, Juan. Take him to a television station and have him make his statement. That's a foolish idea," said the licenciado.

Juan looked directly at the licenciado but addressed Jaime. "We could videotape the DEA Jefe making our demand along with some personal information that only he would have. We would then have the videotape hand-delivered to a television station in some large U.S. city."

Silence fell on the group at the table. Jaime stared at Juan for several minutes. Then a slight smile developed on his face. "Juan, mi amigo, that is an excellent idea." He glared at the licenciado and added, "Not foolish at all."

"I like it also," chimed in the comandante. "Our demands right from the horse's mouth, so to speak."

Having been rebuked for his criticism of Juan, the licenciado wisely decided to remain silent.

Jaime clapped his hands together. "That is what we shall do. We shall make a videotape and send it to a TV station in a big U.S. city."

"Might I suggest we send it to a city far removed from the border," suggested the licenciado. "That could dispel the notion that the DEA Jefe is being held in Mexico."

"Don Jaime, if I could also suggest that we prepare a script that the DEA Jefe should read laying out your demand along with some personnel information that only he would know," interjected Juan.

"What kind of information are we talking about here, Juan?" asked the comandante.

"Maybe just a word to his wife that he is well and not injured. He could address his wife by name."

"Excellent idea, Juan. Licenciado, I want you to put your legal skills to use and draft a script. Comandante, you will see to it that the video is delivered to a TV station. I want this done tomorrow, and I will give the Norte Americanos five days from receipt of the video to meet my demands, or else we shall, as the licenciado has stated, up the ante." Jaime turned back to Juan. "Esta bien, I feel good about this plan, and thank you, Juan, mi amigo. I can see why Miguel Felix put so much faith in you."

At that moment, two waiters appeared with two large trays of food. "Let's eat and enjoy the remainder of this evening." Jaime's joyous mood had returned.

February 4, 1997; DEA Los Angeles, California

It was close to 11:00 p.m. when Tom placed a call to Roger Grey at his Washington, D.C., suburb home. A groggy Grey answered the phone. "This better be damn good. Do you know what time it is?"

"Why, yes, Roger, it's 8:00 here in La-La Land."

"Yeah, asshole, well it's almost eleven here in Virginia. But you already knew that didn't you, butthead?" replied Roger Grey. His speech began to clear.

"Geez, Roger, did I wake you up?" asked Tom with a voice ringing with sarcasm.

"No, wiseass, I had to get up to answer the phone. Yeah, you woke me up.

But then, you know I go to bed early because I get up early. So why the call at this hour?"

"You better sit down for this, Roger."

"Goddamnit, I'm lying down now," answered Roger. His tone indicated that he was starting to get annoyed with Tom. "Now what do you want?"

"Man, you're grouchy when you don't get your beauty rest."

"Screw you, Blaine. Now what the hell do you want?"

"I think I know where Conway is," said Tom barely capable of containing the excitement in his voice.

"What?" exclaimed Roger rather loudly. In the background, Tom heard Roger say, "Sorry, dear. I'll take this call in the den. Tom, wait a minute while I move to my den." Roger soon picked up another phone. "Okay, dear, you can hang up the phone now; sorry for waking you."

Tom heard a click on the line. "Tom, what do you mean you think you know where Conway is?"

"Just that, Roger. I just got off the phone with a CI who is fairly confident that Conway is being held at a ranch near Janos, that's Janos with a J not H, Roger."

"I don't need the spelling lesson right now, Tom. Where is this Janos?"

"Just south of Douglas, Arizona, about eighty kilometers."

"And how does your CI know this, Tom?"

"The CI and I have a history. Evidently, Jaime Gutiérrez the head of the Sinaloa cartel…,"

"I know who Jaime Gutiérrez is," interrupted Roger. "If you recall, we had a recent conversation regarding the arrest of Hector Gutiérrez. At the time, you had no clue it was the Sinaloa cartel behind the killing of those two people in the van in Colorado. Remember that?"

"Seems like I do recall that conversation. Well, anyway, Jaime Gutiérrez needed this CI because the CI had contacts with Colombians from working for Uriarte that Jaime Gutiérrez did not have. To convince the CI, and this is according to him, Jaime grabbed the CI's brother and his family and held them hostage until the CI agreed to return to Mexico. Since August of last year he has been doing for Jaime Gutiérrez what he was doing for Miguel Uriarte."

"Okay, so how does this fit with the kidnapping of John Conway?' asked Roger.

"The CI claims it was Jaime Gutiérrez who kidnapped Conway and is holding him as a hostage until his brother Hector is returned to Mexico."

"No demand like that has been made yet Tom."

"I know, Roger, in fact the CI said that he was calling from a pay phone at a restaurant while Gutiérrez and other members of his organization were dining and planning a strategy about demanding the release of Hector Gutiérrez in exchange for Conway."

"So how is this demand supposed to come about?"

"The CI didn't know, but I suggested that they videotape Conway making the demand himself and send the videotape to a major TV station. The CI was going to suggest that to Gutiérrez."

"Tell me, Tom, why does the CI think Conway is being held at this ranch near um…?"

"Janos, Roger. The CI thinks Conway is at the ranch because of some conversation he inadvertently overheard between Gutiérrez and a comandante, who according to the CI orchestrated the kidnapping. During the conversation, the comandante made mention that they used the tunnel evidently to bring Conway under the border into Mexico. The CI knows that they use a tunnel from Aqua Prieta to Douglas to smuggle large quantities of dope into the United States. The ranch is well guarded according to the CI and would be a good place to hold Conway."

After Tom filled Roger in about Juan, Roger remained quiet on the line.

"So, Roger, what do you think?"

"Jesus, Tom, I think this is probably pretty accurate information. The problem is what in the hell can we do with it?"

"What do you mean, Roger?'

"Tom, if I go to the Attorney General with this information, I can just about bet that their response will be to go the Mexican government with the information and demand they take action. If Gutiérrez is as connected as he must be in order to become so powerful in Mexico, they'll either move Conway or just outright kill him. And it goes without saying that I can't tell this to Peterson. He'll demand we turn this over to the FBI. No, we need a better plan."

"Roger," Tom said. "What if I go get Conway? We won't tell anyone."

"What do you mean, Tom?"

"I mean, we contact my old Snow Cap team and see if they are up for one more trip to Mexico. We don't tell anyone, and just like when we went after Uriarte, we'll be at our own risk."

"Phew," said Roger exhaling the air in his lungs. "I guess that could work. If Conway isn't there, nobody would have to know. Tom, are you sure you're up to this? I mean, that last trip to Mexico took an awful lot out of you."

"Yeah, it did, Roger. I still have the dreams about poor Marcus. But I don't think we have a choice here. Let's face it, the government of Mexico is not going to do anything unless it's forced to, and just as they did with Kiki, they'll allow those who are really behind this to escape any type of punishment. It's basically up to us to bring Conway home; otherwise, I believe he's a dead man."

Roger chuckled. "Ironic, isn't it. Probably the two men who despise Conway and what he stands for the most are willing to risk their careers and maybe their lives to save his worthless ass."

"Yeah, it is, Roger, but in truth, I'm not doing this for Conway, personally. I'm not going to let these assholes come to this country, kill two agents and kidnap an important official without retribution. I also want to send them the message that their government cannot protect them from assholes like me who are willing to disregard the international border, just as they did, to go after them."

"I understand your position. I guess our next step is to see if the other members of your Snow Cap team are willing to risk their careers and lives for Conway."

"Yes, Roger, that's the next step. I'll contact them. What I need from you is the kind of support you gave us for our operations against Uriarte, if that's possible."

"I have some ideas. Let me think about this and we'll talk in the morning. Okay?"

After ending his call with Roger, Tom called Libby.

After a chilly reception, she warmed up a bit. "Okay, so what was so important you had to leave me on hold so long?"

"I got some information about Conway's abduction and needed to get it to Roger Grey right away."

"What kind of information?"

"While I can't go into detail right now, just suffice it to say that Conway is alive."

"Okay, I understand, Tom."

The conversation went back to personal items about their respective days and ended up with them both wishing they were together.

CHAPTER FOURTEEN

February 5, 1997; Main Justice Building, Washington, DC

Marilyn Thomas entered the large brightly lit conference room. "Good morning, ladies and gentlemen." Her pants suit, buttoned to the neck, matched her dour mood. "Please, take your seats," she instructed. An assistant placed some papers, along with a cup of coffee, on the conference table in front of her.

Roger Grey had accompanied Acting Administrator James Peterson and Marsha Grant, the appointed DEA lead person on the kidnapping.

Thomas immediately dispelled any notion as to who was in charge. "Where are we on Administrator Conway's abduction?"

"I'll lead off," began Assistant FBI Director Randal Walsh, dressed in a blue suit, white shirt and dark tie.

Roger made a silent assessment.

"We have received the fingerprints of the dead commando left behind when his mates departed with Mr. Conway. He is not in any of our data bases."

Surprise, surprise, thought a sarcastic Roger Grey.

"There was no identification on the body and all the labels of his clothing had been removed. His weapon, a Beretta 9 MM, is not of record with any of our data bases either, so we cannot determine its origin," continued Walsh.

"So, Mr. Walsh, what you're telling me is that we don't know who this person was nor where he came from. Or if he was, in fact, connected to any of these organizations who have so far claimed responsibility for Mr. Conway's abduction?"

"Uh, yes, Madam Attorney General. Unfortunately, that is the case. However, we do have some other information that I would like to share with you. We, the FBI, have done some checking on Mr. Conway's travel arrangements in an attempt to determine who might have known where he was staying in El Paso. The travel agency that handles most federal travel made the arrangements."

Roger's stomach churned. *Uh, yes, the same travel agency partially owned by a Colombian and who this liberal Administration contracted with when they took office negating the contract with the former travel agency that had been doing the job for fifteen years.*

"While the travel agency made the flight arrangements, Mr. Conway's assistant made the actual lodging reservations. According to her, he has, uh, particular tastes, so she sees to the accommodations rather than leaving it up to the travel agency."

The term *particular tastes* caused the AG to raise her eyebrows, but she said nothing.

"You're not indicating something inappropriate, are you?" asked James Peterson.

"Certainly not, sir," replied Walsh "only that she made the arrangements and not the travel agency which is the usual norm in government travel. So that leads to the question, how did the abductors know his whereabouts? We need to answer that question."

"Do tell," commented the AG.

"Yes, ma'am, our agents in El Paso have interviewed the night manager of the Wyndham Hotel. He told us that around midnight, several hours before Mr. Conway's abduction; the night security officer came to him and said he was ill, the stomach flu or something. This night security officer was a medically retired El Paso police officer. He has not shown up for work since. When our agents went to his listed residence, they discovered he has vacated that location. Additionally, none of the four-member cleaning force that cleans those suites on the top floor has returned to work either. Unfortunately, they all appear to be illegal aliens with fraudulent documentation. None of the addresses they gave as their residences were good.

"So you think it might have been the security officer who tipped off Mr. Conway's location to the kidnappers?" asked the AG.

"It's possible, Madam Attorney General. Either the security guy or the cleaning force."

"What else do we know? What about these groups that have claimed responsibility?" asked the AG with just a hint of desperation in her tone.

"It's too early to determine if any of these claims are legitimate," said Walsh with a tone of false confidence.

"Madam AG, if I might," interjected Roger Grey.

"Yes, Mr. Grey," replied the AG.

"I think we can exclude Khun Sa and the Green Earth Movement for the time being," suggested Roger.

"And why is that?" asked a somewhat defensive Randall Walsh.

"Well, the ethnicity of the deceased commando left at the scene was Latino and the group was well organized. They had very good intelligence, at least concerning the location of Administrator Conway. To me, these facts, along with the proximity of the site of the abduction, which is a stone's throw from Mexico, suggests some type of Latino organization like Los Zetos. And we know from what is occurring in Mexico, at least along the Gulf Coast, that the Los Zetos use kidnapping and murder as a way to spread their influence."

"Those are excellent points, Mr. Grey," advised the AG with just a slight smile on her face.

"But we've not heard from any group in Mexico yet," said Walsh somewhat defensively.

"No, there has been no demand from any groups in Mexico, and so far, none of the sources we have in Mexico have come forward with any information about the abduction," Roger said. "But it's still early, and maybe the persons responsible for this abduction are trying to get organized so they can spell out a demand that can be met expeditiously."

The AG nodded her head in agreement at Roger's last statement. She looked around the large conference table to each participant individually. "So what is our strategy?"

"We are continuing to interview people in El Paso trying to develop any information we can," said Walsh. "We shall investigate every demand that anyone brings forward."

"I think we should advertise a reward for any information leading to the recovery of Mr. Conway and the arrest and conviction of those who did this deed," offered Roger. "That seemed to work in our favor when our agent was kidnapped in Mexico several years ago. Ultimately, it was the idea of a big payday and the relocation of several witnesses that allowed us to recover his body." Thomas nodded her head in agreement. "Yes, I think that is a good idea."

"If we do that, stand by for lots of people coming forward with information. It will bring out all the weirdos, I'm sure," offered Walsh. "And unfortunately, right now, we do not have the manpower to follow-up on all these calls."

James Peterson, who had remained mute for most of the briefing, cleared his throat. "Madam Attorney General, the DEA can help in that regard. At the suggestion of Marsha Grant here," indicating with his hand to Grant who sat next to him, "I've authorized the creation of a Mobile Task Force. Today we'll begin pulling together all information regarding any organization in Mexico who might be behind this. We're also tasking our confidential sources in Mexico through our agents stationed there, and a number of agents are being sent to El Paso to find any information regarding Mr. Conway's kidnapping."

"You'll be sure to pass this on to my agents, won't you, Mr. Peterson," interjected Walsh. "As agreed upon, the FBI is the lead agency on this kidnapping, and all information should be funneled through us."

Marsha Grant answered for James Peterson. "Of course, we will share information with the bureau, just as we expect the bureau to share their information with us in accordance with our Memo of Understanding."

Grant's comments impressed Roger for the first time. *Good for you, Marsha. Stick up for DEA. We have just as much right to investigate this matter, as does the bureau.*

Randall Walsh turned to the AG. "Madam AG, I thought we all agreed that the FBI would be the lead on this investigation?"

Grant did not wait for the AG to reply to Walsh. "Mr. Walsh, I am not suggesting that you are *not* the lead, but we do have a Memo of Understanding that covers matters such as this. DEA expects to be kept fully in the loop on this matter just as we plan to keep the FBI informed of what we develop. We are not just going to sit back and wait for the bureau to try to develop leads on this case when we have the greater presence in Mexico. And as Mr. Grey, I also believe it is more than likely that a Mexican organization is responsible for this abduction," said Marsha Grant.

With battle lines drawn, the Attorney General sought to stave off any more bickering by asserting herself. "I am ordering all of you to cooperate with one another and share all information. If there is a problem with this, I will personally eliminate that problem. Do I make myself clear?

All heads nodded in agreement.

"If there is nothing further, we shall meet again tomorrow, same time— same place."

As Roger Grey rode back to DEA Headquarters with Peterson and Grant, he was distracted from their self-serving conversation with his own thoughts. *I need to make some phone calls and get things going for our efforts to rescue Conway.*

February 5, 1997; Rancho Tierra Del Sol Chihuahua, Mexico

Like Roger Grey, John Conway, a time zone away, had not slept much either. In fact, what little sleep he did get on the bare mattress was fitful and full of terrorizing dreams. The simple dingy woolen blanket was insufficient against the cold night air. When he did drift off to sleep, he would wake either shaking from the chill of the room or a bad dream. During the course of the night, his mental outlook continued on the shifting path it had taken since his abduction. One minute he would be brave and resolute, and then he would lapse into despair and self-pity. During these periods of self-empathy, he chided himself for not being brave. *Have to get hold of myself. Things will work out, and I'll soon be home with Emily and the grandkids.* The thought of his wife and grandkids sent him into another fit of anguish, which frequently caused him to weep silently. Eventually, he would realize that feeling sorry for himself could do no good, and he would snap out of his funk. *Maybe the comandante is right and the AG will do whatever these guys demand. After all, they've never had a person of my stature taken hostage, and it would bode poorly for something bad to happen to me if the Administration refused to deal with these people.*

As light began to creep through the cracks between the plywood covering the single window and with the sound of a rooster outside, Conway realized it was morning. At least he had survived the night.

Conway sat on the mattress with his back against the wall and the blanket pulled up just under his chin. He had dozed slightly but woke to the sound of the door being unlocked. It opened just slightly, and in the limited light, he saw an arm extend into the room and deposit a plate of food and a bottle of water on the floor to the right of the door. The door closed again.

Slowly, he discarded the blanket and rose from the mattress. At the door, he bent down and retrieved the plate of food. It was surprisingly warm to the touch and contained some type of eggs covered with a red sauce. Two tortillas and refried beans were also on the plate. He returned to the mattress with the plate and the bottle of water. When he sat back down, he realized he had no utensils for the eggs. *I guess they don't trust me with anything sharp.* Scooping some of the eggs into a folded tortilla, he took a bite. Instantly, his mouth was on fire, and he frantically spit out what was left of the eggs while at the same time he reached for the water bottle. A long swig of the water tempered the burning sensation in his mouth. He decided to eat only the tortillas. *Apparently, they don't intend to starve me to death.*

As the day progressed, Conway attempted to tune his sense of hearing to any outside ambient noise. He heard muffled sounds of conversation coming from within the house, and what little he could actually hear, was in Spanish, which he did not understand. He also heard heavy trucks or farm machinery at a distance.

He estimated it to be around noon when he heard the distinct sound of several vehicles arriving, followed by someone speaking loudly in Spanish. Judging from the tone of the voice, this person was someone of authority and the person or persons he addressed had done something to irritate him. A few minutes later, the door of his room opened and the comandante entered the room. The comandante wore the same dark sunglasses to obscure his eyes, which Conway assumed was to prevent him from subsequently identifying him.

The comandante looked at the unfinished plate of eggs. "Señor, you don't like our food?"

"Too spicy, just too hot for my tastes, sorry."

"I understand. I shall have them bring you something less hot. Listen, mi amigo, I have come here today to offer you the opportunity to seek your release," began the comandante with a slight smile developing on his heavily pitted face. "If you cooperate, you should be able to return to Los Estados Unidos – the United States unharmed. If you do not cooperate, I cannot guarantee that other more painful methods might be used. Do you understand?"

"What is it that you want me to do?"

"I want for you to state our demands directly to your government in a way that will leave no doubt that we currently have you as our guest and are very serious about our demands."

"And how are we going to do this, Comandante?"

"I want for you to make a videotape which will state our demands to your government. This video will be sent to a television station which will show it to the world and hopefully the right people will act in accordance with our wishes."

"And if they don't?" asked Conway tentatively, fearful of the answer.

"Then, Señor, I will go to what you gringos call Plan B. I'll cut off your pinche fingers and send them, one at a time, to your government."

A cold gut-wrenching fear instantly consumed Conway, and he shivered before he could answer.

"Okay, let's make this video."

"Some rules first, Señor."

"Okay," replied Conway quickly nodding his head in ascent.

"You shall read from a prepared script. If you change this script in anyway, I shall stop the video, and we'll think of another way of convincing your government of our demands."

Conway nodded his head in agreement indicating he understood the ground rules.

"To show we are people of compassion, we shall allow you to tell your family that you are safe and are being well treated. Understand?"

"Yes, yes, I understand. Thank you for your, uh, compassion."

"Once again, I must warn you, Señor. Do not attempt to do anything foolish. If you follow our script, you shall not be harmed."

Conway nodded his head in agreement again. He hoped the AG would accede to their demands.

It took the better part of an hour to arrange the location for the videotape. During this time, Conway read over the script. The first time he read it, he choked up with emotion when he read about telling his wife, who was unnamed in the script, that he was fine and was being treated fairly. Composing himself, he began to think *I need some way to indicate that my treatment is contrary to what I am saying on the video. Hopefully they will realize that they must heed the demands of these people or I will be harmed. I will taint my statement with false information about my family. I hope these kidnappers don't have my correct family information.*

February 5, 1997; DEA Headquarters, Alexandria, Virginia

Roger Grey loosened his tie and sat back in his high-backed leather chair at his office desk. He closed his eyes, which burned from lack of sleep, and sat like this for several minutes trying to collect his thoughts. *Time's a wasting* he concluded sitting upright. He tapped a letter opener on the desk and suddenly felt the tension of all that he had to do in a short period of time. *I have to get this Mobile Task Force Up and Running. At least create the illusion that it will be doing something to help locate and free Conway and not tip my hand that we have good information on his whereabouts. While at the same time, I have to get Tom and his team moving toward Mexico. Time is definitely of the essence here. Who knows how long the Mexicans will hold Conway at Janos.*

He summoned several of his project coordinators into his office. While these coordinators would organize the creation of the proposed Task Force, they would not be privy to the actions of Tom's team. "Go over to operations and look at the records of how Operation Leyenda was set up. Operation Leyenda was the MTF set up during Kiki's abduction. I want this MTF set up the same way with the financing in position to fund travel and other expenses by the end of the day. And we need to name it. Any suggestions?"

"How about Operation? Who gives a shit anyway?" quipped one senior agent.

Drawing chuckles from the other program coordinators and even a smile from Roger he cautioned, "Okay, enough of that crap. I know Conway is not the most popular guy here in DEA, but let's try to forget about him personally and concentrate on what these assholes have done. They killed two agents and abducted the Administrator right here in the United States, not in Colombia or Mexico, but in the United States," Roger emphasized by raising his voice. "Okay, any other suggestions?"

"How about Operation Reckoning?" suggested another coordinator.

"That's better," advised Roger. "Maybe we could soften it a little with the Spanish word for reckoning. Anybody know that word?"

"Calculos," replied another coordinator.

"I like that. Let's go with that for now." Roger stood up to signal the meeting was over.

Roger's next item of business was to place a call to the Special Agent in Charge of the El Paso Intelligence Center (EPIC) in El Paso, Texas. This call resulted in the agreement that EPIC would provide space to house the task force. The Special Agent in Charge also volunteered several of his intelligence analysts to begin research on all information and intelligence that Task Force members might generate. Next, Roger dictated teletypes to send out to solicit all information regarding John Conway's abduction. They would forward this information to the Task Force. Another teletype dictated to the Special Agents in Charge of all DEA Divisions requested that they make personnel available to staff the task force.

Confident that his program coordinators had the Mobile Task Force under control, Roger turned to his more pressing concern – to get Tom Blaine and his team to Mexico to rescue Conway. First, he placed a phone call to his CIA contact and requested satellite imagery of the Janos area. This would give the team an up-to-date lay of the land they would be encountering. Of course, Roger would have to hide his real objective by requesting imagery of several areas in Northern Mexico suspected of being staging and shipment areas of large quantities of drugs destined for the United States. Always amused that the CIA personnel merely answered their phones with their phone number, Roger did likewise. "Good Morning 2112, this is 3314. So, 2112, how are you, this fine day?"

The CIA person on the other end of the line recognized Roger's voice and knew his propensity for humor. "It's a secret, Roger, and if I told you, I'd have to kill you."

"I see," said Roger chuckling.

"What can the agency do for DEA today, Roger?" The CIA person, whose real name was Charles "Chas" Wrigley, no relation to the chewing gum company, had known Roger Grey since Vietnam days when Roger was an Army Special Forces Officer and Chas was an Operative in the Central Highlands of Vietnam working with the Montagnards.

"I need a favor. We have received some recent intelligence that several Mexican ranches close to the Texas and Arizona borders are being used as staging areas for large quantities of cocaine. Can you reorient a satellite and give me some coverage of the Janos, Agua Prieta and just west of Juarez areas.

"I think we can accommodate that. How soon do you need it, Roger?"

"Yesterday would have been good," replied Roger.

"Day and a half is the best I can do right now. We've got a whole bunch of requests for coverage farther south that has to be done first."

"Are you sure you can't do anything sooner? It's kind of important, Chas," asked Roger.

"Important like what's going on in the news important?" asked Chas.

"Could be, Chas," said Roger.

"Okay, late tomorrow is the best I can do,"

"Chas, that would be great. You doing okay?"

"Good days and bad days, Roger. This cold weather wreaks havoc with my back."

Images of the man he was talking with, sitting in his wheel chair, came to mind. He knew his friend had been confined to the chair since Vietnam. "Man, why don't you take a medical? You were seriously injured in Nam, and they'll have to do right by you."

"Yeah, I know, but I'd miss this if I retired. I know riding a desk is not like operating in the field, but at least I am doing something."

"I guess I can understand that. I'd miss the job too much if I had to quit right now myself. Well, you take care and let me know as soon as you have those pictures okay?"

"Ten-four, Roger."

Roger glanced at his watch and decided to kill two birds with one stone. He would make his next call from a pay phone in the mall across the street and get a bite to eat at the same time. Exiting the DEA building, Roger began to question his decision to eat out. The weather had turned frigid, and it was beginning to spit a combination of sleet and snow. He pulled his insulated trench coat up around his neck and bowed his head into the slight wind. With sleet stinging his face, he plunged forward toward the mall across the street from DEA HQs. *I sure wish I could make this phone call from my desk using my personal calling card, but if they ever started checking, they'd discover my long distance calls that would surely sink my career.*

The warmth of the mall not only transformed his physical half-frozen self, but also, energized his spirit. With a spring in his step, he set out to find a pay phone. He found one in a somewhat secluded alcove off the main row of stores. Roger pulled a roll of quarters and his small personal phone book from the pocket of his suit coat. He dialed the phone number of the calling center in New York. Roger waited until the recorded voice instructed him to deposit the amount of change to complete the call. Once connected with the call center, Roger provided his account number and then gave the number he wished to reach. Roger waited to be connected. *Just like the Colombians, I can use this phone service without my long distance phone calls being traced.* When the secret operations ended in Mexico last year, Roger had kept the phone service active paying for it monthly with funds wired from a bank account. By using this service, he could conceal his real calls and any record would reflect only calls to a local number in New York. It would be a good way to contact Tom in Mexico.

When his call was connected, an automated voice solicited his account number and required him to answer a series of security questions. When this was completed, the automated voice advised him to stay on the line for the next available customer representative. A Brahms piece entertained Roger while he waited. *Better than that freaking Barry Manilow,* thought Roger as he listened to the music. After several minutes, Roger heard a few clicks on the other end of the line and then a distinctly British accent came on. "How may the Bank of Grand Cayman help you today, sir?"

"I need to know the balance in the numbered account that I just gave you."

Several seconds later, the British accent answered, "The account has a balance of $1,557,231.22 US."

"Thank you, my good man," said Roger.

"Can I be of further service to you, sir?" asked the British accent.

"Yes. How long does it take to wire money from this account to another account?"

"One business day, sir," answered the British accent.

"Thank you," said Roger. *Man, that's a lot more money in that account. A lot more than I thought,* decided Roger. *My math really sucks.*

Even though Roger had to brave a driving snowstorm on his walk back to DEA HQs, he was somewhat oblivious to the conditions. Instead, the fact that he had the necessary money needed to fund the covert mission to send Tom's team into Mexico seemed to warm Grey. As he stepped into an elevator in the DEA HQS, he decided to forward funds this evening.

February 5, 1997; DEA Los Angeles, California

Tossing yet another signed DEA 6 (DEA's Report of Investigation form, also known as a 6), into his out basket, Tom glanced at his watch. His frustration grew with each passing hour. *Come on, Roger. Christ, it's noon already back there in D.C.* He hadn't been able to reach Roger to get the okay to start contacting the former members of his Snow Cap team. Tom hoped they were all up for another covert venture into Mexico. He had started calling Roger's office at 6:00 a.m. LA time, 9:00 a.m. in DC. Each time Roger's administrative assistant told him that Roger was not in his office. He had also paged Roger several times but had yet to receive a response. Tom knew Roger had a scheduled meeting at the AG's office this morning. "That meeting should be over by now. Check your pager, Roger. I'll bet you forgot to turn the damned thing on again."

"Talking to yourself again, boss?" asked Hawk as he sauntered into Tom's office. Hawk, dressed in his Beverly Hills undercover garb of light green silk shirt, brown slacks and Gucci loafers, had accessorized his attire with a large gold serpentine necklace and rings of gold and multi-colored stones on most of his fingers. "If you start answering yourself, you might want to consider some professional help," he continued as he slipped into a chair in front of Tom's desk.

Irritated and somewhat embarrassed at being caught talking to himself Tom responded. "Ever hear of knocking before entering your superior's office, Hawk, or," after looking him over in his undercover attire, "is it Chad today?"

Hawk looked down at his clothes. "You like?" Then raising his head, he made eye contact with Tom. "I'm supposed to be a minor movie producer. Later on this afternoon, I'm meeting some people who allegedly supply the industry with cocaine over at Señor Pico's in Century City. According to the CI, they're tied directly to a Colombian source."

"Movie producer, huh?" Tom snorted. "You look more like a minor gay porn star."

"One would only wonder how it is that you'd know what a gay porn star would look like, boss." A smirk developed on Hawk's face.

Hesitating just slightly, Tom smiled. "Okay, Chad, enough of this bullshit. How much is this lunch at Señor Pico's going to cost the taxpayers?"

"I'd like to buy a couple of ounces just to show them I'm serious."

"Again I ask, Chad, how much is this going to cost Uncle Sam?"

"Five thousand, twenty-five hundred for each ounce," answered Hawk.

"Let's just do one ounce right now, and if it's good, we'll do more later."

"Aw, man, I need to do more than an ounce to get them to deal with me, boss. They wanted to do a half a k to start," said Hawk with his voice developing a slight whine.

"CI set up the deal, didn't he, Hawk?"

"Well yeah, but I still…" began Hawk before Tom interrupted him.

"Use some of your minor movie producing skills to convince them that you want to do an ounce first to see how good the stuff really is. If it's as good as they say, then we'll do something larger on the next buy."

Hawk sighed. "Okay, I'll call the CI back and tell him to have the crooks bring an ounce." Somewhat dejected, Hawk stood and turned to exit the office.

"Wait, Hawk." Rising from his desk Tom strode to the office door and shut it."

"Uh, oh, I'm in trouble," commented Hawk as Tom walked back to his desk.

Taking a seat, Tom gestured for Hawk to do likewise. "No, you're not in any trouble that I know of. But then the day is still early," answered Tom humorously. "Hawk, I need to talk to you about one of your CIs. But what I am about to tell you will not leave this office. Should you go blab what I have to say to you, I'll deny I ever said it, and I'll make sure you'll do your next undercover assignments in the Bronx, Brooklyn, Manhattan, Staten Island or Queens. Understand?"

Hawk nodded his head. "Yeah, boss, I understand."

"After our deal down in Orange County last night, I came back here to the office to secure the flash roll and was at my desk when I answered the phone. The caller wanted to talk with you."

"With me?" asked a puzzled Hawk.

"Yes, the caller was an old CI you've not heard from in several months. In fact, we had a conversation about him when I took over the group."

"Juan Cervantes?" asked Hawk with the surprise evident in his tone. "I guess he's heard about his indictment and he wants to cooperate now."

"Oh, he's heard about his indictment and yes he wants to cooperate. And man does he have some good information."

"Figures. What kind of information?" asked Hawk.

"More about that in a minute. But first I need to tell you something." Taking a large breath, Tom continued. "Hawk, what I didn't tell you when we talked about Juan Cervantes was that he and I have a history. In fact, I am probably the person responsible for him coming to DEA in the first place."

"Okay," Hawk said with hesitation, "but what do you mean you have a history?"

"This is where it gets a bit dicey, Hawk. And again, if you ever repeat what I tell you here, I'll deny it and then use my influence to make your career take a very unpleasant turn."

"Okay, Tom." Hawk was getting annoyed with Tom's repeating the conditions under which he was going to tell him something. "I understood the first time you warned me."

"Good. I just wanted to make sure I was clear." Tom then went on to detail how he and his Snow Cap team had been operating without DEA's knowledge in Mexico and how he had met Juan when his team raided Miguel Uriate's estanica in an effort to save Marcos Rodriguez who had been grabbed by Uriate's men from a downtown street in Guadalajara. They had not been successful and Marcos was dead by the time they entered the estancia. Juan worked for Miguel Felix-Uriarte in the same role as he currently was for Jaime Gutiérrez. At Tom's direction, Juan had emptied out Uriarte's foreign bank accounts transferring the money to offshore undercover accounts. Tom allowed him to leave the estancia with a large canvas bag of cash and advised him to make his way to the states and become a CI. He could identify numerous real estate holdings in the United States that could be seized. However, Jaime Gutierrez had forced Juan to return to Mexico by threatening to have his brother and family killed if he did not. He had been working for him since.

The astonished look on Hawk's face revealed his feelings. "Jesus, Tom, I can't believe this. It's something out of a novel not real life DEA. How did you get away with this? Weren't you afraid you'd get caught?"

"Hawk, those are all good questions which I'd rather not answer right now because of the others involved. I'm only cutting you in on this information because I couldn't just sit on the information that Juan Cervantes told me last evening."

The raised eyebrows and the penetrating eyes revealed that Tom had Hawk's full attention.

"Hawk, Juan knows where John Conway is?"

"What?" exclaimed Hawk with an elevated voice.

"Shh," cautioned Tom.

"Uh, sorry," said Hawk in a softer voice. "He knows where Conway is being held? How does he know that?"

"According to Juan, Jaime Gutiérrez orchestrated the kidnapping. He plans to hold Conway as ransom for his brother Hector who is being held at Terminal Island awaiting trial. Conway supposedly is at a ranch near Janos, Mexico, just south of Douglas, Arizona. When Hector is returned to Mexico, Jaime will release the Administrator."

"Yeah, I'll bet," said Hawk sarcastically.

"My thoughts exactly. That is why I have made some phone calls, and I'm planning to get the Administrator myself without DEA or anybody else's knowledge before Gutiérrez can kill him. If we wait until the FBI and all the other bureaucrats involved get this information and take action, Conway will be dead."

"I agree, Tom, but I don't know how you're going to do this?"

"I'm going to do it the same way I did Uriarte, with a few select agents who accompanied me from Bolivia into Mexico. I intend to free the Administrator."

Hawk thought for several seconds during which he stared first at Tom then down at his lap and then back at Tom. "Count me in, boss."

"Hawk, I wasn't telling you all this to get you to volunteer but only to advise you because I know if Juan calls and can't get in touch with me, he'll probably ask for you."

"I understand, but I want to be part of this, Tom. Damn it. I feel the same way you do, and besides, he's *my* informant and I have a right to act on his information.

"Even if it could mean the end of your career and maybe prison if we get caught?" Before Hawk could respond, Tom added, "Or you could get killed in the process; you know, that happened in Guadalajara last year."

"I understand that, boss. But I still want in. Hell, I'm just as apt to get killed doing surveillance on these crazy LA highways anyway," Hawk said. "But I can be of assistance to you. No, I was not Snow Cap trained, but like you, I was in the Marine Corps and spent most of my career in the second Recon Battalion. I saw combat in the liberation of Kuwait and the first Gulf War. Furthermore, I speak fluent Spanish like a native speaker."

"You speak fluent Spanish, Hawk?" asked Tom.

"Tom, my Dad worked for Trans-American Fruit, and I spent the first fourteen years of my life in Colombia."

"I didn't know that. How come I never hear you speaking in Spanish, Hawk?"

"I use my Spanish when I need to. Most of the time I just like to play the dumb gringo role and listen to what others say about me in Spanish. Tom, I want to be a part of this, and like I said, I can help."

"You understand you'll not get any credit if we are successful, and you'll probably never be able to talk about it in the future."

"I understand, and I want in."

"Okay, Hawk, but the final decision is not up to me. I'll talk to the man in charge and let you know."

"How soon will you know, boss?"

"I hope within the next couple of hours."

February 5, 1997; Hacienda Puesta Del Sol, La Cruz, Sinaloa, Mexico

"Buenos Dios, Comandante," said Juan when the comandante came on the line. "Como está usted?"

"Hola, Juan. Is Don Jaime available?"

"Sí, Comandante. I will get him for you." Juan's cowboy boots clicked on the Saltillo tiles as he approached the bathroom down the hall where he knew Jaime had spent the last half hour. Juan knocked softly on the rough wood-paneled door. "Don Jaime, are you here?"

"Sí, Juan, what is so important you need to bother me?"

Juan figured Jaime was suffering with an upset stomach from that lousy fish the night before at Los Bandidos. "Don Jaime, I have the comandante on the phone."

"Carajo! Tell the comandante I will be right with him."

Returning to the office, Juan picked up the phone again. "Comandante, Don Jaime will be here shortly." Then daring the opportunity, he asked, "Did all go as planned?"

The comandante didn't hesitate to report. "Sí, Juan, we were able to make a good video of the pinche Jefe de DEA." The comandante laughed.

"That is good; here's Don Jaime, Comandante." Juan handed the phone to a pale-faced Jaime.

Jaime dismissed any attempts at cordiality. "Comandante, I hope you have some good news for me."

"Sí, Don Jaime. The DEA Jefe, after considering my options," he began which he followed with a short laugh, "he decided to keep his fingers and made the video using the script that the licenciado prepared."

"That is good," said Jaime somewhat distracted by an apparent cramping in his abdomen. "Look I don't feel too well right now; can I call you back shortly."

"Sí, Don Jaime, but all I need to know is what to do with the video. Should I bring it there or forward it to that television station in Los Angeles?"

Juan knew Jaime was in deep distress and needed to make an immediate return to the bathroom. He decided to interject his thoughts into the conversation and at the same time more or less confirm the DEA Jefe's location. "Perdone, Don Jaime. Why don't you have the comandante deliver the video to Ramon? He is up there in Juarez. Ramon could make a copy, which the comandante could bring back here. If after viewing it you approve,

Ramon can arrange to have it delivered to the television station in LA. Ramon has enough sense on how to do this without it being traced back to Mexico."

The comandante liked Juan's idea. "Sí, Don Jaime, I could do that. Like Juan said, Ramon is close by."

"Sí, you do that, Comandante." With pain written all over Jaime's face, he dropped the phone, grabbed his stomach and immediately ran out of the office.

The heels of Don Jaime's cowboy boots echoed as he fled down the hallway tiles. Juan smiled to himself. "Comandante, Don Jaime is not feeling well. I think he ate some bad fish last evening."

"Ah. Don Jaime and his fish. I'm glad I had the carnitas."

"Comandante, shall I call Ramon and have him make the arrangements for copying the video?"

"Sí, Juan. I would appreciate that. Give me Ramon's number, and I will head that way right now."

"Can I tell him how long it will be, Comandante?"

"Tell him I'll be there in a little over an hour."

"Sí, Comandante." Juan smiled to himself knowing now that his guess of the location was right. Juan placed a phone call to Ramon and advised him to expect a call from the comandante.

"I shall see that it is hand delivered to KTLA in Los Angeles as soon as Don Jaime approves it," Ramon said. "Assure Don Jaime there will be no way its origin can be traced."

February 5, 1997; DEA Headquarters, Alexandria, Virginia

"It's about time, Roger," said an exasperated Tom Blaine. He stood up at his desk and threw his pen down in disgust. "I've been going crazy here waiting for you to return my call."

Tom's irritated demeanor instantly put Roger on the defensive. "Take your damn pack off, Blaine." Roger regretted losing his patience with his good friend and softened his tone. "Look, buddy, I've been kind of busy since that early morning call of yours. I had a morning meeting at the AG's office and then I had to put together a task force to deal with Conway's abduction. And, oh yeah, I had to make some long distance calls that I couldn't make from my office, if you get my drift. So spare me the bullshit about sitting there going crazy."

Tom regretted venting his frustrations on probably the one person who did not need the acrimony right now. "Sorry, Roger. But I've been sitting here all morning with all sorts of plans and contingencies running through my head."

"I understand that. If I had not been so busy myself, I would have probably been just as frustrated as you, Tom."

"So what do you think, Roger? Are we good to go on this?"

"Let's not speak in specifics on these government lines. You never know who's listening. But in answer to your question, yes, I think we have the funds to do something. One of the things that I did this morning was to check to see if there was any money left over after your last trip. There's about a million and a half in the offshore account."

"Really? I thought all that was doled out last year, Roger."

"I did too, but I wanted to keep a small amount in the account in case we needed it again in the future. My bad math, plus I forgot about the very lucrative interest rates, and low and behold, we have sufficient money."

"That's great, Roger. I think that should be more than enough. I'd like to start calling some of the old team members and see if they want to play."

"Go for it, Tom. But if you call from your office, I recommend you be very careful."

"I thought I'd use a pay phone somewhere, or I'll go to my motel and use that phone. I can put the calls on my calling card."

"Wait, Tom. Use this number." Roger reached for his personal phone book and read the number to Tom. "It's one of those calling center numbers in New York that the traffickers up there use. There's no way to trace a call using this. It's pre-paid; I'll put more money on the account if necessary."

"Thanks. What about equipment, Roger? Is any of that special equipment available?"

"When we ceased operations down south, I had all the equipment moved to Homestead Air Force Base in Florida. It's in storage there. It includes the NEC Digital Satellite phones too."

"Good, that will make communications a lot easier."

"I'm going out and buying another one for my use. I'll let you know the number so when you are operative, you can call me on that."

"Okay, Roger. Let me start calling the guys; I'll get back to you and let you know who's in. Oh, by the way, I had to take one of the agents in my group into our confidence."

Roger paused a moment before speaking again. "You think that's wise, Tom?"

"Yeah, I think it's okay. He's the agent who was working the CI. I can't be sure that when the CI calls he will ask for him if I'm not here. Besides, once I told him the situation, he wanted in."

"Oh?"

"Yeah, but you wouldn't like him; he's a former Marine."

"Wonderful, another stubborn jarhead." Roger gave a short chuckle.

"Another stubborn jarhead who is whiter than you but speaks Spanish like a native."

"Really?"

"Yeah, he spent the first fourteen years of his life in Colombia. His language and recon skills might be very helpful, Roger."

"And you're confident we can trust him to keep his mouth shut?" asked Roger.

"Yeah, I am. He seems to be a standup guy so far."

"Okay, call me at home tonight and let me know how you make out with the calls. Once I know who is in I'll start arranging legitimate travel arrangements to El Paso."

"El Paso? Why El Paso, Roger?"

"That's where the special Task Force is being formed to investigate the kidnapping. If the team members you contact want to play, have their SAC send a reply to the teletype that went out today soliciting volunteers to staff the task force. I can use legitimate travel appropriations to fund their travel there. Once there, you can decide on whatever accommodations you need and how you want to operate."

"Okay, I'll call you tonight."

February 5, 1997; DEA Los Angeles, California

Using his calling card through the New York call center, Tom placed a call to the first former Snow Cap team member from a pay phone on the ground level of the LA World Trade Center. This first call was to an agent he considered his number one priority. Antonio "Tony" Gonzalo, thirty-eight years old, divorced and of Puerto Rican descent, currently worked in the Miami Office. Tom had done two Snow Cap tours in Peru with Tony, and he had proven to be a brave and capable leader during several firefights with the Sendero Luminoso. And more importantly, he had been a bright, courageous and unflappable back-up leader during the Snow Cap operation in Mexico last March, especially during the attempt to rescue Marcus Rodriguez from Uriarte's estancia. Tom considered the thirteen-year DEA veteran, a friend as well as an associate. Tom wanted Tony not only as a team member, but more importantly, for his cool and calm manner under combat conditions. The Antonio Banderas look-alike, a graduate of the University of Miami, had played varsity soccer until a knee injury ended his scholarship and any hope of playing professional soccer. Called to active duty as an officer in the Florida National Guard for combat service in Iraq, he later won the Attorney General's Award for Heroism for actions in Peru.

When Tom explained in general terms what he and Roger wanted to accomplish, Tony uttered only two words. "I'm in."

Tom breathed a huge sigh of relief. "Good, Tony. I need you as my back up."

"I'll have my SAC send a teletype today," he volunteered, "and I'll wait for further instructions from you."

"I'll call you sometime later this evening with the details."

As Tom waited for his next call to be completed, he couldn't help but smile when the face of Rick Lansky, aka "Godzilla," visualized in his mind. The high forehead and deep-set dark brown eyes accompanied by the Fu Manchu mustache gave Lansky a permanent menacing look. Lansky received his nickname, Godzilla, while in basic agent training because of his six-foot-four stature and his naturally intimidating look. Lansky, a DEA agent for seven years, was a thirty-four-year-old former Army Ranger and had extensive combat experience in Iraq. He had done one of his four Snow Cap tours on Tom's team in Peru, and, of course, had demonstrated his courage under fire in the attempt to rescue Marcus Rodriguez last March. If he had a negative quality it was that he subscribed to his own theory about drug dealers. "Shoot em all, and let God sort it out." His quickness on the trigger certainly saved some lives at Uriarte's hacienda. He was fearless and aggressive, just what Tom knew he needed on this upcoming caper. He was currently assigned to the Chicago field division.

"How would you like to get out of the cold for a while?" Tom asked as Lansky answered the phone.

"Do I get to shoot someone," he asked in his usual jovial way.

"I wouldn't rule it out this time," said Tom.

"Count me in. I'll have my Group Supervisor talk to the SAC as soon as I hang up."

"I'll call with details tonight," advised Tom.

Over the next several hours, attempts to reach former team members failed. It wasn't until after 3:00 p.m. that he reached the next prospective team member, Brian Hood. Hood, a six-year DEA veteran who had done five Snow Cap tours, was a former Navy Seal. At five-foot-ten and solidly built, the quiet and unimposing Hood was true to his Navy Seal heritage, fearless. Like Godzilla, Hood had demonstrated his innate courage during the attempt to rescue Marcus Rodriguez, but Hood had also shown his expertise in explosives.

"Brian, it's Tom Blaine. How goes it? Have you been staying out of trouble?" asked Tom. His question about staying out of trouble was in direct reference to an incident in which he punched out his ex-wife's divorce attorney following a court proceeding.

"Hi, Tom," Brian said. "Got a reduced sentence. Her attorney realized that if I had been convicted of assault, I would have lost my job and been unable to pay spousal support or her attorney's fees."

Tom knew that DEA, on the other hand, had suspended him for forty-five days; it was his belief the Administrator wanted him fired from DEA.

"Yeah, I've been keeping kind of a low profile here at DEA since I got back from Iraq."

"I hadn't heard you were in Iraq, Brian?"

"Yeah, did a six month active duty stint with a SEAL team right after we got back from down south. I'm still in the active reserves. In fact, if Conway has his way, and they fire me, I plan to go back to the regulars."

"Speaking of Conway, Brian, how would you like to play a role in rescuing him?"

"Shit, Tom, I'm not sure I'd want to rescue that bastard." Brian laughed. "I don't understand, Tom? How can I play a role in his rescue?"

"I can't go into details on these phones, but if you're interested, I can give you the details tonight. By the way, your favorite Army Ranger said to say hello. He's in."

"If he's in, so am I, Tom."

"Good, Brian; I can really use your talents on this thing. I need your SAC to send a teletype indicating you are volunteering for the task force that's looking into Conway's abduction. I'll call you tonight, and we can talk more freely."

"I'll be waiting."

Tom hung up the phone and made a quick mental count. "That's four," he said aloud.

His assistant advised him there was a call holding on line two.

"Blaine."

"No hello or good afternoon? Just your damned name. Where did you learn your telephone etiquette, Blaine?"

Tom immediately recognized the voice of Wyman Hayes. "I save the etiquette for important people or my friends."

"In that case, it's only for important people, cause you sure as shit ain't got any friends, Blaine."

Tom chuckled. "Okay, now that we've got the necessary insults out of the way, how you doing, Wyman?"

"I'm okay. But I sure hate being here in Atlanta. The white folk here just don't seem to believe that some Negro can actually fly an airplane. I'm always getting the intense questions on where I learned to fly."

"Want a chance to get away for a while and do something for me?"

"What you got in mind, Tom?"

"I can't go into it right now, but I need your aeronautical skills on something similar to what we did last year. You up for it?"

"By the way you're asking, can I assume this flying could get me into a whole heap of trouble?"

"Well, Wyman, what happened to your military career when you flew that F-16 Air Force jet under those high tension wires in the California desert, Wyman?"

"It fucked my career."

"Well, the flying I might need could have that same effect and could also pose some serious risks to your personal self."

"Would these risks be about the same as when we did our thing last year then?" asked Wyman.

"That would be a yes, Wyman."

"So who else would be involved in this caper?"

"Tony, God and Brian have agreed so far."

Wyman needed no more information. "If those guys are in, so am I.

"Can you answer me one quick question, Tom?"

"Sure, Wyman. I'll try."

"Are we going after *him*?"

"Yep, that's my plan."

"Okay, I'll wait for your call tonight."

After hanging up, Tom sat at his desk and pondered his prior association with the feisty and sometimes acerbic Hayes. Thirty-five-year-old Wyman had been with DEA for seven years. An Air Force Academy graduate had, on several occasions, backed up his braggadocio claims that he could fly any type of aircraft. Tom recalled that during a Snow Cap tour, he had taken the controls of a Peruvian helicopter when the pilot had suffered a fatal heart attack. He skillfully flew the helicopter and its passengers of DEA agents and Peruvian military back to their base of operations. Then in Mexico last year, he had flown a King Air, an aircraft he had never flown before, off a dirt strip that he had also never done before. He did this while being shot at by heavily armed drug traffickers. To top this, he had come to the rescue of the team trying to save Marcus Rodriguez at Uriarte's estancia, whisking them away from heavily armed pursuers in a Huey helicopter he had "borrowed" from a local airport. A self-professed computer expert, he used his skills to access Uriarte's foreign bank accounts and relieve him of his vast wealth transferring the money to their undercover account in the Cayman Islands. Hayes, fearless when it came to flying, would be a great addition to the team.

With Hayes volunteering, Tom had just one more person to contact, Kristin Hammond. Kris, an old friend of Tom's, had done two of her four Snow Cap tours with him in Peru. An attractive bodybuilding brunette had just completed seven years with DEA. From having been raised a single girl with five older brothers, this thirty-year-old was not intimidated by her male counterparts. She had demonstrated that on a number of occasions where she showed she could be gutsy and not afraid to use her sexuality to accomplish a task suited for flaunting her physical attributes. She could, however, easily become a supervisor's migraine headache if a tight rein was not maintained on her proclivity to target and seduce males she thought were good looking. There had been one such instance during their last Snow Cap tour when she had slept with a team member. This other team member wanted to develop a deeper relationship with Kris, but in her words, she was just "sport fucking," and did not "desire or need" a repeat episode. But Kris' demonstrated courage in Mexico last year made her a definite advantage to have on the team.

A knock on his office doorframe interrupted Tom's recollection of Hammond's antics while in Bolivia. The massive figure of Jason Wycoff, the one former team member Tom had not sought to include on this team, filled his doorway. A former all-American middle linebacker at Tennessee, Wycoff had been with DEA for six years and had done three Snow Cap tours. Known by the nickname of tree because he was built like a mighty oak, he had been a captain in the Marine Corps before coming to DEA. It was rumored he left the Marine Corps because he had been told that he lacked the intelligence to be promoted above captain. Tom had decided not to approach Wycoff about this mission because during his prior encounters with him, Tom had decided he was, indeed, not the "sharpest chisel in the tool chest." In fact, Tom and the other team members shared the common fear that the tree might someday inadvertently say the wrong thing to somebody about their exploits in Mexico against Uriarte and cause career-ending problems or jail. Besides that, he was the person who had fallen in lust with Kris. When she rejected him after their night of passion, he had become antagonistic toward her, causing her to respond with snide remarks in the company of other team members about his male anatomy and prowess. The encounter caused some initial friction between them, but Tom had nipped it in the bud. "I'll send you both home if you don't knock it off."

"Got a minute, Tom?" asked the Tree tentatively.

"Sure, Jason. Come on in; have a seat," said Tom pointing to a chair in front of his desk. "What's up?"

"Tom, I just got off the phone with God; he asked me if I was going to be involved in a special thing with some of the old Snow Cap Team."

Instantly the irritation with Lansky and his big mouth manifested itself within Tom. But before he could respond, Tree continued. "He didn't say what you guys were going to do, just that it was all hush-hush. But if it's like last year, I'd like to be involved."

"Jason," Tom began trying to pick the right words, "I wasn't going to ask you cause I know you're getting ready for the California Police Olympics. A third gold medal in the power lifting would be unprecedented."

"Yeah, that would be nice, but I'd rather go with you and God and the guys and do whatever it is you're going to do."

Tom stared at Wycoff for several moments. He decided that if he didn't take Wycoff, he might cause more problems than if he went. "Tree," he began trying to choose his words carefully, "just like last year, this mission could be dangerous. It could ruin your career or you could end up in jail."

"I figured that, Tom. I also know you guys worried about me saying something about our mission last year, something that would get us all into trouble. I was worried too, so worried that I saw a therapist and using hypnosis I've been able to put that whole thing in Mexico behind me so that I don't even consider it anymore."

Tom sat upright in his chair. "Jesus, Jason. You saw a therapist and told him about our activities to Mexico."

Tree held his hands up in front of him. "No, Tom, I didn't say anything about Mexico. I told him nothing about Marcus's death that occurred in Bolivia. He just helped me forget about the circumstances surrounding Marcus's death."

Tom stared at Tree. He figured his back was up against a wall, a no-win situation. *If I tell him he can't go, he might blab it to everyone. And if I take Tree, there would be no guarantee he'd keep his mouth shut.* Right now, Tom would rather have him close so he could control him. He decided to include him but not give him any pertinent details until the very last minute.

"Okay, Jason, I'll take you with me. We'll be going to El Paso in the next day or so to be part of the Task Force that's investigating the abduction of the Administrator. I cannot emphasize the importance of not saying a word to anyone. Comprende?"

"Yes, Tom. I understand. And," Tree said as he stood to leave the office, "you won't be disappointed that you included me."

"I hope not, Tree," said Tom with just a touch of malice in his tone.

February 5, 1997; Hacienda Puesta Del Sol, La Cruz, Sinaloa, Mexico

"Esta bien," said Jaime. He clapped his hands together and smiled. "I like it." He whirled around from his stance in front of the projection screen that showed the frozen picture of John Conway. He faced the comandante and licenciado who sat behind him in the office. "Comandante, you did a very good job making this video. And, Licenciado, your script was very good. I like the personal touch at the end. It makes it more personal and should have an effect on those who will make the decision to trade mi hermano for the pinche DEA Jefe.

The comandante nodded his head in appreciation of the positive comments. "Gracias, Don Jaime. But it is mi teniente who deserves much of the credit. He is very good with the video, and we had a very willing subject."

"So he was cooperative then?" asked Jaime.

"Sí, Don Jaime, especially when I explained that he either make the video or I'd whack off his fingers instead and send them to his pinche government."

Jaime chuckled at this last remark by the comandante; Jaime noticed a frown on Licenciado's face. "Licenciado, you seem troubled. You did very good with the script, and the video is excellent. You should be smiling not wearing a frown."

"It's just…it's just that I am concerned about the DEA Jefe's location, Jaime. My sources in the government are already nervous about this matter, and if there is any way that the DEA Jefe's abduction can be traced to Mexico, they may be forced to take actions."

The anger instantly registered on Jaime's face. After an uncomfortable period of silence, Jaime broke the quiet. "Licenciado, tell me who is nervous, and I will take care of his nervousness permanently."

"Don Jaime, it is not just one person, but more like rumors circulating between the Minister of Justice and Minister of Defense's respective offices," advised the licenciado. The sweat broke out on his forehead.

"I guess it is time to send a strong signal then. Tell me, Licenciado, who would you recommend?"

Licenciado realized he would be signing their death warrant if he identified anyone with whom he had been talking to in the Minister of Justice and Minister of Defense's office. Licenciado attempted to downplay the role of his sources. "Jaime, there is no serious talk yet, just rumors as I have said. I don't believe there is a need to take any action right now."

Jaime stared at the licenciado for several uncomfortable moments. "I hope what you say is the truth, Licenciado. If I should hear contrary, I would be gravely disappointed with you."

"Sí, Sí, Jaime," offered a very nervous licenciado. "I promise if I hear anything that is something more than a rumor, I shall advise you immediately so that you can take the necessary steps to protect yourself."

"Bien, Licenciado, I shall trust you on this then."

Juan, who feigned distraction by working at his desk, listened to this contentious dialogue between Jaime and the licenciado. *The licenciado is a dead man. He just does not realize it. Jaime will not put up with him much longer unless he does something to prove himself to Jaime. Jaime seems to be itching to kill someone important just to prove that he has become a very powerful man. Perhaps with his focus on the licenciado, once Tom Blaine and his men act, maybe I can get away quickly with no suspicion directed at me.*

Jaime interrupted Juan's thoughts. "Juan. Oye, Juan."

"Lo Siento, Don Jaime. I was not paying attention to your meeting with the comandante and the licenciado. What can I do for you?"

"Juan, contact Ramon and have that video sent to the television station in Los Angeles right away. And see how long it will take him to do this. We are giving the gringos five days from the day they are notified of our demand to comply, or we shall begin to do something more serious than a video to prove our intent. I am anxious to get this started."

"Sí, Don Jaime, I will call Ramon right away. By the way, with the Norte Americano government slowing down all traffic into the States, we have product backing up at the staging areas. What should we do, Don Jaime? Should we wait or use some alternate method of moving the product?"

"To wait will cost too much money. Let us use the tunnel and move as much as we can that way."

"Sí, Don Jaime, I will so instruct our contacts. And I will contact Ramon right away."

An hour later, after completing a phone call to Ramon, Juan hung up the phone, and addressed Jaime who was in his usual spot in front of CNN. "Don Jaime, the video shall be delivered in a matter of hours to KTLA. Ramon took it on his own initiative to dispatch someone to Los Angeles with the video as soon as the comandante delivered it to him. Ramon said it would be there in several hours."

"Esta muy bien, Juan," said Jaime. "Tell Ramon he did good using his own initiative on not waiting to send it. It will speed up mi hermano's return to Mexico."

Juan knew he had to reach Blaine to tell him the location was definite.

February 5, 1997; Springfield, Virginia

Tom decided to call Roger from a pay phone in the Lobby of the Bonaventure Hotel, adjacent to the World Trade Center. He was anxious to get this organized and off the ground.

"So far, I've gotten commitments from Gonzalo, Hayes, Lansky, Hood," began Tom on the phone with Roger Grey. He hesitated slightly. "And Wycoff."

"Wycoff?" exclaimed Roger. "I thought, based on last year's concerns, we decided he couldn't be trusted to keep his mouth shut."

"Yeah, well, unfortunately he heard from that big mouth Lansky that I was putting together the old team; he came by my office to tell me he wanted in."

"Jesus, Tom, I just don't know about Wycoff," said a skeptical Roger.

"Listen, I think he'll be okay. He admitted to me that he had sought professional help concerning the death of Marcus. He claimed that with hypnosis he has been able to erase from his memory any of the details concerning Marcus' death in Mexico, at least the portion about Mexico anyway."

"He could sink us, Tom," said a somewhat defensive Roger.

"I know, but he could sink us also by not letting him join us. Let me worry about Wycoff. If I see a problem developing, I'll make sure he's isolated from anything we do, so he'll not be able to spill the beans."

"Okay, Tom, but it's on your head." After an uncomfortable pause in which neither he nor Tom spoke, Roger lightened the souring mood. "You haven't said a word about Hammond, Tom. Is she going to join you?"

"I don't know, Roger. I haven't been able to reach her at her office or home. She's evidently on some type of medical leave. I talked with her Group Secretary who would only say that she took some days to recover from a minor surgical procedure. Whatever the heck that means."

"Then I guess she's a no go; we need to get this thing going right now."

"I'm going to try one more time this evening. I still have her mother's number I had for her before we went to Mexico last year. Maybe she can shed some light on Krissy. If I can't reach her, we'll consider her out. But I hope I can; we might need a woman on this thing."

Tom changed the subject in hopes of stemming Roger's darkening mood. "So, Roger, how is this going to work, money wise and equipment?"

"Like last year, I can use Diversified." Roger's voice began to soften from its hardened quality.

"Diversified Exploration Associates?" Tom interrupted. "Do you think that's wise, Roger? I recall that McPherson guy from the bureau telling us the FBI was all over the bank account in Midland. They even contacted the mailbox storeowner who was forwarding the bank statements to Guatemala. Hell, he even correctly speculated that the Patricia Wright, who established the bank account and mail drop, was, in fact, Hammond.

Roger sighed heavily. "Yeah, you're right, Tom. And if you also recall, he had developed a lot of information regarding your team's activities in Mexico identifying several members, including yourself. But thankfully, what he had was mostly his own personal speculation, speculation that obviously did not make it into his official reports. I think if the bureau had solid evidence against Diversified and you, they would have acted by now. Besides, McPherson's no longer with the Bureau. He retired last November to accept a chief of police position back in the Midwest somewhere. I got a card from him at Christmas. So I think it's safe to use Diversified on a limited basis. And I guess we don't have the luxury of a lot of time to set up something new. I'll need a front business like Diversified to handle some of the logistics like plane and car rentals that will arise from our mission. Diversified will allow me the ability to wire money to pay for these things."

"Speaking of planes, I'd like to have an aircraft that can fly some distance if necessary, like the King Air we used last year. Hayes can fly one of those with no problem. If you'd like, I'll have him locate one; you can arrange for its rental or leasing, whatever it requires."

"Fly some distance? Why would that be necessary, Tom?" asked Roger. "I thought the CI said Conway was being held close to the Arizona border."

"Yes, but it might be necessary for us to fly south before we can turn north if we have to fly Conway out of Mexico or just plain escape. I want to cover most contingencies before we go south, and an aircraft that can easily accommodate long distance would be helpful. We both know from last year's experiences that the King Air is a good aircraft for that."

"Okay, Tom, have Haynes find us an aircraft and then have him let me know where to wire the money."

"Milton will be happy to hear that, Roger."

"Milton? Who the hell is Milton?"

"Milton Wojohowski," repeated Tom. "That's Hayes' undercover name." Tom chuckled at the thought of how outraged Hayes had been to use that name as his undercover identity. "Remember, we needed a deceased pilot that was rated multi-engine. The real Wojohowski was killed in Colombia several years ago when he crashed an old cargo plane overloaded with marijuana he was trying to get airborne off an old dirt strip. Hayes adopted his identity and the FAA issued him a new pilot's license in Wojohowski's name."

"Oh, yeah, "agreed Roger. "Now that you mention it, I do recall that Hayes was a bit touchy about his new identity."

"He didn't think the name fit him. I guess there aren't too many black Pollack's," chuckled Tom. "As for vehicles," Tom continued, "I thought I would use my undercover ID and just purchase some used four-wheel drive vehicles either in El Paso or Juarez. We'll just discard them when we're finished."

"Good idea, Tom. Paying cash won't arouse questions."

"Can you get me some money quickly?"

"I could wire some money to Diversified's account in Midland, which I assume is still open. But then you or someone would have to go there to get it."

"I don't know, Roger," began a skeptical Tom. "I'm afraid that would create a paper trail. The bank would have to report any transaction over ten grand to IRS. And while I feel confident our false identities could stand the scrutiny, I prefer not to take the chance. I think we should use something the traffickers are presently using to launder their money."

"What did you have in mind, Tom?"

"Why don't you wire money to several different casinos in Las Vegas? I'll arrange to have one of the team members fly through Las Vegas on their way to El Paso and do a layover. They can change the wired money to chips and then cash out after gambling for a short while. Their remaining chips, in essence, will be clean money. I'll make sure whoever I choose to go will exchange chips for money in denominations less than ten grand. That way there will be no report to IRS. It will just take some time, but at least it will be clean."

"Sounds like it might work, Tom,"

"You said we still had some equipment in Florida. I'll tell Tony to call you and get the details. He can check the equipment and decide what we can use. The only immediate concern is how we'll be able to get it to us in El Paso in an expeditious time frame."

"Tom, what if I have Hayes pick it up in the airplane that he rents? That would certainly reduce our security and delivery to El Paso concerns."

"That's good. I'll have Wyman and Tony get together and work out the details."

"Let me start calling the guys and try to reach Hammond. I'll talk to you later."

February 5, 1997; DEA Los Angeles, California

Back in his office, Tom studied the telephone messages his administrative assistant deposited on his desk before she departed for the evening. The second message gave Tom an instant relief. *Krissy called and left a number where she would be this evening.*

As Tom began to dial Hammond's number, he was interrupted by a knock on his door. Looking up, he saw the smiling face of "Hawk" Henderson. "Got a minute, boss?"

Tom looked Hawk up and down. His light blue print silk shirt opened almost to his navel to expose his heavy gold chains and his tight dress slacks gave Hawk the gaudy Hollywood look. "Sure, Hawk," said Tom. "Or is it Chad now?" They both laughed. "Take a seat," he said as he nodded his head in the direction of a seat in front of his desk.

Hawk looked down at his own attire. "Remember? I was supposed to have a UC meeting tonight with the CI and a minor movie producer, but the movie producer was a no show."

"Oh yeah, I remember. It was just a meet and greet. No drugs right?"

"Right, boss, but I guess the movie producer is still on location somewhere in New Mexico so the meeting was postponed."

"Okay," responded Tom. "What's up then?"

"I was wondering if you had gotten the word if I was going to do this thing with you."

"Yeah you're in, Hawk, Tomorrow we'll get travel orders and appropriation data for us to travel to El Paso."

"Great," Hawk exclaimed.

"Look, Hawk, do you have an undercover identity that you can use if we have to."

"I have an undercover driver's California license, boss."

"Can it be traced back to you?"

"I guess so. I had to make application through a special DMV procedure."

"I'm looking for something that cannot be traced back to you, Hawk? We'll just have to be extra careful on how you use…" Tom began before Hawk interrupted him.

"Nobody knows this, Tom, and I only used it for very limited reasons, but I have a Colombian passport in my mother's maiden name."

"What?" asked a confused Tom.

"Remember, I told you I spent the first fourteen years of my life in Colombia?"

"I recall that."

"I was actually born in Colombia. My mom is Colombian and my dad is American, so basically, I have a dual citizenship. Unlike the US, the Colombian government does not deny you citizenship if you have a citizenship with another country. Anyway, I have a Colombian passport that shows my mother's maiden name as my last name. There is very little chance it could come back to my true identity."

"Hawk, you just keep surprising me, first with the language ability and now with this Colombian passport thing." Sitting there staring at the smug look on Hawk's face, Tom suddenly realized the answer to the problem of moving the money needed for the operation was solved. "Hawk, do you like to gamble?"

"Sure, boss, but I'm not very good. Why do you ask?"

Tom explained the plan to get cash for the operational expenses by going through the casinos. "The money will be wired to several casinos in Las Vegas; you redeem the money in chips, gamble a while and then cash out the chips in quantities under ten grand."

"Why couldn't I just cash out the whole amount?"

"Because the casino would be required to report it to IRS," answered Tom.

"So, with my passport, I'll just be another wealthy Colombian on vacation in Sin City and they can report to IRS all they want," replied Hawk. "There's no way IRS can trace it to me."

"Perfect." Tom felt some relief knowing a major hurdle had just been eliminated. "I'll have you travel to El Paso through Las Vegas; you'll have to figure a lay-over reason if ever questioned."

February 5, 1997; Rancho Tierra Del Sol Chihuahua, Mexico

The ambient light began to fade in John Conway's dingy room. *It must be getting dark outside. I wonder what's going on with that video. Did they get it to a television station and has the AG seen it? I sure hope so and that she acts soon. This not knowing and just sitting here is driving me crazy. I wonder how long it will take them to make arrangements to return Hector Gutiérrez to Mexico so I can be freed. I'm sure that there will have to be some legal details to work out first, like dismissing the indictment against Hector. Is a dismissal necessary? Crap, I can't remember ever having to deal with this type of situation as a U.S. Attorney. And what would the government do if it was the AG who kidnapped…? For that matter, I imagine this situation has never come up before.*

Suddenly a cold wave of dread and fear overtook him and his body tingled with fear. *What if they refuse to deal with these people? Then I'm a dead man.* Conway willed himself to be calm. *How can they not deal with these people? What kind of a signal would that send to the American public—that the government cared so little for one of its executives that it would not deal with kidnappers? Of course, they'll deal with them; I'm worrying for nothing. Maybe I should think of a way to escape. But even if I did, what could I do? I have no idea where I am other than I'm somewhere in Mexico. I don't speak Spanish and have no money to offer someone for help. No, escape is not in the picture right now.*

Lifting his arm, he sniffed his armpit. *Man, I stink. I sure could use a shower, and I'd give anything to brush my skuzzy teeth.* He stroked his face. *A shave would be nice too.*

Sitting with his back against the wall, his thoughts drifted to his family and his home. *I sure hope Emily is holding up okay considering the circumstances of not knowing. At least when she sees the video, she'll know I'm alive and somewhat well. God, I sure hope I survive this.* His last thought brought on the melancholy mood again, and he began to weep silently. This mood did not change as he drifted off to sleep.

He had been asleep for less than a few minutes when the sound of the door opening awoke him. Conway shielded his eyes from the harshness of the light flowing into room. As his vision began to clear, he noted the individual, who he had come to know as the teniente, had entered the room. The teniente threw a blanket at Conway's feet. "Pendejo, here is another blanket to keep you warm," he said with a recognizable degree of hostility in his voice. "You can thank the comandante for this gesture. If it were my decision, I'd let you freeze your pinche ass off, maricón."

Conway crawled slightly forward across the dirty floor to retrieve the blanket, all the while keeping his eyes on the teniente. Just as Conway reached for the blanket, the teniente stomped his foot on it, preventing Conway from pulling it to him. With a slight menacing laugh and a sneer on his face, the teniente slowly removed his foot from the blanket allowing Conway to pull it to him. The teniente turned abruptly to exit the room. When he got to the door, he looked back at Conway. Pointing at Conway, he cocked his finger like a pistol and then mimicked firing at Conway. The teniente's action reduced Conway to a shaking huddled mass. Conway's response to his pantomime made the teniente rear back his head and laugh heartily as he exited the room.

February 5, 1997; Los Angeles, California

"Hey, Blaine, how they hanging?" greeted the jovial and unabashedly brash Kristin Hammond.

Visualizing the fairly attractive face of Hammond on the other end of the line, Tom shook his head from side to side in mild amusement with Hammond's sexual remark. He smiled to himself. "More importantly, Krissy, how are you?" Tom asked. "Your Group Secretary said you were on medical leave recuperating from some type of minor surgical procedure. Is everything okay?"

"Yeah, I'm fine. I had some cosmetic surgery done last week and decided to take a few days off to heal and to get away from those idiots in the Group."

"They still giving you problems, Krissy?" Tom recalled how Krissy had often complained that her Group Supervisor and some of the male members of her enforcement group annoyed her with their less than equal treatment of her because of her sex. Tom suspected that Hammond, who could be brash to the point of being downright insulting, had probably seriously challenged their manhoods by besting them in some type of physical competition. Or she had at least outwitted them in their efforts to categorize and degrade her as a member of the weaker sex.

"Of course, but nothing I can't handle. And I'm sure there will be some more wise ass remarks directed at me once they get a load of my new look."

"Oh? What did you have done, Krissy?" asked an amused Tom.

"I got me some new tits, Tom."

"What?" exclaimed a surprised Tom. "Uh, uh…" Tom stammered searching for the correct response. "And, what was wrong with your old ones, Krissy?" he asked. Before she could answer, Tom chuckled. "As I recall, you used them quite effectively last year when you wanted someone looking at your chest and not your face. And, of course, we won't even mention the affect you had on Wycoff and some of the other team members."

"Wycoff," scoffed Krissy, "that little-dicked jackass. He'd like to get his hands on these new babies I've got now," she concluded. "In answer to your question about what was wrong with my old ones is that they were too small. I needed that wonder bra to make them appear larger than they actually were. Hell, what am I saying? You saw me naked in that shower in Peru and know that my size thirty-four's on my frame were nothing to write home about. But these new babies, well, let's just say I won't need a wonder bra to get someone's attention."

"Wonderful, Krissy, I'm happy if you're happy. Listen, Krissy on a more serious note…"

"These size thirty-eight's are as serious as a heart attack, Thomas," interrupted Krissy.

"I'm sure they are," said Tom with a chuckle. "Listen, Krissy, I'm sure even being on leave you've heard about the kidnapping of Conway and the murder of our two agents in El Paso."

"Yeah, Tom, what a tragedy about those agents. Can't say the same about Conway, but I feel for those agents' families."

"How would you like to get a chance to show those bastards behind the murders and kidnappings that they cannot just waltz into this country, shoot our agents, kidnap a government official and get away with it?"

"What do you have in mind, Blaine?"

"Krissy, we have good information, and this is very confidential right now and cannot be repeated to anyone…"

"Got you covered, boss, my lips are sealed."

Krissy managed to remain silent for the next couple of minutes while Tom explained what had taken place in the last twenty-four hours regarding the kidnapping of John Conway.

"Okay, so how does that affect us?"

"Krissy, with Roger Grey's help I am getting the old Snow Cap Team together and we are going to get Conway. Want to play?"

Dead silence followed Tom's question; he began to suspect the connection had been broken. "Krissy, you still there?"

"Yeah, just thinking," replied Krissy.

"You want in, Krissy?"

"Sure, but that's not what I was thinking about?"

"Oh?"

"I'm just wondering what to wear to get Wycoff hot and bothered," she said with a hint of amusement in her voice.

Tom attempted to ignore Hammond's comments. "Concentrate, Krissy. A teletype will be sent to your office tomorrow with appropriations for your travel to El Paso to be a part of a larger Task Force being formed to look into the kidnapping of Conway."

"Okay. I'll get there as quick as I can, boss."

"We'll stay at the Day's Inn on the West side of El Paso; I'll have a room booked there in your real name. I'll be traveling myself, so if you need to reach me, call Roger Grey at Headquarters. I'll stay in touch with him. And don't forget your undercover ID, BDU's and any firearm you might have that can't be traced to you." Tom gave Roger's number to Krissy.

"Got it, boss. Say, Tom, if I have to use my new boobs on the job, do you think Roger will spring for the seven grand they cost me?" Before Tom could answer, she added, "He did pay for the wonder bra. Remember?"

"I'll let him know of your request, but I wouldn't get my hopes up, Krissy. I'll be in touch."

"Ten-four, boss. And you know what, Tom?"

Tom figured Krissy was going to tell him how much she looked forward to working with him and the team again. "What, Krissy."

"Just like when we went to Bolivia last year, I'll bet you a case of New Castle beer I get laid before you do." Hammond laughed and hung up her phone.

Tom shook his head. "Hammond, you are truly incorrigible," he said to himself.

Over the next several hours, Tom contacted each team member and gave them specific instructions about travel arrangement and accommodations in El Paso. As he did with Hammond, he instructed them to bring their basic duty uniforms (BDU's), their undercover identification and any sidearm not traceable to them. He had additional instructions for several members. "Tony," he said when he contacted Gonzalo, "call Roger Grey and get the details about the Snow Cap equipment stored at Homestead Air Force Base.

"Will do, Tom. How will I get it to El Paso? I mean I can't just ship it."

"Tony, Wyman will be renting us a King Air type aircraft, I hope, and I'll have him come by and get the equipment and you. Stay in touch with him okay."

"Sure, boss."

"And, Tony, time is of the essence. We need to do this thing like yesterday so I want you in route tomorrow. "

"I'll get going on it early in the morning, boss."

Tom's special instruction to Wyman Hayes was to secure a King Air rental aircraft, a plane Tom knew Hayes could fly. "We need to find one that is available tomorrow for two weeks' use. Once you locate one, get the details to Roger and he'll wire the deposit and rental fee from the Diversified Cayman account."

"They'll probably require me to take a check ride with their pilot."

"That shouldn't be a problem for you, Milton, should it?" asked Tom using Hayes' undercover pilot's license name."

"Cut that Milton shit, Blaine, and no that won't be a problem."

"One other thing, Wyman, I want you to coordinate with Tony in Florida. He's getting some of our Snow Cap equipment from storage at Homestead Air Force Base and you'll need to pick up the equipment and him and take them to El Paso."

"Will do, Tom. See you in El Paso," he concluded.

Tom's last call was to Roger Grey at his home. "What's up?" said a groggy Roger.

"Sorry to wake you, Roger, but I wanted to tell you everything is set in motion. Arrangements for the money, plane and equipment have been made."

"Tom, I'll call you in several hours with a satellite phone number I'm picking up around noon."

"That's great; we can have a secure means of communication, Roger."

"I have to get up in a few hours, so I need to get some sleep. And remember, I have a 9:00 a.m. Attorney General's meeting, so I'll be out of pocket for a couple of hours."

"No way! Can't you get out of that, Roger? We need an open method of communication?"

"Afraid not, Tom, somebody from here has to hold Peterson's hand, and I'm it, I guess."

"That bad, huh, Roger?"

"He's a classic example of the Peter Principle. He's achieved his highest level of incompetence. God help us if he has to take over this administration, even on a temporary basis. Got to go, Tom."

"Talk at you in a few, Roger."

Tom had just drifted off to sleep when his pager sounded. He focused his eyes on the lighted screen in his dimly lit room and saw the international number. Tom quickly sat upright in bed and placed the call through the New York number. It took several minutes to make a connection. The phone rang seven or eight times; just when Tom was going to disconnect, the voice of Juan Cervantes answered. "Hola."

"Juan, Tom Blaine."

"Señor Tom, sorry for the late hour, but I had to wait for Don Jaime to fall asleep to make the trip to town to make this call."

"Is it safe for you to be away, Juan?"

"Sí, Señor Tom. Don Jaime was in a good mood tonight and drank much Mezcal. He will not wake for hours."

"Okay, so what's up, Juan."

"Señor Tom, I wanted to tell you that the comandante made the video of your jefe and it is being delivered to a television station in Los Angeles."

"Okay, that's good."

"I also am positive your jefe is at ranchita at Janos, as I suspected."

"Why is that, Juan?"

"The comandante took the video of your jefe to Juarez to have copies made and to make arrangements to have it delivered to Los Angeles. When I talked with him on the phone after he made the video to tell him to take it to Juarez, he said that he was only about an hour or so from Juarez. That could only mean Janos."

"No other place then, Juan?"

"There is the warehouse in Agua Prieta."

"Warehouse?"

"Sí, Señor Tom. It is close to the border, and it is where the tunnel is located."

"A tunnel?" Tom questioned.

"Sí, Tom. A tunnel runs under the border and connects to a warehouse in Douglas, Arizona. Right now, with the borders all but closed because of the kidnapping, Jaime is being forced to use the tunnel to send the drogas to the United States. But I don't think your jefe is there. That note that I found in the office trash can had the J and that could only be Janos."

"Yes, I think you are right, Juan. Anything else?"

"If you are going to do something, you should do it quick, because I think Jaime is very anxious to get his hermano back home. If he suspects your government is stalling, he might do something stupid to your jefe."

"Juan, what about you and your family? If we act, won't it cause you problems?"

"Yes, I am concerned about that, but I think right now, I am safe. Jaime does not realize that I know where your jefe is. I think if you do something like you did against Miguel Felix last year, Jaime will first look at who had direct knowledge of your jefe's location. Hopefully, by the time he focuses on somebody here, I'll be gone."

"Okay, Juan, I promise you I will make that happen. Try to stay in touch. It might take a few minutes, but I'll always answer your page."

"Sí, Señor Tom."

CHAPTER FIFTEEN

February 6, 1997; Main Justice Building, Washington, DC

The morning briefing at the Attorney General's conference room had been in session for just over an hour. Randall Walsh, the Assistant Director of the FBI, while giving details of what his agents in El Paso were doing, pulled back his suit coat and looked down at his pager. He hesitated in his presentation just slightly and read the display on his pager. Looking up, he addressed the AG. "Madam Attorney General, I just received a 911 page. I need to make a call."

"Thomas turned to one of her assistants. "Show Mr. Walsh where he can make a call."

Roger watched this exchange and wondered if the video had made its way to KTLA.

"Let's all hang loose here for a while and see if this is something pertaining to the kidnapping," instructed Marilyn Thomas.

Twenty minutes passed before Randall Walsh returned. By the looks of his face, it was obvious he had bad news. Taking a seat he focused on the Attorney General. "Madam Attorney General, I have both good news and bad news."

Nodding her head, she signaled that she understood and at the same time wanted him to proceed.

"It appears that John Conway is still alive, but in fact, is being held captive."

"Thank god," said Marilyn Thomas.

"The bad news is the call I received was from the Special Agent in Charge of our Los Angeles Office. Early this morning, KTLA in Los Angeles received a videotape from an unknown source. The video is of John Conway advising that he is being held captive and will be released when a major Mexican trafficker, being held in us custody, is returned to Mexico."

"Who is the major Mexican Trafficker?" asked the representative from the U.S. Customs Service.

"I was not told the name of the trafficker. But I instructed the FBI office in Los Angeles to have KTLA transmit the video to its affiliate here in D.C. We should have it within the hour. I've dispatched an agent to wait for its arrival."

Contemplating this development, Marilyn Thomas sat quiet for several moments with her head hanging down slightly. She then looked up and addressed the group. "Let's take a break and wait for the video.

February 6, 1997; Hacienda Puesta Del Sol, La Cruz, Sinaloa, Mexico

Just as the Attorney General of the United States was being informed of KTLA's receipt of the video of John Conway, Jaime Gutiérrez was also being informed. "Don Jaime, I have Ramon on the phone, and he has good news for you. Do you wish to speak with him?" asked Juan Cervantes from his desk in the office of the Estancia.

Jaime stood up from his leather chair in front of CNN, approached Juan's desk and reached for the phone. "Sí, Juan. Let me speak with him."

From Jaime's staggered walk, Juan could detect he was still feeling the effects of too much Mezcal from the night before. His eyes were blood shot and his walk tentative, which to Juan indicated he had one of his intense headaches that normally accompanied the massive imbibing of Mezcal. Juan handed the phone to Jaime. "Don Jaime, can I get you something for your headache?"

"Sí, Juan; it's that obvious?"

"Sí, Don Jaime. You do not look so good today."

Jaime ignored Juan's last comment and took the phone. "Hola, Ramon. Tell me some good news."

As he listened to Ramon, Jaime's face broke into a broad smile. "Esta muy bien, Ramon. When do you think they'll show it on television?"

"Bien, bien. Gracias, Ramon, you did good. I will let you tell Juan what you just told me," said Jaime as he handed the phone back to Juan. But before Juan could talk with Ramon, Jaime offered, "The video was delivered early this morning. It should be on television soon, Juan."

Juan then talked with Ramon and received the details on the delivery of the video. Following this, Ramon and he talked about business and the need to use the tunnel to funnel drugs north and cash south. When he was done, Juan hung up the phone. "Ramon did good, Don Jaime. He set the process in motion and the pinche Norte Americanos not only know your demands but have a set time table in which they have to act."

Jaime had taken a seat in front of CNN with his eyes closed and head resting on the headrest. "Yes, Juan, Ramon did good. Contact the comandante and the licenciado and alert them that the video has been delivered. Things should begin to happen quickly now." As an after-thought, Jaime said, "When you call the licenciado, tell him to come here. I want to talk to him about any problems we might have with our government. I am sure once they hear our demands, the Norte Americanos will place a lot of pressure on them to hold me accountable for the kidnapping. I want to be assured there will be no problems for Hector or me in that regards. I guess the comandante should be here also, Juan. He would be more effective in running interference than the licenciado."

"Sí, Don Jaime, I will make the calls. And, uh, Don Jaime, I have instructed the cook to prepare some Caldo for you. It should make you feel better."

"Gracias, Juan.

February 6, 1997; Rancho Tierra Del Sol Chihuahua, Mexico

With an uncontrollable shivering of his body, Conway realized his body wasn't reacting to the dark, damp coolness of the room, but instead, it was the dream he had just endured before waking with a sudden start. In the dream, an assembly of a few people had collected in a small shabby room. The windows had plywood coverings much like the room in which he was being held and the walls were a dirty gray. The only light in the room seeped through the cracks between the plywood and the window frame. Even in limited light, Conway could see a bare wooden casket containing a body. The people surrounding the casket were there to mourn the deceased. From the comments of the mourners, the closed casket was necessary due to the mangled body caused by days of severe torture. Suddenly, it became apparent the people were there to mourn him. While the mourners showed their respects to the deceased Conway, he noted very little remorse at his passing. The mourners visited with one another in calm and passionless voices.

"He was not a well-liked man," said one mourner. He recognized him to be a junior Assistant U.S. Attorney from his days in Chicago. *I never liked that Harvard-educated jackass anyway* Conway thought.

"Yes, I know, but it is too bad for his wife," said a second mourner. This woman he recognized as an administrative assistant from DEA headquarters. *She's pissed at me because I wouldn't find for her in the bogus sexual harassment suit she filed against her supervisor. Christ, all he wanted her to do was to show up and do what she was being paid to do,* he concluded.

"I sure hope this doesn't jeopardize our good relations with Mexico," said a third mourner. Conway recognized the DEA Country Attaché to Mexico. He couldn't recall his name. *Jeopardize our relations with Mexico? I get kidnapped and dragged to Mexico and held hostage, and he's worried about our relationships with Mexico. I'm glad he quit.*

Conway realized this was just a dream; however, nowhere in the dream was there a single sign of bereavement by his family or friends. Moreover, his wife was absent from the dream. *I wonder what that means,* he thought.

Conway tried to put the dream from his mind, and instead, attempted to concentrate on the here and now. *How long have I been here? It seems forever, but I know it must just be a day or two.* He scratched his face and felt the stubble of the beard. *I have always hated to see beards on agents who thought it was necessary to look like drug traffickers to work against them.* He used his fingernail he scrape off the tarter building up on his teeth. *What I wouldn't give for a toothbrush. I could do without the shave, but I sure would like to brush my teeth.* He smelled his armpits. *A shower or bath would be great also.*

I would imagine the AG has seen the video by now. I wonder what she is doing about it. Most certainly, they would have to cede to the demands of the kidnappers. If they don't, I'm afraid my dream might become a reality. This thought caused a new round of chills and remorse. As tears began to fall from his eyes, his thoughts were of his wife and family. *I had hopes of seeing my grandchildren graduate from high school in several years.* He wiped his eyes with the sleeve of his shirt and silently chided himself. *Stop this negative thinking. It's only dragging you down, stupid. Get a grip, man. Everything will work out.*

He decided to concentrate on what clues he could gather about his whereabouts. The limited light made his other senses more acute. He heard ambient noise better and could tell that Spanish was the only language spoken by others outside. He also heard diesel trucks occasionally passing by the building. Other than that, it was very quiet, no planes overhead or distant sirens. *I must be in a remote area.* His sense of smell had also become better. He could tell when they were bringing him food long before they opened the door. *I wish it was something other than beans and tortillas. If I get out of here...* he had to stop thinking like that, *when I get out of here, the first thing I want is a big juicy hamburger with greasy French fries. A coke would also be nice or a cup of coffee. I'd give anything for a cup of coffee right now.* Leaning his head against the wall, he drifted off to sleep as he contemplated the various places he could get a good cup of coffee.

February 6, 1997; Main Justice Building, Washington, DC

Those who had a role in the investigation of John Conway's kidnapping had reassembled just after noon in Marilyn Thomas' conference room. She pushed the play button on the video recorder that had been rolled into the briefing room. Almost instantly, the screen of the television monitor went from an electronic snowy condition to a fuzzy picture which, when quickly focused, displayed the head and shoulders of John Conway. Conway's face appeared drawn and eyes had become deep set with circles beneath them. His hair was matted, and he looked like he had gone several days without a shave. Without any acknowledgement, Conway cleared his throat, looked down and began to read from an obviously prepared script.

> "I am John Conway, the head of the U.S. Drug Enforcement Administration. I am currently being detained just as the U.S. government is unjustly detaining Hector Gutiérrez. Hector Gutiérrez is a highly successful businessman from Culiacan, Mexico, who has been wrongfully accused of being a drug trafficker by individuals who seek to gain either their freedom from prosecution or financial reward. My hosts have advised me that I shall be released unharmed when Hector Gutiérrez is returned to Mexico. I implore you to release and return Hector Gutiérrez to Mexico and right this wrong. By doing this, I can also be reunited with my family and friends. Additionally, my hosts have set the time limit for the return of Hector Gutiérrez to Mexico of five days from the date that this video is delivered to KTLA television in Los Angeles. On a personal note, Emily, they are treating me well, and I look forward to being reunited with you soon. Please be strong and look after Pedro and Maria, my two Chihuahuas, for me."

As the video concluded, Marilyn Thomas sat silent for several seconds apparently composing herself. During this time, Roger Grey noted that the video had severely affected her as it had several others in the room. The AG's hands shook nervously; Roger thought he detected just a slight tick to her right eye. *Of course, they were not expecting this like I was,* Roger thought. *Had I not known about the video from Tom, it might affected me more.*

The Attorney General interrupted Roger's thoughts. "Mr. Walsh, I suppose there's no way we can get KTLA not to air the videotape for a couple of days while we continue to work on trying to locate John Conway?" asked

Thomas.

"I'm afraid not, Madam Attorney General," replied a somber Walsh. "The video was handed to a cameraman shooting footage at a crime scene just after 2:00 this morning in east LA along with a note that advised KTLA that if the video was not aired by noon LA Time, other copies of the video would be delivered to other television stations in Los Angeles area. To quote their news director: "There is no way KTLA is going to sit on this knowing our competition could beat us to the story of the decade.""

The Attorney General looked around the room from one participant to another. "Okay, then. I've talked with the president, and he wants our input. What do you all make of this?"

"Certainly looks genuine," offered James Peterson. I think we definitely have to consider the demands."

Roger knew Peterson would have been better served if he had just kept his mouth shut. *Jesus, Peterson, will you never learn to keep your mouth shut? God help us if you become the administrator.*

Thomas glared at Peterson. "I wasn't questioning its authenticity, Mr. Peterson," snapped an irritated Thomas. "I think we can all agree that it was John Conway; he was basically pleading for his life. What I need is input on how we deal with this."

"Under normal conditions, we would seek to stall the demands of kidnappers in an effort to determine who they are and where the abducted was being held. Maybe a plea by you to the kidnappers for more time to do everything required to release this Gutiérrez guy legally. That could buy us some time to continue our efforts to locate Mr. Conway," said Randall Walsh.

"We could try that, but how do you know the kidnappers would accede to our request. It's not like we've established a line of communications with them, Madam Attorney General," said Marsha Grant.

"Good point," Ms. Grant," commented the Attorney General.

"If I might," interjected Roger Grey deciding to enter the dialogue.

"Certainly, Mr. Grey," responded the AG.

"The video seems to clear up some questions we have not been able to answer to date," said Roger looking at Randall Walsh.

"Other than their demands, I don't see what questions have been answered," retorted Walsh with a bit of hostility creeping into his tone.

"With their only demand being the release of one of the leaders of the

Sinaloa Cartel, we now know that the Sinaloa Cartel is behind this kidnapping. And I think we can conclude that John Conway is probably being held in Mexico somewhere."

"While I agree that the Sinaloa Cartel is probably behind this, what makes you jump to the conclusion that Mr. Conway is being held in Mexico, Mr. Grey," asked the AG.

"Well, it would stand to reason that the Sinaloa Cartel would remove Mr. Conway to a place where they basically have no fear of interference by law enforcement and that certainly is Mexico. Murder, kidnapping and ransoms have become a cottage industry there. And their bribery and intimidation of high government officials makes them almost untouchable. Besides, John Conway is probably not on any Mexican government officials' Christmas card list with his recent position regarding their in-action against drug traffickers."

"That's just speculation, Grey. And I think if we develop good information, we could force the Mexican government to act," said Walsh.

"When have we ever been able to force the Mexican Government to act in a timely fashion, Mr. Walsh? Even when our agent was kidnapped and brutally tortured several years ago, the Mexican Government was less than cooperative. And as for John Conway being held in Mexico, I think John Conway himself told us he was being held captive in Mexico."

Thomas sat up in her chair. "How is that? I don't recall that on the video." She picked up the remote. "Let's play the video again; I certainly don't recall John saying anything about being held in Mexico."

"Madam Attorney General, he didn't say it directly, he said it by innuendo," replied Grey.

"I don't understand, Mr. Grey," said the Attorney General.

"In his personal statement to his wife, he said he was being treated fairly, which is obviously a lie. He looked terrible, unshaven and rather gaunt looking. But the most telling deception he offered was that he asked his wife, Emily, to look after his two Chihuahuas, Pedro and Maria. John Conway is not an animal lover and does not have any dogs, period. Chihuahuas are dogs routinely associated with Mexicans. I believe by saying this, he was trying to tell us he is being held in Mexico."

"While I think Mr. Grey might have a valid point, we still do not have enough to confront the Mexican Government," said Randall Walsh.

"Confront, no. But maybe," and turning his attention from Walsh to the

Attorney General, Roger continued, "Maybe, Ma'am, you could contact their AG and request they look into this, or if you think it appropriate, have our President call the Mexican President. They seem to enjoy a good relationship, at least that's the way it appears in the press."

"Yes, I think that is a good suggestion, Mr. Grey. I will call their AG, but let me sound the President out on having him contact their President. Politically, it might have adverse reactions if he were to become involved at this stage of the investigation. When I briefed him on the video before this meeting, he was afraid the Mexican President would turn this around and use it to stress his point that we, the United States, are flooding Mexico with assault rifles and other weapons."

"I see," said Roger while he really didn't. Roger then caught himself shaking his head in disbelief. *Typical wishy-washy answer. Just tell the goddamn Mexicans they can't accuse us of creating our own drug problem to justify their countrymen flooding our country with drugs and then not accept responsibility for creating their own gun and violence problems.*

"What have we learned about the video itself, Mr. Walsh?" asked Marilyn Thomas.

"Not much. The original tape, shown to our agents in Los Angeles, is a standard videotape that can be purchased just about anywhere videotapes are sold. And as I said, it was handed to a cameraman who was shooting footage at a crime scene in east LA early this morning. The FBI interviewed the cameraman who said he was distracted from his camera work by a man of Latino descent. The cameraman first thought it might have been a homemade video involving the shooting he was filming. He became suspicious of the contents when he asked the man to follow him back to his mobile unit where they could contact the news director to determine compensation for the video. I guess it's a common occurrence for people to make home videos of newsworthy items then attempt to sell it to the news people at the scene."

"I see," offered the AG.

"When the cameraman got to his mobile unit, he turned and the man had disappeared without making a request for any money."

"And the note?" asked the AG.

"It was taped to the underside of the video and wasn't seen initially by the cameraman. When he played the video in his mobile unit, he immediately returned to the station where the news director eventually contacted our duty agent."

"So there are no leads with the video itself or the person who gave it to the KTLA cameraman?" asked Marsha Grant.

"None at this time, ma'am." Walsh turned to the Attorney General. "Madam Attorney General, what about the press? This video is going to create a crush of press interest; we need to have a common theme."

The Attorney General looked directly at Randall Walsh. "I want all questions regarding this video referred to *this* office." She then redirected her view to all of the assembled agency heads. "I do not want any individual agency to respond to this video or this investigation to date. All press inquiries will be directed to this office, and we shall respond with one unified voice. Do I make myself clear?"

All in attendance nodded their heads in agreement.

"Is there anything else we need to consider right now?" asked the Attorney General.

"The offer of a reward has had the response I predicted, Madam Attorney General," said Walsh.

"We are inundated with calls of people who claim they have knowledge of the kidnapping. My agents in El Paso are trying to prioritize these calls and look into the ones they consider serious. It is really stretching our manpower thin."

"I'll have almost thirty agents there in the next couple of days, and we would be happy to help you sort through and follow up on these calls," suggested Marsha Grant.

"Uh, yes, let me think about that. The FBI is also sending us more help," advised Walsh.

"Mr. Walsh, you will insure that the DEA agents sent to El Paso are used to help in these calls. Am I clear on this?" The Attorney General's stern look at Walsh ended all questions.

"Yes, ma'am," responded a chastised Randall Walsh.

February 6, 1997; Los Angeles, California

The KTLA news teasers had started on the ten o'clock hour with the preempting of a commercial break with the picture of John Conway appearing on the screen followed by a commentator. "This just in, we have breaking news regarding the kidnapping of the DEA Administrator John Conway. More exclusive details and footage to follow at noon."

At noon, the evening news anchor, who had obviously been called in early, reported:

> Good Afternoon, folks. KTLA has received an exclusive copy of videotape featuring John Conway, the Administrator of the Drug Enforcement Agency, who was violently abducted from a hotel room in El Paso, Texas, on February 4. Early this morning one of our mobile cameramen, filming coverage of an east LA shooting, was approached by what was described as a middle-aged Latin man and handed a video cassette. Thinking that the video cassette contained coverage of the shooting he was covering, the cameraman instructed the man to follow him to his mobile unit where he could assess the newsworthiness of the video. The man disappeared somewhere between the shooting scene and the mobile unit. Until receipt of this videotape, there had been no ransom or other demands made by his abductors. I shall warn you in advance, the video, while not showing violence, is of a nature that it could be un-nerving to some.

The video was then aired. As the video faded to electronic snow, the news anchor returned.

"KTLA spoke with Marilyn Thomas, Attorney General of the United States, who advised that she and the President take this video and its demands seriously. They are in the process of doing everything they can to insure John Conway's safe return to the United States. The AG stated that based on the demand for the release of Hector Gutiérrez, who had been indicted for his role in the Sinaloa Drug Cartel, it is fairly obvious that a member or members of the Sinaloa Drug Cartel are behind this abduction. She also advised that she had no knowledge where John Conway was currently being held captive. She further advised that she had talked with the Attorney General of Mexico who promised his full cooperation in this matter. KTLA called the Attorney General's Office in Mexico City this morning. Rueben Echeverra, a Deputy Attorney General, affirmed that while his office promised their full cooperation in this matter, there was nothing to indicate a crime had been committed on Mexican soil. Furthermore, without evidence that John Conway was being held captive in Mexico, his office could do little to help at this time.

For the next hour, KTLA aired its predictable commentary round of talking heads composed of kidnap and Mexican drug-trafficking experts, who each offered their self-considered insightful perspective on the video and its meaning.

While each of these experts had a different take on the video, most agreed that Mexican drug traffickers were behind this kidnapping and that John Conway was obviously being held somewhere in Mexico. They also agreed that if the United States did not meet the demands to release Hector Gutiérrez, John Conway's life was in jeopardy.

In a matter of hours, the video had been shared with other news sources, and it became the lead story on all national nightly news channels.

February 6, 1997; Hacienda Puesta Del Sol, La Cruz, Sinaloa, Mexico

Jaime Gutiérrez's mood shifted decidedly from one of elation, as he witnessed the showing of Conway's video on TeleMundo, to one of intense anger when the News Director read an editorial calling for a full investigation by the Mexican government into the kidnapping of John Conway and the murder of two agents in El Paso.

> Does the present government forget what happened when the American Drug Agent was kidnapped and brutally murdered a number of years ago in Guadalajara? The Norte Americanos closed the border and Mexico's economy felt the damage due for several years. We, as a poor people, cannot afford this to be done to our fragile economy again by traficantes, such as Hector and Jaime Gutiérrez, who amass wealth beyond comprehension even while the border is closed and the poor suffer. It is obvious to this news station that the Sinaloa Cartel, headed by Jaime Gutiérrez, is behind this kidnapping and the murders of two American Drug Agents in El Paso, Texas. While Jaime Gutiérrez might not have been present for the murders and the kidnapping of John Conway, as the reputed head of the Sinaloa Cartel, he obviously ordered it done. Therefore, he is just as guilty as the people who actually carried out his orders. While I seriously doubt it will happen, I suggest that Jaime Gutiérrez be held accountable for these deeds. At the very least, the Attorney General of Mexico should cause his immediate arrest and deportation to the United States to stand trial for the charges levied against him in the U.S. indictment. The Government of Mexico needs to put a stop to this anarchy practiced by these drug cartels. If it does not act, and act soon, the violence is only going to escalate. We welcome all opposing views on this matter.

"Pinche pendejo! Who is this maricón who dares to identify me as a drug trafficker on national television?" screamed a red-faced Jaime at the television screen. He turned to Juan who was in his usual place at his computer. "Juan, get me the comandante. I want him here within the hour. And also call the licenciado and have him come also."

Jaime went to the bar and poured himself a large Mezcal. He drank it down in a single gulp and slammed the heavy glass tumbler on the bar. "I'll show that maricón who has the power in this country. How dare you challenge me?" He poured himself another Mezcal.

Juan knew it would be pointless to try to calm Jaime at this time. Instead, he made the calls to the comandante and the licenciado.

Within the hour, Juan escorted the comandante from the marbled front foyer area to Jaime's large office. "Be careful, Comandante," Juan cautioned. "The jefe is in a really bad mood."

The heels of his snake-skinned cowboy boots clicked on the hard tile surface of the hallway. "Why is he so angry, Juan? I thought with the video on television, he would be very happy."

"Comandante, it was what was said by the Telemundo News Director following the video that upset Don Jaime."

"Juan, those are just hollow words. Don Jaime has nothing to fear from the government. He has become too powerful and many in the government have gotten rich by taking his mordida."

"Yes, I know that, Comandante, but Don Jaime does not like someone accusing him of such things in pubic, even if they are true," said Juan as he opened the door to the large den. "Don Jaime, the comandante is here."

"Ah, Comandante," began Jaime who staggered as he stood up from his large leather couch. With his slurred speech, it was obvious to Juan that Jaime had consumed too much Mezcal in a short period of time. "Gracias for coming right away."

With a simple nod of his head, the comandante acknowledged the thanks offered by the inebriated Jaime.

"Have you seen that Puta on Telemundo who dares to use my name and calls for action by our government against me, Comandante?"

"Sí, Don Jaime. I saw him, but they were just words, Jefe, words that cannot hurt you here in Mexico. I would not concern yourself with that pendejo," answered the comandante.

"I disagree, Comandante. That maricón's words and pressure from the Norte Americanos could cause those in power to forget all I have done for them. This would be especially true if I were to be neutralized somehow and not in a position to exert my influence."

Again, the comandante merely nodded his head to signify he understood Jaime's position. "What is it that you would like me to do, Don Jefe?"

"I want that maricón silenced permanently, Comandante?"

"Who do you want silenced permanently, Jaime?" asked the licenciado who had just entered the room.

"That maricón on Telemundo who dares to identify me as a traficante," said Jaime with a dismissive wave of his hand toward his television.

Unaware of Jaime's angry state, the licenciado chuckled at Jaime's statement. "But Jaime, you *are* a traficante, a very powerful traficante."

Jaime glared at the licenciado for several moments. "You better be careful with that mouth of yours, Licenciado, or I'll silence it permanently also."

The licenciado immediately lost all the color in his face. "Uh, uh, Jaime, I am sorry. I meant no disrespect." With a bead of sweat beginning on his forehead, he continued. "I assure you that you have nothing to worry about here in Mexico. You should not concern yourself with what the pinche news says about you."

"I wish that I shared your optimism, Licenciado, but I cannot afford to, nor will I allow someone to publicly disparage me. It weakens my position," said Jaime.

"Jaime, you should…." began the licenciado in a more conciliatory tone.

"Silence," ordered Jaime interrupting the licenciado. "I have made up my mind on this matter; I want this puta silenced. Not only will it shut him up, but it will also send a signal to others who might be wavering in their support to me."

"Jaime, por favor, please listen. Do you think this is a wise thing to do right now?" implored the licenciado.

"Licenciado I think it is the absolute right thing to do right now. I want to send a signal that I will not be hassled by anyone. Comprende?"

Realizing he might be lumped into the hassling category, the licenciado elected not to argue any further with Jaime. "Sí, entiendo."

"Comandante, do what needs to be done to silence that pendejo. I don't care what it costs. I don't want to see his face again on television, comprende usted?"

"Sí, Don Jaime. I will see to it."

Chapter Sixteen

February 7, 1997; Day's Inn Motel, El Paso, Texas

It was chilly at 7:30 a.m. when Tom, armed with a cup of coffee made from the machine in his room, stepped onto the open catwalk that allowed access to the second floor rooms. Standing at the railing, he noticed the motel formed a U-shape around a centered swimming pool and a grassy children's play area. The bank sign across the street, which could be seen through the open end of the U, blinked forty-two degrees at 7:35 a.m. *Much cooler than LA, Tom* thought *but not as cold as my deck in Elbert County.* This thought brought a bit of nostalgia to Tom. *I sure wish I were standing there with a cup of coffee looking at Pikes Peak. And, of course, with Libby at my side. Oh well, I'll be back there soon enough, I hope.* Continuing his consideration of the limited panoramic view in front of him, he remembered, from his last trip here, that El Paso was a desert with desert flora and fauna. This was especially true of the view from the catwalk. With the exception of the children's grassy play area, everything else was sand dotted with several varieties of cactus, Palm trees and yucca plants.

The ringing phone from his room interrupted his thoughts of home. Pushing the slightly closed door open, Tom entered his room and walked to the nightstand. He sat on the edge of the bed and answered the phone. "Who's bothering me at this hour?"

"This hour? Christ, it's almost 8:30 a.m. here, Tom," exclaimed an amused Roger Grey.

"Yeah, well you're three, no that's not correct, you're two hours ahead of me Roger."

"I guess so. So you made it there okay?"

"I got in early last evening," answered Tom.

"How's the weather there?"

"It's chilly, just like it was last year when we did that thing down south. The clock at the bank across the street says forty-two degrees."

"Consider yourself lucky, Tom. It's fifteen here with the threat of snow."

"Probably the same storm they got in Denver yesterday. Libby says they got about seven inches of snow."

"I suspect that's so. Tom, have you heard from the other team members?"

"Still waiting on Henderson, Gonzalo and Hayes. I'm going to meet with the others in a couple of hours."

"I've heard from all three, Tom. Henderson called me last evening and said it was taking a little longer than anticipated to change the money in Vegas, but he was scheduled to leave at nine o'clock this morning. Both Hayes and Gonzalo are winging their way toward you as we speak."

"So Hayes was able to find a plane then?"

"Yeah, he located a 1980 Merlin IIIB. A lot older than we wanted, but it was available on quick notice and according to Hayes, it's in good shape mechanically."

"Okay, as long as it can stay airborne as long as we need it. Did they say anything about the Snow Cap equipment they were to pick up at Homestead?"

"Yeah, they did. It was not as good as I had hoped. According to Gonzalo, most of the weapons are rusty, but he selected three of the best HK MP5s. Oh, the satellite phones work and should be operational after a battery charge, but the night vision devices are ruined. The batteries have corroded the devices making them unserviceable."

"Shit, those would have come in handy, Roger. What about my favorite weapon?"

"According to Gonzalo, your old M203 was in better shape than the HKs, Tom, but there were no 40 mm rounds for the grenade launcher. There were only five CS gas 40 mm rounds. So I guess it will just be a heavy M16."

"What about gas masks?"

"They're bringing six with them, along with canisters for the masks."

"I don't suppose we were lucky enough to get any C-4 or other type of explosives."

"Afraid not, Tom. While Homestead was accommodating on storing weapons, they were adamant about not storing explosives. I might be able to get you some in a couple of days."

"Forget it, Roger; we don't have the luxury of time. We'll just have to do without I guess."

"What's your plan, Tom?"

"As soon as everyone gets here, we'll develop a more detailed plan, but basically, we'll go into Mexico like we did last year at Zaragosa. We'll recon the area first and then develop a game plan based on what we find."

"My contacts at the agency have promised us some satellite imagery; I'll fax it to you as soon as I get it."

"That might be helpful, Roger, but I trust Brian and God to be able to scout out the ranch where Conway is being held. And like I said, once they have reconned the area, we'll develop a plan."

"I guess I don't have to tell you, Tom, but I don't think we have a lot of time to really scout this thing out?"

"Yeah, I know, Roger. The five-day clock is ticking, but I don't intend to delay. Hopefully, we'll be in Mexico tonight."

Roger paused a moment. "I'm concerned as to how you're going to explain you and your team's absence from El Paso to the ASAC overseeing the MTF. I'm sure he'll want to know what you guys are up to."

"Yeah, I've given that a lot of thought, Roger. I need an excuse to be away from here for several days."

"One of the leads that the bureau has been trying to follow-up on involves the hotel security guy, a former El Paso cop, who disappeared before Conway was abducted and has since vanished. Suppose you got a tip he was hiding out at a relative's home in say southern New Mexico or Arizona and you and your team are going to set up on the relative's residence to see if he is hiding out there."

"Roger, that's a good plan. I'll come up with something like that to distance us from El Paso for several days."

"Stay in touch, Tom."

"You too, Roger; I'll let you know when the satellite phones are operational and we can stay in touch that way."

February 7, 1997; Main Justice Building, Washington, DC

"Okay, what have we got on the abduction of John Conway?" asked an anxious Marilyn Thomas. "I need to update the President in an hour, so I need something." Thomas sat back in her oversized leather chair and scanned the assembled group of agency heads involved in the investigation of the kidnapping of John Conway.

Roger Grey thought Thomas looked particularly bad this morning. *The bags under her eyes are probably a good indicator she's not getting much sleep. Her hands are really trembling today. I'm afraid she's not long for this job. Wish I could share the information about Tom Blaine and assure her that something very positive is being done to rescue Conway. Hopefully, this pressure will be resolved by Monday.*

"Madam Attorney General," began Randall Walsh, nattily attired in a brown pinstriped suit, "the Bureau continues to receive numerous calls with information about the abduction. Most of these calls are not of significance. However, one of these calls was from the Douglas, Arizona, police in response to our BELO, I'm sorry, our 'be on the lookout' for a white van. It's led to the recovery of a van that might have been used in the abduction of John Conway."

"Really?" exclaimed the Attorney General. She sat forward on her chair. "Where and when was it recovered?" she asked.

Walsh focused on a note pad in front of him. "It was found abandoned in a Walmart parking lot in Douglas, Arizona, yesterday. Our crime scene techs searched the van and recovered some blood samples from a pool of blood on the van carpet. The only prints they recovered were not of record with NCIC."

"They recovered nothing else then?" asked the Attorney General.

"No, ma'am, not that I am aware of," replied Walsh.

"What do we know about the van, Mr. Walsh?" asked Marsha Grant.

Walsh disregarded Marsha Grant, and instead, directed his response to the Attorney General. "It was stolen from a used car lot in Las Cruces, New Mexico, the day before Mr. Conway's abduction.

His failure to make eye contact with her caused Grant to develop a slight snarl on her face. Walsh's snubbing of her caused Grant, and while examining her fingernails, to take on a cavalier attitude. "It's a shame we were not able to back off of the van and establish surveillance. See if somebody returns for it."

Good point Marsha, thought Roger.

Walsh glared at Marsha Grant for an uncomfortable period of time. "Unfortunately, that was not practical. The local police had already tipped our hand as to our awareness of the van. Our agents made the decision at the scene to see if the van contained anything that might lead us to the location of Mr. Conway."

"Mr. Walsh, other than the blood and the color of the van is there anything else that might indicate that it was used in the abduction?" asked the representative from U.S. Customs.

"Besides the color of the van, which matches what several witnesses described as fleeing the Wyndham Hotel in El Paso, the fact that it was stolen and the timing makes it seem right that this was the van used. By timing, I mean that according to the Walmart security man, who reported the van to the local police, the van had not been in the lot prior to the night of the abduction," said Walsh.

"What about videotape coverage of the parking lot?" asked Roger. "I know many of the Walmarts have video coverage of their parking areas. Did this one have coverage?"

"Uh, I'm sure our agents checked this out; if there was coverage, they would have reported it," stammered Walsh.

"But we don't know for certain then, Mr. Walsh?" asked the Attorney General.

"Uh, no, ma'am, I'll check and get right back to you on this." Walsh's face began to redden.

"What else do we have?" asked Marilyn Thomas.

"We're still checking leads trying to locate the hotel security man who disappeared the night of the abduction," offered Walsh with a little more enthusiasm in an effort to overcome his embarrassment.

"Madam Attorney General," said Roger Grey, "I have a number of agents who have already arrived in El Paso. They could assist with surveillance on locations where this security man might be frequenting or hiding." Roger knew this would be an excellent cover for Tom's group to absent themselves from the El Paso area and the supervisors of the Mobile Task Force who might question their absence.

"Thanks, Grey, I'll let my agents in El Paso know of your offer," replied Walsh.

"Madam Attorney General, where are we with making arrangements to meet the kidnappers' demands?" asked Marsha Grant.

Instead of answering Grant, Thomas turned to one of her assistants. "Why don't you answer that, Loraine?"

"Yes, ma'am," replied the assistant Attorney General. "We're researching the legal issues involved here. We have no precedence for a situation like this. But we have determined several alternatives. We can have a federal judge in Los Angeles dismiss the indictment based upon a recommendation by the U.S. Attorney in Los Angeles. Also, the President can give him Executive Clemency. In both those instances, the charges would be dismissed, and Hector Gutiérrez would be free to return to Mexico."

"Are those alternatives available to us in keeping with the abductors timetable?" asked Grant.

"Yes, ma'am," replied the assistant Attorney General. "We have people on standby to accomplish either one in a matter of hours."

"Uh, by the way, that's not for release beyond this office," interjected Marilyn Thomas. Scanning the room, she noted the attendees' understanding with nods of their heads. Thomas stood up. "I need to talk with the President. Keep me posted if anything develops. Do not make any plans for the weekend. We shall keep on this thing until it is resolved."

As Roger Grey accompanied Marsha Grant back to the DEA Headquarters, he was sure Tom and his team would have a resolution for Thomas before Monday morning.

February 7, 1997; Rancho Tierra Del Sol, Chihuahua, Mexico

The smell of food awakened John Conway from a light sleep. Sitting upright against a wall, he waited to hear the sound of footsteps approaching his room. He counted the number of breakfasts he had eaten there. *This morning makes three; I've been here three days now. I wonder how much longer it will be? Certainly, the Attorney General has seen the video and knows the demands of these assholes.*

The sound of the door being unlocked and opened slightly interrupted his thoughts. A plate of food was placed on the floor, along with a cup of what appeared to be coffee.

"Coffee!" he spontaneously uttered. The door closed as quickly as it had opened. Conway crab-crawled across the filthy floor and grabbed the cup. He found it warm to the touch and quickly raised it to his mouth taking a big gulp. He instantly regretted his failure to take into consideration that the coffee might be hot. The sudden burning of his lips caused him to jerk the cup from his mouth spilling some of the coffee down the front of his shirt. "Shit!" he muttered. He tentatively brought the cup to his mouth again and blew slightly across the rim of the cup. His taste buds reacted as if he had imbibed some expensive champagne. "Man, that's wonderful," he concluded. *This is the best damn coffee I've ever had. I wonder what kind it is. When I get out of here, or I guess I should say, if I get out of here, I'll have to get some of this.*" Even these thoughts of his immediate future did not dampen the pleasure he derived from the hot coffee.

He set the cup down on the floor carefully so as not to spill a drop of what was left and reached for the plate of food. To his surprise, it contained scrambled eggs, cheese, with some onions and peppers, but none of the mouth-scorching red sauce. He placed some of the egg concoction into a tortilla and munched on the homemade taco. Quickly finishing his food, he slowly sipped the remainder of his coffee. *They must plan to keep me alive for a while. The worse part of this is not knowing what's happening on the outside.*

He heard the sound of someone approaching the door. The door was unlocked and the comandante entered the room.

Conway began to stand slowly.

"Sit down," ordered the comandante. His dark sunglasses again obscured his eyes. The comandante glanced at the empty plate and cup. "I see you had breakfast. Did you find the food to your liking?"

"Yes, uh, today the eggs were good. I'm not used to hot spicy foods, so I was not able to eat the eggs yesterday. I hope I did not offend you by not eating. The coffee was very good also."

"I see," began the comandante. "Would you like another cup, amigo?"

"Uh, sure, if it's no problem?"

The comandante opened the door slightly and spoke to someone. "Mas café, por favor." He turned back to address Conway. "Leche or sucre, uh, perdone, milk or sugar?"

"Uh, no, just black please," answered Conway."

"Negro," advised the comandante to the person on the other side of the door. Several minutes later, a fresh cup of coffee was handed to the comandante, who after receiving it, closed the door. He handed the coffee to Conway and then stared at Conway for several minutes. "You stink, amigo. I can arrange for you to wash a little if you promise to behave and not cause any problems."

"I won't cause any problems, Comandante?"

"Bueno. Several of my men are still very upset with you for the killing of one of their amigos in El Paso. They would not hesitate to kill you should you do something stupid. Entiendo usted?"

"Yes, I understand and will not do anything, uh, stupid as you have said."

"Bueno, I will see to it then." The comandante turned to exit the room.

Conway cleared his throat, almost afraid to speak. "Excuse me, Comandante, have you heard anything about my government meeting your demands for my release?"

Turning his head slightly, the comandante spoke over his right shoulder.

"Unfortunately, not as of yet, but we have been generous and have given your government several days to meet our request so it is still early. I would hope, for your sake, that they meet our demands quickly, so we shall not have to take stronger measures."

The mention of stronger measures caused a wave of instant fear to consume him. Unable to speak any more, Conway shook his head in agreement with the comandante.

The comandante sensed Conway's reaction and turned to face him. He gave a slight smile, more like a sneer. "I will see to allowing you to wash up." He turned and left the room.

The second cup of coffee did not seem as tasty as the first, but then again, maybe it was the comandante's last statement that affected his taste buds.

February 7, 1997; Day's Inn Motel, El Paso, Texas.

"Holy shit, Krissy!" exclaimed a shocked Tom Blaine.

Kristin Hammond entered his motel room wearing a white long-sleeved tight turtleneck sweater that accentuated her brand new thirty-eight inch breasts. She first turned to the right to offer a side profile. "You like?" Placing her left palm behind her head and adopting a modeling pose, she turned slightly to the left offering Tom a different view.

"Uh, uh, ah." Tom could only offer a temporary loss for words. When he finally gained enough composure, he shook his head and laughed slightly. "They certainly are something, Krissy." Tom took in a full view at Hammond from the floor back up again. "If you're trying to distract people from looking at your face, those will certainly do the trick."

"Yeah, I can't wait to use them undercover," she said. She covered the few feet that separated them. "They look and feel real. Go ahead and feel for yourself, Blaine."

"Jesus, Krissy, I can't touch your breasts." Tom pulled back from her and felt the warmth of blush developing on his cheeks.

"Jesus, Blaine, don't be such an ole prude," retorted Hammond playfully. She grabbed both of his hands and held them firmly against her bosoms.

Before Tom could pull his hands away from Hammond's breasts, Rick Lansky kicked open the door to his room. Brian Hood followed close behind.

"Honey, I'm home." Lansky's attempt at humor was stopped short at the sight of Tom with his hands on Hammond's breasts. Lansky, or God, as he was called, chuckled. "Hey, Boss, I know you're a hands-on supervisor, but aren't you carrying it bit too far."

Not to be outdone with God's wit, Brian Hood offered, "Give the man a break, God. He's just being a good supervisor and evaluating the talents of his subordinate."

Tom jerked his hands away from Hammond's breasts. His face, and what was visible of his neck, had turned a beet red. "Haven't you bozos ever heard of knocking?"

Hammond, who seemed to be non-pulsed by the embarrassing moment, acknowledged Hood and Lansky. "Hey, buttheads, how goes it, guys?" She stroke her model's pose. "What do you think of, uh, my changed look?"

Hood nodded his head in approval. "Nice rack, Krissy."

"Yeah, they are something, Krissy," said Lansky. "Has Jason seen those babies yet?"

"Not yet," replied Hammond.

"You'll give him apoplexy, Krissy, you know that?" said Lansky.

"Heart failure is what I was aiming for, God, but apoplexy would be good too," replied a smiling Hammond.

Tom finally gained control of his extreme embarrassment. "Okay, guys, can we get down to business?"

"Geez, I thought that's what you were doing when we walked in, Tom," chided Lansky.

A wave of embarrassment attacked Tom again and the redness returned to his face and neck.

Hammond came to Tom's defense. "Jesus, God, leave the poor guy alone, will ya."

"Has anyone seen Jason?" asked Tom regaining his composure once again.

"Yeah, he'll be right here," said Hood. "He was on the phone to his office when I knocked on his door."

"I wonder who dialed the number for him?" said Hammond.

Lansky and Hood smiled at Hammond's witty remark, but Tom gave a stern glare to all three of them.

"So are we set to go, Tom?" asked Hood.

"Somewhat, but I want to wait until everyone is present so we can discuss our plans as a team. Oh, and listen, we have a new guy joining us. He's from my group in LA. He's an okay guy."

After a moment of silence, Lansky spoke first. "Tom, do you think that's wise right now? Can we trust this guy? What's his background?"

"To answer your questions, God, I feel we can trust him. He's a former Marine who saw some combat in the Middle East, and although he's whiter than you, God, he speaks Spanish like a native."

"Oh, great, another jarhead to contend with," commented Lansky.

"Careful there, big fella, I represent that remark," said Tom.

"Uh, sorry, boss, I was referring to Jason; forgot you were one too."

"Well, anyway, his name is Henderson; he just got here a couple of hours ago from Las Vegas. He had to convert our operating money that Roger had wired to several casinos from an account in the Caymans."

"We still have some money in that account? I thought we cleaned it out last year," asked Brian.

"Yeah, so did I. But I guess Roger's bookkeeping is as lousy as mine. I can never balance my checking; I guess neither can Roger. But thankfully his shortcoming has allowed us enough to do what we need to do," said Tom.

A slight rap sounded on the door and Tom rose to open it.

The bulk of Tree filled the doorframe. Jason Wycoff wore a tight long-sleeve T-shirt that did nothing to hide his massive arms and chest. "Hey guys," he said before instantly halting when he caught site of Krissy. Mesmerized by Krissy's new look, Wycoff stood speechless with his eyes transfixed to Hammond's chest.

Lansky waived his hand in front of Wycoff's eyes. "Earth to Tree; wake up, big fella." Wycoff's eyes stayed on Hammond's chest as Lansky led him to an empty chair. He gave Tree a simple order. "Sit, big fella."

Tom addressed the team and shook his head at Tree whose eyes seemed permanently attached to Krissy's enlarged chest. "Okay, Hayes and Gonzalo are still several hours away, but let's get started. Since Conway's kidnapping, a lot of information has poured into both DEA and the bureau about who nabbed him and where he might be. Hawk, excuse me, Harold Henderson, the agent from my LA Group, has a CI whom you all might recall. When we were at Uriarte's estancia last year trying to save poor Marcus, bless his soul, there was a gentleman present named Juan Cervantes."

"I remember him. Wasn't he Uriarte's assistant or something like that?" offered Hood who simultaneously leaned to his left and snapped his fingers in front of Wycoff's face.

"Yes, that's correct, Brian. If you recall I allowed him to leave the estancia with Uriarte's wife and children and a bag full of cash. At the time, I told him to make his way to the United States and contact DEA there. He had lots of information about Uriarte's assets in the United States that needed to be seized. Well, he did just that, and he ultimately was put in contact with Henderson at the LA DEA office. He began to give Henderson information about Uriarte assets and then suddenly disappeared. Recently, he contacted Henderson and myself and claimed the Gutiérrez brothers, Uriarte's main competition in Mexico, contacted him and forced him to return to Mexico to work for them. According to Cervantes, the Gutiérrez's had taken his brother and his young family hostage and threatened Cervantes that if he did not aid them in developing a working relationship with the Ojedas in Colombia, they would kill his brother and family. He returned to Mexico and has been acting for the Gutiérrez's in much the same capacity as he did for Uriarte."

A slight rap on the room door interrupted Tom. Hood, the closest to the door, stood and opened it revealing Harold "Hawk" Henderson.

Tom stood up and approached Henderson. "Come on in, Hawk. Team, this is Harold Henderson; we call him Hawk."

"Hawk?" questioned Lansky.

"Long story," said Hawk. He took an empty seat adjacent to Tom. "Sorry about not being here on time. It took longer than I thought it would to change the chips back into cash at the casinos."

"How much do we have to use, Hawk?" asked Tom.

"Uh, the whole two hundred grand that was wired to the casinos, Tom," said Hawk who, like Tree, had become somewhat distracted by Hammond.

"You didn't lose any money at all," asked Tom with the skepticism dripping into his voice.

"Nah, boss, I did okay at the craps tables and what I lost at one casino, I seemed to make up at the next."

Hammond returned Hawk's stare with a smile.

"Hawk," began Tom. He waited for Hawk to break his stare with Krissy and to acknowledge him. Tom pointed to each of the other team members as he introduced them. "The big ugly guy is Mark Lansky; we call him God. You already know Jason Wycoff from LA. That's Brian Hood over there and sitting on the bed is the dazzling Kristin Hammond."

Hawk shook hands with each member then took a seat.

"Hawk, I was just bringing the guys up to date on what we have learned from the CI," said Tom to Henderson. Tom refocused on the others and then continued. "Right after they grabbed Conway in El Paso, Hawk and I talked with the CI. He told us that Jaime Gutiérrez, the head of the Sinaloa Cartel, had orchestrated the kidnapping and planned to hold Conway hostage until his brother Hector was returned to Mexico. Hector was arrested around New Year's and is being held without bail pending prosecution of an indictment out of the Central District of California."

"I guess the videotape that's been on the news tends to confirm his information," interjected Lansky."

"It sure does, God, and in fact, it was Hawk and I, who suggested to the CI to recommend that Gutiérrez make the video setting forth his demands and proof that Conway was being held hostage for that reason. This beat Gutiérrez's plan of cutting off some fingers and sending them to the Attorney General."

"Too bad," offered Hood. "The asshole needs to lose more than some fingers if you ask me."

"Now let's be nice, Brian," scolded Hammond. Her words brought smiles to everyone except Tree.

"Yeah, while we might not care much for Conway, personally, and I, for one, definitely have an axe to grind with that prick, these assholes came into our country and killed two of our agents while kidnapping a major government official. I don't know about you guys, but I don't intend to tolerate that," said a righteous-sounding Tom.

"Hey, don't get me wrong, Tom, I'm here to do what needs to be done. Like you, I want to show them clowns they can't hide behind a border," replied Hood.

"Okay, where was I?" Tom questioned himself. "Oh, yeah. The CI feels confident that they are holding Conway on a ranch near Janos, south of Aqua Prieta directly across the border from Douglas, Arizona. The ranch is a staging area for the movement of cocaine and marijuana into the United States and is heavily guarded."

"Like last year at Zaragosa, then." commented Lansky.

"Right, but I'm afraid the guards at this ranch are Los Zetos and not that band of campesinos that we encountered at Zaragosa."

"Okay, so what's the plan, Tom?" asked Hood.

"We're going to Janos and get him, Brian," said Tom with a smile.

"Yeah, I kind of figured, boss, but how are we going to do it?" asked Hood.

"We need to scout the area first, and then formulate a plan. I want to go into Mexico tonight and recon the ranch for a while. Then we can formulate a plan based on what we find out."

"What kind of equipment will we have?" asked Lansky.

"Hayes and Gonzalo picked up some Snow Cap equipment that was being stored at Homestead, but according to them, it's not in the best of shape. I'm going to see the Border Patrol, and see if I can borrow some night vision devices. Brian, I want you and God to get us transportation."

"Transportation?" asked Hood.

"Yes, we'll need two Bronco or Blazer-type vehicles that can carry us."

"Sure, but where? Are we going to rent vehicles or what?"

"No rental vehicles; we might have to abandon them in Mexico. Buy an Auto-trader magazine, find a private seller for either a Bronco or Blazer and pay cash. Hawk will give you the necessary money; plan on spending around ten grand for each."

"How about we also borrow some license plates from another similar vehicle we might encounter in say a shopping center parking lot?" suggested Lansky.

Lansky's use of the term *borrow* brought some smiles from the group and even Wycoff smirked and showed signs of emerging from his mesmerized state.

"God, I just knew you were a juvenile delinquent when you were a kid," chided Hammond.

Tom turned to Hammond. "Krissy, I want you and Hawk to find us a used motor home we can use as a mobile command post and place to crash when not doing surveillance. And like with the cars, I'd prefer a private seller, not a dealer."

"Got you covered, boss. How much should we spend on it?" asked Hammond.

Thirty or forty K would be good," answered Tom.

"What do you want me to do, boss?" asked a now somewhat recovered Wycoff.

"Jason, you'll stay with me and help me get some other things done."

"Ten-four, boss," he acknowledged.

Lansky failed at trying to hide a large smile. "Uh, boss, should these four-by-four vehicles have *large racks*?" Lansky's question brought a round of laughter to the group except for Hawk who looked from one to the other in an effort to determine the cause for the laughs.

Tom's face and neck began to redden again.

"Use your best judgment, God," said Tom "and let me know what you get."

"We'll be sure to keep you *abreast* of our efforts, Tom?" offered Hood, which brought a new round of laughs from the group.

"Get out of here," ordered Tom in mock disgust. "We'll meet here around 7:00 tonight."

Rising from his chair and with a smile developing on his face, Hood announced, "Well, this has been very *titillating*, but, partner, we've work to do. Let's go do it." Again, the group, minus Hawk, laughed at Hood's comment.

Hammond rose to leave the room. "Hold on, Krissy," Tom said. "I want a word with you. Hawk, Krissy will be with you in a minute. And, Jason, I need to talk with you also." Once Hawk had left the room, Tom gave Jason and Krissy a stern look. "Listen, we are on a very short time frame here; I need your full concentration."

"What? I didn't do anything wrong, Tom?" interrupted Krissy.

"I know, Krissy, but I can feel the tension between you two. I know that you two have a history from last year, but I just don't have the patience or time to deal with that right now."

"Again, Tom, I didn't do or say anything," said Krissy defensively.

"Jason, I warned you in LA that I would not tolerate any nonsense from you."

"Uh, sorry, boss, but I was surprised at Krissy's uh, new look," said Wycoff.

"Well, get over it, and let's get down to business," Tom said with authority in his voice.

"Yeah, get over it, Jason, cause you sure as shit ain't going to get beyond the looking stage," said Hammond.

"Krissy," Tom corrected, "that's enough."

Wycoff crossed his massive arms across his chest in a defensive posture. "She's the one causing the problem, boss. Wearing that tight sweater and all. Tell her to tone it down."

Hammond glared at Wycoff. "Tom, tell *him* to tone it down. Wearing that tight shirt to show off his big guns and chest is no better than my wearing this tight sweater to show off my boobs. If you got 'em, flaunt 'em, ain't that right, Tree?"

"Okay, I've heard enough. I'm sending both of you home. I can't put up with this shit."

Tom's proclamation brought immediate responses from both Hammond and Wycoff.

"No, Tom, don't do that. I promise I'll try not to antagonize Tree anymore," pleaded Hammond.

"Ditto on what Krissy said, boss. I promise I won't cause any more problems, and I'll tone down my wardrobe," offered Wycoff.

Tom looked first at Hammond and then at Wycoff. He paused a few moments to let them fret.

"Okay, you've been warned. There will be no more warnings. Do I make myself clear? One more problem and you'll both be out of here."

Both Wycoff and Hammond answered "yes" in unison.

"All right, get out of here," ordered Tom.

February 7, 1997; Hacienda Puesta Del Sol, La Cruz, Sinaloa, Mexico

Jaime paced back and forth from his leather chair to the expansive windows with a panoramic view of the ocean and back to his chair again.

Juan Cervantes stood up from his desk and approached Jaime. "Que pasa, Don Jaime?"

"Oh, nada – nothing's wrong, Juan. I just don't like this sitting around waiting for something to happen. I keep waiting for some type of announcement or statement from the Norte Americanos about answering my demands."

"Jefe, I'm sure the Norte Americanos are working to get Hector released. It probably takes some time to go through the legal steps. Besides, your demand allowed them five days to comply. They are probably using every bit of that time to develop a plan for his release."

"Develop a plan, Juan? Don't you think that pinche female attorney general can just order his release and return mi hermano to Mexico, Juan?"

"I don't know how the system works up there, Don Jaime, but I am sure there are many political ramifications involving his release."

"Their pinche presidente can certainly order his release," suggested Jaime.

"Sí, I am sure you are correct, Don Jaime, but again, I am also sure he has to consider all the political ramifications it will cause."

"I don't care about his political problems. I just want mi hermano back here. Maybe I should do something to get their attention. Something that will cause them to act more expeditiously. That's it; I will do something to get a response from them. Get in touch with the comandante and the licenciado. I want them here as soon as they can get here."

It was a long four hours before both the comandante and the licenciado arrived at the ranch after Juan summoned them.

"What's this about, Juan?" asked the comandante, the first to arrive, as they walked from the front entrance to the office area. The concern was evident in his voice. "Is it about the reporter Jaime wants taken care of?"

"Comandante, I don't think that is the pressing thing on his mind. Don Jaime is a man who always has to be in control, and right now, I think, because there has been no information from the Norte Americanos about their intentions, he feels he has lost control. He wants to do something to get control again."

"Juan, he did give them five days to accede to his demands?"

"Sí, Comandante, but patience is not one of Don Jaime's strong suits."

Turning to Juan, the comandante's usually stoic face evolved into a slight smile. "That is certainly true, Juan, although you never heard that from me."

"Hola, Comandante. What has taken you so long to get here?" Jaime rose his leather chair. With the heels of his boots clicking on the Saltillo tiles, Jaime crossed the room and performed a less then sincere embrace of the comandante.

"Don Jaime, I was up north checking on our…" the comandante suddenly realized that Juan was in the room. "I was checking on our friend and just now flew back here."

Realizing that Juan was in the room, Jaime said, "Juan could you excuse us for a minute?"

As Juan exited the room, Jaime led the comandante to the couch. "I forgot you told me you were going to check on him. Is everything okay up there?"

"Sí, Don Jaime, our friend is fine and is in a secure place."

"Uh, Comandante, I am concerned I have not seen anything on Telemundo about that matter I told you to take care of," said Jaime with a bit of annoyance creeping into his tone.

"I have people working on the matter as we speak, Don Jaime. But, uh, it appears he may have gone into hiding."

"Hiding? Why would he have gone into hiding?" demanded Jaime.

"That's the same question I have asked of my people, Don Jaime? I understand he may have been tipped off about your concern."

Instant anger registered on Jaime's face. "And I think I know who might have been responsible for tipping him off. I shall deal with that shortly, Comandante. "If this reporter was tipped off, as you put it, Comandante, then I am concerned about that pinche DEA Jefe. Maybe we should move him some place where not as many people know where he is.

"Don Jaime, very few people know where we are hiding the DEA Jefe, and he is in a very secure place. The people providing the security are highly trained ex-military and very loyal to us. If you feel that the wrong people know about his location, maybe we should eliminate those people, or at least neutralize them. In either case, just say the word, and I will see to it."

"Gracias, Comandante, I know I can always count on you."

While the atmosphere with the comandante was friendly, it shifted dramatically with the arrival of the licenciado who Juan escorted into the room.

"Buenas tardes, Jaime," greeted the well-dressed Licenciado. Attired in his usual Armani suit, white shirt, tie and Gucci loafers, the licenciado sported a large smile that soon evaporated when confronted by Jaime.

"Oye, Licenciado, what did you do to alert that Telemundo reporter whose commentary I was very displeased with?"

As instant fear registered on his face, the licenciado fought to maintain a calm persona. "I did nothing, Jaime. Why would I do such a thing?" he pleaded. "And what makes you think I would do such a disloyal thing to you?"

A sneer developed Jaime's face. "Oh, I don't know, Licenciado. Money, power or some other advantage. I mean that's why you have, as you say, stayed loyal to me."

"On mi madres soul, it was not I who alerted the reporter that you were displeased with him."

"So he was alerted then, Licenciado," decided Jaime.

"I have received word that he knows you want him dead, Jaime."

"Received word?" shouted Jaime. "From whom?" he demanded. "And when were you going to share this information with me?"

Realizing his own life lay in the balance, the licenciado recalled the recent incident in the men's room of the restaurant. He began to sweat profusely. "Uh, uh, Jaime just within the past several hours, I have learned this from a contact at El Cendro."

"Carajo, Licenciado. I do not believe you." Jaime turned to the comandante. "Comandante, take this piece of shit from my house. He is of no further use to me."

As the comandante stepped forward and grabbed his arm, the licenciado began to plead. "Wait, wait, Jaime. I only informed an associate who in turn told the reporter in order to protect you."

Jaime nodded to the comandante to release his grip on the licenciado. "How would you be protecting me by informing the reporter I intended to have him killed?"

Rubbing his arm, the licenciado's voice broke with emotion. "My source at the Minister of Justice Office advised that the Minister of Justice would be forced to act if the reporter was injured or killed. Public pressure would be too great and he would not be able to shield you."

"I see," said Jaime. Lowering his head, Jaime stroked his chin while he considered what the licenciado had just said. "So you were acting in my best interest then, Licenciado. Is that your position?"

"Sí, Jaime, I only wanted to protect you."

"And I guess I can assume you also told them where I am holding the DEA Jefe, Licenciado, for my protection that is?"

"Jaime, you have not told me where you are holding the DEA Jefe; so how could I share it with anyone."

"Maybe I have not told you directly, but I am confident that you know where I am hiding the pinche DEA puta." Again, Jaime turned to the comandante. "I would like for you to take the licenciado out for a little chat to see if he has told us everything, and please feel free to use your expert interrogation techniques. When you have learned all there is to know about what my loyal friend here has done to us, we should make arrangements to relocate the DEA Jefe."

"Sí, Don Jaime" answered the comandante who then dragged a pleading licenciado from the room.

Shaken by the whole incident, Juan who had been standing next to the licenciado walked to his computer and took a seat.

Jaime sensed Juan's discomfort. "I am sorry you had to witness that, Juan. I know you do not like to be involved in that part of the business. But do not concern yourself. I have previously instructed the comandante not to really hurt the licenciado, but just to get his undivided attention. He still has some value to me."

"Sí, Don Jaime," was all Juan could muster. Juan sat at the computer pretending to input data and considered the near future. *The licenciado is a dead man, and if Jaime intends to move that DEA Jefe, I need to contact Thomas Blaine and advise him of Jaime's intentions.*

February 7, 1997; DEA Headquarters, Alexandria, Virginia

"And that's all we were able to come up with on Blaine, ma'am," advised Riley Wilson. Wilson sat in front of the large oak desk, formerly occupied by James Peterson and now by Marsha Grant, the acting head of the Office of Professional Responsibility or OPR, as it was known throughout DEA. As the acting head of OPR, DEA's Internal Affairs, Grant was responsible for all investigations regarding allegations of misconduct by DEA employees.

Wilson waited for a response to his summation of the investigation regarding Blaine. He noted that Marsha Grant, while not actually a pretty woman, did have a rugged look, but had managed with appropriate cosmetics and a stylish hairdo to make herself somewhat attractive. *And she sure smells a lot better than Peterson. Moreover, she is a damn sight easier to work for than that idiot Peterson,* Wilson silently concluded.

"So what we have is confirmed unauthorized off-duty employment while he was on suspension for violating other DEA rules," said Grant breaking her silence.

"Yes, ma'am. We have Blaine's three-by-five card offering his services, the unwitting witness's testimony on tape that Blaine was performing a service for money - tractor work – and, of course, we have Blaine's bank records that reflect sizeable deposits to his checking account while he was in a non-paid status."

"So tell me again how you think this merits placing Blaine on an indefinite suspension as a prelude to termination?" asked Grant. She shifted her position in the large leather high-backed chair.

"Well, in and of itself, it would not be a cause for recommending termination. However, it was a consensus of Mr. Conway and Mr. Peterson that combined with the fact that he was on suspension for another offense, it showed a flagrant disregard for DEA rules and regulations. That would be the basis for the termination. I think I would concur with their position because I've seen the same position used several times with other troublesome employees."

"I see," answered Grant. She dropped her head as she contemplated what Wilson had just said.

"Ma'am, I also believe that both Mr. Conway and Mr. Peterson agreed that faced with the indefinite suspension, which usually leads to termination, Blaine would retire and DEA would be rid of the problem."

"Yes, I can see how they might be led to that conclusion. I know that others when faced with the same situation have elected to retire. But I also know that both John Conway and James Peterson thought Blaine would elect to retire when they transferred him from Denver to Los Angeles following his forty-five day suspension."

"While I had nothing to do with the decision to transfer him, I thought he might retire also ma'am. In fact, I was fairly certain, until he actually reported that he would pull the pin and retire," said Wilson.

Grant flipped over a document that had been laying face down on her desk. "Wilson, what I have here is a Congressional Inquiry from Senator Jessup Collins of Colorado. He wants DEA to provide him with any and all investigative reports, memorandums and communications regarding the discipline and subsequent transfer of Blaine to Los Angeles."

Wilson jerked his head upright and slightly backwards. "Blaine went to his Senator?"

"Somebody obviously did," retorted Grant. "Why would that surprise you, Riley?"

"I don't know; it's just that knowing Blaine like I have come to know him over the past year and a half, it's not like him to go that route. He's more of an in-your-face kind of guy and is willing to take you on directly like in front of an OPM Merit System Protection Board hearing. I wouldn't think he'd let someone else do his fighting for him," said Wilson. "That's just not his style."

Grant looked down at the papers and began to thumb through them. "Be that as it may, I'll have to respond to this Congressional Inquiry within thirty days. What would you recommend I do?"

Wilson thought for several seconds trying to formulate the right answer.

"Ma'am, can I be frank with you?"

"Well, yes, of course," answered Grant with a slight hesitation in her voice.

"I would pass that Congressional Inquiry on to the man who has caused the Senator's concern. In all honesty, what Mr. Peterson, at the behest of Mr. Conway, has been doing is trying anything and everything to get Blaine gone from this agency. While I cannot actually prove it, I believe their motive is to cull favor from the AG by forcing Blaine to retire as retribution for his lack of support of you in that Denver shooting lawsuit."

"Oh." Grant's simple reply did not match the shock on her face that demonstrated her true feelings.

An hour later, Marsha Grant did exactly what Riley Wilson suggested and passed the Congressional Inquiry on to James Peterson.

Sitting at the massive oak desk strewn with numerous piles of paper, Peterson considered the Congressional Inquiry. He read for what seemed an extra-long period of time. "I don't see a problem here, Marsha. Give the good Senator what he wants. We have done a good job investigating the allegations that Blaine has continually flaunted the rules and regulations of DEA and has been appropriately sanctioned for these infractions," announced Peterson with his usual air of authority in his voice.

"No, James, forty-five days off for a simple misuse of a government vehicle is not what has been the norm in similar cases. Five days has been the custom."

"Minor problem, Marsha. We could stand behind the findings that as a supervisor he should be held to a higher degree of accountability."

Grant allowed a prolonged sigh. "James, we both know what's going on here. Conway wanted Blaine gone because of his open criticisms that Denver shooting involving me. I know Conway was trying to protect me and, of course, he knew that the AG supported my selection as the first female Special Agent in Charge in DEA. I am appreciative of his and your support, but I'm afraid we, DEA, may have gone a bit too far. I think a case can be made for retaliation for Blaine's whistle blowing on the Denver shooting."

"Okay, while I do not agree with your assessment, where does that leave us with this Congressional Inquiry?" asked Peterson.

"The way I see it, we have two options. One, while not actually claiming we were wrong, we could agree to rescind Blaine's transfer, returning him to Denver. We would also advise the good Senator that we would reduce Blaine's forty-five day suspension to five days and reimburse him for lost wages and benefits."

"I don't know. I think that might open us up to a lot of criticism," said a nervous Peterson. "What's option number two?"

"We stand behind our decisions regarding his discipline and transfer and go ahead and put him on an indefinite suspension right now like we planned to do when he was transferred to LA. We would advise the good Senator of our decision and further advise him that DEA's handling of Blaine should be left up to the Merit System Protection Board."

A slight smile slowly developed on Peterson's face as he considered what Grant had said. "I like that. In fact, I'll sign the letter to the Senator. It might not ultimately get us out of the woods, but it will buy us some time."

"Yes, James, and if we prevail at the Merit System Protection Board, it will send a signal to the Senator that we are playing fair with our troublesome employees."

"Yes, I like it, Marsha. I will contact Hugh Gilbert, the LA SAC, and let him know the paperwork is being forwarded to have Blaine placed on an indefinite suspension. Last month, Gilbert asked Conway to hold off a bit on Blaine's suspension until we could get some more experienced supervisors transferred to LA, but these developments will have to take precedence I'm afraid."

"I'll get the proper paperwork prepared and faxed to LA within the next day or so, James."

"Good and I'll be looking for a response to the Senator for my signature.

February 7, 1997; Day's Inn Motel, El Paso, Texas.

With both hands on the metal railing on the catwalk outside his room, Tom watched as the sun dropped below the western horizon. With the sun gone, he could feel the evening chill as the temperature made a quick descent. *Weatherman says high 30s this evening, which means we'll probably freeze our asses off outside tonight. But we've got no choice. Time is not our ally unfortunately,* he concluded silently. Tom glanced at his watch and decided to get ready for the meeting. As he turned to enter his room, his phone rang. He answered on the second ring. "Blaine."

"A man of few words. That's what I like about you, Thomas," quipped Roger Grey.

"Hey, Roger," Tom replied.

"Well, is everything set?"

"Almost. Everyone is here and getting ready for our trip south. I picked up Hayes and Gonzalo at the airport over an hour ago. Hayes is really beat after flying that long, so I told him to get some sleep; I'll wake him when I need him."

"So you have the necessary equipment then?"

"Not really, but it will have to do. I have the satellite phones charging, and I'll let God or Brian check the condition of the weapons. At first glance, they look pretty rusted. There's enough MREs to sustain us if we have to rough it for a day or so, and we have plenty of things like canteens and plastic cuffs for restraints. Oh, I borrowed three night vision devices from the Border Patrol. I told their commander we had a tip about a suspect in Conway's kidnapping and we needed the devices to do nighttime surveillance. Have you gotten anything from the agency?"

"I checked right before I left the office, but my contact still didn't have the satellite imagery of that area yet, so I wouldn't count on it?" said Roger.

"I guess we'll just have to do the best we can without it."

"So what's your plan, Tom?"

"I'm meeting with the team in about thirty minutes, and we'll formulate a plan at that time. But what I envision is that we'll cross over tonight around 10:00 p.m. and make our way to the area of the ranch. I think we can find it; the CI said it had a large stone gate that bears the name of the ranch. I would also suspect that it is pretty well guarded."

"What then, Tom?"

"We'll find a way to get on the ranch and recon the area. Once we know the lay and the opposition, we'll formulate a specific raid plan."

"Can I do anything for you, Tom?"

"Not right now, Roger. Just keep your fingers crossed that we're successful."

Following Tom's last statement, Roger remained silent.

Tom knew Roger all too well. He suspected Roger had more to say. More importantly, he had something more important to say. "You didn't call here just to check on the plans, did you Roger?"

"Uh, no, Tom."

"Spill it, Roger. What's up?" said an annoyed Tom.

"I've got some bad news, Tom."

"Okay."

"Marsha Grant told me Peterson had faxed an indefinite suspension for you to Hugh Gilbert in LA."

"Indefinite suspension?" repeated a surprised Tom. He felt an instant chill sweep through his body.

"Yes. According to Grant, they have a case against you for unauthorized off duty employment while you were on suspension. This, coupled with your other disciplinary actions, has made you a candidate for termination following the suspension."

The body-tingling chill soon gave way to anger. When the anger took over, it took control with a vengeance. "Fuck them, Roger. Let them take their best shot," he said in a loud voice. "Before this is over, they're going to make a rich man out of me. And, Jesus, Roger, why are you springing this on me right now?" asked Tom with apparent hurt in his voice.

"Tom, I wasn't going to say anything, but Grant said that when she talked with Hugh Gilbert he told her you were in El Paso on the Mobile Task Force. She placed a call to the ASAC in El Paso and was advised that you had not checked in with them yet. So she came to me and asked if I knew your itinerary. I told her no."

"So I'm suspended then."

"No, not officially until you are told, and you didn't hear this from me. I'd stay away from the El Paso ASAC if I were you. That's why I'm telling you this now."

"You know what, Roger, fuck it. Fuck Peterson, Fuck Grant and most of all Fuck Conway. I'll just let the Mexicans torture and kill his worthless ass."

"Come on, Tom, you know you don't mean that."

"Why should I try to save that miserable prick, Roger, after all he's done and attempted to do to me?" retorted Tom.

"Because, Tom, you know in your heart, that it is the right thing to do. Conway has been a miserable prick with you, but you need to look beyond that and consider just what these assholes have done. They've killed two of our agents and kidnapped a government official right here in the United States, not in Mexico, but in the goddamned United States. You know you and your guys have the ability to right some of the wrong and send a strong signal to those pricks in Mexico that they cannot import their violence to this county without consequences."

"But give me one good reason why I should give a rat's ass, especially if

I'm going to be terminated?" asked a hostile Tom.

"Tom, we both know they're not going to be successful in terminating you. DEA's track record at the Merit System Board hearings since Conway took over has been abysmal. Conway is grasping at straws in hopes that you will retire which would solve his problem. And besides, you could retire if it began to look like they might succeed."

"So?"

"Tom, I know you too well. You couldn't just walk away from this thing with a clear conscience."

"Roger, I don't know what I'm going to do. I just might say fuck it and go back to Denver tonight instead of Mexico."

"Tom, what about the other guys there? What will happen to them?"

"I'll leave that up to them, Roger. Look, I'm too upset to talk about this anymore. I'll let you know what I decide." Tom hung up the phone.

Following the call from Roger, Tom weighed his options. *Won't these bastards ever just leave me the fuck alone? I just don't know how much more of this shit I can take. I guess I'll just have to give into them this time and quit. The upside of this would be that I could be back in Colorado tomorrow. On suspension, yeah, but awaiting my retirement to click in. Of course, if I quit now, all my efforts to setting the record straight in front of the Merit System Protection Board would be out the window. But I'd still get my day in court on the lawsuits the relatives of those dead Denver officers have filed against DEA and Marsha Grant.*

Following his epiphany Tom sat staring at a spot just above the television where there was a slight blemish in the wallpaper. With a long exhale, he decided to call Libby. Tom reached for the phone and was surprised by its ringing. "Roger, goddamnit, I told you I'd get back to you and tell you what I decided."

"I beg your pardon. I'm sure glad I'm not Roger," was the response he got back from an unknown female voice.

"Oops, I'm sorry. I was expecting somebody else," he offered.

"Obviously," answered the female voice. "This is LA communications center. Is this Group Supervisor Blaine?"

"Yes it is; I'm sorry about that."

"That's okay. I've gotten worse responses especially from Duty Agents at two in the morning. Mr. Blaine, I have a Juan on the phone who insists on being patched to you. He says it's muy importante."

"Yes, please put him through."

After a series of electronic bleeps and clicks, he heard the LA Communications voice again. "Go ahead, Juan. I have Mr. Blaine on the phone."

"Señor Tom," said Juan Cervantes.

"Sí, Juan, Yo estoy aqui," answered Tom.

"Señor Tom, I have información es muy importante."

"Wait, Juan. I need you to call me at another number. Hold on," Tom instructed. He walked to where the satellite phones were charging on the floor near the sink area. "Juan, call me right back at this number," advised Tom. He read the hand written number that was affixed to a piece of duct tape on one of the satellite phones."

"Sí, Señor Tom. I will do it immediately," said Juan who then disconnected his end of the call.

Tom thanked the LA Communications Center lady and hung up his phone. As he waited for Juan to call him on the satellite phone, Tom contemplated his next actions. *Why should I care what Juan has to tell me? Shit, that's not fair to Juan. He's trying to do what he thinks is right and save his poor brother's family.* Tom was separated from his thoughts by the distinct ringing of the satellite phone. "Hola, Juan, que pasa?" he asked.

"Señor Tom, I think Jaime is going to do something stupid to your Jefe?"

"Why would you think that, Juan? It has only been a couple of days since he gave notice to my government about the conditions of the release. His videotape and the note gave them five days."

"Sí, I know, Señor Tom, but Jaime is a very impatient man and there have been some things happening here that have aggravated him and made him very suspicious of everyone."

"How so, Juan? We have done nothing that would lead him to believe that you have been talking to us."

"Sí, that is true, but he is a very suspicious man. He has found that the licenciado has shared too much information about his business with those who should not know."

"The licenciado?" questioned Tom.

"Sí, Señor Tom, Licenciado Gorge Morales. He is the jefe at the Sinaloa State Police and a member of El Cendro. The licenciado is the person Jaime relies on to deal with the Minister of Justice and Minister of Defense. Since Miguel Felix's death, those offices refuse to deal directly with hombres like Jaime."

"I see." Tom recalled the tremendous fallout following the death of Miguel Felix Uriarte last year. The Minister of Justice himself was accused of taking tremendous amounts of mordida from drug traffickers.

"How does this affect us, Juan, this licenciado sharing too much information?" asked Tom.

"Jaime suspects that Licenciado might have discovered that your jefe is at Janos and has shared this with somebody in the Minister of Justice."

"And why would the licenciado do this, Juan? It would not be good for Jaime or him."

"I think the licenciado is trying to protect himself. I think he feels that if something should happen to your jefe, and your government puts pressure on the Mexican government, he can be protected by keeping the Minister's Office informed of Jaime's actions."

"I see," said Tom. "So what do you think Jaime is going to do?"

"I think right now the licenciado is being questioned by the comandante about what he has told his connections in the Minister of Justice and Defense departments. If he has told them that your jefe is at Janos, Jaime will move him right away, and I might not be able to determine where he was moved."

"Okay. So I guess what you're saying is that we need to act quickly."

"Sí, Señor Tom, and even if the licenciado did not give up the location to someone in the government, Jaime still wants to do something to your jefe to force your government to act quicker."

"What do you mean by *something*, Juan?"

"Cut off a finger or more and send them to your government. I heard the comandante say that is what he wanted to do."

"Okay, Juan, you did good by calling me. If something else should happen or you find out something else, call Henderson or me at the last number I gave you. Either Henderson or I will always be by that phone."

"Sí, Señor Tom, and uh, you will do as you promised?"

"What's that, Juan?"

"Take care of my brother and his family. I am afraid that once you do something, Jaime will focus on everybody here, and it will only be a matter of time before he finds out I was talking with you. He will kill my brother and his young family as revenge for my disloyalty. I can take care of myself, but my brother cannot, Señor Tom."

Tom knew now that he couldn't just walk away from this. *Shit! If something happened to Juan or his brother's family because I walked away, I could never live with myself. I have to see this thing through.* "Juan, I promise I'll take care of your brother's family. Give me his name and where I can find him."

After writing down the name and address of Juan's brother, Tom ended the phone call. "Juan, call me anytime if there is something new that develops. If Jaime is planning to torture the jefe or move him, I need to know right away, okay, amigo?"

"Sí, Señor Tom, I shall try."

February 7, 1997; Hacienda Puesta Del Sol, La Cruz, Sinaloa, Mexico

Jaime muted the sound on CNN when the comandante entered his office. Only flashes of light showed as the picture changed on the screen. "What have you learned, Comandante?" he asked as he reached for another glass of Mezcal.

The comandante took a quick sip of the Corona beer Juan handed him and took a seat adjacent to Jaime. He stretched his legs and crossed his snake-skinned cowboy boots revealing tiny red specks on the tops of the boots. "It is as you suspected, Don Jaime," began the Comandante.

"Is that blood on your boots, Comandante?" interrupted Jaime. "I hope it is not the licenciado's blood."

A chagrined Comandante lowered his head slightly and pulled back his legs. "Sí, Don Jaime, it is the licenciado's blood, but I did not seriously hurt him. I just needed to get his attention and have him overcome the superior/inferior relationship he ascribes to us. He needed to realize that I have some authority too."

"I see; so he was not seriously hurt then."

"No, Don Jaime, the blood on my boots came from his nose which bled like a stuck pig when I slapped him to, uh, get his attention."

"So what is it you have learned?"

"It is as you suspected, Don Jaime. The licenciado had the Telemundo reporter informed that you wanted him disposed of, and that is why he has gone into hiding. It is the claim of the licenciado that he only wanted to protect you. He felt that by killing the reporter, too much attention would be directed at you, and your friends in the government might not be able to protect you."

"I see," said a pensive Jaime.

"While I do not agree with his methods, his reasoning might not be too far off, Don Jaime."

Jaime glared at the comandante. "You do not agree with my decisions either?"

The comandante put his hands up as if defending himself. "Don Jaime, I would never question your decisions. However, perhaps the timing is not good right now. Maybe we should wait until tu hermano is back here in Mexico before I see to that reporter."

Jaime stared at the comandante for several uncomfortable minutes. Then his face evolved into a slight smile. "Comandante, you are, of course, correct." Picking up his glass of Mezcal, he raised it in a toast-like fashion. "To you, Mr. News Director. Your day is coming."

Raising his beer bottle, the comandante joined Jaime in the toast.

Setting his Mezcal back on the side table, Jaime asked, "About the other matter, what have you learned from the licenciado, Comandante?"

"The licenciado does know that we have the DEA Jefe at Janos but swears he has told his contacts in the Ministers Office that he does not know exactly where you are hiding the DEA jefe."

"Do you believe what he is saying?"

"Sí, Don Jaime, the licenciado is uh, shall we say, used to fine things and has a very small tolerance for anything unpleasant. For example, he has a very low pain threshold. If he were lying to me, I could have determined it without much effort," said the comandante with the characteristic sneer on his face that substituted for a smile.

Jaime smiled at the comandante's characterization of the licenciado. "Good, I am glad we determined that. But I am concerned that too many people are finding out about where we have the DEA jefe. I want you to go to Janos tomorrow and arrange to move him somewhere else. And I want you to do something to cause the American government to hasten their efforts to return mi hermano to Mexico."

"Sí, Don Jaime, I know just what to do," said the comandante. The sneer once again took form on his pitted face.

Juan Cervantes listened to the exchange between Jaime and the comandante but pretended to be totally engrossed in his work. *I sure hope*

Blaine and his compadres act soon, or it will be too late for their jefe; I need to call him and tell him of Jaime's intentions.

February 7, 1997; Day's Inn Motel, El Paso, Texas.

Tom addressed his team in his motel room. "Let's get started," The team took seats where they could—on the bed, in the two straight-backed chairs that accompanied a table by the widow and on the carpeted floor. "Hayes should be along shortly," Tom advised. "He had a particularly long flight and was exhausted when he got here, so I let him sleep a bit."

As if that were his cue, a slight rap on the door signaled the arrival of Hayes. Gonzalo opened the door and greeted Hayes with a handshake. "Come on in, Wyman. We were just getting started," Tom said.

A dour-faced Hayes greeted everyone else by rapping knuckles with each team member as he made his way to a spot against the far wall. Stopping short in front of Hammond, he broke into his Eddie Murphy-like smile. "Hey, girl, I like the new look."

In response, Hammond, who was sitting on the bed, stood and adopted her model's pose. With one arm cocked behind her head, she rotated her upper body from side to side giving Hayes, as well as the other team members a full view.

"Can we get down to business here," snapped a slightly annoyed Tom as he glared at Hammond. Judging from the stern looks he received from several of the team members, Tom realized his somewhat harsh tone with Hammond was out of line. Just because he was in a bad frame of mind, it was no reason to take it out on these guys. Sighing heavily he apologized. "Sorry, guys, I've received some bad news that only affects me. I should not take it out on you."

"Care to share it with us?" asked Gonzalo.

"No, Tony, not right now, maybe later. Right now, we need to concentrate on our mission. I had a recent conversation with the CI. He thinks Gutiérrez may be planning to move the Administrator from his current location. Even worse, he might be planning to maim him in some way to speed up the response from our government."

"Does the CI know where they might move him, Tom?" asked Hood.

"No, and even more ominous is the fact that Gutiérrez suspects somebody on his staff is leaking information about the abduction to the Mexican government," replied Tom.

Hammond interjected using a motherly tone. "Now, Jason, ominous means something bad."

"I know what it means," snapped an irritated Wycoff.

"Well, I know how you have problems with big words and for that matter other big things," answered Hammond with a slight smile on her face.

Her sarcasm earned her smiles and several chuckles from the other team members and a "Zing," from Lansky. Wycoff glared at Hammond.

Tom attempted to mask a smile. "Krissy," he said, followed with a slight shaking of his head. "As I was saying, we need to do this right away. I think, for the most part, we're ready to go." Tom nodded first at Hood and then at Lansky. "Brian and God, I hope you were able to get us some cool transportation for this afternoon. Tell us what you got."

"We got a '91 Ford Bronco, in really good condition, and an even better '92 Chevy Blazer," said Lansky. "We bought both of these vehicles from private parties for cash this afternoon."

"Cool transportation? Man, those cars ain't cool. A Mercedes or Cadillac, now that'd be cool," interjected Hammond.

"Hey, dumbass," said Lansky, "by cool, Tom meant untraceable."

"Yeah, I know, God, but I just thought I'd offer you white folks the Negro take on cool," quipped Hayes.

Hood shook his head in mock disgust at Hayes. "We swapped license plates from some similar vehicles we found in a Walmart parking lot."

"That's good. Krissy, why don't you and Hawk tell us what you guys found."

"Like Brian and God, we were also able to purchase a vehicle from a private party for cash. It's a smaller model Winnebago. Right after this meeting, I'll find a similar vehicle and swap plates."

"With your background, you'd be able to find a home with wheels," piped up Wycoff.

"Zing," repeated Lansky.

Non-pulsed, Krissy quickly retorted, "Well, yeah, Tree, a trailer home is a lot better than living under a rock."

"Double Zing!" said Lansky.

"Let's stay focused here," Tom said, but his tone was more of amusement than authority. "The Winnebago will be our mobile command post. It will also serve as a place where we can get in out of the elements when we are able.

It's supposed to be very cold tonight with temperatures in the low thirties," said Tom.

"That's not cold, Tom," said Lansky who was from the Chicago area.

Hammond, who had just arrived from the Detroit area, nodded her head in agreement with Lansky. "It's downright temperate."

"Well, it's cold for some of us not used to this weather," suggested Hawk.

"The Winnebago will give us some comfort for those who want it and a place to crap out if we get the opportunity," said Tom.

"And what about the mode of transportation I just took ten hours to bring here?" asked Hayes pretending to be insulted for being slighted.

"I didn't forget about you, Wyman. I was saving the best for last. Tell us what you brought," Tom said.

"Yeah, right," Wyman retorted to Tom's comment. "We have a Merlin, twin engine. It's an older aircraft and not as nice as the King Airs we used last year, but it will do the trick. Tony and I also brought some of the old Snow Cap equipment with us from Homestead."

"It was in pretty shitty condition, but some of it might be salvageable," offered Gonzalo.

"Brian and God, check out the weapons and see what we can use," directed Tom. "Also, check the other equipment and see if we can use any of that. I was able to borrow some night vision devices from the Border Patrol."

"Got you covered boss," answered Lansky.

"Wyman," began Tom as he turned his attention to Hayes, "I want you to fly south and see if the small airport that I see on the map at Nueva Casa Grandes, can be of use to us. It's directly south of Deming, New Mexico, and just south of Janos." Tom then turned his focus to the other team members shrugging his shoulders. "Sorry, guys, but the only map of the area I could find on such short notice was an Atlas. Roger Grey was trying to get us some aerial photography from the agency, but it was too short a notice."

"I'll check it out, boss," said Wyman. "If it looks vacant or not too busy, should I just set down there?"

"Yes, if you think it's a good place where we won't draw too much attention for a day or so. If it is, I'll have Krissy and Hawk bring the motor home there. We'll try to operate out of that area. If the place is not safe, we'll have to stage somewhere else.

"So how we going to do this, Tom?" asked Gonzalo.

"Okay, starting at 9:00 tonight, we'll go south into Mexico here at Juarez. Krissy and Hawk will lead off in the motor home. If questioned about where you're going, tell them you're heading for Guaymas on the coast; you're on vacation."

"Why Guaymas?" asked Gonzalo.

"It's a popular tourist location and a favorite spot for many Americans," answered Hawk for Tom."

"Yes, that's right, Tony. In fact, each of you should use that same excuse if questioned by Mexican Customs or immigration. Oh, I almost forgot. I'm going to give each of you three thousand dollars in currency. Use it as needed including bribing Mexican officials."

"What about the U.S. authorities, Tom? I hear they're still checking cars going south," Gonzalo asked.

"Yes, they are still checking cars, but it's been several days now since the kidnapping and U.S. Customs and Immigration have slacked off a bit and aren't doing detailed searches. Just try to be Americans going south for some fun," said Tom.

"I know I plan to have some fun," said Lansky with his typical scowl lighting his face.

Tom chose to ignore Lansky's comment, which he understood was Lansky's way of saying he intended to hurt or kill someone. "Jason and I will go next in one of the cars that Brian and God bought. Brian and God will come after us." Tom turned to Gonzalo. "Tony, I want you to stay with Wyman until we get south. Wyman, you think you'll have a problem flying into Mexico?"

"No, not at all. Mexico, unlike the U.S. doesn't really give a shit about who flies into their airspace. But just to make sure, I'll fly west, turn off the transponder and then drop down and fly amongst some of those canyons I used last year."

"Okay, once you get on the ground, let us know if that place is safe for us to set up our operation. If it isn't, we'll have to find another place."

"Ten-four," answered Wyman.

"Once inside Mexico, we'll try and stay in a loose convoy. We'll take Highway 2 to where it T's at Highway 10 at Janos. The ranch is supposed to be a few miles north of Janos."

"How will we know the ranch, boss?" asked Gonzalo.

"According to the CI, it has a large stone gate, and has the name Tierra Del Sol on it. I would suspect it is the only ranch in the area with guards at the gate. Evidently, Tierra Del Sol is similar to Zaragosa, the ranch we, uh, visited last year except it doesn't have an airstrip."

"So we just might have to take someone out?" offered Lansky half in jest and half seriously.

"You just might," said Tom. "According to the CI, the troops protecting this ranch are not like those campesinos we encountered at the ranch at Zaragosa last year. These are more than likely members of Los Zetos, or at least, a trained para-military organization. Most probably have military experience and are armed. They are probably the same crew that grabbed Conway and killed our two agents in El Paso. We know those guys had AK-47s."

"Mexican Military, isn't that an oxymoron," suggested Hood chuckling as he did so. His characterization of the Mexican military as something less than competent brought chuckles from several team members.

Wycoff first looked perplexed, then so as not to be excluded from the apparent joke, also chuckled, but he obviously had no idea what oxymoron meant.

Krissy looked at Wycoff and began to say something derogatory, but Tom interceded. "No, Krissy, don't even go there."

"The first order of business is to locate the ranch. We will then determine how we can bypass the gate and gain access to its interior. Once on the ranch, we will recon and locate where Conway is being held and what kind of opposition is present. Right now, I plan to use tonight and into early morning to do the recon. Then tomorrow night we'll act."

"Are we all going to do the recon boss?" asked Lansky.

"No, God. You, Brian and I will do the recon. Tony, along with Krissy, Hawk and Jason will be a reaction team if we get into trouble and need help."

"What about me, Mistuh Blaine, don't this token Negro get to join the white folk?" asked Hayes.

Ignoring the sarcasm, Tom looked at Hayes. "Wyman, I want you airborne; we can use you to bounce a radio signal to use our handhelds. You'll be our eyes from above. You might also be needed to do an emergency extraction."

Hayes nodded his head in ascent.

"These are just tentative plans; we'll be flexible and adjust as necessary."

"If we have to act quickly, what's the plan to get Conway off the ranch and out of Mexico?" asked Gonzalo.

"I hope the recon will answer the first part of your question, Tony. I hope we can whisk Conway off the ranch and get him to wherever Wyman can land. Wyman will fly Conway and some of us to the states," said Tom.

"Sounds like a plan," Gonzalo said.

"Any questions so far?" asked Tom as he looked from one team member to another.

Getting several no's and some negative shaking of heads from various team members, Tom sat for several minutes before he continued. "Team, just like last year, this is a dangerous mission, and we're very likely to meet with opposition. If any of you want to back out, you can do so now or at any time. No one will hold it against you if you do." He waited for a few seconds to see if anyone had a response to his last statement. When no one offered any comments, he said, "Just like last year, I promise I will not leave anyone behind in Mexico. I want you to be prepared to defend yourself. These bastards have already killed two of us, so if need be, err on the side of caution. His words were met with simple nods of the heads from the team members.

"Okay, I suggest you all get some sleep and something to eat; this may be your last of food or sleep for a couple of days. We'll meet here at 8:30 p.m. ready to go south. Oh, I almost forgot, take your BDUs and we'll change once we get in the vicinity of the ranch."

"What should we do about our guns, Tom? Do you think the Mexicans will check for those when we cross the border?" asked Hammond.

"Good question, Krissy. I suggest we either hide the weapons on the motor home which has a lot of places to hide things, or we could have Wyman take them with him in the plane."

"I, for one, do not want to be without my gun in Mexico, boss," said Lansky with a sense of finality in his tone.

"Okay, God, I'll leave it up to each of you individually what you want to do."

"Tom, let's have Wyman take the long guns. Individually, we each secret our handguns in the vehicles that we'll cross in," suggested Gonzalo.

Turning to the team, Tom asked, "Are you all cool with that?"

With the nodding of heads, the team all agreed.

As the team members began to file from the room, Lansky turned to Tom. "Hey, boss, several of us are going to check out the local Hooters for dinner. Want to join us? We know how much you are into Hooters."

Lansky's commentary was met by laughs from Hood and Hammond who, even at her own expense, enjoyed the slight embarrassment that Lansky's comment had caused Tom."

"Get out of here," Tom said.

Tom's final action before leaving his motel room that evening was to place a call to Libby in Colorado. Tom patiently listened to her miserable day, and her problems with the justice system, particularly the Federal justice system in Colorado. "Look, sweetie, I'll be out of pocket for a day or two and won't be able to call you."

"What? What do you mean by out of pocket, Tom?"

"I can't say too much, but basically we have an informant who might know the location of John Conway. We're going to check it out. It may take a day or two of surveillance. So I may not be able to get to a phone."

"You mean you might actually know where Conway might be located?" asked Libby.

"Yes, but it is speculative, and we need to do some good ole fashioned surveillance to confirm the CI's information. So don't worry if you don't hear from me. No news is good news, okay?"

"Uh, I guess so. But please be careful." Libby chuckled. "Jesus, look who I'm telling to be careful. Please call me as soon as you can."

"I promise," answered Tom.

February 7, 1997; Los Angeles, California

"There have been no new developments in the abduction of John Conway, the Administrator of DEA," began the evening KTLA news anchor. "Other than the videotape that was first exclusively aired on this station, there has been no other recorded communication from the adductors. With the five-day period given by the abductors to meet their demands of returning suspected drug trafficker Hector Gutiérrez to Mexico into its second day, there does not seem to be much information coming out of Washington on its efforts to meet these demands. For more information, we have Carla Roan of our Washington, D.C., post. Good evening, have there been any new developments?"

"Good evening Brian. No, there have been no new

developments here in D.C. Attempts by this station to interview Attorney General Marilyn Thomas regarding the efforts of the U.S. government have resulted in only a written news release advising that anything and everything is being done to seek the release of Administrator John Conway. Any further information at this time could jeopardize these efforts. Our White House liaison officer advises only that the President is being kept informed of the situation. All our attempts to talk with the FBI, whose responsibility includes investigating kidnappings, have been deferred to the Attorney General's office."

"Thank you Carla. We now have Ricardo Escalante of our Mexico City News Bureau on the line. Good evening, Ricardo. What do you hear from the Mexican Government on this abduction?"

"Good evening, Brian. The position of the Mexican Attorney General's Office has not changed and contends that until there is information, which indicates that Mexican Laws have been violated, their hands are tied. When pressed that there certainly is information present that Jaime Gutiérrez and the Sinaloa Cartel was behind this abduction, their representative further advised that this was pure speculation based upon demands that were made in the United States and not in Mexico. No Mexican law seems to have been violated at this time."

"Thank you, Ricardo. In other news…"

CHAPTER SEVENTEEN

February 8, 1997; Janos Chihuahua, Mexico

"I'm too old for this shit," uttered a very tired Tom. He mechanically put one foot down in front of the other. This line, one of his favorites, was a lament frequently expressed by Danny Glover while playing the role of Detective Murtaugh in the *Lethal Weapon* movie series. This morning, it seemed to correctly sum up both Tom's physical and mental states as he trekked cross-country to the waiting Chevrolet Blazer driven by Tony Gonzalo. Tom retraced a route, which, along with Lansky and Hood, he had traversed several hours previously in route to the interior of the Tierra Del Sol ranch. Their several-mile trek through rock-strewn arroyos and sandy washes was dotted with cholla, yucca and other species of cacti that threatened one with bodily harm if contacted. Thankfully, a full moon offered enough light to assist them in their march and allowed them to see the potential hazards in advance. Hazards also included the sudden changes in the terrain and the wildlife that called this area home. He had spooked several coyotes and a mother Javalina with several sucklings spooked him. She had first developed a threatening stance but backed off when Tom did likewise alternating his course just slightly. Added to the wildlife threats and the rough terrain was the temperature, which Tom estimated hovered in the low thirties. He noted the frost on the vegetation. *Damn it's cold out here. I forgot just how cold it got here in northern Mexico at night. At least with this time of year and this cold, I won't have to worry about stepping on a rattlesnake. Thank God, it's not too much farther. I sure hope they have some hot coffee in the motor home.*

As he continued his trek to the pickup point, Tom recycled the events of the past nine hours. The movement of the team south into Mexico was easier than anticipated. The only vehicle that either the U.S. or the Mexican authorities elected to search at the border was the motor home. And even that was lacking conviction on the part of both American and Mexican Immigration officials. Of course, Krissy, wearing her tight white turtleneck sweater, imposed her new physique on the inspectors distracting them enough that they elected to forgo a detailed search. Ignoring Tom's directions to wait until first light, Hayes went airborne in the Merlin while the other team members entered into Mexico. When the convoy of the three vehicles was approximately halfway to Janos, Hayes came up on the radio and advised them that the airport at Nueva Casas Grandes looked deserted. Using his airborne position, he guided the three vehicles to the small airport and with the aid of the headlights from the three vehicles to light the runway, he landed the Merlin with little effort, parking the twin-engine plane between two older hangars, which also appeared to be deserted.

While Krissy, with Hawk in the motor home, remained at the airport along with Hayes and Gonzalo, Tom, Wycoff, Hood and Lansky drove to Janos to find the Tierra Del Sol ranch. They found the ranch just as the CI advised. It was a short distance north of Janos and was readily identified by the massive stone gateway. Below the stone gateway, a heavy metal gate limited access to the ranch. Further restricting access to the ranch was a lighted guardhouse, manned with two guards. The obvious security of the ranch entrance and the security lighting that gave the ranch a glow caused it to stand out from the adjoining properties, which appeared to be dirt-poor ranches in comparison.

Tripping over a large rock, Tom's review of the past few hours was brought back to the present with a loud "son of a bitch." *Jesus, I don't recall the trip in to be this strenuous, but then again, the adrenaline and the anticipation of what we might encounter probably had a lot to do with masking any physical exertion last year.*

Access to the interior of Tierra Del Sol was limited to the front entrance by a six-foot chain link fence that ran the length of the property that bordered the paved road in front of the ranch.

When Tom asked if Lansky and Hood were sure they could gain access to the interior of the ranch by navigating across, Lansky and Hood both bragged. "We'll use the land navigation skills we learned in the military and used quite successfully recently on a number of occasions in the Gulf Wars."

However, after several aborted attempts, Hood and Lansky elected to follow Tom's suggestion.

"Listen, you knuckle heads. I'm too old to keep traipsing all over this damned countryside. Why don't we just follow the fence line that separates the Tierra Del Sol from the ranch to the east? We can head north until we see the light from the main ranch area and then go west into Tierra Del Sol." Tom's suggestion proved to be a winner, and they were able to traverse the neighboring ranch and then the Tierra Del Sol. The only significant obstacle encountered by the three was an electric three-strand barbed wire fence that separated Tierra Del Sol from the neighboring ranch. Concluding that it was probably alarmed, they elected not to try and defeat the fence by cutting or laying something across it, but instead, they would circumvent it by actually digging a hole and squeezing under the hot wires. "I sure hope I can find that hole again," Tom thought aloud as the fence line became visible in the limited light.

When the dawn began to break to the east, Tom found, not only the hole under the fence, but he was also able to make his way to the road where he found Gonzalo dozing in the Blazer parked off the road in a strand of trees. Tom pounded on the hood as he walked by the front of the vehicle.

Startled, Gonzalo woke with a start and with his pistol in his hand. "Whoa there, Tony," cautioned Tom as he opened the passenger door of the Blazer.

"Fuck! You'd like to give me a heart attack, Tom," complained Gonzalo. "Where's Brian and God?" he asked looking around the area from where Tom had emerged.

Tom welcomed the warmth of the Blazer and began to unbutton his field jacket. He rubbed his hands to speed the warmth. "Man, that heat feels good. Uh, change of plans, Tony. Brian and God stayed behind on the ranch to watch what goes on in the daylight and see if they can determine just how much opposition we're up against."

"Was that wise, Tom? It's not like we can just rush in and rescue them if things go to shit."

"Not to worry, Tony. Brian and God are hunkered down in a large barn and can see most of the main area of the ranch from different points in the barn. The Navy Seal and the ex-Army Ranger are in their element there. I left them the satellite phone. Oh, and by the way, there appears to be several tons of grass in the barn."

Gonzalo shook his head in acknowledgment. "So the CI was right; this is a staging area for shipments of marijuana and cocaine to the states."

"It appears that way, Tony, but right now our main concern is John Conway. If we can see our way clear to do something extra-curricular with this find, we'll do it. Of course, only after we have Conway safe in our company."

"So what's the situation, Tom?"

"It looks a bit challenging, but let's wait until I can get the team together.

I can brief everyone at once on what we found during our initial recon." Tom continued to rub his hands to spark some warmth back into them. "I sure hope there's some hot coffee in the motor home."

"Yeah, I'm sure there is. Krissy made a last minute Walmart run before we came south and picked up some junk food items as well. Nobody really wanted to live on Meals Ready to Eat."

"Tell that to Brian and God. When I left, they were haggling over which MRE was the best."

"Figures. I'm surprised God didn't want to find a snake to eat," offered Gonzalo with amusement in his tone.

Tom's face broke into a slight smile. "Actually, Tony, God was disappointed that there were no snakes he could skin and eat. Claims it's like eating chicken."

"I've eaten snake during survival training in the Army, and it sure as shit don't taste like chicken, Tom."

Forty minutes later, fortified with hot coffee and two packages of powdered sugar donuts, Tom addressed the assembled group of Hayes, Gonzalo, Hammond, Henderson and Wycoff in the cramped confines of the combination dinette and living room of the motor home. Tom passed around a hand-drawn diagram of the ranch headquarters. "Here is the main ranch house, a smaller building, what I would call a bunkhouse, and a large barn in the central area of the ranch. The main ranch area is lighted with those large dusk-to-dawn lights powered by a large generator adjacent to the barn. Military sentries are patrolling the area. They find places and ways to take forty winks when they can. Capitalizing on this human foible, Brian, God and myself were able to get close to all three buildings to check them out. From what we discovered, we think Conway is being held in a back bedroom in the main ranch house."

"What makes you think that, Tom?" asked Hawk.

"There's plywood covering a window in the rear of the ranch house; the rest of the windows are normal with glass. If I were a betting man, I'd wager the plywood is a quick attempt at creating a cell or holding room. Also, a guard with an AK is positioned at the front entrance to the ranch house and not the other smaller house. So I think Conway is in the ranch house."

"How many people do you think are on the ranch, Tom?" asked Hammond.

"Yeah, what are we up against?" echoed Hayes.

"I estimate ten to twelve. There seems to be a lot of coming and going from the bunkhouse area but not as much from the main ranch house. So I would assume most of the guards reside in the bunkhouse. As for the barn, it's a large metal building with sliding doors on the front. It contains what we estimated to be several tons of marijuana in large burlap bags. There might be other drugs there, but we weren't able to search it in the limited time we had. Brian and God found a small alcove in the rear of the barn that offered them a concealed position to make it possible for them to stay in the barn. They can move about and will update us if they find anything else.

"So what's the plan, Tom? How are we going to do this?" asked Gonzalo.

"Because of the number of guards and their weapons, we need to use surprise and speed to our advantage. As I said a few minutes ago, things and people tend to become slow and lazy in the early morning hours. I know in Vietnam, the NVA and VC used these hours to their advantage on us, and we were highly trained. So morning would be the best time to act. That is unless we hear or observe what we believe is Conway being moved. Then we'd have to readjust our plans and do something else."

"Okay, speed and surprise. How do we accomplish that? Are we all going to enter the ranch like you, Brian and God did?" asked Wycoff.

"One problem with that, Jason, would be exit transportation. We need to exit as fast as possible, and I'm sure the Administrator will be in no condition to travel over land. No, we need to do a two-pronged assault. One team to breech the front gate area will provide us with exit transportation, and one team will neutralize the opposition at the main ranch house and rescue Conway."

"So are we just going to go in there with guns blazing and hope we can overcome the resistance? I mean, I heard you say you saw the guards were armed with AKs. The only automatic weapons we have are the two H&K MP5s that Brian and God cleaned and elected not to take with them," said Hayes.

"I haven't finalized a plan yet," Tom said. "Let me think about how we can do this. And if any of you have any thoughts on this let me know."

"Have you given any thought about how we would get the Administrator out of Mexico once we grab him, Tom?" Hayes asked.

"Yes, right now my plan is to get him to you and the Merlin as fast as possible and for you to fly him directly to the states setting down at any available airport. Once there, we'll have to develop a cover plan."

"Cover plan?" questioned Hammond.

"Yes, Krissy, just like Mexico last year. We need to keep our actions in Mexico off the skyline. It would cause all sorts of international problems and would focus too much attention on us. Right now, I'm planning to stick with the story that we acted on information from a CI and found the Administrator in the United States and not Mexico. But we've got to get him to the United States first." Tom turned to the others individually. "Are we clear on that?"

Getting agreements from all, Tom then suggested, "Okay, I want you all to take some time and think about how we can do this thing. I need to get some rest; then we'll have another planning session."

February 8, 1997; Main Justice Building, Washington, D.C.

"Thank you for being here on this miserable morning," began a haggard-looking Marilyn Thomas. "There's some talk of shutting down the government on Monday if it keeps snowing through today like it is forecasted."

Roger Grey silently assessed the Attorney General. *I don't think I've ever seen her looking so bad. Her reddened and sunken eyes look like she hasn't slept in a week or was on a terrible drunk. Knowing her, it's definitely not the latter. Her hands are shaking. I fear she's not long for this job. Hopefully, Tom and his crew, wherever the hell they might be right now, will act and be successful. Recovering Conway will definitely take some of the pressure off the AG.*

Grey turned toward Randall Walsh, who today unlike everyone else, had not dressed casually for the severe weather. On this Saturday morning, Walsh wore a Hoover blue suit with white shirt and tie, along with the characteristic wing-tipped shoes.

"I understand there has been a development in the kidnapping, Mr. Walsh," said the AG. "Please share it with us."

Roger sat forward on his chair. Looking to his left, he noted the AG's announcement of a development had also caught the attention of Marsha Grant who began to stare daggers at Walsh. *She's pissed that we were not told of any developments. But I can't say I have been forthright, so who am I to cast stones at the bureau.*

"Well, it's a sort of development," started Walsh who thumbed through some papers on the conference table. "We, the FBI, have found the missing night security guard from the Wyndham Hotel."

"Really!" exclaimed a surprised Marsha Grant. Before she could consider the fact that it really was the Attorney General's call to be questioning Walsh and not hers, she demanded an answer in a tone that could only be considered curt and impolite. "What has the Bureau learned from him?"

"I'm getting to that," retorted Walsh glaring back at Grant. "Anyway, acting on an anonymous tip, we found the night security man, an Anastasio Perez, hiding at his cousin's house in Anthony, Texas, which is between El Paso and Las Cruces, New Mexico."

"And what has he told us?" asked Thomas.

"Well, Madam Attorney General, as you probably recall, he's a former El Paso Police Officer who reportedly resigned before being fired and is no stranger to the legal system. As the saying goes, he knows his rights and chose to invoke the right to remain silent."

"So we have nothing that will help us locate John Conway?" asked Marsha Grant again not waiting for the Attorney General to ask the question.

"Well, uh, no, but several hours after invoking his right to remain silent, we Mr. Perez's attorney contacted us and wants to be Monty Hall and play *Lets Make a Deal.*"

"A deal? What kind of a deal?" asked the Attorney General who sat forward in her chair while at the same time glaring at Marsha Grant.

"Yes, Walsh, just what kind of a deal would he expect for his complicity in the killing of two agents and the kidnapping of our Administrator?" asked a brash Marsha Grant who refused to be stared into silence, even if it was the Attorney General doing the staring.

Returning Grant's hostile look, Walsh answered the AG's question. "He wants immunity from prosecution for the murders and the kidnapping."

"What? Surely you've got to be kidding," retorted Grant. She turned to the Attorney General. "Ma'am, we can't really be considering giving this man total immunity."

Having been relegated to silence by Grant while Walsh and Grant went head to head, the Attorney General asked, "What can this Mr. Perez give us? Can he tell us where John Conway is being held?"

Walsh shrugged his shoulders. "I don't know what he can tell us, Madam Attorney General. And uh, immunity is not all that he wants."

"And what else does he expect from us?" asked the AG.

"According to his attorney, he wants us to convince the El Paso Police Department to reinstate him in his position as a detective."

"Oh, for Christ's sake, I'm surprised he only wants to be reinstated and not promoted to Chief of Police," said an exasperated Grant. "I think what we should promise him is that we won't seek the death penalty against him," continued Grant. "And would we even be considering making a deal if it were two dead FBI agents involved?" demanded Grant as she threw her pen down in apparent disgust.

"Marsha, please, let's try to be civil here," suggested the Attorney General.

"So he wants us to make assurances to him, but yet, he refuses to give us anything? Is that about right?" interjected the head of the Customs Branch of Immigration and Customs Enforcement.

"Yes, that's about right," said Walsh.

"Well, I certainly cannot agree to anything like that," said Thomas. "If he wants any kind of a deal from the U.S. government, he needs to give us something that would indicate he has relevant information that might help us recover John Conway." Thomas waved her hand in a dismissal manner.

After a strained silence among the assembled executives, Roger, who had remained silent watching the verbal gymnastics between Grant and Walsh, made a suggestion. "Maybe we need to take a different tactic with him." All eyes turned to Roger.

"Mr. Grey, what is it that you would propose?" asked a weary AG. "And why do I suspect I am going to regret asking you to explain yourself?"

Non-pulsed at the Attorney General's somewhat demeaning response, Roger placed his folded hands on the large oak conference table in front of him and looked from the Attorney General to Randall Walsh. "I think we should simply tell him either he cooperates with us and tells us what he knows, or we'll just kick him loose without any charges being filed against him."

"I don't understand. What will that accomplish?" asked Walsh.

"Figures," mumbled a sarcastic Grant.

"Simple, Mr. Walsh," said the head of the Customs Branch. "If he has any real information regarding the kidnapping and we just kick him loose, it might signal to those who did the kidnapping that he cooperated with us. He'd have a lot more to fear than prosecution by us."

"Yes, it might be a death sentence," added another representative from the Customs Branch.

"Surely, you jest, gentlemen!" exclaimed Thomas with surprise evident in her tone. "I cannot be a party to something like that," she cautioned. With obvious irritation developing on her face and body language, she looked first at Roger and then to other assembled executives. "We need to play this thing straight up. We charge him based upon what we have and see if he'll proffer something we can use. If he does so, we'll talk about a deal at that time."

"And if he doesn't?" asked Roger.

"We'll have to just do the best we can, Mr. Grey, and we'll do it according to the law and not some street thug method you would employ." With her patience obviously waning, the Attorney General asked, "Is there anything else?"

Seeing that no one had anything else to add to the meeting, the Attorney General said, "Depending on the weather and any further developments, I'll keep you posted on whether we'll meet in the morning. I know we are getting close to the end of the timeframe imposed by the kidnappers. We'll need to act in the next day or so, but if there is nothing new for us to discuss, I don't see the need to have you venture out in this weather if it is not necessary. So be by a phone where you can be reached on short notice."

"For what it's worth, Roger, I liked your idea," said Marsha Grant to Roger as he maneuvered the government vehicle through the snow-covered streets of DC heading toward the DEA headquarters building in Arlington. "Without some type of leverage like that, the hotel security man is not going to give us any information. It's too risky for him."

Roger glanced at Grant then back at the road. "I seriously doubt he has information that could tell us where Conway is being held. I'd bet the farm he was given a shit pot full of money to finger the room where Conway was staying and then told to be absent during the night."

"You're probably right about that," said Grant. "Can you believe that asshole Walsh? Sitting on that information until the meeting this morning instead of sharing it with us?"

"I'm not surprised, Marsha. The Bureau never seems to be able to play nice."

"Say, on another matter, the ASAC in El Paso has not heard from Blaine. Have you heard from him or know how we can get in touch with him?"

"No, I haven't heard from him since he said he would be leaving LA for El Paso, but then again, I would not expect to hear from him unless he had something that needed my approval or input." Roger hoped his facial expression would not reveal his lies.

"Well, I know you two are buds and all, but if he calls you, I want you to tell him to contact the ASAC of El Paso right away. Am I clear on that Roger?" challenged Grant.

"Yes, ma'am," was Roger's simple reply.

During the remainder of the trip, Roger and Grant rode in silence, which allowed Roger time to think. *I sure wish I knew where and what Tom and his team was up to. Damn, I guess I should have kept my big mouth shut about the suspension. But I really had no choice. If I hadn't said anything and he contacted the El Paso ASAC, he'd be on suspension right now and not wherever he might be. When I get home, I'll try the satellite phone again.*

February 8, 1997; Nueva Casas Grandes Chihuahua, Mexico

"Tom, wake up," insisted Tony Gonzalo as he nudged Tom's left shoulder.

Disoriented, Tom woke with a start. As his eyes began to adjust to the light, he realized he was lying prone on the bunk in the Winnebago. He rubbed his eyes to force them into focus. Glancing at his watch, he realized he had been asleep for just short of four hours. Slightly shaking his head and continually rubbing his eyes, he attempted to rid his head of its groggy state. Tom sat upright on the bunk with his legs hanging over the side. "What's up, Tony?"

"Tom, I have Lansky on the sat phone; he wants to give you an update on the ranch."

"Oh, good," said Tom as he took the satellite phone from Gonzalo. "What's up, God?"

"Hey, boss, lots of activity around here today," said an upbeat Lansky.

"Oh, what's going on?" Tom's head was now fully clear of the cobwebs.

"Man, this place is an armed camp, boss," emphasized Lansky. "Brian and I have seen at least a dozen individuals who all seem to be wearing various pieces of uniforms and carrying AKs."

"Shit, that's not good, God," Tom said.

"It might not be as bad as you would expect," answered Lansky.

"Why is that? A dozen armed men seem as bad as a heart attack," replied Tom.

"Yeah, that would be true in most instances, but these guys don't seem to be concerned with security. They just seem to wander around the area of the main ranch house and the bunkhouse without much concern."

"While that's good for us, God, it still worries me that there are so many, and we are definitely grossly outgunned."

"Yeah, but with the element of surprise, we might be able to even the playing field," said Lansky. Addressing Hood in the background, he asked, "What's that, Brian? Okay, I'll tell him. Boss, Brian wanted me to tell you we need to develop a plan that will satisfy one of Sun Tsu basic principles he put forth in the Art of War. A principle that he and his buddy Navy Seals frequently employed in the middle east."

"Okay, and what is that?" asked Tom expecting something off the wall from the Navy Seal.

"Bring war material with you from home, but forage on the enemy," said Lansky. "Brian thinks that with stealth and surprise, we can separate a number of these clowns from their AKs and make the odds a little more in our favor – automatic weapon-wise."

"God, that's actually a very excellent idea. Why don't you and Brian work on that?"

"Uh, it might mean we'd have to use, uh, deadly force, boss," said Lansky with hesitation in his tone.

Tom sighed deeply and took some time before he responded. "God, I harbor no illusion that this rescue mission is going to be without bloodshed. Let's just make sure it's not our blood that gets shed. Okay?"

"Got you covered, boss," answered Lansky.

"What else have you determined?"

"Most of the activity is around the bunkhouse. There has been a changing of the guard at the main ranch house about every four hours. And Brian and I have identified who we think is one of the guards' leaders."

"Why do you think he's the leader?"

"He seems to command the respect of the guards who almost assume the position of attention when he approaches them. But more importantly, he is frequently in and out of the main ranch house."

"I don't suppose you've seen Conway?" asked Tom.

"We should be so lucky, boss."

"What else?" asked Tom.

"Not much else, boss, except that Brian and I had to relocate in the barn because there's a flatbed stake truck backed up to the front door and several of the troops are loading bales of marijuana on the truck."

"Is that so? I wonder what that's about."

"I would imagine they're moving the marijuana north to smuggle it into the United States," Lansky suggested.

"Yeah, you're probably right. Even with this kidnapping, the drug business has to go on sending dope north and keeping the money flowing south."

"I guess you're right."

"Okay, you guys stay cool. I'll talk to you in a couple of hours," said Tom. Then as a second thought, he asked, "Say, God, what color is that truck?"

"It's yellow and red and has the name Los Productos De Sonora on the doors. Why do you ask?"

"Hold on a minute, God," said Tom. He turned to Tony who had maintained a close vigil while Tom was on the phone. "Tony, God said they're loading a truck with bales of marijuana right now. The CI said that the Cartel has a tunnel up near Aqua Prieta, sixty or seventy clicks from here that they use to smuggle the drugs under the border into Douglas, Arizona. It's a cinch, with the number of guards and their apparent firepower at the ranch, a daylight intervention would be suicide. What do you say we do some good old-fashioned surveillance and follow the truck and see if it leads us to the tunnel? We might be able to determine where it comes out on the U.S. side and give the info to the local DEA to work."

"I'm game, and we have Wyman with the plane. A loose surveillance would be all that is necessary. Besides, it beats just sitting here until tonight," said Gonzalo.

Tom picked up the satellite phone headpiece. "God, let us know if and when the truck departs."

"Ten-four, boss," answered Lansky.

Thirty-five minutes later, the satellite phone rang. "The truck appears to be leaving, boss," said Hood. There's a driver and one guy riding shotgun. Oh, and they didn't even bother to cover the bales of marijuana. Pretty brazen, if you ask me."

"I guess they have nothing to fear, Brian…"

"Oops, wait one, Tom," interrupted Hood. "Okay, looks like they'll have company; a green suburban with a driver and a passenger is leaving with the truck."

"Okay, you two be careful; we'll be in touch," said Tom as he ended the call. Tom turned to the group lounging in the motor home. "Listen up," Tom said. "Brian just advised that there is a truck loaded with marijuana and an escort suburban leaving the ranch right now. According to our CI, this organization has a tunnel up near Aqua Prieta that they use to smuggle the dope under the border. It's a cinch we can't attempt a rescue during daylight hours, too many armed guards present. I suggest we do some surveillance and determine where the tunnel is located and where it might come out in the U.S. We could give this info to the local DEA or Customs to work once we are through here. What do you guys think?"

"We'd need to be real careful, so we don't get burned. If they made our surveillance, it might make them hinky and move Conway," offered Gonzalo.

"Good point, Tony."

"Listen," said Hayes. "I can get airborne in a few minutes. I could allow you guys to stay way back. Hell, from the air, I might even be able to determine where the tunnel comes out on the U.S. side," offered Hayes.

"Wyman, why don't you take Krissy as an observer? Tony, you and Wycoff can take one car, and Hawk and I can take another. Remember, be careful, and break off surveillance if you think they're getting hinky. Whatever we do, we don't want to jeopardize our real reason for being here. And let's only use one radio per vehicle. Keep the others turned off. That way we'll still have fresh radios for later."

Once airborne, it took Hayes less than twenty minutes to locate the truck and the suburban heading north toward Aqua Prieta on the road ten. "Okay, we've got 'em," Hammond said over her radio. "I can see what is probably Aqua Prieta to the north. They seem to be moving pretty fast."

"Good, Krissy," said Tom. "We're a ways back; we'll try to catch up as soon as we can. Fortunately, there doesn't seem to be too much traffic on this road."

"Not to worry," said Krissy calmly. "I think we've got some time before they get to Aqua Prieta, and we have a good eyeball on them. Besides, I think we'll be able to pinpoint the location where they stop. It will be up to you guys to get a definite location from the ground."

Thirty minutes later, an excited Krissy came on the radio again. "Okay, the truck and suburban have pulled into a fenced yard. The truck is backing up to a large warehouse-type building; now it's backing into the building and the suburban is parking adjacent to the building. The driver and the passenger of the suburban are entering the building. The garage door is being pulled down."

"Good job, guys. We're a few minutes away; can you give us some directions?" asked Gonzalo.

"As you enter Aqua Prieta, stay on the main road until you reach the north end of the town. At the far end of the commercial area, take a right. That will lead you to a warehouse area. Our truck entered the, one, two, three, the third warehouse on the north side of the road, approximately three hundred yards from the international border," said Krissy. "Oh, and Wyman says to be careful. There's not much traffic on the road in front of the warehouse."

"With this being a border town, no one would suspect us with U.S. plates, but let's be careful," suggested Tom.

Several minutes later Hawk said, "Bingo, the name on the warehouse is Los Productos DeSonora, same as on the truck."

"There's a warehouse on the U.S. side about 250 to 300 yards in a direct line from this warehouse," said Krissy. "I'm willing to bet that's where the tunnel comes out."

"Oh, and looky there, Krissy," Hayes said in the background.

"What do you see?" asked Tom.

"Tom, there's a large ravine that seems to form the border between the U.S. and Mexico. Behind our warehouse there's a tremendous amount of fill dirt in the ravine."

"I do believe we have found the tunnel, guys," exclaimed a jubilant Tom.

February 8, 1997, Rancho Tierra Del Sol Chihuahua, Mexico

John Conway sat huddled against the wall opposite the door. He pulled the dirty blanket up around his neck to ward off the chill. *Jesus, what's taking them so long in meeting the demands of these thugs? I thought I was more important than that. What's taking the AG so long to act?* The chill of an immense fear suddenly consumed him. *Shit, what if she has refused to give into these people or even worse, what if she has already acted and these assholes have no intention of honoring their end of the deal? I'm a dead man in either case.* He shivered uncontrollably now, more from fear than from the actual chill of his cell-like room. As the fear ran its course, he was overcome with self-pity. He began to sob audibly. After several minutes of sobbing, he willed himself to become calm. *Don't be stupid. Of course, the AG will negotiate for my release and these people will honor their end of the ransom. They've gone to great lengths to keep me alive and somewhat comfortable – food and water and even some coffee. If they were just going to kill me, they wouldn't care how I was treated. It's just this not knowing and waiting. It's preying on my mind.* He sat upright. *Be strong, stupid, and don't let your imagination get the better of you. Everything will work out.*

With his emotions in check for now, he judged from his apparent hunger that it was about dinnertime and within the hour, his nostrils alerted him that food was on the way. Standing up slowly, he watched as the door opened just slightly and a tray containing food was set on the floor just inside the door. The door then closed.

The food, a concoction of chunks of meat with beans and other vegetables, was tasty, and again, there was a cup of hot coffee. Using a corn tortilla to package the meat and bean mixture, Conway ate ravishingly until the plate was clean. He sipped what was left of the coffee. *All that worry was for nothing. They are feeding me well and wouldn't be doing that if they just intended to kill me.*

The heavy meal on his stomach caused him to become drowsy, and he fell asleep. He had not been asleep long when the sound of footsteps outside the door awakened him. He expected to see one of the guards who would collect the empty food tray and take him to the bathroom. Instead, the comandante entered the room and ordered one of the guards to take the empty plate. The comandante wore his ever-present heavily-tinted sunglasses. "Was the food to your satisfaction, Señor?"

"Yes, it was very good, Comandante," answered Conway striving to be thankful and respectful.

"Bueno, I am glad they are treating you well here."

"Yes, I guess they are treating me good," Conway replied as he began to stand.

The comandante waved Conway to remain seated. "Tell me, Señor, are you not a very important person in your government?"

Perplexed by the question, Conway had to think about his response for a minute or two before replying. "Uh, I guess you might say that," said Conway with some hesitation.

"Then I am confused," began the comandante. Looking down at the floor, he stroked his chin; he then looked up. "Why is it your government has not acted quicker in meeting our demands then? If you are so important that is?"

Conway was unable to read the comandante's eyes through the dark sunglasses. "Comandante, I think what you have done and what you have demanded has not been done before. My government, while it might seem to be acting slow, I am positive they are doing everything that is required to meet your demands in the time frame you have established."

"I see. And why is it they do not say that on the television?" asked the comandante.

"Uh, I don't know, maybe they feel too much publicity is not in the best interests of either you or me?"

"I see," said the comandante who turned and said something in Spanish to someone standing outside the door.

After staring in the direction of Conway for some time, the comandante finally said, "Well, amigo, unfortunately my jefe does not like the slowness in which your government is responding."

A cold dread began to build within Conway. "I don't understand. Has the time frame you gave them elapsed?"

"No, but my jefe has heard nothing and fears that your government does not take him seriously."

The fear of where this was leading began to take hold. "Comandante, please," Conway begged, "I am sure they are going to agree to your demands. It just takes time to do everything properly."

"I don't agree…" began the comandante. Several guards entered the room.

"Oh, God, no!" cried Conway when he saw one of the guards carrying a large set of bolt cutters.

The comandante nodded his head, and the guards converged on Conway, who began to struggle and resist the guards' efforts to take control of him. With twisting of arms and wrists into a painful angle, the guards easily succeeded in getting control of Conway. Now controlled by his captors, he cried out, "Oh no, God, please, please I beg you. Don't do this. Don't hurt me. My government is going to meet your demands."

Conway continued to struggle against the superior number of guards as he cried and begged them not to hurt him.

"I am sorry, friend," said the comandante void of any emotion, "but I think your government needs more convincing." With that said, he nodded to the guards again. With several guards holding the still struggling Conway, who now was emitting sounds like an injured animal, another guard pried opened his right hand. With bolt cutters, another guard then with very little effort snipped off Conway's right index finger.

The intense pain wracked Conway's brain, such pain he had never before experienced in his life. He heard himself scream in pain, which he followed by vomiting his recently digested meal. Mercifully, he lost consciousness excusing him from further pain.

Across from the ranch house, Lansky and Hood continued their surveillance. "Jesus, was that a scream?" asked Hood.

"I think it was," said Lansky, as he scrambled closer to the front doors of the barn.

"What are they doing to him?" asked Hood.

"I imagine something that has to do with the bolt cutters we saw one asshole carry into the ranch house."

"Jesus, we can't just sit here and let them torture that poor bastard, God," said Hood.

"Yeah, I know Brian, but there are just two of us and a dozen of them with automatic weapons. It would be foolish for us to try something."

"But we can't just stand by and let them do this."

"I know, buddy. Let's get Blaine on the sat phone; maybe he'll have a plan."

Several minutes later, Tom was on the phone. "Tom, something bad is happening here."

"What's going on, God?"

"About an hour ago, a green Range Rover arrived at the ranch with three men. One seems to be a honcho of some sort."

"How do you know that, God?" asked Tom.

"Everybody seems to show him respect, even the guy we thought was the guards' leader. One of the men carried what looked like bolt cutters into the ranch house."

"Oh shit, that's not good."

"Yeah, it gets worse, boss. Ten minutes ago, Brian and I thought we heard someone scream."

"Fuck!" Tom exclaimed. "The CI said their original plan was to cut off a finger or fingers of Conway to prove they had him."

"Well, somebody obviously screamed in pain, boss. What should we do?"

"How many guards present there right now, God?"

"Ten, maybe twelve, and the activity in the ranch house has brought most of them out of the bunkhouse." After several moments of dead silence, Lansky asked, "Are you still there, boss?"

"Yeah, God, I was just thinking. Hold on a minute let me talk to the others here."

Tom turned around and told the assembled team members what Lansky had reported.

Gonzalo was the first to speak. "Was there just one scream or repeated screams?"

Picking up the phone Tom asked Lansky, "Was there just the one scream or repeated screams God?"

"We just heard the one scream, boss."

"They only heard the one scream."

"Tom, I think if they were actively torturing him, we would hear more screams. That's their system—keep the victim conscious so he can get the full effect of the pain that they inflict. My best guess is they either killed him or cut off a finger as they originally planned," said Gonzalo. "I think it's too late to save him from that fate. I suggest we just wait until tonight and do as we planned using darkness as our ally."

"I agree with Tony, boss," said Hawk. "It would be suicide for us to attempt a rescue mission in broad day light."

Hammond, Wycoff and Hayes agreed with Gonzalo's assessment.

"If the screaming begins again, we'll have to rethink this," said Gonzalo.

Tom turned back to the satellite phone and told Lansky of their assessment of the situation. "If you hear more screaming, let me know right away."

"Ten-four, boss."

February 8, 1997; Hacienda Puesta Del Sol, La Cruz, Sinaloa, Mexico

Juan Cervantes hung up the phone and turned to his computer to input data. *Jaime seems to be feeling the effects of too much Mezcal again* he thought. *This is becoming an all too frequent occurrence. This thing with Hector has played heavily on his mind I guess. Well, Jaime, I sure hope you have a large stock of Mezcal, because unless I am wrong, I think Thomas Blaine and his men are going to create a lot more problems for you.*

Jaime walked tentatively back into the office and settled slowly into a large leather chair. "My head is killing me," Jaime said. He muted the sound of CNN and asked over his shoulder, "Juan, have we heard from the comandante?"

"No, Don Jaime, not since I've been here. But I did hear from Ramon."

"And what did Ramon have for us?"

"He just wanted you to know that they moved 2,000 kilos north earlier today?"

"White or green, Juan?"

"Green, Don Jaime."

"Good, there is a good market north right now. The cold weather there creates a demand for our product." He rested his chin on his chest.

"Don Jaime, can I get you something? Something for your head?"

"Sí, por favor. I am drinking too much with worry over Hector."

"Entiendo, Jaime." Juan left the office and returned shortly with aspirin and some bottled water. He handed both to Jaime who had remained slumped in the leather chair.

"Gracias, Juan." He palmed the aspirin into his mouth and washed them down with the water.

"Ramon also said he has taken in two million that he will move to the Caymans this week."

"Bueno," replied a distracted Jaime.

"Don Jaime, he has suggested that we need a new banker, one who will not demand the percentage that the Juarez person is demanding."

"He thinks we are paying too much?"

"Sí, Don Jaime. He feels with the volume we are doing, we should be getting a much better rate."

"Let him check. If he thinks I should have a chat with the banker we use to get us a better rate, I can do that too."

"Sí, Don Jaime, I will talk with him."

"And, Juan, try to contact the comandante. I need to know what he is doing."

"Sí, Don Jaime," said Juan.

February 8, 1997; Nueva Casas Grandes Chihuahua, Mexico

"It should be dark in a few hours; we'll start making our move," said Tom Blaine to the assembled group. In the past hour, they had developed a plan to rescue John Conway. "We should…" The ring of the sat phone interrupted Tom.

Hammond answered it. "What's up?" After listening to the person's quick response, she said, "I'll let you talk with the boss. It's Hood, Tom," she said as she passed the phone to him.

"What's happening, Brian."

"Boss the Range Rover and the three guys who arrived in it are leaving. They were carrying the bolt cutters and a small package."

"Okay, anything else going on? Any more screams?"

"No, boss, it's actually become quiet here since the Range Rover departed ten minutes ago."

"Hold on, Brian." Tom turned to the team and reported what Brian had said.

"Gee, I wonder what's in the package?" asked Hawk feigning ignorance.

"If I were a betting man, I wager it's one of John Conway's fingers," said Gonzalo.

"I'd take some of that action myself," said Hayes.

Tom scratched the side of his head, "The CI said a comandante who works for the Gutiérrez's wanted to cut off Conway's fingers to prove they had abducted him. God and Brian think one of the men in the Range Rover was some type of honcho because of how the people at the ranch treat him. Maybe this person is Gutiérrez's comandante.

"Could be," said Gonzalo. "So what? There's not much we can do to him right now."

"I'm not so sure, Tony," began Tom. "If it is the comandante, he's also the same prick who orchestrated the kidnapping of Conway and the killing of our agents." Tom turned to Hayes. "Wyman, get airborne while we still have some daylight."

"Got you covered, boss. Then what?" asked Hayes.

"See if you can find us a green Range Rover on the road from Janos to Juarez or Janos to Agua Prieto."

"What are we going to do, Tom?" asked Hawk.

"Yeah, what you got in mind, boss?" added Gonzalo.

"If this guy *is* the comandante, he might be the key to the front door of the ranch where they're holding Conway. We could use him just like we used Uriarte last year to gain access to his estancia."

"Oh, yeah, I see," said Gonzalo. A large smile formed on his face. "I like it, Tom."

"Yeah, I think that's a good plan too," offered Hammond. "Particularly if I can get a chance to kick him in the nuts like I did to get Uriarte's undivided attention last year."

The infamous kick Hammond had used with Uriarte to overpower him long enough for Tom and his crew to capture him, brought smiles and chuckles to the group members who had been present to witness Hammond in action.

"I'll keep that in mind, Krissy," said a smiling Tom. "Let's see if we can arrange a meeting with the comandante."

Thirty minutes later, Hayes came over the radio. "Tom, I've checked the roads north and south of Janos and almost to Juarez. I don't see any green Ranger Rovers."

"Shit, Wyman," exclaimed a frustrated Tom. "He couldn't have driven too far in the short time from when he left the ranch until you got airborne. Even if he was driving like hell, he could not have made it to either Juarez or Agua Prieto."

"I know. He must have pulled off the road somewhere," said Hayes.

"I think I have him, boss," interrupted Hammond who was with Gonzalo. "There's a green Range Rover parked outside a restaurant just outside of Janos on the road to Juarez."

"Good work, Krissy. We'll be there in a couple of minutes."

As they headed toward the restaurant, Tom reached behind the seat and grabbed the satellite phone. He waited several minutes before a groggy Hood whispered, "Hello."

"Brian, sorry to wake you, buddy."

"S'okay, boss, God and I were trying to catch some sleep before it gets dark."

"Good idea, Brian. Listen, describe the person who you said looked like he was the jefe who arrived in the Range Rover."

"Lansky, it's the boss. He wants to know what the guy who arrived in the Range Rover looked like."

After a short delay, Lansky came on the phone. "He was about six foot tall, dressed in dark leather jacket and trousers. I think he had medium length dark hair, but it was hard to tell because he had on a dark-colored cowboy hat.

"Anything distinguishing about him, God?" asked Tom.

"No, not really, only that he had on those reflective mirror sunglasses, the kind you can't see into."

"Okay, good. Get some sleep; I'll get back to you with a plan shortly."

"What's up, Tom? Why the questions about this guy?"

"God, I can't go into that right now, but I think I've found us a way to gain access to the ranch without me having to make that cross-country trek again."

"Ten-four, boss. We'll be waiting to hear from you."

February 8, 1997; Janos Chihuahua, Mexico

As Tom, Hawk and Wycoff approached the east terminus of Janos, Hammond came on the radio. "The Range Rover is parked between the two buildings on the right, just up ahead, Tom."

"Okay, we'll check it out," said Tom.

"Wait one, boss," ordered Krissy with a note of excitement in her tone, "there appears to be someone standing outside the vehicle near the driver's door. He's smoking a cigarette."

"Doesn't he know that's bad for his health?" interjected Hayes circling above the area in the Merlin.

"He's probably an ayudante; he's watching the vehicle while the others eat," offered Gonzalo.

"We need to get a look into that vehicle to see if it's the right one," suggested Tom.

After several minutes, Krissy broke the radio silence. "Let me see if I can distract him. Be ready to move fast once I act."

Gonzalo, who was driving the Bronco, stopped the vehicle just behind the Range Rover and Hammond departed it from the passenger door. She walked directly toward the suspected ayudante and in her best attempt at Spanish called to him. "Dispense me, Señor – excuse me, sir."

The suspected ayudante turned toward Hammond and dropped his cigarette. He used his boot to ground it out. "Sí – que pasa, señora? Yes, what's up, Miss?"

"Donde está el camino a Juarez – Where is the road to Juarez?" she asked as she closed the distance between herself and the suspected ayudante.

"Ah, señora…" began the ayudante. When he turned his head away from Krissy and began to point the proper direction to Jaurez, it gave Krissy the slight distraction she needed. Reacting immediately, she drove her knee up directly into the ayudante's groin causing him to fold over like a pocketknife. Her next knee thrust caught the ayudante directly under the chin causing him to right himself and then fall to the ground.

"Ouch!" exclaimed Gonzalo who witnessed Krissy's actions from their vehicle. "Knee to the nuts, guys. Let's go," he said over his radio as he exited his vehicle.

The remainder of the team quickly exited their vehicles and were to Krissy's aid in a few seconds. Using plastic cuffs, Tom cuffed the ayudante who was retching violently.

Hawk opened the Rover's back door. "Got the bolt cutters, boss," announced Hawk.

"Geez, for this guy's sake, I'm glad of that. I would hate for Krissy to do that to an innocent guy," quipped Wycoff.

"Yep, you were right, Tom. The box contains a bloody finger, looks like a fore finger," said Tony as he exited the driver's side of the Range Rover examining the contents of a small box.

"Ugh," offered Krissy as she looked into the box at the severed finger.

With his retching subsiding, the ayudante began, "Pinche puta," which earned him a swift kick in the side of the head from Wycoff. "Only I get to call her dirty names, asshole."

"Silencio," ordered Gonzalo. He bent down so that he was face-to-face with the ayudantes. "Oye, amigo, if you do not want me to have the señora give you another kick to the juevos, you will answer some questions."

Shaking his head in ascent he said, "Que quire – what do you want?"

"That's better, amigo," said Gonzalo as he patted the ayudante on the cheek. "Is the comandante in the restaurant?"

The ayudante looked from Gonzalo to Tom, who had moved in closer. Instead of verbally responding, he merely nodded his head in ascent.

"You did good, amigo," said Gonzalo and again patted the ayudante on the cheek. "You saved yourself considerable pain."

Tom stood and turned to Wycoff. "Tree, I'm afraid you'll stand out like crazy if you go in the restaurant with us. I want you to take our friend here and put him in the blazer. Stay there unless you hear shots fired, then come on in. Understand?"

"Got you covered, boss," said Wycoff. He bent down, and, with one hand, effortlessly lifted the moaning ayudante off the ground, and shoved him toward the Blazer.

"Hawk, you and Krissy enter the restaurant first. Tony and I will be right behind you," instructed Tom.

"Tom, why don't we just wait for him to exit?" asked Gonzalo.

"Might take too long, Tony, and I think with him sitting down, we'll have a better chance to take him without a fuss."

"Okay, boss," replied a less than convinced Gonzalo.

"Besides, Tony, I want to have a word with the comandante," said Tom as he grabbed the box containing the severed finger.

He looked at Tom with an expression of mild disbelief. "Aw, shit, is this going to be another Saurez-Saurez incident, boss?" he asked. His question was a direct reference to a confrontation that Tom orchestrated between himself and a major Bolivian drug trafficker in a Cochabamba restaurant the year before. During that confrontation, Tom first had drinks sent to the table of the drug trafficker who was dining with his lady friend. Tom then joined the couple at their table and told the trafficker that he, Tom, had been responsible for the destruction of one of drug trafficker's major cocaine-producing labs in the jungles several weeks prior.

"Tony, don't you know that all work and no play makes Tony a dull boy."

Gonzalo shook his head. "Okay, what's the plan?"

"It all depends on the situation inside the restaurant," Tom said.

The restaurant was larger than it appeared from the outside. The interior walls were a beige stucco with red brick accents, similar to the exterior walls, and the floor was a highly polished Saltillo tile. Booths lined the windowed wall that fronted the street and the other interior walls with numerous tables scattered in the middle. A sweeping curved stucco and brick arch divided the main dining room into two separate areas. Paintings of matadors engaged in combat with large bulls and Mexican landscapes adorned most of the interior walls.

Entering the restaurant to the sounds of Latin music, Tom's nostrils immediately came alive. "Man, I'm hungry," he commented to Gonzalo who merely smiled and nodded his head in reply.

Gonzalo quickly scanned the patrons and spotted the comandante. With his head, he nodded in the direction of the comandante. The comandante sat in a booth against a far wall at the back of the restaurant drinking a beer. His distinctive sunglasses and cowboy hat sat on the table. One other person accompanied the comandante. He appeared to be at ease with the comandante while they drank beer together. *Must be an ayudante or police officer* Tom concluded silently.

A quick look around the restaurant and Tom determined only a couple of booths and tables were occupied. Pleased that there would not be many witnesses, he whispered to Gonzalo, "Tony, follow my lead." He turned to Hammond and Hawk. "Stay behind us and take the table next to their booth. Be ready to make a quick exit."

"Ten-four," Hawk said quietly.

As he approached the comandante's booth, Tom observed a waitress carrying a tray of plates of food heading toward the table. Following the waitress, Tom waited while she placed the plates of hot food in front of the comandante and his companion. When the waitress turned and walked away from the table, Tom dropped into the booth beside the comandante forcing him to move closer to the wall so that Tom could be seated on the outside of the booth.

Gonzalo followed his lead and did the same on the other side of the booth to the comandante's companion. The surprised comandante demanded, "Que pasa – what's happening?"

Tom picked up a tortilla chip from a bowl, dabbed it into a small dish of salsa and popped the chip into his mouth.

Annoyance quickly developed on the face of the comandante. "Who are…?"

Holding up his index finger to signal that he needed a minute, Tom chewed the tortilla chip and swallowed. "Wow! That's good salsa."

Again, the comandante, whose annoyance had turned to anger, began. "Who are…?"

Once again, Tom signaled he needed a minute. He then placed the small box on the table, pulled out Conway's severed finger and deposited it in the middle of the comandante's refried beans. "I thought you'd like some finger food with your meal, Comandante," said Tom sporting a large smirk.

Looking at the finger, then at Tom, the comandante hesitated for just a second before he began to squirm and struggle for his pistol in his belt against his back. Tom, who had placed his gun in his belt in front before entering the restaurant, beat the comandante to the draw and jabbed his Glock .45 pistol in the side of the comandante. "Don't be foolish, Comandante, or your kidneys will meet that wall."

Mimicking Tom's actions, Gonzalo did the same to the comandante's companion. "What he said." He indicated Tom by shrugging his shoulders in Tom's direction. "Don't be stupid, señor."

"Who are you, pendejo?"

"Aw, now is that nice, Comandante? Name calling, and after I brought you a special treat for dinner?" said Tom with the sarcasm dripping from his voice.

"You have made a very bad mistake, señor," spit the comandante.

"Won't be the first time and probably not the last time, Comandante," retorted Tom with a slight grin lighting his face. "But unless I miss my guess, you are the comandante who caused two of my pals to be killed up in El Paso the other day. And, then, you kidnapped John Conway. While I don't really give a shit about John Conway, I'll be damned if I'll let a piece of shit like you come to my country and kill agents and kidnap government officials."

From the visual expressions, Tom could see the comandante's anger had turned to rage.

"You are a dead man, hombre," threatened the comandante through clenched teeth.

Tom took on a nonchalant air. "Yes, it is a fact of life that we shall all die. But I suspect that's not what you meant." Getting serious, Tom looked at the comandante. "Listen, hombre, lots of better men than you have threatened me and so far none have succeeded. I think you better start worrying about how you are going to survive the night."

"Meeting Tom's glare with a menacing look of his own, he demanded, "Who are you?"

Tom reached up and put on the comandante's sunglasses. "I'm your worst nightmare, Comandante. I'm the man who is going to take John Conway home, and guess what, mi amigo; neither your government nor mine knows that we're here. So we can do whatever the fuck we want to do to get the job done. Comprende, amigo?"

The comandante's anger gave way to a sneer. "You have not succeeded yet, Pendejo."

Tom ignored the last comment. "Okay, dinner's over, I guess. I think we shall be leaving. Tom looked over the top of the sunglasses at the comandante. "Do as you are told, and you might survive tonight. Be stupid, and I'll shoot you right here." Tom leaned over toward Hammond, who sat with Hawk at an adjoining table. In a low voice, Tom said, "Krissy, you and Hawk create a diversion."

"Gotcha covered, boss," said Hammond. Waiting a few seconds, Krissy then challenged Hawk in a voice meant to carry through the restaurant. "You son of a bitch. Are you looking at the waitress's butt? We haven't been married a month, and you're already looking at other women's asses."

Krissy's loud accusation had the desired effect. She could see that she had gotten the attention of everyone in the diner.

Hawk quickly dropped into the role of the husband with a wandering eye and begged innocence. "Don't be silly, dear. I was not looking at her butt."

"Bullshit, and don't honey me. I saw you gawking at her fat ass. She jumped to her feet upsetting the table as she did so and thrust her chest at Hawk. "Aren't my girls big enough to satisfy you that you have to ogle another woman's ass?"

The domestic commotion Krissy created resulted in the restaurant patrons, staff and management to focus on Krissy and Hawk paying very little attention to Tom and Tony as they escorted the comandante and his associate from the restaurant.

Seeing that Tom and Gonzalo had made it out of the restaurant, Krissy picked up a water glass and threw it at Hawk. "I'm out of here. I'll be in the car, jerk."

Hawk's face had actually reddened in embarrassment while playing the role of the philandering-eyed husband. He withdrew two hundred dollar bills from his wallet and threw them on the table. "I'm sorry for that folks," he announced to the restaurant in perfect Spanish. "Dinner's on me." With his head hanging, he quickly exited the restaurant.

Outside, the team members greeted Hawk with laughter and congratulated Krissy on her grand performance.

"Good job, Chad," said Tom. "You two certainly created enough of a diversion to allow us to slip out unnoticed."

With the comandante and his two associates restrained with plastic cuffs, Tom gave the plan. "Let's transport these guys back to the motor home."

Tom then radioed Wyman. "Wyman, we're returning to the motor home. Do you have enough light to land or will you need us?"

"I can see the runway is lit right now. I guess someone who knows how to key the runway lights is using it. See you at the motor home," said Hayes.

During the trip to the airfield, Tom sat in the back seat to watch over the comandante while Gonzalo drove. He looked around the commandeered Range Rover and then turned to the comandante. "Nice car. Sure is a lot better than what we've been driving."

February 8, 1997; Hacienda Puesta Del Sol, La Cruz, Sinaloa, Mexico

Jaime paced back and forth in front of CNN news. He stopped and looked up at Juan who was at his desk. "Juan, the comandante still has not called?"

"No, Don Jaime, he has not."

"I am concerned; he should have called by now. I hope nothing has gone wrong," said Jaime as he looked from Juan to the floor in front of him.

"Perdone, Don Jaime can I be of assistance?" asked a pensive Juan Cervantes. "Did he take the jet? If he did, I can page the pilot and see if he has heard from the comandante."

"Sí, Sí, Juan. That is a good idea. The comandante took the jet up to Juarez to check on, uh, ah… something for me."

"I will page him right away. Don Jaime, should I also call Ramon to see if the comandante has checked in with him?"

"Sí, Juan. That is even a better idea, mi amigo."

Mi amigo, I don't think you will be using those terms with me very shortly if Thomas Blaine does as he plans.

"So you have not heard from the comandante?" asked Juan who received a call from the pilot shortly after paging him.

"Uh, no, Juan I have not heard from him, and I am concerned," said the pilot.

"Concerned? What concerns you?"

"The weather, Juan. It is beginning to rain here in Juarez and the prediction is that it will turn to freezing rain in a few hours. If it does, I will be grounded here in Juarez."

"I see," said Juan. "Don Jaime is very anxious to hear from him, so if you hear from the comandante, have him call here right away. If he is unable to call, you call."

"Sí, Juan, I will call. Should I stay here even if the weather starts to get bad?"

"Let me ask Don Jaime." Juan turned to Jaime. "Don Jaime, the pilot has not heard from the comandante; he is concerned about the weather."

"The weather?"

"Sí, Don Jaime, it is raining slightly in Juarez, and they predict it will turn to a freezing rain in several hours. If that occurs, according to the pilot, he will be grounded in Juarez. Should he stay there?"

Jaime was silent for a few moments. "Yes, tell the pilot to stay there. He can get a room if necessary, but I want him available for the comandante."

"Don Jaime wants you to remain there in Juarez," he told the pilot. "He said you may get a room if the weather prohibits you from flying. And be sure to call as soon as you have word about the comandante."

Next, Juan called Ramon in Juarez. "Hola, Ramon," began Juan.

"Hola, Juan. I have become very important with two calls from you in the past few hours?" said Ramon chuckling.

"Ramon, you will always be important to me," kidded Juan in response. "Oye, Carnal, listen buddy, we've still not heard from the comandante. Has he been in touch with you in the past several hours?"

"No, Juan, I have not heard from him. He called me this morning, said he would be bringing something for me to handle, and wanted to be sure I would be here around dinnertime. But since then, I have not heard from him."

"Okay, Ramon. I will tell Don Jefe this information. If the comandante does contact you, have him call right away, Don Jaime is very concerned."

"I will do that, Juan, and give Don Jaime my regards."

Juan hung up the phone. "Don Jaime, Ramon sends his regards and advises that he has not heard from the comandante since early this morning. He was expecting him by dinnertime, but he has not arrived nor has he called."

"Gracias, Juan. I guess I will wait another hour or so before I take some action."

"Don Jaime, I'm sure the comandante has a very good reason for not calling; he is a very reliable individual."

"Sí, Sí, of course you are right, Juan, but I am very anxious to take the next step necessary to bring mi hermano back home."

"Entiendo, Don Jaime."

February 8, 1997; Nueva Casas Grandes, Chihuahua, Mexico

Tom came out of the rear bedroom after checking on the three prisoners just as Hayes entered the motor home.

"We have a problem, Tom," Hayes said.

"A problem? What kind of a problem?" Before Hayes could answer,

Tom challenged him. "Don't tell me there's something wrong with the plane, because I'm relying on that to get Conway out of Mexico."

"No, Tom, there's nothing mechanically wrong with the Merlin, but we do have a problem with the weather."

"The rain?" asked Tom.

"Yeah, boss. But it's more than just rain. According to the National Weather Service, this drizzle will probably turn to freezing rain by midnight, which will effectively ground all general aviation aircraft along the border area. I'm afraid we can't count on using the Merlin to fly Conway out of here."

"Well, shit!" exclaimed Tom. "That creates a new set of problems for us. I was counting on you flying us to El Paso once we grabbed Conway."

After a prolonged period of silence, Gonzalo asked, "What now, boss? Can we wait a day and do this thing tomorrow night?"

"Yeah, Tom, we could wait one more night. Maybe the weather will be better," offered Hammond.

"What'll we do with our friends back there?" asked Tom as he jerked his thumb toward the motor home bedroom. "I'm sure the comandante was in touch with Gutiérrez and when he just disappears, it will be noted. Gutiérrez may send more people here looking for the comandante. We don't need more armed people at the ranch to contend with right now."

"I guess we shouldn't have confronted the comandante and left well enough alone," offered Gonzalo.

"Wait a minute, Tony, that's not fair," Krissy said coming to Tom's defense. "Tom's decision to grab the comandante and use him as a shield to gain access to the ranch was a good one. How was he to know the weather was going to put a crimp in our plans?"

Gonzalo shrugged his shoulders. "You're right, Krissy. Sorry, boss, I'm just frustrated."

Tom nodded his head accepting Gonzalo's apology. "One other factor is against us waiting guys. We're up against the time limit imposed for the exchange. Come Monday morning, the AG will have to order the release of Hector Gutiérrez. We can't afford for something to happen tomorrow evening that will delay our arrival in the US. It could result in them killing Conway once Gutiérrez has been released."

"It's a cinch we can't just drive up and cross the border with him. That's way too dangerous for him and, of course, us," concluded Gonzalo.

"Yeah, Tony, I agree. We don't know how much influence Gutiérrez has on the Mexican immigration, and I'm not willing to take that chance." Tom looked down while thinking for several moments, then he slowly raised his head as a smile began to spread across his face. "Maybe we can't take him across the border, but we can take him under the border."

"Under the border?" questioned Hammond.

"The tunnel!" exclaimed Gonzalo.

"Right, the tunnel. We definitely know where it begins. The only question is where it ends and we think we know where that is," said Tom.

"I'm sure it will be guarded," offered Hawk.

"I guess that's the chance we'll have to take. Just like when we go in to take Conway away from them, we'll also have to be prepared for resistance at the tunnel." Tom turned to Hayes. "Do you think you can get airborne?"

"Sure, boss, the rain's not freezing yet."

"Okay. Think you can fly to Douglas?"

"Douglas? Sure, I planned to fly north toward New Mexico anyway. When I get to the border, I'll turn off my transponder, drop down low and follow some shallow canyons to avoid the radar like I did last year. I'll just fly further north once I cross into the US, and then turn south and west and head toward Douglas."

"Sounds good."

"Well shit, boss, I feel like I'm leaving you guys high and dry," said Hayes regretfully.

"That's not true. Unlike the cars we brought with us, we can't just abandon the plane here. There will be too many questions asked on both sides of the border. Besides, I need someone to get us motel rooms so we have a place to reorganize and rest. You can rent a car so we'll have transportation. Stay in touch with us on the sat phone, and if the weather breaks, you can return and help us."

"Ten-four, boss," said Hayes as he stood to leave. "Good luck, guys, I'll be waiting in Douglas for you."

February 8, 1997; Rancho Tierra Del Sol Chihuahua, Mexico

A very despondent John Conway lay curled up in a fetal position in the far corner of his cell-like room. With the dirty blanket pulled up around his chin and his right hand, minus its forefinger, throbbing with a dull pain, Conway sobbed quietly. Slowly shoving the injured hand from under the blanket, he examined it. The rag that somebody had placed over the wound while he was unconscious had staunched the bleeding. *It has just begun. Deep down, I knew it would come to this. I, I just don't know how much more pain I can take* Conway thought. His shoulders shook from his sobs. *Why hasn't the AG acted? She's had enough time to get me out of here. I guess they have written me off. I'll never get to see Emily or my grandkids again.*

His last thought brought another round of self-pity and he began to sob again. The sound of footsteps outside the door interrupted his sobbing. Marshalling what little resolve he still had, he gave himself a quick pep talk. *Be strong, John. Don't give these assholes the benefit of seeing you cry.* Steeling himself, he waited while the door opened.

"Crying like a niño, hombre?" asked the teniente.

"Let me whack off one of your fingers, asshole, and see how you act, hombre," retorted Conway vehemently surprising even himself in the strength of his response.

Laughing as if Conway had said something funny, the teniente looked at Conway. "If I'd had my way, I'd have cut off more than your pinche finger, maricón. But it's not up to me at this time. Let me see the hand," he demanded. He grabbed Conway's injured hand and removed the rag to display the bloody stump where the forefinger had been. He nodded his head. "The bleeding has stopped. Can't have you dying from loss of blood, carnal." He threw his head back and laughed a deep laugh, then exited the room.

Several minutes later, the door reopened causing Conway to shrink into the corner where he had taken refuge. A tray of food was placed on the floor just inside the door. Conway made no movement toward the tray, and instead, slumped against the wall hoping some sleep would block out the pain.

Not one hundred yards away, hidden in the large metal building, the vanguard of his rescue team enjoyed a meal of MREs comparing the tastes of one variety over the other.

"I really like this spaghetti," commented Hood.

"Yeah, me too," answered Lansky. "But I also like the beef stew."

Hood glanced at the luminous dial on his watch. "What time do you think we'll get going?"

"I would imagine some time after midnight, but with this slight rain maybe Blaine will join us sooner."

Hood spooned spaghetti into his mouth and chewed for a while before swallowing. "This drizzle will benefit us, buddy."

"Think so?" asked Lansky.

"Sure, God." He used his plastic spoon to punctuate his point. "Knowing human nature, I'll bet that guard on the front porch of the ranch house will spend more time inside than outside in an attempt to keep warm."

"So how does that benefit us?" asked Lansky shrugging his shoulders.

"Simple, it will allow us to get close to the porch while he's inside. When he steps outside, his eyes will take several minutes to get accustomed to the dark. We'll jump him then."

Lansky pointed his own spoon at Hood. "That's a good idea, Brian, and…." Before he could finish his thought, the satellite phone interrupted him. Lansky picked up the phone. "A Team."

"Real cute," replied Tom with a chuckle. "What's going on there, God?"

"It's quiet, boss. The rain and cold is keeping everyone inside?"

"Everyone? There's no outside guards?" asked a surprised Tom.

"Well, there's a guard on the front porch of the main ranch house, but he's been spending more time inside than out, I guess trying to stay warm. In fact, Brian and I were just discussing how this weather will benefit us by keeping everyone inside."

"Well, God, the weather may help us on that end, but it's screwed us on getting Conway out of Mexico."

"How so, boss?" asked Lansky.

"We can't use the plane. This drizzle is predicted to become freezing rain which will ground all general aviation."

"Well, shit, that's not good. What are we going to do, boss?"

"I have an alternate plan I'll explain when I meet with you guys."

"So when are we going to get going, Tom?"

"God, we have the key to the front gate; we'll try to enter around midnight."

"A key to the front gate? I don't understand, Tom."

Tom explained how they had taken the comandante into custody and how they planned to use him as a decoy to broach the front gate of the ranch."

"While that's a good plan, Tom, I don't think Brian and I can control this end while you do that. If something goes wrong with your plan or if word comes back to the ranch house that somebody is at the front gate, even if it is this comandante, it might get things stirred up here. There are way too many folks here for just Brian and me to handle with killing them all."

"Okay, God, then what would you suggest?"

"I think we're gonna need two more people here at the main ranch area before you attempt the gate thing. Four people should be able to control the situation here, especially if we use surprise and something to debilitate the main body of the reaction force."

"Debilitate? What did you have in mind, big guy?" asked Tom.

"Chemical warfare, boss, just like we did in Mexico last year at Zaragosa."

Tom considered for a moment what Lansky had just said. "Well shit, God, I wasn't looking forward to schlepping cross-country back into the ranch, especially with this rain. But your plan sounds a hell of a lot better than ours. I'll let you know when Wycoff and I are in route. And I'll bring the debilitating agent."

"Ten-four, boss, we'll be waiting; if things change on this end, I'll let you know."

"Good, you guys stay dry and be careful," Tom said as he ended the conversation.

February 8, 1997; Hacienda Puesta Del Sol, La Cruz, Sinaloa, Mexico

Jaime had decided to wait one hour before he took action to determine the location of the comandante. He spent fifty-five minutes of that hour, looking out on the ocean and pacing in front of CNN. Finally, not able to wait another minute, Jaime commanded, "I can't wait any longer. Get Miguel on the phone, Juan."

"Sí, Don Jaime," answered Juan. He picked up the phone and punched in Miguel's number. Juan had memorized this number having used it on a daily basis to discuss the smuggling operations for Jaime's organization.

"Miguel, please hold for Don Jaime," announced Juan into the phone. Juan turned to Jaime. "I have Miguel on the phone, Don Jaime."

"Miguel," asked an impatient Jaime, "who is in charge at Tierra Del Sol?" After hearing Miguel's response, a frustrated Jaime answered, "No, no, Miguel, I want to know who is in charge of security at the ranch." After a short delay, Jaime yelled into the phone. "Carajo, Miguel! I know the comandante is in charge of security for the ranch. Who is there right now? Who makes sure security is doing its job? Do you understand what I'm asking you?" Before Miguel could answer, Jaime, whose face had reddened with anger, demanded, "I want to know who to talk to if I call the ranch right now."

As Miguel answered, Jaime grabbed a pencil and jotted down the name of Teniente Ochoa. "So this Teniente Ochoa is in charge? Who is this teniente? Do I know him?"

While waiting for Miguel's response, Jaime leaned over and whispered to Juan, "Call the ranch, Juan." Then speaking back into the phone, Jaime said, "I see. So he is Los Zetos, huh? I hope he has things under control for everyone's sake." Jaime listened again to Miguel's reply. "I don't have time to explain, Miguel. And, no, there is nothing you can do right now. I will talk with you later."

"The phone is ringing on the ranch, Don Jaime," advised Juan as Jaime drummed his fingers on the desk. "I have Don Jaime on the line," Juan said to the person who answered the ranch phone. "He wants to talk with Teniente Ochoa." Juan turned to Jaime. "They're getting him, Don Jaime."

"Hola," said a male voice.

"Is this Teniente Ochoa?" asked Juan.

"Sí, it is. Who is this?" answered Teniente Ochoa.

"Don Jaime wishes to speak with you, Teniente," said Juan.

Jaime took the phone from Juan. "Teniente, do you know who I am?"

A placating teniente offered, "Sí, Sí, Don Jaime. How can I be of assistance to you?"

"I am trying to get in contact with the comandante and have not been able to reach him for several hours. Has he been there today?"

"Sí, Don Jaime, he was here, but he left several hours ago."

"I see. Did he say where he was heading?" asked Jaime.

"Sí, Don Jaime, he said he was going to Juarez to deliver that finger..."

"Uh, Teniente let's not get into specifics on the phone," interrupted Jaime.

"Oh, sí, sí, Don Jaime, perdone. He left several hours ago with the, uh, object from our pris... uh, our guest," said the teniente.

"And you have not heard from him since?"

"No, señor, maybe he stopped for dinner along the way, Don Jaime. There is a local restaurant where he frequently dines when he's here," volunteered the teniente.

"Yes, perhaps, but it is strange he has not called. He knows how anxious I am about what he was doing."

"Don Jaime, it is raining right now; maybe the weather has delayed him."

"Sí, Sí, that could be so, but I am, uh, just concerned I have not heard from him. You said he left with what he came for?"

"Sí, Don Jaime, he did."

"And how is our guest, Teniente?"

"He continues to sob like a niño, Don Jaime."

"Well, I am sure your actions were painful for him," offered Jaime.

"Yes, that is so, Don Jaime, but he was sobbing before we took our action."

"I see. Tell me, Teniente, how many men do you have there to watch over the ranch?"

"There are fourteen men here usually, but two needed to take care of family matters. Right now, I have twelve."

"Teniente, I want to emphasis what you are doing right now is very important. There will be no mishaps, entiende usted?"

"Sí, Don Jaime, I have good men and they are alert."

"Bueno, but If you feel you need more support, call me, and I will arrange it right away."

"Sí, Don Jaime, I will do so."

Jaime handed the phone back to Juan. "I do not like it. I have a bad feeling about this, and I have a bad feeling about this teniente.

Juan knew Jaime had every right to be concerned. *You think you have a bad feeling now, wait until Thomas Blaine pays a visit to the ranch. If it is like his visit to Miguel Felix's estancia last year, you shall be very unhappy.*

"Juan, have the car brought up. I want to visit with the licenciado and have him call his contact at the Minister of Defense."

"Sí, Don Jaime," said Juan with some surprise in his tone. "Should I just call the licenciado and have him come here?"

"No, Juan. The licenciado has not been feeling too well since his conversation with the comandante. I thought it would be best that he stay under a doctor's care until he feels better."

"Sí, Don Jaime, I understand," said Juan as a cold shiver coursed his spine.

CHAPTER EIGHTEEN

February 8, 1997; Rancho Tierra Del Sol, Chihuahua, Mexico

It was a wet and chilled-to-the-bone Tom Blaine who keyed the transmit button on his hand-held radio. "We're outside the barn, guys."

"Come around to the back, boss. There's a small door near the generator; I'll let you in," replied Lansky.

Several minutes later, Tom, accompanied by Wycoff, entered the barn and greeted Hood and Lansky. While the metal, unheated barn was chilly, it was considerably warmer than outside, and it offered shelter from the freezing rain.

"Man, is it ever shitty out there, guys," Tom said. He shed his field jacket and shook it to rid it of some of the sleet.

"And dark," volunteered Wycoff.

"The cross-country trek back here seemed a lot longer than I remembered," added Tom. He looked around the barn at the numerous stacked bales of marijuana visible in the limited light. "Kind of pungent in here, isn't it?"

"Yeah, it is," said Hood as he chuckled. "God and I estimate about sixteen tons of grass here, boss." They all scanned the stacked bales of marijuana.

"If we get a chance, we'll have to do something about this," Tom said. He turned and faced Lansky and Hood. "How you two holding up?"

"Anxious to get started, Tom," replied Lansky.

Hood nodded his head in agreement.

"Because of the weather, we're going to start around midnight, which is…" He glanced at the luminous dial on his watch. "Thirty-five minutes away."

"What's the plan, boss?" asked Hood.

"I want to do a coordinated attack. While we're taking care of the opposition at this end, Tony, Hawk and Krissy will broach the front gate."

"Do they have enough people to do that, Tom?" asked Lansky.

"I think so. We grabbed the folks in that Range Rover. Turns out one of the guys is a comandante who according to our CI orchestrated the kidnapping of Conway. Oh, and they did whack off his index finger. We found that in the Range Rover."

"Bastards!" exclaimed Hood.

"Yeah," agreed Tom. "Tony and Hawk will have the comandante with them when they approach the gate. Hopefully, the gate guards will recognize the Range Rover and the comandante, and will open the gate."

"And if they don't?" asked Lansky.

"Plan B is to take out the gate guards. Tony will let us know if they have to go to plan B before they do so."

"Tom, I planned on killing the power to the ranch and bunkhouse when we do our deal," said Lansky. I think we can do it by shutting down the generator. Will that interfere with Tony and the guys at the gate?"

Tom thought for a minute. "Actually, I think that's a very good idea. The limited light might benefit our guys. It might draw the guards in closer to the Range Rover where our team can overcome them more easily. Tree, you'll be the electrician. We'll give you the word, and you'll shut down the generator."

"Won't the darkness hamper our efforts, too, Tom?" asked Wycoff.

All three other team members looked at Wycoff amazed he could think of that consequence on his own. But it was Tom who answered. "Tree, that's an excellent question." Pulling his pack closer, Tom reached in and pulled out the night vision devices he had borrowed from the Border Patrol in El Paso. "We only have three of these; Tree, you'll have to either stay put or wait until your eyes get accustomed to the dark."

"All right!" said an enthused Wycoff as Tom handed him the night vision device.

"Okay…" began Tom before he was interrupted by Hood.

"Sh…," commanded Hood as he put a finger to his lips. "Somebody's opening the front door."

The slight squeak of metal in need of lubrication grew louder as the large sliding door opened slightly.

Lansky crawled forward and peered around some bales of Marijuana. Turning toward Tom and the others, he held up one finger. Tom scooted toward Lansky, and Lansky pointed out the outline of a figure bent over something near the barn door. "He's filling a five gallon can of fuel, probably for the generator," Lansky whispered.

Tom nodded his head in agreement and scooted back to the others. "Let's take him out," suggested Hood. "One less we have to deal with in thirty minutes."

"Good idea," said Tom.

"It's fairly dark; we'll jump him at the generator. We won't be seen by the ranch or bunkhouses on the back side of the barn." Waving his hand in the direction of the rear door, Tom ushered Hood forward. "Tell Brian what we intend to do. You guys stay put unless I yell for some help."

"Ten-four, boss," replied Wycoff.

Tom and Lansky took position in the shadows. The noise of the generator would surely mask any sounds that either the guard or the men might make; they waited. They didn't have to wait long before the guard approached the generator carrying a five gallon can of gas. He also had what appeared to be an AK-27 slung over his shoulder. With hand gestures, Tom positioned Lansky so the guard's back would be to them as he poured the fuel into the generator.

With his undivided attention focused on lifting the heavy five-gallon gas can, combined with the noise of the generator, the guard didn't hear Lansky's approach from the rear. Standing right behind the guard, Lansky reached forward and tapped him on the shoulder, startling the guard and causing him to jump and drop the gas can. As the guard spun around to see who had tapped him on the shoulder, Lansky caught him directly on the right temple with the butt of his Berretta pistol sending the guard sprawling sideways to the ground. He attempted to recover from the blow but was struck by Lansky with a gloved hand to the left side of his face. Shoving a rag in the guard's mouth, Tom used a set of plastic flex cuffs to manacle his wrists. Tom and Lansky then dragged the guard into the metal barn where they deposited him in a rear corner. Looking at their captive, Tom asked the others, "Think he'll give us some information?"

"Yeah, boss, I'll bet he'll be willing to talk with us," said Lansky.

Taking out a large K-Bar knife the Fu Manchued Lansky bent down so he was eye level with the captured guard. In his limited Spanish, he advised the guard that he was going to answer some questions, and if he refused to answer or did not tell them the truth, Lansky would begin removing body parts from him. He also warned that if he yelled when he removed the rag from his mouth, Lansky would be quick to cut out his vocal cords. The guard looked from Lansky's menacing face to the large knife, and with a furious nodding of his head, he indicated a willingness to answer questions.

Tom pulled the rag from the guard's mouth. "Donde está el jefe del DEA – Where is the DEA boss?"

He looked at Lansky and then at Tom and answered in a low and halting voice. "En la casa principal – In the main house."

"Quantas hombres en la casa principal? – How many men are in the main house?" Tom inquired.

"Tres personas—three people" replied the guard.

"Tres personas?" repeated Tom.

"Sí, dos guardias y el teniente—Two guards and the lieutenant," answered the captive.

"Quantas personas en la casa otra – How many people in the other house?" asked Tom.

"Cinco personas – Five people."

Tom shoved the rag back in the guard's mouth and turned to the group. "That makes eight people we have to deal with. Any ideas?"

"I suggest God and I take up positions on each end of the porch while the exterior guard is inside taking one of his frequent breaks to warm himself. Tom, you and your little friend, "as Hood pointed to the M203 Tom had brought with him on his return trip," cover the bunkhouse. That way, if necessary, you can lay down a covering fire."

"Or, I could use the M203 grenade launcher to put the CS gas into the bunkhouse. That will certainly slow down any reinforcements."

"Yeah, that will work," agreed Hood. "Once we're in position and the guard returns to his position on the porch, we can use our radios to signal Tree to cut the power to the generator. Tree, we'll key the radio three times. Okay, big guy?" asked Hood looking directly at Wycoff.

"Got it, Brian," replied Wycoff.

"The back-up plan, in case we miss the keying of the mike, will be, uh, how about the word blackout," offered Tom.

"Good idea," said Hood as Lansky nodded his in head in agreement."

"We'll use the night vision devices to take out the guard on the porch who should be temporarily blinded by the sudden darkness. Hopefully, we can do it quickly and with a minimum of noise. We'll then enter the main house and reduce any resistance in there."

"What should I be doing while you're doing the main house?" asked Wycoff.

"Make your way to Tom's position, if you can. Remember, it will be very dark, so if you can't safely move that way, just stay by the barn," answered

Hood.

"Actually, maybe Tree," Tom began as he pointed at Wycoff "should stay by the generator and he could turn the power back on if we need it, once we have the situation under control. Without a night vision device he'll not be of much use at the main or bunkhouse."

"Yeah, that's a better idea," said Hood.

"Yep, that's why they pay me the big bucks, guys," quipped a smiling Tom trying to ease the mounting tension with a little levity.

"Tom, do you think you can still use that M203 like you once did?" asked Lansky.

"It's like riding a bike; once you learn, you never forget. I'll put the CS grenades into that bunkhouse with no problem," Tom said with just a bit of braggadocio in his tone.

"The CS will certainly roust them from the house, and they should be blinded by the gas. We can wait outside and take them into custody as they exit the bunkhouse," said Hood.

"Yep, it should be effective in doing that. But remember guys, be careful not to get a snoot full yourself. We don't need any of us becoming casualties," cautioned Tom.

"Okay, once we have both buildings secure, we'll get Conway and get the hell out of there."

"Sounds like a good basic plan, Brian. We might have to modify it as we go to accommodate unexpected contingencies, but basically, we'll try to stick with the plan," concluded Tom as he looked at the three other team members. "Okay, let me call Tony and let him know when we're doing our thing, so he and his team can get ready to do their thing at the front gate."

February 8, 1997; Hacienda Puesta Del Sol, La Cruz, Sinaloa, Mexico

A highly agitated Jaime Gutiérrez, several hundred miles away from Tierra Del Sol, was the first person outside of the ranch to learn that something was amiss at the ranch. As had been his routine since the early evening hours, he had called the ranch on the hour in an effort to determine why he had not heard from the comandante. While on the phone talking with the teniente, they both heard several shots in the background.

"Are those shots?" shouted Jaime.

"I've got to go," advised an excited teniente; the phone went dead.

Jaime called the ranch repeatedly resulting in the phone ringing continually. Jaime turned to Juan and cursed. "Carajo!"

Juan was glad he had decided to stay at the hacienda to keep an eye on Jaime and his reaction to any developments at the ranch. Juan jumped up from his computer and advanced toward Jaime. "What is wrong, Don Jaime?"

Jaime continued to redial the ranch. His tone and body language indicated disbelief at what he had just deduced. "Something is going on at the ranch, something bad I think."

"What could be happening this late at night, Don Jaime?" asked a concerned Juan.

"I don't know, but I heard shots when I was talking to that pinche teniente.

"Shots?" questioned Juan.

"I knew something bad was going to happen when I did not hear from the comandante. I just knew it, and I did nothing to prevent it," he ranted.

"How can that be, Don Jaime? Isn't the ranch protected?"

"Sí, Juan. The ranch is well protected. The comandante has Los Zetos at the ranch, but something has happened; I can't get hold of either the teniente at the ranch nor the comandante," By this time, Jaime was almost frantic.

"What can I do, Don Jaime?"

Jaime pulled a slip of paper from his shirt pocket. "Juan, call this number. It's to the Deputy Minister of Defense. He's the person the licenciado has looking after our interests. I will talk to him once you get him on the phone." Jaime turned and walked to the large mahogany bar and poured himself a large helping of Mezcal.

"Don Jaime, I will certainly call this Minister, but would it not be better to have the licenciado call?"

"Yes, Juan, it would," said Jaime, between gulps of Mezcal, "but unfortunately, I believe the licenciado is the cause of this problem. Besides that, he is in no shape to make calls right now. Make the call Juan," said an annoyed Jaime.

"Sí, Don Jaime," said a contrite Juan. While dialing the number, Juan suddenly realized something. *He suspects the licenciado is the person who gave out information about the DEA jefe being at the ranch. He doesn't suspect me. I'm safe for the time being and so is my brother and his family.*

After dialing the number, Juan had to wait several seconds while the phone rang before a groggy voice answered. "Sí, quien es – Yes, who is it?"

"I have Jaime Gutiérrez who wishes to speak with you, señor."

The groggy voice took in a large breath of air. "Are you sure you have the right number, señor?"

"Is this the Deputy Minister of Defense?"

"Sí, I am the Deputy Minister of Defense, but I don't know why you are calling me. And at this late hour."

"Hold one moment," said Juan who handed the phone to Jamie. "I have him on the phone, and perdone, Don Jaime, he appears to be confused as to why you are calling him."

Jaime grabbed the phone from Juan as the veins in his neck began to pulsate. "Mr. Minister, I got your phone number from Licenciado Gorge Morales. I believe you know him, señor?"

"Sí, I know the licenciado, but I am confused as to why you are calling me and not the licenciado if there is a problem. That is our normal arrangement."

"Well, Minister, the licenciado is not available right now, and I need for you to do something for me."

"Can't this wait…" began the Minister.

"No, this can't wait," interrupted Jaime. "I need for you to send someone to check on my ranch at Tierra Del Sol near Janos. I think there's been a serious breach of security there. I need troops to secure the ranch."

"Uh, señor, I think you have the wrong person…" began the Minister.

"No, Minister, I have the right person, the pinche person whom I pay considerable amounts of money to insure the security of my business." When there was no immediate response from the Minister, Jaime continued. "And let me be perfectly clear about this, Mr. Minister, if I don't get your immediate support, you should start worrying about more than a lack of financial support from me."

After a short period of silence during which Jaime could hear heavy breathing on the other end of the line, the Minister said, "The ranch at Janos you said?"

"Sí, Mr. Minister, I was on the phone with someone there and heard shots fired and now no one answers the phone."

"Let me see what I can do. What is your number where I can call you back, señor?"

Twenty minutes later, the Minister called Jaime. "Señor, I have made some calls and have been told that the weather is very bad up there right now. It is freezing rain, and the roads are icing over. It's also a Saturday evening, and many of the security forces are enjoying a night off."

"Carajo," shouted Jaime into the phone. "Are you telling me that you cannot get troops to the ranch?"

"Uh, no, señor, I am just stating it will take some time to get troops there. The roads...."

"Pendejo, you get me some troops there, or there will be consequences that you and your boss will not like," shouted an enraged Jaime before slamming the phone down. Stomping across the tiled floors, he went to the bar, poured himself another hefty glass of Mezcal and downed it in short order.

Juan decided to make a suggestion that would not be viable but would put him in good stead with Jaime. "Don Jaime, let me call Ramon. Maybe he has some contacts locally who might be able to get some security type people to the ranch right away."

Jaime gave Juan a dismissive wave of his hand. "Sí, Juan, see if Ramon can do something. But I'm afraid it will be too late by the time we can get someone to the ranch."

February 9, 1997; Rancho Tierra Del Sol, Chihuahua, Mexico

The gunshots Jaime heard while on the phone with the teniente were an audible sign that Tom and his team's well-laid plans to rescue John Conway had faltered. Much like a cheap Walmart Chinese-made garment that when you pull on a loose thread more thread follows and ultimately the garment falls apart, so were the initial plans that the team had established. The first loose thread involved Wycoff and his radio. As soon as Lansky and Hood were in position on opposing ends of the front covered porch, they signaled to Tom they were ready. Tom, who had taken up a position to cover the front door of the bunkhouse, keyed the mike on his handheld radio three times in succession to signal Wycoff to kill the generator. After a minute when the sound of the generator could still be heard in the distance and the lights had not been extinguished, Tom repeated the signal with the radio. Once again, there was no response to the signal. Placing the radio close to his mouth, Tom said, "Blackout," the backup audible signal to Wycoff to turn off the generator. When this command was not heeded, Tom repeated the word *blackout*, one more time. What Tom, Lansky and Hood did not know was that Wycoff's radio battery had gone dead.

Tom looked at Brian. "What the hell is wrong with Wycoff?" But before he could decide if he should go see what was wrong, Lansky whispered into his radio. "Front door's opening. Be ready, Brian. If he looks your way, I'll take him and vice versa."

Hood keyed the handheld radio twice to indicate his understanding.

Tom could just barely make out both Lansky and Hood hidden in the shadowed ends of the front porch.

At that moment, a guard, armed with an AK-47, exited the front door. As he did so, he turned his head back toward the open door and said something over his shoulder to someone inside.

Quick as a cat and almost as quiet, Lansky mounted the porch and closed the several yards' distance between him and the guard. He was almost on the guard, when he turned and saw Lansky. The guard's surprise and hesitation was all Lansky needed to close the distance and grab the front end of the AK-47. With an almost fluid motion, Lansky jerked the barrel of the AK-47 upward and away from himself. The surprised guard, whose finger was on the trigger, squeezed off a burst of several rounds before Lansky ripped the AK-47 out of his hands. In a continual motion, Lansky performed a perfect vertical butt stroke upward with the AK catching the guard under the jaw. The force of the weapon, driven up under his jaw, lifted the guard up almost off his feet. As he began to settle back down, Lansky again used the butt of the AK and struck the guard directly in the face, rendering him bloody and dazed.

Hood, who had jumped onto the porch as Lansky took on the guard, heard the distinct sound of smashed bone and quickly closed the distance to the front door.

The burst of automatic weapon fire did what the keying of the handheld radio and the audible signal of *blackout* failed to do, and Wycoff shut off the generator.

The second loose thread in the plan then became manifest. The generator controlled only the exterior lighting and the lighting in the barn. The lights in the ranch house and bunkhouse continued to burn, until the inhabitants extinguished them.

Flipping down the night vision goggles, Lansky and Hood prepared to enter the main ranch house to reduce the resistance that would come from that building. After wiping the sleet from his face, Tom, across the compound, did the same, and sighted in the M203 at the bunkhouse. As the door to the bunkhouse opened slowly, Tom squeezed off two rounds from the M-16 part of the M203 striking the door about waist high.

The door slammed shut in response.

Positioning themselves low and on either side of the front door, Lansky and Hood slowly pushed the door slightly ajar. When no gunfire met their efforts, they shoved the door open. Instantly, a burst of automatic weapon fire exited the door opening. The light hit the sensors of the night vision goggles and temporarily blinded both Lansky and Hood who lay prone on the porch. Both Lansky and Hood flipped their night vision goggles up and focused their attention on the spot where the automatic weapon fire had originated.

Lansky answered with a burst from the AK he had liberated from the guard. Lansky and Hood then saw a shadow jerk backward. Sensing they had struck the shooter, Lansky and Hood bolted through the door and fired several more rounds into the area where they suspected the guard had fallen. Lansky flipped the night vision goggles back down and was the first to determine they had eliminated the interior source of the weapon fire.

Meanwhile, Tom began taking on sporadic rounds from the bunkhouse. As several rounds snapped over his head, he said to himself, "That's enough of this shit," and dropped a 40-millimeter CS gas projectile into the grenade launcher beneath the rifle barrel. Carefully aiming the M203, he squeezed off a round, feeling the recoil and instantly regretted not holding the weapon tighter into his shoulder. The large bullet-like grenade easily splintered the front door.

Another loose thread became apparent at this time. The round was a dud and did not expel the CS gas, as it should have. Reloading the launcher, Tom fired another round, which actually entered the bunkhouse through the large hole in the door created by the first grenade. "Man that's some shooting," whispered Wycoff, who had quietly snuck up on Tom.

Startled by Wycoff's sudden words and appearance, Tom jumped. "Jesus, Tree," Tom whispered, "you scared the shit out of me. And what the hell happened with the generator?"

"Sorry, boss. Battery in my radio went dead."

Tom focused back on the bunkhouse and determined the second grenade had functioned, as it should. Just to be on the safe side, he decided to fire a third round. Aiming for a widow to the right of the door, he squeezed the trigger. The sound of breaking glass preceded a loud painful scream.

Almost instantly, the broken door opened and a man stumbled from the bunkhouse shouting, "Don't shoot, don't shoot, I give up" in Spanish. Suffering from the effects of the CS gas, the person was blinded and choking from a lack of oxygen. A second and then a third individual did the same, blindly bumping into objects and each other before falling to the ground.

Tom and Wycoff watched them.

One final individual stumbled from the bunkhouse blinded and retching violently. Keeping an eye on the main ranch house and the bunkhouse, Tom and Wycoff cautiously approached the first person who was thrashing and rubbing his eyes and the snot from his nose. "Resist and you're a dead man, hombre," advised Tom in Spanish.

Tom and Wycoff grabbed his arms and cuffed him with plastic cuffs. They did the same to the three other individuals trying to avoid the CS gas in their clothing.

"You stay here and watch these clowns and cover me while I make for the ranch house."

Back in the ranch house, Lansky and Hood slowly entered and began to search the structure one room at a time. The front door to the ranch house opened to a large front living area with a small kitchen off to the left. It was sparsely furnished with an old couch, ripped and threadbare in several places, a large wooden box, which served as a coffee table and a television atop the wooden box. A hallway, situated to the right of the kitchen, led to the rear of the house. After cautiously making their way across the living room, they began to clear the rooms in the hallway. The first room to the right was a bathroom and empty. The next room on the left side of the hall and directly across from the bathroom had a large padlock attached to a hasp on the closed door.

Lansky put his ear up to the door and heard slight noises like an animal whimpering. He motioned for Hood to listen. Both Lansky and Hood decided this was probably where Conway was being held. They passed this room and continued down to the end of the hall to a rear bedroom. They cautiously approached this room noting that the door to this room was also closed. Taking up defensive positions against short walls on either side of the door, Hood reached over and slowly turned the knob on the door. Even before the bolt was disengaged, the door suddenly exploded as rounds exited from within the room. Lansky and Hood hugged the wall as bullets whizzed by them traversing the length of the hall. Lansky waited until the firing from the room stopped, then turned and faced the door. Using the AK, he fired the rounds remaining in the twenty-round magazine through the door and the portion of the wall he had used as a shield. Hood did likewise with an AK he had taken from the dead guard in the living room.

Hugging the wall again, Lansky waited while Hood inserted a fresh magazine into his weapon. Lansky then fronted himself on the door, and with his foot, kicked it just above the door handle splintering the doorframe and causing it to fly open. Dropping to his knees as the door flew backwards, Lansky fired his pistol into the darkened room.

Hood, who had taken a position above and behind Lansky, fired his into the same area. When there was no return fire, Lansky and Hood checked the room and found the shooter, slumped against a far wall pulsating blood from several wounds. Lansky and Hood watched as the life drained from the teniente.

February 9, 1997; Springfield, Virginia

Roger Grey glanced at the luminous face of the clock radio on the nightstand. *Just past 2:00 a.m.* His restless sleep caused his wife to wake.

"Roger, what's wrong? You have been thrashing about for the past two hours."

Roger sat up and dropped his feet over the side of the bed. His toes searched for his slippers. "Sorry, dear, must have been something I ate." He kissed his wife softly on her cheek. "Go back to sleep. Think I'll get a glass of water."

Roger closed the bedroom door softly and headed to the kitchen sink where he drew a glass of water. *I wonder what Tom and his team are doing. I wish he would call me. This not knowing is killing me. I'm calling the satellite phone.*

Roger entered his den and sat down at his desk to place the call through the New York calling number. Drumming his fingers on the desk, Roger waited as the electronic noises changed as the call was being forwarded. The phone rang just twice before a female voice answered. "What's up?"

Recognizing the voice of Hammond, Roger said, "Krissy, this is Roger Grey. Is Blaine available?"

"We're kind of busy right now Mr. Grey," Krissy said.

"Look, Krissy, I know you don't want to say too much on the phone, but can you at least tell me if you guys are doing your thing?"

"We're in the middle of it now."

"So it's going according to plan then?" asked Roger.

"Not really, the weather turned to shit with a major cold front blowing in. It's sleeting and the roads are icing over as we speak."

"Crap that's not good. What…" He started to continue but was interrupted by what sounded like gunfire.

"Was that gunfire?" shouted Roger. His question went unanswered and he was left holding a phone whose connection had been broken. "Holy shit!" he exclaimed aloud to himself. *I sure hope that is not what I think it was.*

February 9, 1997; Rancho Tierra Del Sol, Chihuahua, Mexico

When the gunfire erupted at the main ranch house, Gonzalo and Hawk, riding in the Range Rover, had just stopped at the main gate of Tierra Del Sol. Gonzalo, attired in the comandante's leather jacket, cowboy hat and mirrored sunglasses, stepped from the Range Rover and stood by the passenger door. In the freezing rain and limited light, he had initially fooled the guard who approached the front gate from a small gatehouse.

Thinking Gonzalo was the comandante, who in actuality lay cuffed in the rear of the Range Rover, the guard started to swing the large metal gate open. The sound of gunshots from the main ranch area stopped him. Gonzalo, having reentered the vehicle leaned out and commanded the guard to "Rapido, rapido – quickly, quickly."

Looking first at Gonzalo, and then toward the ranch, the guard quickly complied and swung the gate open, just as the overhead lights went off. Plunged into darkness, Gonzalo and Hawk pulled into the ranch and exited the Range Rover. Once out of the vehicle, they quickly approached the guard and disarmed him with little resistance. They were not as fortunate with another guard who exited the gatehouse.

Upon seeing Gonzalo and Hawk subdue the other guard, he retreated into the gatehouse and began shooting wildly in their direction.

Gonzalo and Hawk dropped down and low crawled to a position behind several large rocks piled on the opposite side of the road from the gatehouse.

Hammond, following the Range Rover in the Blazer, took up a stationary position where the road to the ranch intersected the highway running parallel to the ranch. When she heard the sound of gunfire, she decided to provide backup to Gonzalo and Hawk. With her vision partially obscured by the freezing rain and the dark, she attempted to close the distance between her and the gate with her headlights off. Finding little traction on the slick pavement, she used a trick one of her older brothers had taught her while growing up in Michigan. She allowed the Blazer to drift to the gravel shoulder of the roadway where the tires were able to dig in and propel the vehicle forward. As she neared the gate, she flipped on her high beams at the last possible minute, bathing the gatehouse in light.

The guard stopped shooting at Gonzalo and Hawk and took her under fire. In her efforts to avoid the bullets slamming into the Blazer, she swerved to the left and felt the Blazer begin to skid on the slick pavement. Spinning the wheel from left to right to compensate for the skidding movement, Hammond regained some control. At the same time, she aimed the Blazer at the gatehouse with the intention of putting the Blazer between the guard and Gonzalo and Hawk. After firing several rounds at the Blazer bearing down on the gatehouse, the guard had to stop shooting to insert a fresh magazine. He was still reloading when Hammond stomped on the brakes to stop her forward motion.

Krissy failed to compensate for the slick roadway. The sudden braking movement caused Hammond to lose control of the Blazer, which began to skid. Spinning completely around, the Blazer slammed rear-end first into the front of the stucco and wood-framed gatehouse.

Unable to jump out of the way of the skidding Blazer, the guard fired wildly again at the Blazer. When the left side of the Blazer crashed through the flimsy door, the collapsing wall and roof buried the guard when it came crashing down.

The impact of the Blazer with the gatehouse not only disabled the guard, but it also threw Hammond onto the four-wheel drive lever on the transmission hump bruising or fracturing her ribs and rupturing her left implant. With a painful rib cage and an intense burning sensation to her left side, Hammond crawled from the Blazer through the right passenger door.

The two cuffed ayudantes, captured in Janos and riding in the rear of the Blazer, were dazed by the crash, but not seriously hurt.

Gonzalo and Hawk ran to Hammond's aid as she exited the Blazer. Gonzalo helped her to the Range Rover while Hawk checked on the guard buried in the remains of the guardhouse. Determining that the guard no longer posed them a threat, Hawk entered the Blazer through the right passenger door. After several attempts, he got the Blazer started. By shifting quickly from drive to reverse and rocking the Blazer back and forth, he was able to dislodge it from the guardhouse. He loaded the captured guard into the Blazer and followed Gonzalo and Hammond, who were in the Range Rover, toward the main ranch house.

February 9, 1997; Hacienda Puesta Del Sol, La Cruz, Sinaloa, Mexico

Fueled by his inability to get answers about the comandante and the Rancho Tierra Del Sol, Jaime's anger continued to burn. A more than healthy amount of Mezcal helped to increase the anger. Red-faced and slightly inebriated, Jaime Gutiérrez decided he would get answers and would not wait a second longer. It didn't matter that it was past midnight, if he wasn't going to get any sleep neither was anyone else in his organization or in the government contacts he owned. In call after call, he demanded something be done to find out about the activities at the ranch. He used his tried and true methods of first trying to bribe or induce the recipient of his call with money. When that failed, he resorted to what he considered a more positive method: He threatened them and their families.

"Maricón," he screamed into the phone to a high-ranking deputy Minister of Justice, "you readily have taken my money to protect my interests, and now you tell me there is nothing you can do?"

The Deputy Minister pleaded with the inebriated Jaime. "Señor Gutiérrez, it's not that I don't want to do something it's…uh…the weather. There is nothing moving in the northeastern part of the county because of the treacherous roads."

"Carajo! I find that hard to believe, Mr. Deputy Minister. I know somebody has managed to get to my ranch and is, as we speak, probably stealing the very product I distribute that pays you so handsomely," said Jaime through slightly slurred speech. "If you know what is good for you and your family, you better take some action right now." Jaime slammed down the phone before the Deputy Minister could respond.

Jaime stumbled to the bar and poured himself the last of the Mezcal bottle. After downing his drink, he attempted to pour another before he realized the bottle was empty. "Carajo," he uttered through clenched teeth. He searched the cabinets for another bottle of Mezcal. "Juan, is there more Mezcal here somewhere?" Juan had decided to stay at the hacienda and close to Jaime during this night for two reasons. First, he wanted to be in a position to learn any information that might adversely impact Thomas Blaine's attempts to rescue his jefe. And, second, to defuse any suspicion that he was the one who provided the information concerning the DEA Jefe's whereabouts.

Juan rose from his desk and approached Jaime. "Why don't you sit down, Don Jaime? I'll see if there is more Mezcal." Juan searched all the cabinets above and below the bar area. "Lo siento – I am sorry, Don Jaime, there is none. Would you like some coffee?"

"No, Juan," Jaime yelled, "no café; I want Mezcal."

"Don Jaime, it is past midnight and all of the local stores are closed, or I would send someone for it."

"Call that pinche manager of my hotel. Wake that maricón and tell him to get me some Mezcal from the bar."

"Sí, Don Jaime," answered Juan. He returned to his desk, but before he could dial the number, the phone rang.

"Put Señor Gutiérrez on the line, por favor," said the caller.

"Quien es? Who is this?" asked Juan.

"Uh, let's just say I'm the person Señor Gutiérrez spoke with several minutes ago," said the tentative voice.

"Don Jaime, I think it is that Deputy Minister of Justice who you just talked with."

Jaime walked unsteadily across the office and grabbed the phone from Juan. "Que? – what?"

"Uh…Señor Gutiérrez, I have made the appropriate calls and have closed the border crossings at Juarez and Agua Prieto. Nothing will cross the border for the next several hours. I have also instructed the comandante of the local federales in both areas to establish roadblocks several miles from each border crossing. While the roads are impassible right now, they will do so as soon as the roads open."

"Bueno. And what about my ranch?" demanded Jaime.

"I have talked with the Army; they will dispatch a unit to check the ranch and will attempt to get there, weather permitting, as soon as possible."

Jaime shook his head in disgust. "If we were invaded, the Army could only respond weather permitting, Minister?"

"Señor Gutiérrez, the Army does not anticipate an invasion from the Norte Americanos; there are no combat units in that area. Lo siento, señor, it is the best we can do right now."

"I see," said Jaime. "But let me make myself clear. If anything happens to what is at my ranch, there will be serious consequences. Entiendo, hombre?"

"Sí, Señor Gutiérrez. Pero…"

"No buts. I have made myself clear," Jaime said before hanging up the phone. "Closed the border, set up road blocks, send an Army unit, weather permitting – pinche maricóns," Jaime muttered as he staggered back to his leather recliner.

In actuality, the U.S. government closed the border crossings at Juarez and Agua Prieto and not due to any effort of the Deputy Minister of Justice. The bad weather and road conditions made it impossible for on-coming shifts of U.S. Immigration and Customs personnel to make it into work. As for the roadblocks, the comandantes of both areas told the minister it was foolish to establish roadblocks on roads already impassible. Furthermore, they both voiced their extreme displeasure at being awakened in the middle of the night for something as foolish as this. When the minister made his next call to the head of the Department of Defense, he found that noon on Sunday would be the earliest an Army unit could be dispatched to the ranch.

Not knowing any of these misrepresentations made to Jaime by the Deputy Minister of Justice, Juan became concerned. *I need to warn Thomas Blaine about the border and roadblocks. Do I risk calling from here?* His answer came with the next call, which was from the manager of the Jaime's hotel. After talking with the manager, Juan turned to Jaime. "Don Jaime, that was the manager of your hotel; he will get some Mezcal from the bar and have it delivered. Maybe I should go get it from him. It would be quicker," said Juan.

With the effects of the Mezcal and lack of sleep, Jaime had started to nod off. "Sí, Juan, that would be good," he said in a slur.

February 9, 1997; Rancho Tierra Del Sol, Chihuahua, Mexico

"Two dead inside, boss," greeted Lansky as he stood in the ranch house doorway.

Tom climbed the porch to the main ranch house, and before he could say anything, Lansky shrugged his shoulders. "They didn't give us much choice; began firing on us as soon as we entered the house."

Tom nodded his head that he understood. He turned his head back toward the bunkhouse. "We have four in custody so far, but we haven't been able to check it out because of the CS gas. What about Conway? Any signs of him?"

Hood came out of the ranch house to join Tom and Lansky on the porch. "There's a bedroom that's padlocked; we heard whimpering sounds coming from inside. We didn't check it out yet; we wanted to see if you and the Tree needed our help."

"Let me check on Tony and his guys first. I heard gunshots from the front gate area…"

"You there, boss?" asked Gonzalo over the radio.

"Yeah, Tony, we're ten-four here. How about you guys?"

"We're okay, Tom. We had some resistance at the gate, but we're safely through it. Is it safe to come to your position?" asked Gonzalo.

"It should be. We think we're secure here, but be careful. We haven't thoroughly checked the bunkhouse."

"Ten-four, Tom. Hammond is hurt," said a tentative Gonzalo.

"What? Did she get shot?" he asked. The question and tone of his voice immediately got the attention of both Lansky and Hood.

"Krissy shot?" asked Hood moving closer. Tom put up his finger to silence Hood.

"No, she didn't get shot. She slammed the Blazer into the gatehouse when we were taking fire from it. She either bruised or broke some ribs, and she thinks she punctured one of her new boobs."

"How bad is she?" asked Tom.

"She's in pain; I think we need to get her medical attention as soon as possible."

"Okay, Tony, we'll get out of here as quick as we can."

"Have you got, Conway?" asked Gonzalo.

"We're about to check out the room we think he's been held in. Keep on coming, and we'll get together once you get here."

"Ten-four. Oh, and I have some more good news, Tom. The roads are really slick with this freezing rain."

"And the shit just keeps on coming," was Tom's simple reply.

"Krissy had some type of accident with the Blazer and injured some ribs and maybe punctured one of her implants," Tom told Lansky and Hood after shoving his radio back in his rear pocket. She's in pain; we'll need to get her medical attention as soon as we can." Tom said. "Let's go check out this room."

Tom watched as Lansky, using the butt end of the AK-47, smashed the padlock of the door. Opening the door slowly, Tom entered the darkened room. The stench of human waste immediately assaulted his nose. He tried to hold his breath while he scanned the room. The sound of a whimper coming from a far corner drew his immediate attention. As his eyes adjusted to the dark, he could see a form huddled and cowering against an exterior wall. Slowly approaching the form, Tom noted the form attempted to draw further back against the wall. Realizing that Conway was probably petrified from the shooting and what he had endured these past several days, Tom spoke to him in a soft voice. "Mr. Conway, we're here to take you home. Don't be afraid John; we're DEA, and you're safe now."

The use of his first name and the words DEA seemed to, momentarily, quiet and halt the form's attempt to become part of the wall. Bending down to get on eye level with the huddled form, Tom repeated himself. "Mr. Conway, it's me, Tom Blaine. You remember me, sir? We're here to take you home."

Conway stared at Tom for several moments before recognition registered in his eyes. His head dropped to his chest, and he began to sob uncontrollably.

Tom moved closer to Conway and placed his hand on Conway's shoulder being wracked by his sobs. Tom allowed his hand to remain there for a moment. "It's okay, John. You're safe now. We're going to take you home." Slowly he encouraged Conway to stand. As he turned away to tell Lansky to find some clean clothing, Conway latched onto Tom's arm and would not let go. Turning back to Conway, Tom said, "Don't worry, Mr. Conway, I'm not leaving you. I just want to get you something clean and warm to wear. Do you understand, sir?"

Conway nodded his head that he understood. Conway then pleaded in a hoarse voice, "Yes, but please, don't leave me. Look what they did to me." He extended his right hand covered with a bloody rag.

Tom nodded his head in ascent. "Don't worry, I won't leave you, but we need to get you something clean and warm to wear; it's really cold and wet outside. We'll look after that hand. Lansky, go search this place and see if there's something clean for him to wear. His clothes are filthy."

"Ten-four, boss." Lansky left the room.

"Brian, I saw a kitchen on the way in here. See if there's some coffee we can heat for the Administrator. It might calm him a little to have something warm to drink."

Hearing the exchange between Hood and Tom, Conway said in a very weak voice, "Coffee, they have coffee. They gave me coffee once."

"Brian, get some coffee." Tom placed his arm around the back of Conway. "Let's you and I get out of here."

A completely submissive Conway held tight to Tom's arm as Tom escorted him from the filthy room he had called his cell for the past four days.

Passing the bathroom, Tom asked, "Do you need to use the bathroom, sir?"

Conway shook his head no. "Not right now. I guess the gunfire startled me, and I couldn't hold it."

"I understand. We're going to find you some clean clothes so you can change," advised Tom as he guided Conway to the couch.

It took a few minutes before Hood found some instant coffee and boiled some water on an electric hotplate. He handed a cup of hot coffee to Conway. "Here, sir, it's hot, so be careful. I couldn't find anything like cream or sugar; you'll have to drink it black."

"Black is fine." He nodded his head in thanks and took several sips. He slowly looked around the room, and then focused on Tom who sat next to him on the couch. "How did you guys find me, Blai…uh…it's Tom, isn't it?'

"Yes, sir, call me Tom. It's a long story, and we'll have time to go into that later, but we need to be going pronto."

Lansky entered the living room carrying some clothing that included a field jacket. "These will probably do for the time being."

Tom noticed Conway's immediate withdraw from the jacket as Lansky laid it in front of Conway.

"What's wrong, sir?" he asked gently.

"That jacket. It's the one the teniente was wearing"

"The teniente?" asked Tom.

"Yes, he was one of the people in charge here, one of the bastards that chopped off my finger—him and the comandante."

"Well, the teniente won't be cutting off any more fingers, Mr. Conway," offered Lansky. "He's leaking blood in the back room."

"And we have the comandante in custody also," added Tom.

"God, you and Brian go check on Tree. He's keeping an eye on the prisoners from the bunkhouse. And be careful, we haven't checked the bunkhouse because of the CS gas."

"Will do, boss," answered Hood for both.

Before they could exit the ranch house, they heard the sound of vehicles approaching. One of the vehicles sounded loud with its muffler missing along with the squeal of metal rubbing upon metal.

"Jesus," exclaimed Tom. He turned to Conway. "Relax, sir, those are some of our guys. Finish your coffee while I go check on them." He turned to Hood. "Brian, you stay here with the Administrator. When he finishes his coffee have him change clothes and see if you can clean his hand also."

"Will do, boss."

Tom and Lansky exited the ranch house and greeted Gonzalo who was halfway between the parked Ranger Rover and the Ranch house. "Tony, we're Ten-four here."

"Did you find, Conway?" Gonzalo asked.

"Yeah, and he's pretty emotional right now. How's Hammond?"

"She's in pain, Tom, but insists she'll be able to hold off on medical care until we finish here. She's in the Range Rover."

Hammond sat slumped in the Range Rover with her head against the headrest when Tom opened the passenger door. "Hey, Krissy, you doing okay?"

"Shit, no I ain't doing okay, Blaine. My chest hurts like hell, and I think I busted my left tit. And, Christ, I haven't even finished paying for them yet."

"Not to worry, Krissy. We'll get you to medical aid as soon as we can and, tell you what, I'll talk to Roger Grey about paying for the implants."

His statement brought a slight smile to her face. "Oh, he called just before the shooting began."

"He did, huh? What did he want?"

"Just wanted to know if we were doing our thing yet? I didn't get to finish with him because of the shots fired."

"I'll call him as soon as I can."

"Oh, and Wyman called right after you and Wycoff took off from the motor home for the ranch. He flew the Merlin to Douglas and was able to get us four rooms at a Motel 6. I've got the number written down for the motel. He'll wait for us to call him there."

"Okay, that's good," commented Tom.

"And another thing, he said the weather in Douglas is really shitty. The roads are iced over and nothing is moving."

"Great, just what we need. Okay, Krissy you sit tight and we'll be out of here in a very short while," Tom said patting Krissy on her right forearm, which earned him a grimace sort of smile.

Tom examined the damage to the Blazer parked behind the Range Rover. "Well, we certainly can't use that."

"What are we going to do, Tom? We can't all fit into the Range Rover," Gonzalo said.

"No, we can't, Tony." agreed Tom.

"Should I take Hawk and go back to get the Bronco and the motor home at the airport?" asked Gonzalo.

"Shit, Tony, we don't have time for that. The roads are bad, and we need to get moving north heading toward the border as soon as possible. No telling what we'll encounter along the way; I definitely want to be back in the states once daylight hits.

Lansky decided to offer an idea. "Sun Tzu, Tom. Bring war material with you from home, but forage on the enemy…" offered Lansky.

Gonzalo seemed perplexed until Tom smiled. "Hood's Navy Seal philosophy. Bring your own guns but also take advantage of the enemy's munitions, and I guess, equipment. Let's see if there's another vehicle here we can use."

"I have a suggestion, boss?" offered Lansky again. "After you left, Brian and I watched while they loaded another stake bed truck with marijuana. It's parked in the barn, ready to go. And I'll bet the keys are already in it or nearby. It would definitely accommodate all of us and might be a good decoy vehicle. I don't think they'll be looking at a truck like that as a likely escape vehicle."

"Good point, God. Go check it out."

"Let's go check on Tree," Tom suggested to Tony.

Wycoff met them halfway to the bunkhouse. "I think we have a dead guy inside the bunkhouse, boss. I couldn't go in; the gas is still too strong, but looking in the window, I could see a guy lying on the floor."

"We need to check that out, Tree. We also need to check the bunkhouse for weapons. Open all the doors and break out some of the windows so we can air out the house."

While Wycoff took care of the bunkhouse, Gonzalo and Tom watched over the prisoners who lacked outer clothing, and shivered quite noticeably. "While I would normally feel sorry for those poor bastards," Tom said, "I keep thinking they probably were the ones who killed our agents in El Paso."

"Yeah, let them freeze to death," concluded Tony.

"Keys are in the truck and looks like it has three-fourths tank of fuel," said Lansky as he rejoined Gonzalo and Tom. "What's the Tree doing, boss?" he asked as he turned his head toward the bunkhouse.

"He's airing out the bunkhouse, so we can check it out for suspects and weapons," replied Tom.

"That could take all night. I'll go check it out," he offered, pulling a gas mask from a container strapped to his multi-pocketed utility trousers.

Looking first at Lansky, then at Tom, Gonzalo shook his head. "Figures. He's ready for any combat situation, isn't he?"

"Yeah, at times it's actually scary how ready he is to do combat," said Tom.

Lansky had not been in the bunkhouse very long when he exited with several AK-47 rifles, slung over one shoulder and two tube-like devices slung over his other shoulder. As he neared Gonzalo and Tom, Tom could see the tube-like devices were, in fact, light anti-tank weapons, more commonly referred to as LAAWs. He recalled using these in the Corps toward the end of the Vietnam War.

"Got one dead inside, boss," offered Lansky. "Looks like your CS grenade slapped him in the chest. The projectile was laying at his feet. These babies just might come in handy."

"Sure hope we don't need them, God." Gonzalo stated with some emphasis.

"Okay, let's get all these clowns into the ranch house," directed Tom. "Get the comandante out of the Ranger Rover and his ayudantes from the Blazer. "We'll make sure they're shackled really well and leave them in the ranch house."

"If it were up to me, I'd leave their drug-dealing murdering asses out here to freeze to death," quipped Lansky.

"Yeah, I hear you, God, but let's do it my way, okay?" Tom turned to Gonzalo "Let's get the truck out of the barn and put the Blazer in its place."

"Huh?" exclaimed Gonzalo in confusion.

"Put the Blazer in the barn, Tony. We're going to torch it anyway; that way, we'll burn up any evidence there might be in the Blazer."

"Oh, I see. Good idea, boss," said Gonzalo.

"God, take Tree and go douse that marijuana in the barn with the diesel fuel in the storage tank just inside the barn. I'm not leaving that shit here for

Gutiérrez to send to the US."

"Sure, boss, come on Tree," said Lansky.

When all the prisoners were secured in the ranch house, Tom walked over to the comandante who had been placed slumped against one of the filthy and hole-marked walls in the bedroom, which, until recently, had been John Conway's cell. He bent down so he was eye to eye with the comandante. "Listen, Amigo, let this be a lesson to you and your bosses. Don't ever come to the United States and kill our agents again. If you do, expect a visit from someone like me."

"You're a dead man, señor," said a surly comandante. "You'll never get out of this county alive."

"Like I said, I've heard that before, mi amigo." Then reaching forward, Tom patted the comandante on the cheek. "Hasta luego, amigo." Tom stood up. "Let's get going." He turned to John Conway. "Mr. Administrator, you'll ride up in the cab of the truck with Henderson and me. Tony, you drive the Range Rover with Krissy. And, unfortunately, guys," he turned to Lansky, Hood and Wycoff, "you'll have to ride inside the back of the truck. If it gets too cold, we'll switch off with Henderson and myself." Tom looked back at Conway. "Mr. Conway, let's get you home."

With the Range Rover leading the way, Tom drove the stake bed truck, following at a distance as they slowly exited the ranch by the front gate. The severely damaged gatehouse showed no signs of life.

"Hey, Krissy," Gonzalo said, "I guess that guard you trapped inside when you did your race car driving is either dead or running for his life."

"Shit, I ain't getting out to check," advised Krissy.

Gonzalo agreed with a simple affirmative nod of his head.

The tandem of vehicles had just reached the main roadway that would take them north to the border, when the skyline behind them erupted in a large fireball. The distance and the damp atmosphere muted the sound of the explosion, but the team could still hear it.

Tom looked over to the administrator and Hawk. "That will be the gas tank on the Blazer. Hood's a genius when it comes to blowing things up."

Hood and Lansky, riding in the back of the truck, signaled their approval by banging on the metal wall separating the cab from the cargo compartment. They yelled in unison. "All right!"

CHAPTER NINETEEN

February 9, 1997; Agua Prieta, Sonora, Mexico

The eighty-plus-mile drive from Janos to Agua Prieta that should have taken an hour and a half under normal conditions proved more of a challenge than anticipated. Creeping along at ten to fifteen miles an hour, they had barely covered twenty miles after an hour. With visibility severely impaired by freezing rain and sleet, the sheet of black ice covering the highway made travel treacherous at best. An assortment of vehicles littering the highway and its shoulders added to the mix. Most of these vehicles were abandoned, but others were still occupied by drivers and passengers who huddled inside to keep warm. The Range Rover and stake truck weaved a path around them employing Krissy's tried-and-true technique of using the gravel shoulders and inched their way north.

During the trip north, John Conway, initially succumbed by the warmth of the cab of the truck and a sense that for the first time in days he was safe, fell asleep. He awoke after forty minutes with a better grip on his ragged emotions. He looked around him and then engaged Tom Blaine. "How did you guys find me?"

Tom looked from the road to Conway, and then back to the road again. "Hawk and I have a CI who is very close to Jaime Gutiérrez, the head of the Sinaloa Cartel, and the one who orchestrated your kidnapping. He was able to determine where they had taken you when they grabbed you from your hotel in El Paso."

"I see," Conway said nodding his head slightly in understanding. "Uh, Tom, I don't want to seem unappreciative, but why you? With our history and all, I can't understand why the AG would send you or why you'd agree to do this." Before Tom could answer these questions, Conway continued. "And why did the AG take so long to act? She was cutting it kind of close, wasn't she? I mean, today is the fourth or fifth day; I've kind of lost track of time."

Daring to take his eyes off the road again for several seconds to look at the administrator, Tom tried to formulate a response that would elicit the needed cooperation from Conway. He refocused his eyes on the road ahead. "Uh, Mr. Conway, we were not sent here by the AG. In fact, the AG has no knowledge about where you were being held or the fact that we have come to take you home."

"What?" asked Conway in a somewhat elevated tone. He struggled to sit up on the bench seat of the truck and looked at Tom. "I don't understand. What do you mean the AG didn't know where I was being held and about you guys coming for me?"

"When we found out about where we thought you were being held, we decided that if we told the AG, she would have insisted that she contact the Mexican government. Had that occurred, Gutiérrez would have had you moved before the Mexican government could act. Let's face it, Mr. Administrator, Gutiérrez is a very powerful man in his country. The obscene amount of money he pays to bribe government officials at all levels makes him untouchable. Then there is the fact that you are not a very popular individual with the powers-to-be in the Mexican government. Oh, I'm sure the Mexican government would have eventually raided the ranch, but not until long after they had moved you. Then they would have issued a statement that our information was obviously false, and there were no signs you were ever there. One merely has to recall the Mexican government's response when our agent was kidnapped in Guadalajara a number of years ago. I know you were not in DEA then, but I was, and I was outraged at the actions, or more correctly, the lack of actions by the Mexican government. So we were afraid that if we had told the AG and she advised the Mexican government, we would not have gotten another chance to rescue you alive."

"I see," said Conway deep in thought.

"And to answer your question, well, uh," began Tom hesitating to choose the right words, "I'll be goddamned if I was going to let these drug trafficking assholes come to my country, kill two of our agents and then kidnap you and not do something that was in my power to do." He punctuated his last by slapping his palm against the steering wheel of the truck.

Conway sat silent for several minutes considering what Tom had said. "Thanks for doing this. I know you and your men did this at great personal risk to yourselves."

Again, Tom just shrugged his shoulders in acknowledgment of Conway's remarks.

Conway sat silently again for several minutes. "You keep saying we. Does this include James Peterson or others in DEA?"

A look of amusement developed on Tom's face that could be seen in the limited light reflected off the instrument panel. Tom shook his head slightly. "James Peterson? With all due respect, give me a break, sir. From what I have been told, that clown has been totally overwhelmed by this. He has deferred any action to the FBI. While there is somebody in DEA who is involved, I'd prefer to leave him out of this until he agrees to be identified. Suffice it to say that with the information about where you might be located, I was able to organize this team of volunteers and come here to rescue you without the knowledge or help from the U.S. government."

Conway stared at Tom for a while. "Again, Tom, I am extremely grateful to you and your men. And, uh, I want you to know, I am sorry for what I have done to you. I obviously misjudged you. You definitely are what others have been telling me all along—that you are a stand up guy."

"Thank you, sir," was all that Tom could manage in reply.

"So are we heading for the border?" asked Conway.

"Sort of, sir," replied Tom.

"Sort of?" asked Conway who seemed confused by Tom's answer. "What does that mean?"

"Let me ask you this, sir? When they brought you into Mexico, did they take you across the border at a border crossing?"

"Uh…no. Uh…they took me through a tunnel, I think. They put a pillowcase over my head, so I don't know for sure what they did. However, I recall being shoved down a ladder, then riding on a cart of some sort, then back up another ladder; I imagined we were going under the border. Why do you ask?"

"Before I answer, let me ask you this. How long did it take them to get to this tunnel after they grabbed you in El Paso?"

"Uh…I don't know; it seemed that we rode for a long time. I'd guess about three or four hours. I was pretty scared to really keep track of time."

"I see. We suspect they brought you through a tunnel that runs from Agua Prieta to Douglas, Arizona. Gutiérrez and his organization use a tunnel to smuggle drugs into the country," advised Tom.

"I see," said Conway.

"We're pretty sure we know where that tunnel is located and that's where we're heading."

"How do you know that? Your CI?"

"Nope, just good old fashioned surveillance. We followed a truckload of marijuana to a warehouse located in Agua Prieta and feel pretty confident based upon info from our CI and our observations that the tunnel is located at this warehouse."

"And if it's not?" asked Conway.

After considering Conway's question for several minutes, Tom said. "I guess then we'll go to plan B, sir."

"Okay, what's plan B?"

"We'll have to figure that out when plan A does not work, sir."

"So it's the tunnel or nothing then," said Conway.

Tom saw the concern on Conway's face and smiled. "Look, sir, the tunnel was not originally plan A but became plan A when the weather prevented us from using our original plan A. And just as the weather has affected our original plans, it is also affecting the Mexicans' actions to prevent you from leaving this country. Not to worry, sir, we'll get out of here safely."

Conway seemed to accept Tom's statements by nodding his head. "What happens once we get across, or under, the border?"

"The first thing we'll do once we are safely back in the U.S. is get you medical care. While we're doing that, we'll also have you call your wife, sir, and let her know that you are safe. We have a satellite phone and can call from just about anywhere."

With the mention of his wife, Conway's emotions again took control of his demeanor. Tears rolled down his cheeks. "Thank you," he whispered.

Tom allowed Conway a moment to compose himself. "Look, sir, there is something I need to discuss with you that will require your total cooperation."

"What's that, Tom?"

"We need to fudge the truth about where we rescued you?"

"I don't understand. Why can't you just explain what you told me about how you located me and then came and got me?"

"It would probably cause an international incident, sir. I'm afraid the Mexican government might consider armed troops coming into their country, killing several of their countrymen and then leaving as an act of war. At the very least, our actions will cause the Mexican government to determine all DEA personnel persona non grata in Mexico. And while I am just as offended by the amount of money we give them and their often lack of cooperation in stemming the flow of drugs going north, we still need to have agents in Mexico. The intelligence we gain just by having a presence there is invaluable."

"Okay. I am sure you're probably correct about the international incident. I can understand that, but what do you intend to say about where and how you located me?"

"I don't have a definitive cover story yet because a lot depends on how our escape pans out. I want the cover story to be that acting upon informant information, we established surveillance on a location in Douglas, Arizona. Then acting upon visual observations, we decided to raid a certain location where we found and rescued you."

"So let me get this straight. We will say that I, and for that matter you and your team, were never in Mexico."

"Yes, sir, that's what I'd like to say."

"While lying really goes against my personal beliefs, I can see where we really have no choice in this regard."

"That's the way I see it too, sir."

"Looks like Gonzalo and Krissy are stopping, boss," interjected Hawk.

"Yeah, I see. I wonder what's up."

February 9, 1997; Hotel Los Mares Azul, Mazatlán, Mexico

With the lack of traffic out at this time of the morning, Juan made good time traveling from the Hacienda Puesta Del Sol in La Cruz to Mazatlán and Jaime's hotel. Upon entry into the hotel, the front desk clerk directed him to the manager's office. "The manager is in his office waiting for you, sir."

Entering the large wood-paneled office, Juan saw the manager, who had obviously been aroused from his bed, was asleep slumped in a large leather chair behind his massive oak desk. The manager, who always seemed to wear an expensive suit, was this morning wearing a sports shirt with jeans.

Careful not to be seen by the front desk clerk, who appeared to be the only person moving about at this hour, Juan took this opportunity to slip through the lobby to the bank of pay phones lining the alcove hidden from the lobby. Dialing the number he had memorized, Juan waited while the call connected. What seemed like an eternity, but in fact, was less than a minute, a female voice answered. "What?"

Befuddled by the terse answer and that a female had answered the phone, Juan hesitated, and then stammered, "Uh, Señor Thomas Blaine, por favor?"

"Is this Juan?" asked the female voice.

"Sí," answered Juan cautiously.

"Wait one, he's not in this vehicle but is close by," said the female voice. In the background, Juan heard her say, "It's the CI for Blaine. We need to stop."

Juan heard a male voice. "Krissy, give me the phone."

"Juan, this is Tony. I met you last year at Uriarte's Estancia. We are driving right now, and Tom is in another vehicle. The roads are bad so unless this is really important, I'd rather not stop and go get him. Can you tell me what you need him for?"

"Sí, Tony. Tell Señor Thomas that Jaime has had the borders at Agua Prieta and Juarez closed. Also the Federales in both those areas are going to set up road blocks and the Mexican Army is sending a unit to the ranch."

"I see, Juan," said Tony. Can you hold on while I go get Tom for you?"

"I can't wait too long because I need to see someone for Jaime. Then I need to get back to his hacienda. If I am gone too long or if this person I am here to see catches me on this phone, I might have problems."

"I understand, Juan," said Tony. Red flags went up for Tony. *This is a little strange for the CI to call at this hour when we're right in the middle of this thing. While he may be actually giving us good information, what if he's been compromised and is trying to get information from us. I'll give him some information that if he is under duress or should find the need to tell anyone about our whereabouts, he'll speak what he thinks is the truth.* "Thanks for the information, Juan, but don't be concerned. This bad weather forced us to head south. I doubt Jaime's men would expect us to head away from the border. We plan to hold up somewhere and figure a new way to get out of Mexico. But should you develop any more information please call right away."

"Sí, Señor Tony, I will."

As Juan exited the alcove, the hotel manager met him. "Are you lost Juan? My office is back over there."

"Uh, no señor, I had to use the bathroom," said Juan as he pointed with his finger to the rest rooms at the back of the alcove.

"You should have awakened me. You could have used my private bathroom. Let us go get the Mezcal from the bar."

Juan followed the manager. *That was close. A few seconds earlier, and he would have caught me on the phone. I must be more careful from now on.*

February 9, 1997; Agua Prieta, Sonora, Mexico

Tony handed the satellite phone back to Krissy and slowed the Range Rover to a stop. "I need to talk with Blaine. I'll be right back."

Slumped against the seat in a position that seemed to ease the pain in her chest, Krissy mumbled, "Okay."

He pulled his coat up around his neck, and lowering his head into the pelting sleet, Tony carefully walked from the stopped Range Rover to the stake bed truck, which had pulled up close to the Range Rover. Signaling with his hand for Tom to roll down the window as he approached the truck, he jumped up on the running board. "CI just called, boss. He wanted to tell you that Gutiérrez has had the borders closed at Agua Prieta and Juarez and there are supposed to be federale road blocks between here and there. Oh, and the Army has sent a unit to the ranch."

"Shit, the road blocks could be a problem. We'll just have to deal with them when we encounter them," said Tom. "Okay, if we should come across a road block, stop far enough back so we can formulate a plan to either circumvent or breech it. We've come too far in this shitty weather to turn around."

"Ten-four, boss; maybe God will get to use those LAAWs he liberated at the ranch."

"Yeah, he might, but I'd rather he not have to, Tony. How's Krissy holding up?"

"She's in a lot of pain, boss, but has been very helpful in guiding us around the obstacles along the road. And her technique of running on the gravel shoulder is really helping us."

"Yeah, it has. Well, let's get going."

Gonzalo began to step down from the running board, then hesitated and turned back to the window. "Tom, I told the CI that we changed our plans and because of the weather we decided to head south."

"Oh?" exclaimed Tom in slight surprise.

"Yeah, I figured if he is compromised or gets compromised, he can truthfully tell Gutiérrez that we told them we were going south not north."

"Good thinking, Tony. I hadn't thought of that."

During the remainder of the trip to Agua Prieta, the occupants of both the Range Rover and the stake bed truck remained alert for possible roadblocks. However, the bad weather was the only roadblock they encountered. Ice covered both the roads and the surrounding landscape as they moved further north. The vegetation, including both trees and bushes, as well as the buildings they passed lay in a blanket of ice, which at times took on the appearance of snow in a classic Currier and Ives winter landscape. As they closed in on Agua Prieta, some four and half hours after leaving the Rancho Tierra Del Sol, the amount of disabled and abandoned vehicles increased, and at times, the tandem of vehicles had to weave its way carefully in and around these temporary obstacles. Five miles outside of Agua Prieta and with lights from the city illuminating the horizon, the Range Rover ran out of gas. "Shit!" exclaimed Gonzalo as he edged the sputtering Ranger Rover to the side of the road.

Krissy rose slightly and winced from the pain in her chest. "What's up, Tony?"

"We're out of gas."

He echoed his remarks when Tom appeared at the driver's door window.

"Okay, let's all get into the stake bed. We're almost there now, Krissy, so it won't be too bad," Tom said.

Wycoff lifted and helped Krissy to settle into the rear of the stake bed truck. Hawk moved to the back of the truck, vacating his seat for Gonzalo.

They had been driving only a few minutes when Gonzalo asked, "Remember where we're going, Tom?"

"I think so, Tony. If I remember correctly, we go all the way through the center of the town and take a right at Calle Uno at the north end. It runs parallel to the border."

"That's how I remember it too, boss," agreed Gonzalo.

Thirty minutes later and following these directions, Tom slowed the stake bed truck as it approached the warehouse bearing the sign Productos De Sonora. "I guess we should check it out before we approach it," said Tom reaching for the door handle of the truck. Gonzalo did likewise. As he began to exit the truck, Tom turned to John Conway. "Sit tight, sir. We'll be right back."

Nodding his head in ascent, John Conway said, "Be careful."

Tom opened the back of the truck. "We're just down the street from the warehouse with the tunnel. At least we hope the tunnel is in this warehouse. God, Brian, Hawk, I want you to come with Tony and me to check it out. Krissy, Tree, you stay here. We won't be long. Oh, and Conway is settled in the cab and should be okay. Monitor your radios, folks; I'll keep you posted on what we find. Any questions?"

While moving toward the warehouse, Gonzalo looked to the sky. "At least the freezing drizzle has stopped."

They moved cautiously in the direction of the warehouse. "I would imagine there is a guard at the location," said Tom, "especially if there is any quantity of marijuana in there."

"There also might be canines," suggested Henderson.

"Yeah, good thought, Hawk. You watch for them. And remember guys," as he looked at the

rest of the team, "we should consider ourselves in enemy territory until we get to the U.S. side of the border. We shall do whatever it takes to accomplish this task."

It took less than fifteen minutes to determine that a ten-foot high chain link fence, topped off with strands of barbed wire, circled the warehouse. Access to the warehouse grounds was through a large sliding chain link gate that appeared to be automated and would slide to the right on small metal wheels mounted on a track when being opened. Even in the limited visibility, exterior lights on the warehouse itself flooded the grounds. Two large roll up doors were on the front of the warehouse, as well as a smaller regular door. To the right of the smaller door was a bank of windows and a faint light could be seen coming from this window.

"What do you think, guys?' asked Tom when they had gathered back at the stake bed truck.

"I think this truck," as Hood slapped the side of the truck "can ram that gate and easily knock it off its track."

"That's providing we can get up enough speed first. I think the black ice and lack of traction could be a problem," offered Lansky.

"What if I use one of these babies on the gate," volunteered Lansky as he un-shouldered one of the LAAWs he was carrying.

Gonzalo smiled at Lansky's suggestion. "Let's save those things for tougher targets. I think we should try the truck first."

"Well, however the hell we're going to do it, let's get going. I'm freezing my ass off out here," said a shivering Hawk. "I didn't see any dogs running around, but if they're not dumb like us, they're probably in out of this shitty weather."

Tom ignored Hawk's complaint. "Okay, we'll use the truck to ram the gate. I want God, Brian, Tree and Hawk to take up positions on either side of the gate and cover us. If there are guards here, they're more than likely in the warehouse."

Entering the truck, Tom took the driver's seat and as Gonzalo made himself comfortable in the right passenger side, Tom turned to Conway. "Hold on, sir. We're going to use the truck to ram the gate. And we don't know if there might be a response from somebody in the warehouse. If shooting does start get down as low as you can and try to use the engine as a shield."

"Okay," Conway said nervously.

As they started to roll forward on the slick pavement, Gonzalo said, "This is where it gets dicey, guys."

The slick road did not offer much in the way of traction. "Shit," Tom muttered, "I hope we can build up some momentum."

As they neared the gate, Tony sat up in the seat and looked at Tom. "Say, Tom, instead of trying to ram the gate, why not try rolling up to the gate and leaning on the horn. Maybe somebody inside will recognize this truck from the ranch and open the gate."

"Certainly worth a try," Tom said. "If it doesn't work, I can always back up and then ram the gate."

Up to this point, Conway had remained mute during the exchange between Gonzalo and Tom. "Why don't you try using that garage door opener on the driver's visor," he suggested.

Tom looked first at Conway and then at Gonzalo. "I'll be damned! I didn't see that thing there."

"Change of plans, guys," Tom said as he stepped down from the truck. "We're going to see if this opens the gate." He displayed the garage door opener he held in his hand.

"Figures. It's like all those unlocked doors we've kicked in when all we had to do was try the knob first," said Lansky with a sneer-like smile.

"If it doesn't open the gate, I'll honk the horn and see if that will get a response from the warehouse. But be on guard, it might elicit the wrong response."

Slowly rolling up to the gate, Tom pressed the button on the door opener. The sound of an electric motor being activated began. The gate shook slightly but did not retract. Pressing the button again, the motor activated and continued to do so without a response from the gate.

"Shit, it's frozen shut, Tom," said Gonzalo who peered out of his side of the truck. "I can see the arm trying to move, but the wheels are frozen to the rail. It's not going to budge."

"Okay, then let's go with honking…" began Tom.

Gonzalo interrupted him. "Tom, somebody's exiting the warehouse. Shit, he's carrying a rifle, looks like an AR-15."

"I was afraid of this," Tom exclaimed as he tried to back up the truck. In his haste, he gave the truck too much gas and succeeded in only causing the rear tires to spin without gaining traction. Allowing the wheels to stop, Tom tried backing again, this time using very little pressure on the accelerator. Slowly, the truck inched backwards.

"The guard's watching us, boss. I guess he doesn't know what to make of us yet."

"Tell Brian and God to take him out if he decides to become stupid."

"Ten-four, boss," said Gonzalo who then relayed Tom's instruction to Hood and Lansky.

Tom backed the truck about twenty yards from the gate, when he stopped and shifted the truck into a forward gear. Slowly, the heavy truck began forward, but it soon became obvious that he could not build up enough speed to ram the gates and force them open.

The guard, who was watching this action, also concluded the truck was going to ram the gates, and that something was amiss. He placed the AR-15 into his shoulder and began to close the distance between him and the gate.

Lansky watched as Tom tried to gain traction while the armed guard approached. "Fuck this," he said. Taking a LAAWS from his shoulder, he extended the tube, pulled the disarming pin and sighted the front sight on the gate motor housing. With a whoosh, the rocket cleared the tube and seconds later, a tremendous bang quickly followed a brilliant flash of light.

The occupants of the truck, initially startled by the flash and bang, felt the shock waves of the explosion. "Jesus Christ. What the fuck?" Tom exclaimed.

The gate, knocked off its track by the explosion, slowly fell away and backwards into the warehouse yard. The guard halted his progress for a moment surprised at the exploding gate. Seeing Lansky, Gonzalo and Hawk scrambling toward the gate, he began firing at them and the truck with his AR-15. His initial rounds struck the ground around Hood, the front motor area and the windshield of the truck causing Tom, Gonzalo and Conway to duck down to the floor of the cab.

Responding to the guard's attempts to halt the progress of the truck,

Hood and Lansky fired upon the guard with the AKs from the ranch. Their aim was much better than the guard's and the majority of both Lansky's and Hood's bullets struck the guard. Hood, Lansky and Henderson, now accompanied by Wycoff, rushed to the gate and dragged it away from the road allowing Tom to guide the big truck into the warehouse yard. The truck had no sooner cleared the gate than a fusillade of bullets, originating from the opened door, struck it. Lansky and Hood responded to this new threat and took the warehouse under fire. When the rounds continued from the warehouse, Lansky un-shouldered the second LAAW, extended the tube, sighted the weapon and fired. Again, they heard a loud whoosh followed by a brilliant light and bang, as a large hole appeared where the small door on the front of the warehouse had once been. The rifle fire from the warehouse ceased. In a leapfrog maneuver, Lansky and Hood moved forward toward the warehouse from one covered position to another, while Henderson and Wycoff covered them also from covered positions.

Inching the truck forward, Tom was able to get it to the first roll up door where he killed the engine. "Wait here, sir," he instructed Conway. "We need to make sure it's safe."

It took just several minutes to determine the guard outside, shot by Lansky and Hood, was dead. Two additional guards inside had been killed by the exploding round from the LAAWs. Once secured and after switching on the overhead lights, Tom and Tony led the remainder of the team in searching the warehouse.

It was a large metal structure, similar to the barn at the ranch, and like the barn, contained a mountain of stacked burlap-covered bundles of marijuana. "Must be several tons of grass here," concluded Gonzalo.

They found an overhead winch set directly over an opening in the concrete floor toward the rear of the warehouse. "I do believe we have found the tunnel, guys," said Tom.

After carefully checking the opening, Tom descended a twenty-five foot aluminum ladder affixed to the wall of the tunnel. In an animated voice, Tom yelled up to the others. "Holy shit, this is something else."

The rest of the team members soon joined him. The tunnel, as sophisticated as any mining tunnel in the United States, was six feet tall in height; only Lansky had to duck to prevent striking his head on the heavy oaken beams that supported the tunnel. The width of the tunnel accommodated a steel rail on wooden ties and a battery-powered motorized cart used to move both drugs and personnel through the tunnel. A light bulb hung from a wooden beam every twenty-five to thirty feet. While not bright enough to read by, they certainly provided sufficient light to navigate the tunnel. A ventilation system provided clean air for the tunnel. A breaker box mounted on the wall next to the ladder controlled both the lights and ventilation system.

"This is a professionally made tunnel," offered Gonzalo. "Gutiérrez obviously had someone with tunnel or mine experience to construct this."

"Should we check out the tunnel, boss?" asked Lansky.

"I don't think we have too much time, God. The shooting and explosions are sure to have attracted someone's attention. I think we need to go for it. We know this is how Gutiérrez smuggles dope into the US, so it has to come out somewhere across the border. And if it doesn't, we're fucked anyway."

"I think you're right," said Gonzalo. "We need to get going."

"Let's get Krissy and Conway down here. They can ride on the cart. Hawk, you and I will lead, and Tony and Tree can follow the cart." He turned to Lansky and Hood. "God, you and Brian provide us with a rear guard. Give us thirty minutes, unless you get some unwelcomed company, and then join us in the U.S."

Ten minutes later, Conway and Krissy managed to descend the ladder and sat in the cart. As Tom started to descend the ladder, he looked at Lansky and Hood. "Listen, guys, no heroics, okay? If company comes, don't stick around to greet them."

"About that boss, God and I were talking and how about we do the same thing on the grass in this building like we did at the ranch. We can pull that truck in here and torch it like we did the Blazer at the ranch. That would certainly delay anyone trying to pursue us down in the tunnel."

"Go for it guys, but be careful."

February 9, 1997; Hacienda Puesta Del Sol, La Cruz, Sinaloa, Mexico

At the same time that Jaime's recently-freed hostage was crossing under the border into the United States to freedom, Jaime learned, not only the fate of the comandante, but also, news of the apparent failure of his plan to exchange John Conway for his bother Hector.

It began with a telephone call, not from any of the Mexican government officials who enjoyed a more than comfortable lifestyle due to the largess of mordita paid by Jaime Gutiérrez, but instead from Ramon Acevedo, his trusted and reliable Juarez-based accounts manager.

"Hola, Juan, began Ramon who lacked the usual spark Juan had come to appreciate. I see you are at the estancia early, mi amigo."

"Sí, Ramon. In fact, I have not left and have spent the night waiting with Don Jaime on word of what is happening at the ranch."

Ramon gave a long sigh. "Juan, that is why I am calling. I have very bad news for Don Jaime."

"Oh?" exclaimed Juan. He attempted to inject enough of a surprised concern to disguise his real feeling.

"Sí, it is very bad, Juan. But I should have the comandante talk with Don Jaime first."

"You have located the comandante, Ramon?" This time he did not have to pretend to be surprised.

"Sí, I have found him," answered Ramon with a hint of excitement returning to his voice.

"Where was he Ramon?" asked Juan not able to control his continued surprise.

"He was at the ranch here in Janos."

"So you are at the ranch then?" asked Juan.

"Sí, Juan. I was able to gather some men who work security for me from time to time and we made the drive here from Juarez arriving only twenty minutes ago. It took us most of the night with the bad weather and really bad road conditions."

"I see, Ramon. Let me wake Don Jaime. He is uh…resting."

"Drunk?" asked Ramon.

"He has been drinking Mezcal, as usual, but I think it's more exhaustion than passing out from alcohol. He has slept little the past several days."

Setting the phone aside, Juan proceeded to the dark leather recliner that was currently serving as the makeshift bed for Jaime. He gently shook Jaime. "Don Jaime, perdone, but I have Ramon on the phone. He is at the ranch in Janos."

"Uh…what?" asked a groggy Jaime still more asleep than awake.

"I have Ramon on the phone, and he is at the ranch in Janos. He has found the comandante."

The words *ranch in Janos* and *Comandante* seemed to do the trick in awaking Jaime. He struggled getting out of the recliner, then took a minute to steady himself. He crossed the room for the phone on Juan's desk. "Ramon, tell me what's going on," he demanded.

"I am sorry, Don Jaime, but the news is not good."

Jaime sighed heavily. "Tell me, Ramon."

"Sí, Don Jaime. Armed men, who the comandante believe were DEA, attacked the ranch and took the DEA jefe with them."

"Attacked the ranch and took the DEA jefe?' asked an astonished Jaime.

"Sí, Don Jaime," replied Ramon.

"When did this occur, Ramon?" asked Jaime.

"Around midnight, Don Jaime," replied Ramon.

"Juan said you found the comandante?"

"Sí, Don Jaime. He was at the ranch. He and the rest of the guards were handcuffed with those plastic restraints the police use. The attackers killed several of the guards including the teniente."

Jaime fell into Juan's desk chair. Jaime, who under normal circumstances would have become violently angry, merely said, "Let me speak with the comandante, Ramon."

"Uh por supesto – of course, Don Jaime. He is right here and while he is shaken up by what has happened, he is physically okay."

"Carajo!" exploded Jaime into the phone in instant anger. His face and neck instantly turned scarlet. "I don't care if that pendejo is shaken up. Get him on the phone."

A moment later, the comandante took the phone. "Don Jaime, Lo siento, señor pero - but…."

Before he could continue, Jaime, whose anger and lack of patience was obvious in his tone interrupted him. "What happened, Comandante?"

"Uh, ah, I don't know how, but some DEA putas found out where we were hiding their jefe," replied the comandante coming directly to the point."

"DEA? How do you know they were DEA?" asked Jaime with some of the anger leaving his tone.

"Just by the way they talked, Don Jaime. I am very sure they were DEA."

"What happened, Comandante?"

"Well, they overpowered myself and one of my men in Janos and then took us with them to the ranch," said the comandante not wishing to provide the details on how they easily captured him.

"So they knew about the ranch when they, how did you say it, overpowered you, Comandante?"

"Sí, Don Jaime, they knew about the ranch. They attacked the ranch just after midnight. They killed several of our men including the teniente and took their jefe with them when they left."

Jaime paused several moments to process the disastrous news. "I am very distressed with this, Comandante. I trusted you to protect my ranch, and you obviously have not done what I expected."

"Don Jaime," pleaded the comandante "This is not my fault. I hired the best security. These men were Los Zetos and highly trained."

"Highly trained!" exclaimed Jaime. "I think not. If they were highly trained, I would have dead DEA putas at my ranch along with their jefe right now."

"Pero, Don Jaime, the DEA acted like trained commandoes, and the weather worked to their advantage."

"Carajo! The weather! I am sick and tired of hearing about the weather. Why did it only affect you and your highly trained security? It did not seem to affect the DEA did it?" mocked Jaime.

"Uh, no, Don Jaime, I guess not."

"Comandante, I want you to find those DEA putas and their jefe before they get out of this country. Then I want you to deal with whoever did this to me. If you fail in either of these efforts, do not bother to come back here for I will consider you a dead man. Entiendo?"

"Sí, Don Jefe," gulped the comandante. "I will look to it right away."

"Put Ramon back on the phone, Comandante."

"Sí, Don Jaime," said the comandante.

"Uh, Don Jaime," began Ramon when he came back on the phone, "the comandante is telling you the truth about the apparent DEA commandoes."

"Oh?" questioned Jaime.

"I talked with several of the guards, and they said they overpowered them with tear gas; the commandoes were very well prepared," offered Ramon.

"I see. They must have had good information then," decided Jaime.

"Sí, Don Jaime. To determine their jefe was here and then conduct a coordinated attack on this ranch, they had to have very good information."

"Sí, Ramon, I agree. Somebody who had knowledge about our business has been talking to DEA."

"I would agree with you, Don Jaime."

"Ramon, did you see any Army units at the ranch or while in route to the ranch?"

"No, señor, I did not see any Army units," replied Ramon.

"It seems my contacts in the government could only close the borders and have the federales set up roadblocks."

"Close the borders?" questioned Ramon. "The Norte Americanos closed the borders because of the weather, not the Mexican government. And, uh, Don Jefe, I did not see any road blocks between Juarez and here."

"Pendejos!" cursed Jaime. "I pay all this money to protect my interests, and I get nothing from them. I will deal with those pendejos. By the way, Ramon, I want to thank you for taking it upon yourself to go to the ranch."

"It was nothing, Don Jaime. And while I do not want to upset you any more than you are already, I think you should know that the people who conducted the attack here also burned the barn."

"Burned the barn?" questioned Jaime not seeming to understand the significance of what Ramon was telling him.

"Sí, Don Jaime, they burned the barn with all of our product."

Instant anger arose in Jaime. "Carajo!" he shouted. "How much was lost, Ramon?"

"I need to check, but I think about sixteen megagrams—short tons of verde—green and fifteen hundred units of white," said Ramon using the code words green for marijuana and white for cocaine.

Dumbfounded would best describe Jaime's response to this news. He merely dropped the phone and walked to the bar where he raised the bottle of Mezcal to his lips and drank deeply from the bottle.

Juan picked up the phone. "Ramon, que pasa - what's happening? What did you just tell Don Jaime?"

Ramon repeated what he had just told Jaime.

"Oh, that's not good," Juan exclaimed. "Oye—listen, Ramon. Why don't you stay there at the ranch while Don Jaime sorts things out? I'll get back to you shortly."

"Sí, Juan. I do not wish to leave right now even if I was able. The weather and roads are just too bad. We shall wait until the sun comes up and the ice melts before we attempt to go anywhere."

"Esta bien - that is good, Ramon," said Juan as he hung up the phone.

Juan watched as Jaime continued to drink from the bottle of Mezcal and as he navigated a path back to his recliner. Jaime dropped down into his chair and spoke rhetorically. "Who would do this to me?" He took another swig of Mezcal. "Whoever did this to me shall pay."

His proclamation sent a cold shiver coursing through Juan. *I'd better think about getting out of here soon. I hope Thomas Blaine and his team are successful and will help get me out of here before it is too late.*

CHAPTER TWENTY

February 9, 1997; Douglas, Arizona

It had taken approximately forty minutes to traverse the almost three hundred-yard tunnel from its beginning at Productos De Sonora in Agua Prieta to its end in Douglas, Arizona. Initially, the tunnel descended on a very gentle slope as it wove its way north. After what Tom estimated was fifty yards, the tunnel leveled off and, for the most part, was almost a straight shot with just several slight turns as it made its way to its terminus in Douglas. The last twenty yards of the tunnel erased the descent by a slight incline which ended in a medium-sized underground room with a metal ladder fixed to the wall that led up to ground level. It took forty minutes because of a concern for the potential threat of armed guards. Because of this concern, Tom had decided he and Hawk would lead the electric cart containing the injured Hammond and John Conway.

While Hammond seemed focused, even while suffering the severe pain in her rib cage, Conway seemed to be overwhelmed at the level of violence expended to rescue him. His current mental state now required his being treated much like an adult would treat a young child.

Gonzalo and Wycoff brought up the rear following the cart that Hammond was controlling with an extended handheld control module. Making their way north toward Douglas, Tom and Hawk would move to points where one of the tunnel's slight curves obscured the vision ahead. After checking out what lay ahead they would signal for the cart to move up to their position.

Encountering no resistance, Tom gathered the team beneath the ladder leading up to ground level. "Listen, guys. I've checked and there seems to be some type of hatch door at the top of the ladder. I wanted to wait until we had everybody here before I checked it out. Tony, Hawk, Tree, I want you guys to cover me while I go up and check the door."

Scaling the ladder, Tom examined what was blocking the way to the ground level. He shouted over his shoulder. "It looks like the bottom of a wooden pallet. And it looks like there is something stacked on the pallet." Using his shoulder, he pushed with all his weight. "I can't budge it."

"Holy shit, what are we going to do?" asked Wycoff. At the start of the trek through the tunnel, Wycoff confided in the team that he suffered from mild claustrophobia. Even in the cool air of the tunnel, perspiration dripped from his forehead.

"Calm down, big guy," said Gonzalo, "we'll figure something out here." He patted Wycoff on the arm. "Take some deep breaths."

"Yeah, we can always retreat back down the tunnel…"

A rumbling sound, followed by the ground trembling like a minor earthquake, interrupted Tom. Several seconds later, the lights in the tunnel and room went out, pitching the team into complete darkness. As some dirt dropped from overhead, Tom pulled a small-stream light flashlight, turned it on and focused it on the ceiling of the room. Gonzalo and Hammond did likewise with their lights creating an eerie shadow effect on the ceiling and walls.

Tom looked up at the ceiling. "Jesus, I certainly hope that was God and Brian doing something to delay any pursuers."

"Holy shit, Tom, what if this tunnel collapses?" asked Wycoff.

In the limited light, Tom could see the look of fear in Wycoff's eyes. He had seen this look before when Wycoff, hanging on the back of the pilot's seat, watched as Hayes piloted a stolen aircraft down a dirt runway last year in Zaragoza, Mexico.

"Yeah, we'd best be checking out what's above the ladder, pronto," advised Gonzalo.

"Let me check out the trap door, Tom," volunteered Wycoff pushing by Tom to get to the ladder.

With Tom focusing his flashlight on the top of the ladder, Wycoff quickly scaled the ladder. At the top, he examined what was blocking the exit to the tunnel. "I think you're right, Tom," he called back down to Tom. "It's a wooden pallet all right, and there appears to be something on it. Let me see if I can move it." He climbed the ladder so he could position himself in a crouching position and then placed his shoulders against the pallet. With his knees, he attempted to power-lift the pallet. After several attempts, and with slight panic in his tone, he shouted down to the others. "No go; it's too heavy for me. I can't get a steady base position."

"What do we do now?" asked Gonzalo.

As Tom considered Gonzalo's question, they heard the sound of footsteps moving north along the tunnel and rapidly toward them. Taking up defensive positions, they waited. Several minutes later, they saw flashes of light.

"Don't shoot; it's us," Hood said. Both Lansky and Hood, wearing miners' helmets with lights emerged from where the tunnel made a slight bend.

"Nice hats," quipped Hammond as they entered the room.

"Yeah there was a whole bunch of mining equipment in the small building outside the big barn. I thought these might come in handy," said Hood as he tapped the miner's helmet.

"Was that you we heard, the rumble and shaking," asked Gonzalo.

"Uh huh," answered Hood. "I also found these while we were checking out the miners' equipment." He displayed several sticks of dynamite. "It sure helped in torching the marijuana."

"You used dynamite?" asked a slightly perturbed Tom. "Weren't you afraid you'd collapse the tunnel, Brian?"

"Give me some credit, boss. I know explosives," replied an indignant Hood as he used the light on the miner's helmet to check out the small room. His light focused on something fixed to one of the main overhead support beams, "In fact, I know that large white softball sized chunk of putty looking substance stuck up there on that beam is probably Semtex, a Czech-made explosive used by Arab terrorists."

All heads turned to the beam Brian had in his light.

"Shit, I didn't see that," exclaimed Gonzalo.

"Me either," said a chagrined Tom. "I guess they booby trapped this place so they could blow it if the cops ever discovered the tunnel."

"That would be my guess, boss. It also looks like it has an electric blasting cap and a delay fuse. I'm sure glad you didn't try to use that breaker box over there to turn the lights back on in this room," said Hood.

As all heads looked from the apparent booby trap to the breaker box, several team members expressed their collective concern and relief with words like "Jesus, holy shit and fuck me."

"So what's the story here? Why are we waiting?" asked Lansky.

"Slight problem guys," said Tom.

"Oh?" questioned Lansky as he looked from Tom to Gonzalo.

"Seems the exit up at the top of the stairs is covered with a pallet and there is something heavy on the pallet," offered Gonzalo.

"We can't move it at all?" asked Hood.

"Even the California Police Olympic two-time Power-Lifting champion could not budge it," Tom said looking at Wycoff.

"I couldn't get a good platform position," said Wycoff in his defense.

"Can we retrace our steps and get out at the other end, guys?" Tom asked Lansky and Hood.

"Not unless you're a mole or have mining equipment, Tom," said Lansky. "I'm fairly positive that Brian's handiwork collapsed a good portion of the tunnel at the other end."

"Mind if I check it out, Tom," asked Hood pointing toward the pallet covering their exit. "Maybe I can rig something to move or reduce that pallet."

"Help yourself Brian," said Tom.

Hood climbed the ladder and after several minutes of looking over the pallet with his headlamp, he pulled a K-Bar knife from its sheath strapped to his calf and began to hack away at the pallet. Wood chips began to fall to the tunnel floor, followed by an off-white stream of granules.

Tom examined and sniffed the granules as they began to collect at the base of the ladder. "I think it's fertilizer."

"Maybe he can lighten the load by puncturing all the bags stacked on the bottom. It might reduce the weight enough for us to lift the pallet off," suggested Hawk.

"Good idea, Hawk," said Lansky. "Come down here a minute, Hood, I think we can hasten up this process of puncturing those bags."

Looking first at Lansky then at Gonzalo, Tom shrugged his shoulders not understanding what Lansky was going to do.

After Hood returned to the ground, Lansky moved to a position that would offer him an oblique angle up the shaft to the covered hatch and cautioned the remainder of the team. "You guys might want to stand back a bit. And cover your noses and ears."

Inserting a fresh magazine into the AK-47 he still carried, he began blasting away at the pallet. Wood chips and fertilizer began to trickle down to the floor of the tunnel. The trickle then became a heavy shower creating a heavy fog-like cloud mixed with the odor of cordite from the expended rounds from the AK-47. When the shower slowed, Lansky removed his miner's helmet, donned his gas mask and climbed the ladder. Pulling partially empty bags through the slats in the pallet, he exposed new bags, which began to seep fertilizer through exiting bullet holes. Stepping closer to the wall and while hanging on the ladder he used his K-Bar to expand the holes in the bags. Again, there was a shower of fertilizer falling to the ground.

As the shower diminished to a trickle, Wycoff, who had covered his nose and mouth with a bandana said, "Let me see if I can move it now."

After Lansky returned to the ground, Wycoff carefully climbed the ladder expressing his dislike of heights as he did so. Positioning himself directly under the pallet, once again, he used his legs to lift as he straightened. The pallet lifted slightly from the floor above. "Hey, guys, I moved it a little." He lifted again.

Hood scrambled up the ladder and managed to take a position next to Wycoff balancing one foot on the ladder while the other swung free. "Tree, when you lift again, I'll try to shove the pallet sideways."

"Let's do it," said Wycoff.

The two-time California Police Olympic Gold Medal winner then gave another gold medal performance and pushed up with all he had while Hood shoved against the pallet. The pallet moved a foot sideways. "One more time, Tree," shouted Hood.

Grunting and sucking in air once again, the duo managed to lift and move the pallet a foot or so. A third time resulted in creating a small opening.

"Hey, let me see if I can slip through that opening," said Henderson, the smallest male of the group. He took off his coat while waiting for Wycoff and Hood to descend the ladder and stuck his Beretta 9 mm in the small of his back. He nimbly climbed the ladder and with much pushing with his feet and sucking in of his breath, he managed to squeeze through the opening. After surveying what he could see in the warehouse above, he yelled down to the others. "Appears to be abandoned up here."

The team waited while Hawk removed the remaining sacks of fertilizer from the pallet. While waiting, Hood examined the Semtex booby trap.

The sound of the pallet sliding across a concrete floor signaled the opening was clear.

"Tony, take God and Hood up with you and check out the warehouse," said Tom. "Tree, you help Krissy; I'll see to the Administrator."

Wycoff helped Krissy to a standing position. "Do you think you can climb the ladder?"

She winced noticeably as she attempted to raise her arms. "Shit, it hurts like hell to raise my arms, Tree."

Wycoff bent down. "Get on my shoulders, Krissy."

Slowly and as pain caused her to cry out "Ouch, fuck that hurts," she mounted Wycoff's shoulders. Standing upright, he walked to the ladder and began to climb. Halfway up, Krissy, even in pain, found resolve to quip, "I'll bet you never thought you'd get your head between my legs again, Tree."

"Wrong head, Krissy," replied Wycoff.

"In your dreams, big guy," said Krissy as she playfully slapped Wycoff on the top of his head and then cried "Ow" in pain from her actions.

Tom helped John Conway, who had remained huddled on the cart and seemed to be in a mild state of shock. "Welcome back to the United States, Mr. Administrator."

Tears rolled down his cheeks. "Thanks, Tom." Then the administrator began the climb back to the United States.

February 9, 1997; Hacienda Puesta Del Sol, La Cruz, Sinaloa, Mexico

As John Conway stepped onto U.S. soil for the first time since being kidnapped four days prior, Jaime Gutiérrez sprang to his feet, belying the fact that he had consumed half a bottle of Mezcal. "Juan, get Ramon on the phone. He should still be at the ranch."

"Sí, Don Jaime." Juan dialed the number to Tierra Del Sol.

A male voice answered the phone on the second ring. "Hola."

"I have Don Jaime for Ramon."

"Sí, señor, he is lying on the sofa. I shall get him."

Several minutes later, a groggy sounding Ramon answered. "Hola, Don Jaime."

"It's me, Ramon," said Juan. "He is right here." Juan passed the phone to Jaime. "Ramon is on the phone, Don Jaime."

"Ramon, I have been thinking about what you said about the weather and the roads around the ranch. I don't think those pinche DEA commandoes could get very far; they'll have to wait for the roads to clear."

"Sí, Don Jaime, I would agree they would have to wait somewhere."

"I am also thinking they have not told anyone in the American government that they have rescued their jefe. If they had notified their government, I think the world would know by now. It would be all over the news. At least I would hope that my sources in the government would have contacted me."

"Sí, señor, I think you might be correct. I would agree they would wait until they cross the border before they tell anyone in their government also," agreed Ramon.

"Yes, of course, you are probably right, Ramon. Tell me, does the comandante still have the DEA jefe's finger?"

"I do not know, Don Jaime. Let me ask him; he is right here."

Jaime could hear Ramon asking the comandante in the background. When he could not hear the comandante's response, he became agitated. He yelled into the phone. "Ramon, put that pendejo on the phone."

"Sí, Don Jaime, here he is."

"Don Jaime, I was explaining to Ramon…" began the comandante before Jaime interrupted him.

"Do you have the finger or not, Comandante?"

"No, the DEA commandoes took it from me," said the comandante telling Jaime only half of the truth.

"Carajo," blurted Jaime. "Put Ramon back on the phone."

"Sí, Don Jaime and I am sorry for…"

"Put Ramon back on the phone, Comandante," yelled Jaime before the comandante could finish his apology.

The comandante handed the phone back to Ramon.

"Oye, Ramon, get a message to the press that we will give the pinche American government until 4:00 p.m. Mexico City time today to return my brother to Mexico, or we shall kill the DEA jefe. Tell them we have changed our minds about the five-day waiting period, because they have not been honorable with us. They have been deliberately delaying Hector's return while they try to locate their jefe. Four p.m. today, Mexico City time, comprende carnal – understand buddy?"

"Sí, Don Jaime. I will get word to the press immediately."

"Esta bien, Ramon." After hanging up the phone, Jaime turned to Juan. "If the pinche gringos have not been informed that I no longer have their jefe maybe I can bluff them into thinking I still do and force them to return Hector before they find out."

"Sí, Don Jaime, it is certainly worth a try," agreed Juan.

"Oh, and Juan, you did good, mi amigo, bringing Ramon into our business. He has done a lot for us, a lot more than the people I pay good money to do what he does on his own initiative."

"Gracias, Don Jaime. Ramon is a very smart and loyal hombre," said Juan. *Jaime will not be thanking me when he discovers I was the one who told the DEA about the location of their jefe. By then, I hope to be long gone with my brother and his family living our lives in peace where no one can bother us.*

February 9, 1997, Douglas, Arizona

Following John Conway up the ladder from the tunnel, Tom stepped into a large warehouse. The semi-darkened cavernous building was considerably larger than the last two warehouses. This one also differed in that it was semi-heated by a forced air unit suspended from a ceiling beam. It blew warm air and made the building comfortable. The warehouse, an open bay affair, had a walled-off office area toward the front of the building. From the contents stacked on nearby pallets, it appeared the building housed an agricultural supply business. Many of the items on the pallets bore the label of Pan American Wholesale Agricultural Supply, Douglas, Arizona.

Wycoff assisted Krissy to a picnic table in a worker's break area while the rest of the team searched the warehouse. After ten minutes, each of the team members returned to the break area.

Hood and Lansky, the last to arrive, headed directly to a refrigerator. As they rifled for something to eat and drink, Lansky reported to Tom over his shoulder. "Warehouse and surroundings are clear, boss. There's an office up front. We didn't find any more dope here, but it does have the smell of marijuana up near the loading dock doors."

"Anyone want a Coke?" Hood pulled one from the refrigerator and snapped the top tab resulting in the usual gushing sound. He took a large drink then retrieved several more and handed them to the other team members.

Tom surveyed the assembled team and John Conway, who seemed less emotional now that they were back on U.S. soil. After several minutes, Tom addressed the team. "Well, guys, I guess we did it." He held up his Coke in a toast. "We successfully showed those dope-dealing pricks they can't just come into our country, kill our fellow agents and kidnap one of our leaders without consequences. Maybe they'll think twice before trying something like that again.

"Yeah, we can all hope, but I doubt it, Tom. With the way things are going in Mexico, I think this is just the beginning," said Gonzalo.

Tom nodded his head. "You're probably right, Tony." Tom took a large swig of the Coke. "Okay, we need to get our story straight before we move on to the next step, which is getting to the motel and notifying the world that Mr. Conway is safe."

John Conway sat with his head hanging down with his chin resting on his chest. When Tom mentioned his name, he lifted his head. With tears in his eyes, he addressed the group. "Ahem, listen guys and gal," as he motioned toward Krissy, "I just want you all to know there are no words to convey my sincerest appreciation for you risking your lives to save mine. So thank you."

"No thanks is necessary, Mr. Conway," said Tom. "We are always committed to do the right thing." Tom looked back to the team. "I've had several hours during our trek to think of our story. Feel free to jump in here at any time, if you have a better idea." Tom took in a deep breath. "Hawk was contacted by a reliable informant who is obviously close to Jaime Gutiérrez."

"You're talking about Juan, the guy we all met in Guadalajara last year?" asked Krissy.

Irritated that Hammond would offer this information in front of Conway, Tom gave her a menacing look. "His name needs to be forgotten by all of us, Krissy. Let's just say that the CI had provided reliable information in the past. "Anyway, this CI provided us with information that Mr. Conway was possibly being held in an Agricultural Supply warehouse near the border in Douglas, Arizona. This warehouse, located at the northern end of a drug-smuggling tunnel used by the Sinaloa Cartel, is connected to a warehouse directly across the border in Agua Prieto in Mexico. Based on this information, we drove over here from El Paso on Friday. After doing considerable surveillance on this warehouse, we determined Mr. Conway was possibly being held here."

"What do we say caused us to focus on this particular warehouse, boss?" asked Henderson.

"Yeah, boss, why this warehouse and not another one close by," added Hammond.

While Tom considered this question, Hawk spoke up. "Because I'm willing to bet if we check the neighboring businesses, this is the only Agricultural Supply business on this street. Once we established surveillance on this suspect building, we noted armed guards protecting it. We saw them coming outside to check the area. Additionally, these guards had a system of relief with new guards arriving every eight to ten hours. All the other surrounding businesses were closed. That's what drew our suspicion to this place."

"That's good, Hawk," said Tom, "and consistent with what the CI said. Around 10:00 p.m. last evening, the CI called and advised us of Jaime Gutiérrez's concern with how many people seemed to know the location of Mr. Conway. He decided to move him but couldn't because of the shitty weather. Not wanting to chance that they'd relocate him, we moved in," Tom continued.

"Did we meet any resistance from the guards?" questioned Lansky.

"We could say we met some resistance, but when we returned fire, the guards fled using the tunnel. After making entrance to this warehouse, we found Mr. Conway down there in that room at the head of the tunnel," said Tom. "When we found Mr. Conway, we decided not to pursue the guards."

"Don't you think they're going to want to talk with the CI and confirm the story?" offered Gonzalo. "They certainly will need him for an indictment against Gutiérrez."

"Let me answer that, boss," offered Henderson.

"Go ahead, Hawk," Tom said.

"Truthfully, I have no way of contacting the CI. He has to call me. Besides, he has already told me he will never agree to come forward for any interview. He fears for his brother's young family who Gutiérrez has threatened to kill in the past. And I would imagine that once the Gutierrez's hear about this on CNN they'll put two and two together and know that it's Juan. Besides, even if we were to offer him and his family witness protection, he probably would not take it. What he wants to do is fade off into the sunset with his family and never be heard from again."

"What's in it for him then?" asked Lansky.

"I promised I would try to have the indictment against him dismissed for his cooperation so if he wanted to come to the US, he could. I think he also expects a sizeable reward for his efforts in helping us rescue Mr. Conway. That reward will help him disappear."

"What do you think about this so far, Mr. Conway?" asked Tom.

"While I'd like nothing better than to indict Jaime Gutiérrez for what he did to me and those agents in El Paso, I also understand what you promised to this CI to gain my release. I can live with this idea, and I will certainly do everything in my power to insure that he gets any reward that he has been promised."

After a few moments of silence while everyone considered the plan, Tony raised his head. "Tom, Mr. Conway was supposed to be held here for four days. How are we going to explain that if the room below us does not look like it was being used as a cell?"

Dead silence followed Gonzalo's question until Hood spoke up. "Maybe

I can be of assistance there. If the room and tunnel were to disappear, then there would be no place for anyone to search for evidence."

"How would you do that, Brian?" Tom asked. "The dynamite?"

"Naw, I'd use the Semtex that's already in place. I'd just put a delay fuse on the blasting cap that will allow us to get away from here." Hood pulled a section of fuse from his pants' pockets. "I also found this back in the warehouse in Agua Prieta. I have enough to give us a twenty to thirty minute delay."

"Will it do the trick, Brian?" asked Tom.

"It will collapse the room, a portion of the tunnel and probably a large section of the floor here."

"How do we explain the explosion, guys?" asked Gonzalo.

Lansky decided to answer this question. "I think we should say that the guards, who escaped down the tunnel when we hit the place, initiated the booby trap as they fled."

"Why didn't we wait for a search warrant before we secured the building? I'm sure they'll want an answer to that question," asked Gonzalo.

"Simple, I saw the Semtex and warned everyone we needed to move away from here, pronto," said Hood.

"And once the building blew, there was no more need to secure it for evidentiary purposes. At least, evidentiary purposes regarding Mr. Conway's abduction," added Gonzalo. "I like it."

"Okay, this plan sounds workable to me. Any questions or concerns?" Hearing none, Tom continued. "I'll take the lead with Henderson and write the report. Each of you will initial my final report of investigation adopting it as your own. All right, we need to get out of here."

"Let me call Hayes at the motel," said Krissy. "I talked with him just before we went into the tunnel in Agua Prieta; he's waiting for our call." She picked up the satellite phone. "Fuck, the battery's dead."

"I saw a phone in the office up front," volunteered Henderson.

"Give me the number; I'll call him," said Tom.

"Ten-four, boss," replied Hood.

February 9, 1997; Hacienda Puesta Del Sol, La Cruz, Sinaloa, Mexico

Juan shook Jaime's shoulder gently. "Perdone, Jefe, I have Ramon on the phone."

Jaime, who had fallen asleep in his leather recliner, blinked open his eyes.

He raised the recliner to a sitting position and spoke in a groggy voice. "What time is it, Juan?"

"It's just past 8:00 a.m., Don Jaime."

Rising from the recliner, Jaime noted the sound had been muted on CNN. "Has there been anything on the television, Juan, about the rescue of the DEA jefe or our new demands?"

"No, Don Jaime, I have not seen or heard anything yet? But it is still early."

Jaime accepted the cordless phone from Juan. "I hope you have some good news, Ramon."

After a short silence, Ramon sighed. "Unfortunately, Don Jaime, I have both good and bad news."

"Carajo! That pinche DEA puta is back in his country safe, Ramon? Is that the bad news?" asked Jaime, jumping to the conclusion that his bargaining chip in the kidnapping had been lost.

"No, Don Jaime, we have not heard if the DEA jefe has made it back to the United States."

"What is the bad news, Ramon?" demanded Jaime.

"The comandante has just heard from his man in Agua Prieta that armed men attacked the warehouse covering the tunnel?"

"What?" shouted Jaime. His face and neck reddened and his nostrils flared in instant anger. "How did they know about the tunnel, Ramon?"

"I do not know, Don Jaime, but if it is the same commandoes that raided the ranch here, they evidently have very good information about our organization and have already succeeded in getting the DEA jefe into the Los Estatos Unidos."

"Yeah, by using my pinche tunnel, Ramon?" Jaime replied sarcastically.

"Sí, Don Jaime, my source thinks that is so, but he cannot be sure."

"Cannot be sure? Why is that?"

"Uh…Don Jaime, they blew up the warehouse and probably collapsed the tunnel in the process."

"Blew up the warehouse?" repeated Jaime. His anger switched to a sense of hopelessness.

"Sí, Don Jaime, they blew up the warehouse and killed three guards protecting it."

"Did we lose more product, Ramon?"

"Sí, Don Jaime, several megagrams had just been delivered there yesterday."

"Cabron. So we do not know if they blew up the warehouse and tunnel before or after they used it to escape?"

"Sí, Don Jaime, but I would suspect they blew it up to cover their escape."

"But there is no word from the gringo press that the DEA jefe has been rescued?"

"No, Don Jaime, I have several people monitoring the Norte Americano Press and there has been no mention of his rescue yet, which I think is strange if he is back safe in Los Estatos Unidos."

"Sí, Ramon, I agree with you. If he was back there safe, they would certainly broadcast it at the first opportunity. Ramon, you said you had some good news?"

"Sí, Don Jaime, I just heard from a contact in Los Angeles. The call has been made to the news station that first broadcast the videotape of the DEA jefe's abduction. They have successfully conveyed your recent conditions to the news director."

"And they took your contact seriously and will broadcast the new demand?"

"Sí, Don Jaime, when my contact told them exactly how they received the videotape, which is information only known to the person who delivered it and the reporter who received it, they realized this new demand was genuine."

"Okay, Ramon, but I fear that 4:00 p.m. this afternoon will be too late, especially with this latest information about the tunnel. Have your man re-contact them and tell them I want Hector delivered to the Tijuana border crossing by noon today, Tijuana time. Tijuana is only a short distance from Los Angeles. They could drive him there in a little over two hours. That gives them almost four hours to comply. That should be enough time."

"I will call my contact right away, Don Jaime."

After a short silence, Jaime asked, "Tell me, Ramon. Why are you calling me and not the comandante?"

"Uh…well, you see, Don Jaime, the comandante knows he has let you down and is afraid that you will hold him responsible for what has occurred."

"I certainly do hold him responsible," Jaime chortled. "It was he who contracted with Los Zetos to protect my ranch and the tunnel."

"Yes, he agrees with that, but in his defense, Don Jaime, the Los Zetos have been the best security for us in the past, much better than using ex-police types."

"Sí, Ramon, I guess you are right. Tell the comandante I am still angry, but maybe he can be of further service to me."

"I will tell him, Don Jefe," promised Ramon.

After disconnecting the call, Jaime stood and stared into the rug, apparently deep in thought. He shook his head slightly, walked to the bar and poured himself a large crystal glass of Mezcal. Still in thought, he sipped the Mezcal and talked to himself aloud. "It could only be the licenciado."

"Perdone, Don Jaime?" said Juan.

"I was just thinking out loud, Juan, about who in our organization would know about the ranch and the tunnel, and who would sell us out to the gringos.

A cold shiver coursed through Juan's body. *I hope he does not realize that I, too, have this information.*

February 9, 1997; Douglas, Arizona

The resourceful Wyman Hayes once again proved his worth at providing transportation under trying conditions. However, unlike the year before when he borrowed a Hughes Helicopter to whisk Tom and his team from Miguel Uriarte's surrounded Estancia in Guadalajara, this time he borrowed a twelve passenger van from the motel where he had secured lodging for himself and the team. While he quickly borrowed the van with relative ease, the trip from the motel to Pan American Wholesale Agricultural Supply proved to be otherwise, taking close to two hours.

It took Lansky and Hood a while before they managed to force open the frozen sliding gate at the front of the warehouse.

"The roads ain't for shit, boss," said Hayes, when Tom greeted him. "The city and the state highway crews have been sanding and treating the main roads with chemicals since midnight but the side roads are pure ice."

Tom acknowledged Hayes with a simple nod of his head. "Nice van, Wyman. Is it uh…borrowed?" he asked as he slapped his arms in an effort to warm himself in the frigid morning air.

"Of course," Hayes said.

"And it won't come back on us, will it?"

"Not unless we're unlucky and get caught in it. I borrowed the keys from the motel early this morning when the girl working the front desk from four to midnight didn't get relieved because of the weather. She put a note on the counter that she was sleeping on a lobby couch and to wake her if necessary. I saw no need to wake her and just helped myself to the keys. I figure I'll have the van back before anyone needs it. They'll just think that whoever drove it last left the keys in it."

"Then let's get everyone loaded and get the hell out of here," said Tom as he turned to re-enter the warehouse.

"So you guys were successful then?" asked Hayes.

"If you mean, did we rescue Conway, the answer is yes, but it was at some cost."

"Oh?" exclaimed Hayes. He looked at Tom.

"Don't worry, Wyman, the good guys are okay; however, Krissy suffered some broken or cracked ribs and a possible ruptured boob? I can't say the same for about a half dozen of the bad guys who decided to fight us."

"How did Krissy hurt herself?"

"She wrecked the Blazer trying to dodge some bullets," said Tom as he continued into the warehouse.

"Ah, woman driver," Wyman jested.

Tom entered the warehouse. "Transportation is here; let's mount up."

"About time, Hayes," said Hammond. With pain etched in her face, she struggled to stand up from the bench seat."

"Nice to see you too, Sunshine," began Hayes. "At least I managed to get here without wrecking my ride or injuring myself in the process, unlike others present."

"Fuck you, Wyman," she said with a smile. He gave her his hand to assist her in standing.

Lansky stuffed another corn tortilla that he had found in the break room in his mouth. "Sure took your sweet ass time getting here, Wyman."

Wyman looked at Lansky with one of his classic Eddie Murphy wide-eyed looks. "I sure is sorry, Master Lansky. I would have been here sooner, but I had to stop and have some watermelon and fried chicken for breakfast first. You know what they say. Breakfast is the most important meal and you shouldn't skip it. And you knows how us black folks likes our watermelon and chicken."

"Jesus Christ, Hayes, I was just kidding. Don't take it so personal," said Lansky realizing that his attempt at dry humor had failed.

"Knock off that crap. Both of you," Tom said. "I know our nerves are a bit raw, but we're almost home free. So let's just get loaded into the van and get to the motel where we can get showers and rest." Tom turned to Hood. "Brian, go do your thing. Give us about thirty minutes. That should be enough time to get us away from here," Tom instructed.

For approximately ten minutes, the team waited in the van for Hood and Lansky to exit the building. "What the hell are those bozos doing, Tom?"

"They're getting rid of the alleged crime scene, Wyman," replied Tom. He then told Hayes about the booby trap and the need to destroy the underground room to hide the obvious lack of evidence that it had been Conway's cell for several days.

Finally, Hood and Lansky appeared and jumped into the van. The van had departed the yard and had almost made it to the main road, when they heard a slight explosion followed by a larger one several seconds later.

Tom looked at Hood. "I know explosives?" Tom said, repeating Hood's previous words following the blowing up of the warehouse in Agua Prieta.

"Must have been a defective fuse," said Hood in his defense.

"Two explosions? Why two, Brian?" asked Gonzalo.

"I put the dynamite about twenty yards down the tunnel, so a good portion of the tunnel would collapse. I think that was the first one that blew and probably triggered the Semtex."

On their way to the motel, they passed several police units responding to the explosion. The main road to the motel was in much better shape than any of the other roads the team had driven on in the past eight hours. The team arrived there approximately thirty minutes after the explosions.

Hayes parked the van in the spot from where he had borrowed it. Then he distributed the keys to the four rooms he had reserved. "You'll have to double and triple up, unless we can get more rooms. I need a separate room for Mr. Conway, and Krissy should have a separate room until we can get her to a hospital," said Tom.

"I'll see about more rooms," offered Hayes who headed to the lobby.

With the key Hayes had given him, Tom opened the door and ushered John Conway into the cold room. He turned on the combination heater beneath the window, and the room began to slowly warm. Assisting Conway with a blanket to wrap around his shoulders, Tom said, "Let's make that phone call I promised."

Tom used the number Conway provided to dial the phone. A female voice answered. "Mrs. Conway?" Tom asked.

With a slight hesitation, the female voice answered. "Yes. Who's calling?"

"Ma'am, my name is Tom Blaine; I am a Group Supervisor with DEA. I have someone here who wants to say good morning to you."

He handed the phone to Conway. As he exited the room, he heard a sobbing Conway greet his wife. "It's me, dear. I'm safe."

Tom closed the door behind him, and made his way toward the lobby where he met Hayes in route to his room. "I was able to only get one more room, boss."

"Give it to Krissy. I think she's in the room with Gonzalo. Wyman do you have the other satellite phone? The one that Krissy has is dead."

"Yeah, it's in my room; the battery should be charged by now."

In Hayes room, Tom dialed the New York number and then the home number for Roger Grey.

"He's at an emergency meeting at the Attorney General's Office. They called here early this morning and told him to come in right away. Something about the kidnappers had changed their demands," advised Roger's wife.

Tom thanked her for the information and then dialed Roger's pager number several times leaving the 911 number signifying it was an emergency each time the number connected.

While waiting for Roger to return his call on the satellite phone, Tom used the motel phone in Hayes' room to make a long over-due call to Libby in Colorado.

"Hey there, kiddo," Tom said when Libby answered the phone.

"Tom, oh thank God! I was worried sick about you." Tom could sense Libby was close to tears.

"I told you that I would be out of pocket for a while, kiddo," Tom said trying to defuse her emotions.

"Yes, but I thought maybe a day but not two days. I haven't heard a word from you since Friday evening. I've been worried sick about you. When the phone rang just now, I knew it was going to be bad news."

"Sorry, kiddo, had I been able to call, I would have, but I have not had the opportunity until right now. I've been…pre-occupied." Then after a short silence, Tom continued. "We rescued John Conway, Libby."

"Does this we mean including you or is it euphemistic?" asked Libby.

"It includes me. That's why I've not been able to call. We got some information and had to act on it. It required a lot of continual surveillance and then this morning we acted and rescued him."

"Where, Tom? Where did this all take place?"

"I'm in Douglas, Arizona, right now. I'd rather tell you in person about the rescue than over the phone."

"You were in Mexico, weren't you, Tom?"

"Listen, Kiddo, I don't want to talk about that right now. I'll explain it to you when I come home."

"Come home? You're coming home to Colorado, Tom?"

"Yes, I am. Roger told me I'm on an indefinite suspension, which ultimately leads to termination. So tomorrow, I suspect I'll get the official word, and I intend to come home and decide whether or not to fight this or just retire."

"What can I do at this end, Tom?"

"Nothing at this point, I guess."

"Well I intend to contact the AUSA handling those civil suits and advise him of what they are doing to you. He told me they were ready to sanction Conway the last time they suspended you. I'm sure he'll go directly to the judge with this."

"Let me talk with my attorney first, kiddo."

"Okay, but I still might talk with him and give him a heads up. When do you think you'll be home?"

"I'll need to fly back to LA first to get my belongings. Then I'll fly directly to Denver. I should be home tomorrow evening late or early Tuesday."

"I'm so relieved and can't wait for you to get home."

"Me too, kiddo."

"Manfred will be happy too. He hasn't been the same with you gone."

"I'll be happy to see that fur ball. Listen, I have to run. I'll call later and let you know what's going on."

"I'll be waiting," answered Libby.

February 9, 1997; Main Justice Building, Washington, DC

"So there have been no new leads as to the location where Mr. Conway is being held?" asked a stern-faced Marilyn Thomas. She addressed the assembled senior executives who constituted the kidnapping task force. Dressed in casual attire and less makeup this Sunday morning, she looked even more haggard and severe than normal with a noticeable twitch in her face and hands.

"No, Madam Attorney General," began Randall Walsh, "While we have received and pursued numerous leads, nothing definitive has resulted."

"Nor have we developed anything substantive," answered Marsha Grant for DEA. She, like the Attorney General, had dressed in casual clothing; however, Marsha had spent some time on her makeup.

"Then, I guess we have no choice but to comply with the cartel's most recent demand to produce Hector Gutiérrez at the Tijuana border crossing by noon today, which leaves us…" she looked down at the gold watch on her left wrist, "about three hours from now."

Roger Grey's frustration grew as he watched this exchange—Frustration due to the fact he had no word from Tom as to whether they had rescued Conway or not. Nor could he be sure the team successfully got him back to the United States. His mind kept recycling the sound of gunshots he heard while talking with Hammond on the phone earlier this morning. He looked at his pager for probably the twentieth time since this meeting began. *Come on, Blaine. Just call and let me know what's happening.*

The AG turned to Sidney Hawkins, the representative from the U. S. Marshall's Office. "Sid, how is this going to happen?"

"Madam Attorney General, we have tried to arrange for an aircraft to fly Gutiérrez from Los Angeles to Tijuana, but as you know, the Mexican government prohibits Federal Law Enforcement Aircraft to enter Mexican airspace. Our efforts to obtain a charter aircraft on such short notice, and on a Sunday morning, have not been productive. We did find one charter service that could do it, but by the time they have an aircraft and pilot ready, we would be pushing the time deadline." He shrugged his large shoulders evident through his sweater. "So I have arranged for the Marines to fly Gutiérrez from Long Beach to the Naval Base at Coronado in a helicopter. The U.S. Marshals will pick him up and drive him to the San Ysidro Port of Entry. There we will surrender him to Mexican authorities, much like the return of illegal aliens to Mexico. I need to contact our Immigration people so they can arrange for the transfer."

"I can help in that regard, Madam Attorney General," volunteered the Representative from the U.S. Customs Service. "I'll have one of our liaison reps in San Diego take care of Mexican Customs and Immigration."

Thomas shook her head in agreement. Her facial and body posture indicated a sense of defeat. "Okay, then, make the call and get this rolling."

"Excuse me, Madam Attorney General," began Randall Walsh as he sat upright in his chair, "but are we doing this on the hope that Mr. Conway is still alive? Don't you think we should at least demand proof of life before we do this? And how do we know they will honor their end of the deal and release him unharmed?"

With a look of astonishment, Marsha Grant turned to Walsh. "Jesus Christ, Walsh, are you kidding me? We don't have the luxury of time, and let's face it," she turned and faced the Attorney General "the ball is definitely in the cartel's court, not ours. We have no choice but to accede to their demands and release Hector Gutiérrez and hope they will do the same for John Conway."

"Yes, I agree, Marsha," replied the Attorney General. "That's all for now, but don't stray too far in case I need your collective input."

"Can you believe that idiot, Walsh?" asked an irritated Grant as she and Roger Grey walked down the empty corridors of the Main Justice Building to the underground parking. "Can you imagine him wanting to ask for a proof of life when we barely have enough time to meet the cartel's deadline?"

"Yes, I know…" began Roger. His pager began to vibrate. He pulled the pager from his belt. Roger could hardly contain his excitement when he saw the familiar satellite phone number followed by 911. "I've got to make a phone call, Marsha…" he began but a second page interrupted him, which repeated the first page. This time, two 911s followed.

"We'll be back at DEA in thirty minutes, Roger. Can't it wait until then? I have a luncheon engagement and…"

"No, ma'am, it can't wait. It might have something to do with John Conway," said Roger as he rummaged through his briefcase and extracted his satellite phone.

Stepping outside the Main Justice Building in the cool brisk air, Roger dialed the satellite phone number displayed on the face of his pager.

Marsha looked at the satellite phone, and then at Roger. "Where did you get one of those, Roger?"

He held up one finger to silence Grant and waited for the phone call to connect. "Buenos Dios, good morning," greeted a jovial Tom Blaine.

"Did you do it, Tom? Do you have Conway?" asked an anxious Roger.

"What, no greeting? No foreplay, just wham bam thank you ma'am? Your wife was right; you must be lousy lover," kidded Tom.

"God damn-it, Blaine, I need an answer right now," Roger retorted.

"Jesus, Roger, don't get your skivvies in a knot."

"Tom, you don't understand, the AG has just ordered that Hector Gutiérrez be released and taken to Tijuana." When there was no response from Tom, Roger added, "The cartel changed their demands and gave us until noon today to have Hector at the Tijuana Port of Entry. Otherwise they'd kill Conway."

"When did this all take place, Roger?" asked Tom.

"It happened early this morning. We're not sure why the change in demands."

"I know why," volunteered Tom before Roger could finish his statement. "Well, relax, we've got Conway. We're at Motel 6 just north of Douglas, Arizona."

"Oh, thank God, Tom," said a relieved Roger. "Is he okay?"

"Physically, he's okay, but emotionally he's a wreck right now, but most people would be having gone through what he just did. The bastards whacked off his right forefinger."

"Why did they do that?"

"I don't know. I can only guess they intended to use it for a proof of life."

"Listen, Tom, I have to get back to the Attorney General so she can stop the transfer of Hector Gutiérrez. I'll call you back in a little while to get the details."

"Sure, but just so you know, it did get bloody."

"None of our guys, I hope."

"No, but Krissy cracked or broke some ribs. We can talk about this when you call back."

"Okay. So I'm good to tell the AG that John Conway is safe in a Motel 6 room, in Douglas, Arizona?"

"That's where he is. He was talking to his wife when I left him several minutes ago. What should I do with him?"

"Stand by there. I'll get back to you shortly, Tom."

Roger quickly turned around and headed rapidly back toward the Attorney General's Office. "Come on, Marsha," he yelled back when he realized Marsha still stood back where he first received the call. "We've got to stop them from releasing Hector Gutiérrez. John Conway is safe in a hotel in Douglas, Arizona, thanks to Tom Blaine."

Marsha ran to catch up and stay with Roger. "Tom Blaine has the Administrator? I don't understand, Roger."

"I don't have time to go into the particulars right now, Marsha. We need to get the AG to stop the release of Hector Gutiérrez."

CHAPTER TWENTY-ONE

February 9, 1997; Los Angeles, California

Upon receiving the new demands regarding the release of Hector Gutiérrez from the Sinaloa Cartel, KTLA, the all-news Los Angeles radio station, had immediately contacted the local FBI who in turn contacted the U.S. Attorney General's Office. And for its cooperation, the Attorney General's office allowed KTLA to do an exclusive release of the demands and the fact that the Attorney General had ordered Hector Gutiérrez transported to Tijuana to satisfy the new demands. This release began a news-feeding frenzy. All the major news media in the greater LA area converged on the Federal Correctional Facility on Terminal Island in Long Beach, vying for a position to video Hector Gutiérrez being escorted from the prison to Tijuana.

Their actions created an almost comical spectacle, much like the one created in the slow pursuit of O.J. Simpson in the white Bronco prior to his arrest several years previously. However, Hector Gutiérrez rode in a dark-colored Chevrolet Suburban with heavily tinted windows in the middle of a convoy of marked and unmarked U.S. Marshals, police and sheriff vehicles. With news helicopters hovering overhead and ground units all shooting live feeds back to their respective studios, the movement of Hector Gutiérrez from Terminal Island to Tijuana beamed throughout the world. Added to these live pictures, each station's commentators and talking heads provided a verbal narration about the movement as well as the significance of the release of Hector Gutiérrez and the forced compliance with the cartel's demands. These talking heads interviewed experts on terrorism who warned that the U.S. was setting a dangerous precedent by "caving into the demands of drug terrorists."

Several hundred miles south of this motorcade, Jaime Gutiérrez, sipping coffee while seated in his recliner, watched the live television feed of the Suburban carrying his brother. He watched with a smug look on his face only breaking into a frown when news reporters described his brother, and ostensibly himself, as drug-dealing terrorists.

"Oye, pendejos, we are simple businessmen providing a product that your pinche countrymen crave," he shouted at the television challenging the commentators. He turned slightly and spoke to Juan over his right shoulder.

"Is everything set at Tijuana?"

"Sí, Don Jaime, the pilot called to say he is only thirty minutes from touchdown at the airport. I have also contacted our people in Tijuana. They have assured me they will have security there to prevent any unforeseen problems," Juan continued.

"Esta bien amigo," said Jaime as he turned back to the television. "Soon, mi hermano will be back home safely."

February 9, 1997; Douglas, Arizona

"Hey, Wyman, mind if I make myself a cup of coffee?" asked Tom Blaine as he pointed to the coffee pot located on the bathroom sink counter.

"No, go ahead, boss," replied Hayes.

"I guess we got Conway back here just in the nick of time," said Tom as he poured water into the coffee maker.

"What do you mean in the nick of time?" asked Hayes.

"Roger Grey just told me the cartel changed its demands. They want Hector Gutiérrez delivered to Tijuana by noon today, or they'd kill Conway. The Attorney General ordered his immediate transport. I guess he's in route right now."

"Well, shit! Are they going to be able to stop his being set free?"

"I sure hope so, Wyman," advised Tom as he filled his cup with coffee. "Now that I've told Roger we have Conway here, I suspect things will get real busy here soon.

"You think so, Tom?"

"Bet on it, Wyman, we'll be swarmed by anyone and everyone of importance in the Department of Justice who wants to be seen as a part of saving Conway."

Tom took a sip of the freshly brewed coffee and screwed up his face. "Man, this shit is terrible." He set the cup down on an end table. "I guess I better go warn our guys to refer anyone who contacts them to me." He took a pad of paper and a pen from the nightstand. "What are the room numbers?"

After writing down the team members' room numbers, Tom headed to the door. He turned back at the door. "Why don't you check on the weather and see when we might be able to fly back to El Paso."

"Ten-four, boss. I checked an hour before I came to get you at the warehouse, and the National Weather Service advised that this cold front should be mostly past us by noon. If that holds true, I would expect that we might be able to get airborne in the early afternoon."

"That's good, Wyman. It sure will feel good to get back to a change of clothes, a long hot shower and some real food. Oh, and Wyman," began Tom, "I may not get another chance to say this, but you did real good. You came through again when we really needed you."

"Shit, Tom, I feel like I haven't done a thing," said a chagrined Hayes.

"Don't be silly, Wyman," refuted Tom waving his hand in a dismissive manner. "You got us transportation when we needed it the most and got the plane to a location where it would be available to us. Shit, we could still be stuck in that warehouse at the border with no means of getting to El Paso. No, you did good, buddy."

"Thanks, boss," said a humble Hayes.

Tom went to each room on his list with the same message for them to refer, anyone who asked, to him. "I'm in room 214 with the Administrator."

The common question from the other team members was when they could expect to leave for El Paso.

"Hayes thinks sometime around early afternoon," Tom told them. "The cold front should be past us around noon; the roads and runways should be passable shortly thereafter."

He visited Krissy's room last. He found her in obvious pain. "Krissy, let me get you to a hospital."

"Tom, I'd rather wait until we get back to El Paso. Any idea when we'll be leaving here?"

"Hayes thinks it might be shortly after noon. But listen, if the pain gets too bad, let me know and we'll get you to medical help."

"Okay."

"Can I get you anything, Krissy?" asked Tom.

"Something stronger than aspirin would be nice. And I'd kill to take a hot shower."

"Well go ahead, Krissy. We've got plenty of time…"

"It's not the time," interrupted Krissy, "it's the pain. It hurts like hell to move. I've tried taking my shirt off, but I can't raise my arms above my midriff."

"I wish we had another female agent with us to help you, Krissy. A hot shower might help with the pain. It might at least make you feel better."

"You're right, Tom, a hot shower might help," said Krissy struggling to stand up. She fumbled with the buttons on her shirt. "Help me with this shirt, will ya?"

Tom unbuttoned the shirt. "Okay, all done."

"Well, don't just stand there; help me take it off, Tom?"

Tom's face reddened in embarrassment. "Krissy, I can't help you undress."

"Jesus Christ, Blaine don't be such an old prude. Besides you've seen me naked before."

"Yes, but..."

"Please help me," pleaded Krissy interrupting him. "I really want to get some hot water on these ribs."

Tom tried to avoid looking at Krissy as he helped her undress. Just the act of helping her shed her clothing caused him to get aroused. Hammond, who also noted his condition, said, following a short pain-filled chuckle: "I'd like to help you with that problem, big guy, but it would be way too painful."

Tom's ears reddened to match his neck and face. He assisted Krissy to the shower, where after adjusting the water, he exited the bathroom to allow her some privacy and himself some relief from embarrassment. The embarrassment returned when she shouted for him to return to the bathroom and help her dry off and replace her clothing. That act completed, he departed her room with the warning, "and I'd prefer this not be put out for public knowledge, Krissy."

"My lips are sealed, Blaine, except for maybe Tree. I may tell him. Because he wasn't available, I had to resort to using you. You know just to antagonize him a bit."

"Real nice, Hammond, get some rest; I'll let you know when we're ready to leave."

February 9, 1997; Main Justice Building, Washington, DC

"Is she in?" Roger Grey asked the Attorney General's Administrative Assistant as he barged into the outer office.

"She's on the phone right now. Please have...."

"I'm sorry, this cannot wait," interrupted Roger. Without waiting, he entered the door to the Attorney General's large office followed by Marsha Grant. Seated behind her massive desk with the phone to her ear, she looked up at Roger Grey and with an immediate look of anger. She mimed the words: "Get out of here. I'm on the phone to the President."

Without acknowledging her command or at least delay her call, Roger advised in a loud voice: "Madam Attorney General, we have rescued John Conway. He's alive and safe in Douglas, Arizona."

With her look of anger changing to one of surprise, Thomas said into the phone, "Mr. President, I have just heard that John Conway has been rescued and is alive and safe. May I call you right back when I have the details? Thank you, sir, I'll call you right back." She turned to Roger Grey. "Grey, you have my attention. This better be true."

Winded by his rapid trip from the bowels of the Main Justice Building, Roger paused to gulp in air. "Madam Attorney General, I've just received word from a DEA supervisory agent assigned to the kidnapping task force that John Conway has been rescued. He's alive and safe in a Motel 6 in Douglas, Arizona."

"Alive and safe," said Thomas repeating Roger's words. "When and how did this happen and how come we did not know this was happening, Grey?" asked Thomas whose inquisitive mood was switching to one of annoyance.

"Ma'am, I don't know all the details, but I suspect that this was a very fluid action. It's my guess that when the agents received the information, they had to act quickly without a chance to notify anybody. But at least John Conway is safe."

"Yes, yes, of course, Mr. Grey," admitted Thomas softening her tone with Roger. "He's where?"

"He's in a Motel 6 in Douglas, Arizona. We need to get in touch with the Marshals transporting Hector Gutiérrez and have then stop the trip to Tijuana."

"Yes, yes, we certainly do," said Thomas as she stood up at her desk. She looked beyond Roger at her Administrative Assistant, who had followed Roger and Marsha Grant into the Attorney General's Office. "Reach out for Sidney Hawkins and have him immediately terminate the movement of the defendant to Tijuana. Have him call me after he has done so." Thomas turned to Roger. "Please get me the details on his rescue so I can brief the President. I should also call Mrs. Conway with the good news."

"Ma'am, I'm told Mr. Conway has already called his wife; I'll get you the details on his rescue immediately."

February 9 1997; Hacienda Puesta Del Sol, La Cruz, Sinaloa, Mexico

With his eyes glued to the large projection television, Jaime watched with baited breath as the large Marine helicopter containing his brother flew along the Southern California coast. With live shots of the southbound helicopter beamed from a pursing posse of news helicopters, the anticipation that he would be successful in getting his brother returned to Mexico increased. Not wanting to miss a minute of the trek, he squirmed in his seat and shifted his position in hopes that he could delay a long over-due trip to the bathroom. Finally, his overfull bladder won out, and he bolted to an adjacent bathroom to relieve himself. While Jaime was not gone but for several minutes, it was sufficient enough time for the live scenario on television to change drastically. Returning to the office, Jaime saw Juan had moved from his position at his desk and was now standing next to Jaime's recliner with his eyes glued to CNN. The look on Juan's face was more than enough to tell Jaime that something was amiss.

"Que pasa – What's happening?" asked an anxious Jaime as he quickly crossed the room and took up position on the other side of the recliner.

"No se – I don't know, Don Jaime," offered Juan as he turned to address Jaime. "They say the military helicopter has slowed down considerably."

Sliding into his recliner without removing his eyes from the large screen, Jaime demanded from the television, "Que pasa – what's happening?"

As if to answer Jaime directly, the female commentator addressed a person in the news helicopter who was following the Marine helicopter. "Chuck, any idea why the Marine helicopter has slowed down?"

"No, Maria," replied Chuck. "Oh, wait one, Maria." Then in the background, the television audience heard, "Okay, roger that." Chuck returned to his television mike. "Maria, our pilot has just been advised by San Diego air traffic control that the Marine helicopter is diverting to the Marine Base at Camp Pendleton. That is restricted air space, and we will not be able to follow."

"Has there been any reason given why the helicopter has been diverted, Chuck," asked the commentator Maria.

"No, Maria, not at this time. It could be a number of things ranging from mechanical problems to some other on…" Chuck began before Maria interrupted him.

"Chuck," said Maria drowning out Chuck's voice "the U.S. Marshals Service in Los Angeles has just informed us that the flight with Hector Gutiérrez is being diverted to the Marine Base at Camp Pendleton to await further instructions. Our news director is on the phone with the Marshals

Service right now. As soon as we know why the flight is being diverted, we'll let our viewing audience know."

"Carajo!" exclaimed Jaime. He pounded the arm of the recliner.

Juan sensed Jaime's temperament was vacillating from anxious concern to anger. Juan tried to calm Jaime. "Don Jaime, it just might be something simple like a problem with the helicopter."

"Sí, por supuesto – yes of course, Juan, but I am getting a bad feeling about this," said a pensive Jaime over his shoulder.

Jaime's bad feeling was well founded and became manifest when Maria, the commentator, made another announcement a short time later. "This just in: Marilyn Thomas, the U.S. Attorney General, has announced that John Conway, the Administrator of DEA who was abducted several days ago from an El Paso hotel room has been rescued. He is alive and well and is being cared for in a location in Southern Arizona. More details will be made available as they are received."

Juan anticipated Jaime's typical outburst of rage. However, Jaime surprised him when Jaime merely rose slowly from his recliner and walked to the bar. Pouring himself a large tumbler of Mezcal, he raised it to his mouth and downed it. With his face reddening slightly, Jaime poured a second drink and sipped it. Jaime looked across the drink at Juan. "Juan, call the ranch," Jaime said in a calm, clear voice. "I want to talk with the comandante." Jaime then went to his recliner, grabbed the module that controlled the big screen television and extinguished the picture.

Several minutes later as Jaime sat quietly in his recliner, Juan said, while cupping his hand over the mouthpiece of the phone, "They are getting him now, Don Jaime."

Nodding his head in understanding, Jaime rose from the recliner and approached Juan's desk. He took the phone from Juan and waited.

"Hola, Juan."

"No, Comandante, this is Jaime."

"Lo siento –I'm sorry, Don Jaime, I was told it was Juan on the phone," said the comandante.

"Never mind that, Comandante. I have decided to give you one more chance to redeem yourself. I want you to go to Juarez. The plane will come for you to bring you back here. I expect you to do whatever you need to do to find out who did this to me. Entiendo? – Understand?"

"Sí, Don Jaime. I will not disappoint you again," promised the comandante. "I will head to Juarez as soon as the weather and roads clear ..." began the comandante.

"Oye – listen, Comandante," interrupted Jaime. His voice began to take on an edge and his face and neck began to redden. "I want you to leave right now. The weather and the icy roads did not deter those DEA putas from coming into my country and taking their jefe from me." Then in a voice that was almost a shout, he next demanded, "Have you not heard, Comandante?" But before the comandante could answer, Jaime continued in a tone filled with rancor. "The pinche DEA jefe is safe and back in Los Estados Unidos, Comandante."

The comandante instantly realized he had said the wrong thing to Jaime. "Don Jaime, I will leave for Juarez immediately."

February 9, 1997; Douglas, Arizona

"So that's the version we are going with, Roger," said Tom Blaine after he explained the previously agreed upon scenario of where and how they rescued John Conway from an underground room beneath Pan American Wholesale Agricultural Supply warehouse in Douglas, Arizona, and not the ranch at Tierra Del Sol in Janos, Mexico.

"Everybody is cool with this plan?" asked a skeptical Roger Grey. Before Tom could answer, he added, "Even Conway?"

"I think so, Roger. I had a long talk with Conway during our drive from Janos to Douglas. I think I've convinced him of the need to go with our story as opposed to what really happened. But he's pretty beat up emotionally right now; I guess he could say just about anything." After several seconds of silence Tom suggested, "I'll go have another talk with him when we are done here and try to convince him of the need to keep to our story."

"Okay, Tom. And all the other team members are cool with this story?" asked Roger.

"Yup, even Tree. I grilled him for several minutes an hour ago, and he was fine. I'm not worried about the team, Roger, just Conway. I plan to do a collective report on our activities which all the team members will adopt as theirs by signing the report with their initials."

"Sounds good, Tom. So what's your plan?" asked Roger.

"I guess we'll relocate back to El Paso when the weather clears, Roger. Hayes will fly us back there later this afternoon. Krissy needs medical attention but wants to wait until we get back there. What should I do about Conway, Roger? We sure as shit can't take him on the plane with us."

"Yeah, you're right, Tom. I'm sure that once I tell the AG and all the high-powered brass here, they'll have ideas on how to handle Conway."

"Oh, I'm sure they will," advised Tom with a hint of sarcasm creeping into his voice.

Following his conversation with Roger Grey, Tom returned to his room where he found John Conway resting on one of the double beds. Sitting down on the adjacent bed, Tom addressed Conway who was drifting in an out of consciousness. Leaning toward Conway, Tom quietly addressed him. "Mr. Conway, are you okay?"

Conway opened his eyes and did a quick survey of the room. He then sat upright on the bed. "I must have dosed off." He looked at Tom. "What time is it?"

"It's a little after 9:00 a.m., sir. How are you doing?"

"I'm okay, I guess. He looked at his hand missing the finger. "My hand throbs a little."

"I've notified Washington and am waiting for instructions from them as we speak. I imagine we shall have lots of help here soon."

Conway nodded his head. "I'm sure you're right."

"Sir," began Tom, "before we are descended upon, I want to discuss again what we talked about during the ride from the ranch to the border early this morning."

"Okay," was Conway's simple but hesitant reply.

"Are you still okay with our story about finding you in the room beneath the warehouse in Douglas and not the ranch in Janos?"

After several minutes of contemplation, several minutes that caused Tom some concern, Conway replied. "Certainly, Tom. You guys risked your lives to save me and I'll do anything you ask to protect you and your team. I plan to rely on the stress of the entire situation that will cause lapses in my memory and will suggest they refer to you for the details, if that's all right with you."

"Perfect, sir."

February 9, 1997; Main Justice Building, Washington, D.C.

Roger Grey watched Marilyn Thomas thumb through some papers scattered on the large oak conference table in front of her. *It's amazing what an hour can do once a tremendous burden has been lifted from your shoulders.*

The color has returned to her face, and she seems to have lost some of that haggard look.

The Attorney General sensed Roger's stare and looked up from her work. "Let's just give the other members of our task force a few minutes to get back here, Mr. Grey. I'm sure, like me, they'd like to know the details of the rescue of Administrator Conway.

"Yes, ma'am," stammered Roger feeling his face redden after being caught staring at the AG.

One by one, the task force participants wandered into the conference room and took a seat at the table. Most were jovial and upbeat with the news that Conway had been successfully rescued. Taking a seat next to Roger the representative from U.S. Customs leaned over. "I guess some of your guys did good, Grey," he said in a loud whisper.

With a slight smile Roger answered, "Yeah, they did. Not bad for Brand X, huh?"

Laughing slightly at Roger's use of the Custom's derogatory term for DEA, Brand X, the Custom representative patted Roger on the shoulder. "Grey, you'll wish Brand X is all you'll be called when the FBI arrives."

Roger's reply was an affirmative nod of his head.

Several minutes later, the conference room door opened and Randall Walsh, accompanied by several other men Roger recognized as FBI senior supervisors, entered the conference room. Unlike the other executives who had arrived, Walsh was not jovial, nor did he exhibit any upbeat signs. With his eyes focused straight ahead, Walsh walked with a determined pace to a chair at the conference table where he seated himself and placed a leather binder on the table. He then raised his head and glared at Roger.

Roger made eye contact with Walsh. *He looks pissed. And I'll bet I know why. He can't bear the fact that somebody other than the bureau successfully rescued Conway. He'll be gunning for me I guess, as I'm the most visible target. Take your best shot, buddy, but you can't beat the fact that DEA, not the bureau, rescued Conway.* This thought brought a smug smile to Roger's face. He hoped his look was not wasted on Walsh.

"Now that we're all here, I want Mr. Grey to brief us on the successful resolution to the kidnapping of John Conway," began the Attorney General. She turned to Roger. "Proceed, Mr. Grey."

Roger used Tom Blaine's contrived version and briefed the assembled executives. During the briefing, Roger could feel the heat from the glare of Randall Walsh and knew that before this meeting was over that he and Walsh were going to do battle. When he concluded his briefing, he turned his attention to the Attorney General. "That's the gist of the rescue, Madam Attorney General. My agents are standing by for instructions on what they should do with Mr. Conway."

"Thank you, Mr. Grey," said the Attorney General. She turned her gaze from Roger to the rest of the attendees. "Before we discuss the logistics of returning Mr. Conway to Washington and, of course, his family, are there any questions?"

Waiting and watching to see if the others had any questions, Randall Walsh remained mute. When there were no questions, he sat up in his chair and looked at Roger Grey. "I have a question," he said. "If this action began on Friday evening, why weren't we all advised sooner?"

"Well, Mr. Walsh, as I..." began Roger.

But before he could finish his explanation, Walsh exploded. "We almost blew it and returned, uh…what's his name, that cartel boss." He searched through his notes in his binder for the name.

"Gutiérrez, Hector Gutiérrez," offered Roger Grey.

"Yes, Gutiérrez, thank you. We almost returned Gutiérrez to Mexico when we were not informed of the possible rescue efforts that were ongoing."

Roger returned Walsh's menacing glare and stood his ground. "As I explained, Mr. Walsh, there was no time. This was a fluid thing, and once the action began, there was no time to step back and notify anyone."

"I don't believe that for a minute, Grey," said Walsh. "You said this whole thing began on Friday evening, and Conway was not rescued until early this morning. During this time frame, there was not time to make a call and let people know what was going on or get some help?"

Roger met Walsh's glare head on. "If my supervisor on the scene said there was no time, then there was no time. I won't Monday-morning quarterback him. And help? What kind of help could have been provided?"

"We could have gotten a Hostage Rescue Team to the area and they…" Walsh began to explain.

"Give me a break," interrupted Roger. "The ice storm grounded all aircraft and made the roads nearly impassable. There's no way you could have gotten an HRT to Douglas in time to be of help."

"That may be the case, Grey, but as the Federal Agency charged with investigating kidnappings, the FBI should have been notified of this information. Instead, the Director had to hear it from John Conway's wife who called him as soon as he called to tell her he was safe and in Arizona."

Before Roger could reply, Marsha Grant placed a hand on his arm. "Mr. Walsh, John Conway was safely rescued, and we were able to stop the transfer of Hector Gutiérrez to Tijuana. Therefore, it was a successful conclusion to this whole kidnapping affair. Let's be happy it ended well and save the sour grapes for later."

"Well said, Marsha," offered the Attorney General. "The only thing that really matters is that John Conway is safe and will be returned to his family soon. On that note, what is the normal course of events in such cases, Mr. Walsh?"

"Normally, Madam Attorney General we have a plan in place, but in this instance where we did not participate in the actual rescue, we don't have a plan," said Walsh with a bit of sarcasm creeping into his tone. "Maybe DEA has a plan," he suggested.

Anger registered instantly on the Attorney General's face. "You know what, Mr. Walsh, I am really tiring of your attitude. If I can't work with you on this matter, I'll just get hold of your director and see if he can help me."

Realizing he had gone too far, Walsh quickly backed down. "Uh, ma'am, that won't be necessary. I will have our agents in Douglas, Arizona, on the scene within the hour. They'll take custody of Mr. Conway and arrange for his safe transportation back to D.C."

"That's better, Mr. Walsh." The Attorney General, with a slight hint of a smile at the corner of her eyes, turned to Roger. "Please advise your agents on the scene in Douglas to cooperate fully with the FBI, who will take over the investigation from here on and arrange for John Conway's safe passage back here to DC."

"I'll notify them right away," said a smug Roger.

As Roger and Grant walked to their vehicle in the underground garage of the Main Justice Building, Roger had all he could do not to laugh. He looked at Marsha Grant a couple times.

Marsha, sensing Roger's stare, turned to him. "What?"

"Uh…nothing, I guess," said Roger. He shook his head and decided he just couldn't hold it back any longer. "I was just thinking how ironic it is that it was Tom Blaine, the one person both you and the Administrator have made a career of trying to force from this agency, who came to the rescue. And he did it knowing he is going to be suspended indefinitely on some bullshit thing."

Grant's face instantly reddened in either anger or embarrassment. "He knew he was to be suspended, Roger?"

"Yep, I felt compelled to tell him when he launched into this rescue effort."

Stopping short, Grant stared at Roger for several seconds and then placed a hand on her hip in a defensive posture. "So let me get this straight, Roger. You knew there was something going on but decided not to confide in me or anyone from the task force?"

"No, Marsha, I did not know there was anything going on until early this morning. Once I told Blaine about the suspension, which was on Friday, he hung up on me and would not answer my calls. I had no contact with him from Friday evening until he called me this morning to tell me that he was in Douglas and had the Administrator with him. My only prior knowledge was that he told me he had a CI who was giving him information about the possible location of Conway. Nothing else."

"Well, you could have at least shared that with me," retorted Grant. She turned and walked toward the parked cars.

Yep, I could have, and you or Peterson would have done something stupid that would have jeopardized Blaine's efforts to do what he needed to do.

February 9, 1997; Douglas, Arizona

The loud pounding on the motel room door woke Tom from a deep sleep. Disoriented, it took him several minutes to realize where he was. He threw back the bedspread that he had pulled to cover his still-clothed body and rose slowly from the bed. John Conway, on the adjacent twin bed, continued to sleep through the pounding. Tom looked at his watch as he went to open the door. *Jesus, I've been asleep for over an hour. It seemed like just a few minutes.* When Tom opened the door, the massive bulk of Jason Wycoff blocked his view to the parking lot.

With his hair askew, Tree's rumpled appearance seemed to match his rough demeanor. "Sorry, boss, but this arrogant prick is looking for you." Tree then moved slightly to the right allowing Tom to see a much smaller white male standing slightly behind Wycoff.

While the man was the same height and weight proportion as Tom, anyone would seem smaller when standing next to Tree. With the flat top haircut and characteristic wing-tipped shoes, Tom guessed he was FBI.

Then the arrogant prick, as identified Tree, removed all doubt about his being the FBI. "I'm Maynard Jennings, the Resident Agent in Charge of the Douglas Office of the FBI," he said with a Brooklyn accent. "I have been directed to assume the investigative jurisdiction of this kidnapping case. He turned to Tree. "And I don't particularly like being called an arrogant prick."

"Then don't act like one," Tree said as he wheeled around and headed back toward his motel room.

After demanding and seeing Jennings's FBI credentials, Tom waived his hand and said, "Come on in." Tom stepped aside from the doorway to allow Jennings to enter the room. "That's Mr. Conway," said Tom as he motioned toward John Conway who had awakened and was sitting on side of the bed.

Quickly crossing the room, Jennings extended his hand to Conway. "Sir, I am Maynard Jennings of the FBI. I am here to get you back to Washington and your family."

Extending his uninjured hand, Conway shook the hand extended by Jennings. He looked back at Tom. "Tom, how come you don't get to take me back to DC?"

Before Tom could answer, Jennings continued. "Sir, I have been advised by my director that it was the AG's decision for us to assume control of this investigation. Kidnapping is an offense under the purview of the FBI, not DEA."

Rubbing the sleep from his eyes, Conway looked at Jennings. "Listen; uh…what did you say your name was?"

"It's Jennings, sir, and I am the Resident Agent in Charge of the Douglas FBI office."

"Listen, Jennings, I'm a former FBI agent myself, and I know your jurisdiction, so don't be patronizing. I also know it was my agents who rescued me and not the FBI, so you better tone down your attitude."

Tom watched the exchange between Conway and Jennings. *He might be beat up emotionally, but he still has some fight in him. And what's this my agents crap. I'll bet it's the first time he has actually claimed us as his own. A good sign for sure.*

"Uh…sorry sir, I meant no offense, but I have been directed to take charge here. I'd like to get you back to DC and your family as soon as possible.

"Uh…Jennings," began Tom trying to maintain a civil tone, "Mr. Conway has been injured and needs medical attention before any travel. I think he would probably like to return to El Paso for his things that were in his hotel room, or at least have his things brought here. He needs clean clothing."

Jennings looked at Tom with an *I don't need your help* expression. "Of course. I'll arrange for both of those things."

"Well, if you have things under control, Jennings, I'll just take my things and move to another room," said Tom. He addressed Conway. "I'll be in the room with Hayes. I'm not sure of the number, but they'll know at the front desk." As Tom prepared to leave the room, he walked over to where Conway was standing and extended his hand. "Mr. Administrator, I'll leave you in the capable hands of the FBI. Have a safe trip home."

Conway ignored Tom's extended hand, and instead, embraced Tom. "Thank you; I won't forget what you did for me."

Tom nodded his head and turned to leave the room.

"Uh, wait one, Blaine," Jennings said. "I want a word with you." The two men stepped outside onto the open-air catwalk. "Blaine, I have agents in route to take statements from you and all your agents."

Tom looked at Jennings for several seconds before replying. "Ain't going to happen, Jennings."

"What do you mean?" Jennings' screwed up face showed his confusion. "I have been directed to get statements from all your men."

"I don't give a good shit what you have been directed to do. My guys are Special Agents, just like you. We don't do statements; we do reports of investigation. I shall do a collective report for my team that will cover all aspects of our rescue of Mr. Conway."

"But I have been directed…"

"Have a nice day, Mr. Jennings," interrupted Tom. As he began to walk away, he turned and said, "You'd best leave my agents alone. They might not be as cordial as me."

Tom had been asleep on one of the double beds in Hayes' room for a short time, when he felt a slight shaking of his shoulder. "Hey, boss, wake up. You've got a visitor."

Sitting up, Tom rubbed his burning eyes. "Who is it? Not another FBI guy, I hope."

"Nope," said Hayes. "He's one of us."

Tom stood up by his bed and noted a stranger standing by the door. "I'm Art Sanchez. I'm the Resident Agent in Charge of the DEA office here in Douglas."

Tom met Sanchez in the middle of the room and extended his hand. "Tom Blaine, pleased to meet you."

Sanchez ignored Tom's extended hand. "Could I have a word with you in private," he said in a curt tone.

"Okay, let's step outside," said Tom grabbing his coat from a chair.

Once out on the open-air catwalk, Sanchez began. "I'll come right to the point, Blaine. I don't like outside agents coming into my area of operations and conducting investigations without my knowledge. As the senior DEA presence here, I need to know what is on-going so other investigations are not jeopardized."

"I see," said Tom.

"Your actions have seriously jeopardized my investigation into the smuggling activities of the Pan American Wholesale Agricultural Supply which my agents have been working on for months. Now their efforts is all for nothing. I intend to take this up with the Director of Operations first thing tomorrow," ranted Sanchez.

When Sanchez appeared to have finished his diatribe, Tom asked, "Is that all?"

"Yes," spit Sanchez, "except what do you have to say for yourself."

"I say go fuck yourself," Tom replied. Tom turned around, reentered the room and slammed the door in the process.

Tom had just calmed himself down, when there was a knock on the door. Upon opening the door, Tom faced a tall Hispanic Police Officer in uniform, and judging from the stars on his collar, a high-ranking officer. And judging from the frown on his face, he had not come to offer congratulations on a job well done.

And the hits keep on coming, thought Tom. "Can I help you?" asked Tom barely able to keep his voice within a cordial range.

"Are you the agent in charge of the group that blew up the Pan American Wholesale Agricultural Supply warehouse?" demanded the uniformed officer.

"And you are?" questioned Tom.

"I am Felix Castaneda, the Assistant Chief of Police of Douglas. And you are?"

"My name is Blaine, Thomas Blaine, and you are incorrect in your assumption that it was my agents who blew up the warehouse. It was booby-trapped to blow and fleeing suspects blew it up as they escaped down a tunnel that I assume connected to somewhere in Mexico. We barely made it out and away from the warehouse when it exploded."

"Oh, okay. How come you didn't see fit to check in with my department before you raided the warehouse?"

Tom knew the chain of command. He liked using the term "territorial prerogative" with supervisors who demanded prior approval before outside agents conducted missions in their area. Tom sighed heavily. "Look, chief, I'm sorry the warehouse was destroyed and has caused you some concern, but it was beyond our control. And as to checking in with your department, I'll offer two things. First, and foremost, we did not have the time to do so. It was a fluid and continuous operation that ultimately terminated before we could seek assistance from other agencies. I made the decision to act in order to save the life of a kidnapped victim, which we did by the way, without injury to the victim or any of my agents. And, finally, the last time I looked at my badge, it contained the letters U.S. embossed directly in the center. It does not say U.S. except for Douglas, Arizona, so I don't need to check in with you to get your approval to do my job here. Now if you'll excuse me, I need to get some rest." Tom returned to the room and fumed to Hayes. "Jesus, Wyman, you'd think somebody would come by to shake our hands and tell us what a great job we did instead of chewing our asses because we forgot to involve them or ask their permission to do our job."

"I'm glad it's you and not me they're chewing on, boss. I don't think I'd be so genteel," said Hayes with a slight grin on his face.

"Yeah, well, I've done used up all my genteel, Wyman. Check the weather again and see if you can get us out of here pronto."

February 9, 1997; Day's Inn Motel, El Paso, Texas

It had been early afternoon before the weather cleared sufficiently making it possible for Tom and his team to fly back to El Paso. Hayes decided he should make two trips so as not to push the weight limit of the plane. Tom went in the first group along with Hammond, Hood and Lansky. Gonzalo, Henderson and Wycoff waited for the second trip.

Once back in El Paso, the first order of business was to get Krissy medical attention, which Tom did as soon as they had both changed into clean clothes. At a local hospital, doctors diagnosed Krissy with a cracked sternum, and the implant under her left breast had ruptured sending saline solution into her body. They decided she would stay in the hospital overnight for observation and see a specialist the next day.

Tom returned to his motel from the hospital and retrieved several phone messages from the front desk. One message, from Jennings of the FBI, Tom immediately discarded in the trash. Another message was from Roger to call him in DC. Two messages, from the Assistant Special Agent in Charge of the El Paso DEA District Office dated the seventh and eighth of February, directed Tom to call as soon as possible. Sensing that the call would not bode well for him and his career with DEA, Tom decided to ignore the command to *call as soon as possible.*

After a futile attempt to nap, he gave up and sat upright in bed with the pillows propped behind him. He found the remote and turned on the television. Surfing the channels, Tom's attention was drawn to CNN and its lead story regarding the rescue of John Conway. Switching between still photographs of John Conway and actual footage of the destroyed warehouse in Douglas, Arizona, the anchor advised,

> "Early this morning, federal agents acting upon reportedly reliable information, raided the warehouse of Pan American Agricultural Supplies in Douglas, Arizona, and rescued John Conway who was kidnapped from a hotel in El Paso on February 4. According to informed sources, the agents moved in exchanging gunfire with the abductors and rescued Conway before the fleeing suspects detonated the booby-trapped warehouse. The FBI is continuing its investigation."

"I guess their informed source is the FBI. And there's no mention that it was DEA agents who rescued Conway," Tom said aloud with just a hint of disgust in his tone. He chuckled to himself. *Good luck with your continuing investigation, FBI. Fat chance a crime scene even exists. Brian's handiwork did more damage to the warehouse than I thought.* Wide-awake now, Tom moved from the bed to the table where he wrote a detailed report of the rescue of Conway. The report, of course, advised that Conway had been rescued from the warehouse in Douglas, Arizona, and not the ranch in Janos, Mexico. Just as he finished the report, Hood and Lansky knocked on his door. At the same time, they yelled for Tom through the door. "Hey, boss, we're going for drinks and dinner someplace nice. Want to join us?"

A few minutes later, the team, minus Krissy, piled into two cars and drove to an upscale steak house west of El Paso in the town of Anthony. Tom had eaten there on several occasions when visiting the DEA Office in Las Cruces, New Mexico, and knew that their steaks excelled above most.

After consuming two beers, Tom decided to remain sober to serve as a designated driver as did Gonzalo. Both of them switched to a soft drink engendering the barbs of their fellow team members who all got drunk. Rowdy at first, the drunks fell asleep during the ride back to El Paso. Tom gave up trying to wake them when they arrived at the motel. *If they get cold enough, they'll wake up and go to their rooms* he silently concluded.

As Tom lay in bed later that night, a feeling of intense gloom swept through him. The possibility of his career ending made him sad; he would no longer enjoy the camaraderie he had just experienced. A dichotomous combination of feelings ranging from a foreboding of what he faced beginning tomorrow and a resolve to fight to keep his job quickly replaced his melancholic feeling.

CHAPTER TWENTY-TWO

February 10, 1997; Over Eastern California

As the sound of the large jet engines ebbed and the plane leveled-off, Tom sensed the Denver-bound United Airlines 737 aircraft had gained its proper altitude. The pilot switched off the seatbelt sign and flight attendants began moving down the aisle taking beverage requests. He purchased a double scotch and water from the flight attendant and quickly downed it. He then started on the second, which he sipped slowly allowing the liquor to have its desired numbing effect. Reclining the seat slightly, Tom leaned his head back against the headrest and contemplated the events of the day.

After a fitful night of trying to sleep, he had finally drifted off into a deep sleep around 4:00 a.m. devoid of any dreams. Loud salsa music from the clock radio, set for 6:00 a.m., woke him with a start. For a fleeting minute, he imagined he was back at the ranch at Janos, and he had overslept resulting in him being late for the raid on the farmhouse. As his head cleared, he realized he was in his motel room in El Paso. He reached over to turn off the annoying music that the maids had no doubt tuned to while cleaning the room.

After showering and shaving, Tom dressed in casual attire and went to Gonzalo's room where he woke Tony. "Tony, I'm heading into the El Paso D.O."

"Uh…do you want me to go with you, Tom? I can be ready…" he began as he stood up and began to search for his jacket.

"Not necessary," Tom interrupted. "Listen, there's something I didn't tell you guys before we went into Mexico; I didn't want it to be a distraction."

"Oh?" Gonzalo stopped searching for his coat and faced Tom.

"Last Friday, Roger Grey told me that Peterson ordered an indefinite suspension for me."

"Suspended indefinitely, Tom?" exclaimed Gonzalo. "Jesus, Tom, that's tantamount to firing."

"Yes, I know, Tony."

"Why? What did you do, Tom, to cause them to want to fire you?"

"Well, the initial charge is that I worked while I was on suspension, and as you know, unapproved off-duty employment is prohibited."

"They can't fire you for that, Tom?" said Gonzalo with anger in his voice.

"Peterson and his people are saying my actions are part of a continuum of conduct that is a flagrant disregard for DEA policy and procedures. That can be a firing offense."

"Jesus, Tom, how can they do this to you, after what you just did? Doesn't that count for something?"

"Not in their minds, I guess, Tony."

"Are you going to fight it? You certainly have enough time that you could retire, right?"

"Yeah, I can retire, and I don't know if I'm up to fighting them again. Right now, I plan to go into the El Paso Office and be formally suspended. Following that, I'll fly back to LA, get my personal belongings and then fly on to Denver. I'll talk with my attorney and then decide what I'm going to do."

Gonzalo looked down and shook his head from side to side. "I just can't believe they would do this to you after what you just did. And to think you risked your life and your career knowing they were going to suspend you." He raised his head. "Listen, can I do anything for you?"

"Yes, that's why I dropped by. Roger Grey and I think it's best that the team get out of Dodge, so to speak, as soon as possible. That way you won't be readily available for grilling by DEA or the Feebs for that matter. I want you to make sure that happens."

"Ten-four, Tom. I'll take care of that."

"Oh, and could you check on Krissy? Make sure she's taken care of."

"Yeah, I'll see to that also."

Tom extended his hand. "It's been a pleasure, Tony. Have a safe trip home."

Gonzalo brushed Tom's hand aside, moved in and hugged Tom. "You too, Tom. Keep me posted on what you intend to do."

"Will do, Tony."

Following his conversation with Tony, Tom drove one of the rental cars to the El Paso DEA District Office where, after identifying himself to the receptionist, he was ushered into the office of Terrell Rowland, the Assistant Special Agent in Charge. While Tom had never personally met Rowland during his career, he knew of him. Rowland, a large black man whose most distinguishing feature was his shaved head, was a celebrated amateur boxer who had spent most of his career in offices on the East Coast beginning in Philadelphia a year or two after Tom came on the job. The wall behind his desk was certainly a testament to his work done in the City of Brotherly love with "atta boy" plaques for the good work done in the Philadelphia Division. This Monday morning, Rowland looked like he had just stepped off the page of a GK magazine with a precisely tailored three-piece gray pinstriped suit, white shirt and dark gray tie. However, his sartorial elegance was lost on Tom, who was extremely nervous.

Rowland's menacing glare did not help Tom's nervousness. "Blaine, I don't like being ignored. I left several messages at your hotel to call me ASAP and, at a minimum, you should have kept me advised as to what you were doing. I don't like being blind-sided and having to hear about the exploits of agents under my supposed control from CNN."

Rowland's menacing manner seemed to have the opposite effect on Blaine. Instead of being intimidated, if that was Rowland's intentions, it was not working, and Tom could sense his anger replacing the internal nervousness. Without uttering a word, he reached into his coat pocket and removed his black leather bi-folded credential case. He removed his badge from his belt and tossed them on Rowland's desk. Patting his hip, Tom said, "The gun is mine and not DEA's so I'm keeping it. Oh," he said reaching into an inside coat pocket. He extracted the handwritten report of the rescue of Conway and dropped it onto Rowland's desk. "That's the Six on the rescue of John Conway. Now I think there's a form I need to sign that spells out my suspension. Let me sign it, and I'll spare you any further aggravation, unless there's something else you need from me."

Rowland looked first at the handwritten report and then at Tom. "Uh, I'll have this typed right away and then you can sign it," Rowland said slowly. "We can finish up with the necessary suspension forms after your report is signed."

Tom waited outside Rowland's office while the Administrative Assistant typed his Report of Investigation.

The assistant attempted to make small talk with Tom about the rescue of Conway as she typed the report. She ultimately decided he preferred to remain silent and gave up. When the report was complete, she excused herself and took it into Rowland. Ten minutes later, the Administrative Assistant ushered Tom back into Rowland's office.

"This is a good report, Blaine," offered Rowland in a somewhat friendlier tone.

Tom took his change in tone as an attempt to make amends for his earlier rough demeanor. However, Tom was having none of it. "I think there's a form I need to sign."

Without saying a word, Rowland slid a sheet of paper across the desk. The single sheet of paper informed Tom of his indefinite suspension and outlined his rights to contest the suspension.

After looking it over, Tom signed where designated. He stood up and turned to leave.

"I'll arrange for a ride back to your motel, Blaine," Rowland said.

"Don't bother; I'll arrange for my own transportation," Tom replied in a curt tone.

Rowland shook his head. "You know, Blaine, I've talked to a number of people about you, and they were right. You are some piece of work."

Having made it to the door, Tom turned and said, "Yeah, and it wouldn't surprise me if those same people believe this is how they should reward an agent for taking some initiative and saving the life of the Administrator. Oh, and if you don't like getting info on agents under your supposed control from CNN, stop watching CNN." Before Rowland could reply, Tom, with a heavy sarcastic tone advised, "Have a nice day."

Tom returned to the motel following his meeting with Rowland, collected his belongings and took a cab to the airport. His flight from El Paso through Phoenix to Los Angeles put his arrival in the City of the Angels around 3:00 p.m. He took a taxi to his long-term suites-type hotel, collected his possessions and returned to Los Angeles International Airport where he caught a flight to Denver at 8:00 p.m. Prior to boarding, he called Libby and told her he was coming home.

"It's too long a story, sweetie, and too involved to go into right now. We'll have plenty of time once I'm home," Tom offered to her when she questioned why he was coming home.

Resting his head against the back of the seat, he considered *Yes it had been a long day.* And as the plane knifed through the cumulus clouds over the California desert winging its way eastward toward Denver, he pondered *Who knows what the future will bring.*

Glossary of Terms and Acronyms

The Federal Government and its many agencies use a variety of terms and acronyms that can be confusing. In order to reduce the confusion, the terms and acronyms used in this book are listed below.

AG - Attorney General
ASAC - Assistant Special Agent in Charge
AUSA - Assistant United States Attorney
CI - Cooperating Individual or Informant
DA - District Attorney
DEA - Drug Enforcement Administration
FBI - Federal Bureau of Investigation
LAB - Lloyd Aero Boliviano, the National Airlines of Bolivia
NAFTA - North American Free Trade Agreement
OPR - Office of Professional Responsibility (DEA's Internal Affairs)
RAC - Resident Agent in Charge
SAC - Special Agent in Charge
SES - Senior Executive Service
SMG - Submachine Gun
SWAT - Special Weapons Attack Team
UMOPAR - Unidad Movil De Policia Rural, the Bolivian National Police

9 781941 516164